Praise for *Fetish Fantastic*

"S/M is staking its claim in the next millennium . . . and *Fetish Fantastic* may well be its handbook."—*Lambda*

"*Fetish Fantastic* is a perfectly mixed cocktail of hot SM action and sci-fi scenarios that lingers delightfully on the palate, leaving you craving another taste."—*Skin Two*

"*Fetish Fantastic* is a captivating anthology of futuristic SM fantasies . . ."—*XTRA*

"The best [stories] fully integrate sex with SF/fantasy and provide erotic heat . . . imaginative and a cut above most . . ."
—*Publisher's Weekly*

Praise for *S/M Futures*

"*S/M Futures* is the latest book in a series of innovative and boundary-breaking science fiction collections. Cecilia Tan . . . persists in tackling material that is too hot for the mainstream."
—Pat Califia, author of *Public Sex, No Mercy,* and *Macho Sluts*

"If you like either SF of SM you are bound to find something of interest here."
—*Fetish Times European*

Color of Pain,
Shade of Pleasure

Color of Pain, Shade of Pleasure

edited by
CECILIA TAN

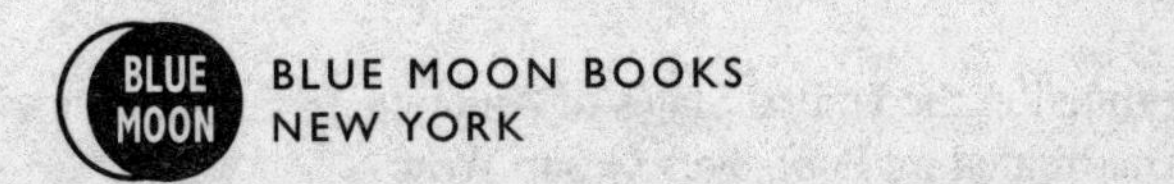

BLUE MOON BOOKS
NEW YORK

Color of Pain, Shade of Pleasure
Compilation copyright © 2004 by Cecilia Tan

S/M Futures copyright © 1995 by Circlet Press, Inc.

Fetish Fantastic copyright © 1999 by Circlet Press, Inc.

Individual copyrights to the works represented in this volume are held by the respective authors and artists of the works.

Published by
Blue Moon Books
An Imprint of Avalon Publishing Group Incorporated
245 West 17th Street, 11th floor
New York, NY 10011-5300

All rights reserved. No part of this book may be reproduced or transmitted in any form without written permission from the publisher, except by reviewers who may quote brief excerpts in connection with a review.

ISBN 1-56201-399-8

9 8 7 6 5 4 3 2 1

Printed in the United States of America
Distributed by Publishers Group West

S/M Futures
Erotica on the Edge

Contents

Introduction

When I first set out to collect the stories for this anthology, some time in 1993, I asked authors to imagine how developments in various areas might affect the way we play with S/M in the future. Medical, societal, legislative, technological... any kind of change. I didn't know if people would tend toward pessimistic futures or bright ones, whether they would envision dystopias where S/M players are persecuted by witch hunts, or S/M paradises. All I figured was that by asking some big "what if?"s, we could set the stage for some very erotic stories that could delve into the workings of sadomasochism, dominance and submission, and so on.

I was right about that. What I didn't expect was that in the time that passed between beginning to collect these stories and their publication, that we would enter the future itself. One of the first stories I bought concerned a dominatrix participating in a scientific experiment. At one point she thinks to herself "*This may be the only chance to get in on the ground floor* ... If she pulled this off, S&M might end up on the OK list, and not the sicko list." I am happy to report that in 1994, thanks to the dedicated effort of several individuals, the most recent edition of the Diagnostic and Statistical Manual (DSM) utilized by mental health professionals has removed consensual S/M from the "sicko" criteria, much as it did for homosexuality some time ago.

There is not a direct causal relationship between these two particular cases, and yet I feel somewhere underneath it all, in the synchronistic gestalt of human existence, that when we imagine a better future for ourselves, we are taking the first step toward achieving it. There are still plenty of reasons to be pessimistic about the state of erotic and sexual freedom in the English-speaking world—in England the Operation Spanner men are still serving jail time for their consensual S/M activities, Amnesty International has thus far refused to recognize them as prisoners of conscience, two different college campuses have forced their student-run BDSM support groups out of official recognition, the Canadian border is virtually sealed against anything seeming to do with S/M including magazines and books like this one... And yet, the stories in this book seem to have come down on the side of optimism, *better living through S/M*, if you will. The authors have done their part by writing them. Now it is your turn. So, read and enjoy!

Cecilia Tan
Boston, MA

One Day in the Life of the Landfords

Tammy Jo Eckhart

You sit down in your favorite chair and switch on the TV set to find a perky blonde dressed in a navy blue suit, a belt of handcuffs encircling her waist.

"Hello, Catena. This is Lori Grant speaking to you on WXXX, the TV news station that brings you the local dirt. Behind me is the home of one of our most successful business owners: Mary Landford."

The camera turns its lens to a large mansion resting gracefully on a sloping hill.

Lori Grant's fist knocks on the large black door.

A man in his mid-thirties, with dark hair, wearing brown cotton pants and a brown and green checkered shirt, opens the door with a smile. "You're Lori Grant," he states, bowing to the reporter. "Please come in."

The camera pans down to show that the man is barefooted. As the camera enters the home, it sweeps across the entryway. Part of the living room can be seen. The camera turns to focus on a sign by the door:

Rules of the House
1. Mary is always right.
2. Ask before you make a mistake.
3. Begging can get you some things.
4. Be honest.

"Please follow me," the man's voice is heard.

The camera turns to follow the man through the elegant living room down another short hallway to a very large kitchen. A young blond man kneels on the floor near an auburn-haired woman in a business suit and leather boots who is glancing over the shoulder of another man looking into the microwave oven.

"I can't fix it, Mary," the man says as he takes his head out of the microwave. He runs a hand through his black hair. "I doubt anyone can."

"Shit!" the woman looks down at the blond on the floor. "You two go to the appliance shop over your lunch breaks and get a new one."

"I'm sorry, Mistress." The man on the floor looks down at the woman's boots.

"I don't have time now," the woman says, turning away. She pauses, then smiles as she walks toward the camera. "You must be the TV people?"

"Yes, I'm Lori Grant from WXXX. You agreed to let us observe your family for a day."

The woman nods. "Yes, of course. I'm Mary Landford." The woman motions to the man who opened the door. "This is Jeff. He takes care of the house." She motions to the two men by the microwave. "This is Brad." She places a hand on the black haired man's shoulder. "He's a professor in the electrical engineering department of the nearby state university. This is Kyle," and she motions to the blond. "You've probably seen him on *Day to Day*. My other man is Nick, and he takes care of the farm so he's already out."

The camera follows Mary as she grabs her purse. "I have to get going. Join me in my car."

Lori Grant appears on the screen once more. "The rest of this documentary was edited from tape shot by five different film crews who interviewed all of the Landford family members. We'll look at each member's day at work after a word from our sponsors."

A man and woman dressed entirely in black leather smile as they stand in front of the camera. "Hi, I'm Ron."

"And I'm Rita. Owners of," and they step in opposite

directions to reveal a building with a big pink neon sign, "Ron and Rita's Rings and Things."

Suddenly Rita is sitting on a stool next to a bare chested woman lying on a table. "I'm a certified piercer with a degree in psychology," Rita says.

The woman sits up, two large hoops hanging from her nipples. "Rita did my nipples and made it one of the most enjoyable days of my life." The camera zooms in to focus on the two women kissing passionately, their tongues touching and probing.

Ron appears on the screen. "This is our retail room." He walks alongside the displays as he speaks. "We carry a wide variety of rings for all piercings. All of them are either fourteen-carat gold or hypoallergenic. And if you don't see anything you like, I can custom-make a pair to your design."

Ron and Rita are outside their store again, both smiling as they are joined by several other people all wearing name tags. "Come down!" they all shout.

Lori Grant's smiling face returns to the screen. "Now we will see how each of the Landford family members spends a typical work day."

"This is my office," Mary Landford announces to the camera as she pushes open the door. She nods to the man sitting at the reception desk and walks into the larger office, where rows of desks and their occupants are spaciously located. "Everyone, this is the day that I told you all about. Just behave normally for the nice TV people," she announces.

At the end of the office space is another hallway lined with open doors to various private offices. "This is my secretary, Jenny," Mary introduces the woman standing next to a large desk at the entrance to a set of double doors.

"Ms. Landford," the secretary bows and holds some letters up.

"What appointments are on my schedule?" Mary asks as she opens her office's double doors and walks in to sit at her large wooden desk.

"One in ten minutes with the consumer affairs people about the survey results. One at ten thirty with Ed about the personnel training manual. Phone conference at two with the lawyers. The final one at three with the discipline board." The secretary glances back at the camera.

"That will be all, Jenny," Mary says as she looks through her mail.

The camera follows Mary into her office. After sitting down in her large comfortable executive chair, Mary motions to the unseen reporter. "Please sit down over there. You can observe all day if you wish."

"Actually," you hear Lori Grant's voice, "I'd like to ask you about the accident this morning."

Mary's eyes narrow, then she smiles. "The microwave. Yes, Kyle put some aluminum foil in there and well," the executive pauses with a tired shake of her head, "everyone knows that you don't put that kind of stuff in microwaves."

"What do you do now?" the reporter asks.

"Get a new one and punish Kyle." Mary shrugs and picks up her mail again. "There's nothing else to do," she mutters.

"This is Kevin O'Donald," a man standing in a corn field announces. "Let's go see how Nick spends his day." Kevin walks through the corn stalks, his leather biker boots squeaking with the contact. After a few seconds the camera leaves the corn field and enters a grassy area housing a barn. The camera approaches a tractor with two feet sticking out from under it. "Hey, Nick!"

The man with his head under the tractor pushes himself out to look up and wave. "You're that TV news guy," he says as the camera moves in closer.

"Yes. We're here to do a documentary of your family. So, Nick, what do you do around here exactly?"

"Well, I'm responsible for the farm, which is only five hundred acres," Nick replies with a grin. He grabs another tool from a nearby tool box. "She bought this land for me to work on," he adds with a hint of pride in his voice.

"Really?" The reporter crouches down in the grass next to the tractor so the camera can focus on both men. "Why did she do that?"

The farmer's grin widens. "I think she was very pleased with me."

"Can you be specific?" the reporter presses with a smile.

"Not on a family show, I can't," the farmer states and pushes himself back under the tractor.

Jeff, the man who opened the door to the Landford home, turns around from the sink. "I let them air-dry."

"What's your day usually like?" a woman's voice asks. You recognize the voice of Nina Blackwood, one of the station's newest reporters.

Jeff dries his hands off on the towel hanging down from a cupboard handle. "It depends on the day." He leads the way to a stairway and heads downstairs. "Different chores for different days. Today is laundry day. Every day I take lunch to Nick and Mary. And I make most of the meals."

"Sounds like a lot of responsibility," the reporter comments. "How do you feel about it?"

"I love it," Jeff says, looking over a basket of dirty clothes. "When we first got married I offered to stay home after we had kids and Mary got her degree. She's much more career oriented than me."

"Married?" the reporter asks, her voice sounding incredulous. "You're married to each other? A legal marriage?"

Jeff laughs as he puts the clothes in the washing machine. "Yeah, regular vows and everything out in the regular world. I wore a tux and Mary wore the white dress."

A photo of Jeff and Mary at their wedding appears on the screen for several seconds as the man continues speaking.

"The only difference was that she didn't change her name; I changed mine after I moved here. That's when we discovered that we both liked S and M." He smiles as he puts in liquid detergent and starts the machine. "We both always wanted to have this type of a relationship."

"With Mary as the dom?" the reporter inquires and is answered by a nod. "Did you both want the other men?"

Jeff's face clouds for a moment. "It's been a fantasy of Mary's for years. It makes her happy." He pushes past the camera and heads back up the stairs.

The camera follows him as the reporter asks, "How do you feel about what happened with the microwave this morning?"

Jeff glances over his shoulder as he takes a basket of towels from the kitchen hamper. "It was an accident. But Kyle's had a lot of accidents since he arrived here."

"When was that?"

"About six months ago," Jeff says with a small sigh.

"How many classes do you teach, Brad?" a woman's voice, whom you recognize as senior reporter Barbara Wheaten's, asks the black-haired professor as he walks down the hall.

"I teach three a semester. Right now we are headed to the intro class for non-EE professionals." He opens the door and lets the camera in ahead of him. The camera turns slowly around to show the rows of desks in the small lecture hall before focusing on the professor, now standing behind a podium.

"Do you enjoy teaching?"

"Very much," he states as he pulls down the projection screen behind the podium. He faces the camera. "I'm very lucky that Mary lets me continue working here."

"So, you met Mary while you were teaching here?"

Brad nods, with a roll of his eyes. "Yeah. I was up for tenure that semester. I took a real risk when I went to that lecture."

"Which lecture?" Barbara asks.

"Oh, there used to be a student support group for alternative sexualities here on campus, and they invited

Mary to come and speak about Catena." He walks to the chalkboard, shaking his head at the writing from a previous class before erasing it. "I had heard about the place on the computer networks, so I wanted to hear her speak. But the lecture was right after a lunch meeting with the rest of the EE faculty. So I had to make a choice." He turns back around to smile at the camera. "I was a few minutes late to the lecture. Good thing too."

"How so?"

"Well, at the end of the meeting they said that I needed to get more involved with students, so by going to the lecture I did," Brad says.

"They didn't care what type of group this was?"

"The club lasted another couple of years, before the fundies got it removed. But at that time, they didn't care." Brad laughs as he writes on the board. "There are lots of science geeks into S and M."

"Anything else good come from going to the lecture?" the reporter asks, looking into the camera for a second to wink at the audience.

"Oh, yes," Brad glances back over his shoulder. "Mary noted that I was late and approached me after the lecture. She told me to get down on my knees and beg her forgiveness," he adds with an awed look.

"Did you?" The reporter's voice sounds breathless.

"Yes, I did." Brad turns around. "It was the beginning of paradise for me."

"Is it difficult to deal with your many fans?" asks Rick Montens, one of the reporters at WXXX. Around him you see the backstage of some television show, which you assume is *Day to Day*, Catena's most popular soap opera.

Kyle rolls his eyes as the makeup artist finishes his face. "Sometimes, because they think I'm really Mike Frost—you know, my character on the soap. So I always send a brief description of myself, which includes the fact that I'm in a permanent relationship. But sometimes they keep writing," he adds, a sudden look of terror in his eyes.

"And you don't like that?"

"Let's just say that I've had trouble with fans before," Kyle states. He manages a smile and nod to the makeup artist. "Mary never saw the show, so I felt safe getting involved with her."

"How did you meet her?"

"I'd rather not talk about that," Kyle snaps as he takes the comb from the hairstylist and finishes the job himself.

There is an awkward pause, then the reporter asks, "So what happened with the microwave this morning?"

Kyle frowns and stands up. "Oh, Goddess! Don't ask me now, I have a scene to do." The camera pans down his body as he walks away, pausing on his shapely butt barely covered by the torn and worn jeans.

The screen goes black for a brief moment, then a middle-aged man with slightly graying hair appears on the screen. He spreads his arms, and the camera zooms out to show him surrounded by a variety of beating instruments. "Hi, I'm Roger Whitecrest of Whitecrest Hand-Crafted Whips. I personally design and hand-craft each whip with the finest leather available. I also employ ten other leather artists who can help you create that special toy for your partner. We offer on-site demonstration rooms and several employees who will happily help you try out each item."

Roger Whitecrest smiles as a man and woman, both dressed very scantily, come into view and kneel at his feet. "Come down to my studio. If you mention this commercial, we'll give you five percent off the total purchase price."

The screen blackens briefly then returns to Lori Grant sitting in the WXXX studio. "Now we'll see what a typical lunch hour is like for the Landford family." The screen turns blue, and the following words appear: *Sexual Content. Parental Guidance Is Advised.*

The camera follows Jeff through the tall corn field.

"Nick," he calls out as he nears the building where the tractor still stands.

The other man moves into view from under the tractor. "Here!" He rises and wipes his hands on a rag at his belt.

"I packed two lunches," Jeff states, handing the farmer the larger metal meal box, "one for you and the other for Kyle."

"Wait a minute," Nick says and pushes himself out from under the tractor. "That's not your job."

"No, Brad just called and says that he had a prearranged meeting at school so you need to take Kyle to the appliance shop over lunch," Jeff says.

"Why?" the farmer asks, his voice with a harsh edge to it.

"He broke the microwave by putting metal in it," Jeff simply states.

"Oh, damn." Nick wipes his sweaty chest off with his shirt as he sets the container down. "That fool. A new one's going to cost a bundle." He puts his shirt on. "You know, things were a lot better around here before he came along."

Jeff glances at the ground so the microphone barely picks out his words. "They were best before any of you came."

"You got the car keys?" Nick requests, holding out his hand and refusing to look at the other man.

"You can have the pickup keys," Jeff says, handing the other something. "I got to go take her lunch to her."

"Have fun," Nick says half-heartedly as the other turns to leave.

"Don't I always," Jeff calls back as the camera watches him wade through the corn field.

The camera follows the professor out of the Electrical Engineering building. "I'm meeting a few students for a study lunch. I think one of them has potential."

"To be a new addition to your family?' the voice of the reporter asks.

"Not exactly." Brad checks his watch. "I'd have to

clear things with Mary before I could tell you more."

The professor nears a large table where several younger men and women are gathered. He sits at the head of the table, where a seat has been saved. "I have your papers for you with comments." He hands around several large envelopes, which the students pass around.

The camera follows his eyes to a blonde woman sitting a couple of seats from him. She takes a paper from the envelope and blinks at it. Slowly she lifts her eyes and nods.

The camera refocuses on the professor. "Now, will anyone need to see me alone about the comments," Brad says after several minutes pass.

"I do, right after lunch." The camera turns to find that the speaker is the blonde whom the camera had just focused on.

"That's fine," Brad's voice is heard. The blonde smiles.

The camera follows Jeff down through Landford Enterprises' offices. As he walks, the camera turns to look at the activities going on over the lunch hour. Most desks are empty, but over one a female secretary is eagle spread on her front, wrist and ankles tied to the desk legs. Her short skirt is hiked up to expose her round buttocks as a man, his pants around his ankles, is pumping into her.

Past the desks, one of the office doors is partly open, and the camera peeks in. A man is kneeling, arms tied behind his back, in front of a woman sitting on the edge of her desk. The woman moans as the man buries his head in her crotch.

The camera hurries down the hall to find Jeff backing into the executive office, his arms balancing the covered tray. Jeff enters the office silently. He sets the tray on the desk and lays the platters on it onto the table. He takes a bottle of wine from the bag over his shoulder and pours one goblet, setting it on the table. He kneels by the side of the desk, legs spread slightly, arms clasped behind his back, head bowed.

The camera focuses on the back of the leather executive chair, which faces away from the desk. After a few moments, the chair turns around to show Mary Landford sitting confidently in her business suit but holding a Y-shaped leather leash. "Do it," she says as she takes her goblet of wine.

Jeff rises as music seems to fill the room from nowhere. Slowly, swaying to the music, he unbuckles and steps out of his sandals. Next he slides out of his pants to reveal white bikini briefs. He unbuttons each button on his shirt and slides it off. Each nipple displays a ten-gauge gold ring. Then the camera focuses on his firm ass as he slips out of his briefs. Slowly, the camera turns to a PA piercing on his cock as it stands erect, waiting for the next command.

The camera follows Jeff as he returns to kneel next to Mary's feet. The Y-shaped leash is clipped to each nipple ring; the hand grip is looped over the chair arm. Jeff removes Mary's boots and rubs each foot as she eats.

Clearly, time has passed, because Mary sets aside the last empty platter and looks down at Jeff. "Now for the dessert." Her voice is barely heard.

The camera pulls back to display the entire desk. Mary leans back in her chair, putting one leg on the desk. Her skirt is lifted by Jeff, who buries his head in her crotch. Mary closes her eyes and sighs. She removes the leash from the arm of the chair and gives it a pull. Jeff moans.

"Wow," an unidentified male's voice is heard. "This is some lunch break."

Lori Grant's face suddenly appears in front of the lens. "Shhh. They need some privacy, I think."

"Four hundred and fifty-nine dollars!" Nick states angrily as he opens the pickup door for Kyle, who is struggling under the weight of a microwave. "She is not going to be happy."

Kyle sets the microwave down on the seat and glares at the other man. "You know, if I've pulled a muscle, the producers won't be pleased."

Nick grabs the blond by the collar of his shirt and shoves him up against the open pickup door. "I am getting tired of you thinking you're so hot." He shoves the now shaking blond into the pickup. "You're carrying it into the house too, pretty boy," he orders as he slams the door shut.

Brad opens his office door and steps aside to let the blonde student inside. He faces the camera. "If you came in it would only make her uncomfortable."

"We placed a camera in there over the lunch hour," the reporter states.

Brad looks at the young woman waiting inside. "Well, OK. But you'll have to get her permission before you air anything," he whispers.

"We always do," the reporter assures him.

The hidden camera displays most of the office from the angle of the door. The young woman's back is visible. Brad walks in and sits on the edge of his desk. "Did you want to see me about something, Miss Taylor?"

"Yes, this note you gave me." She holds up the small piece of paper.

"Is that something you'd want?" he asks as he loosens his tie.

"Well," and she crosses to sit in the professor's chair. "I thought you were married or gay or something. I wouldn't want an angry SO coming after me with a gun, Professor Landford."

"I'm in a permanent relationship, that's true." Brad stands up and faces the desk. "However, it's an unconventional situation."

"In what way?" she asks as she puts her legs up on his desk. Her skirt falls down, revealing the top of her stockings and the garter straps.

"Well," Brad says as he takes off his tie and lays it on the desk, "I'd like to show you something that may help explain it, if you don't mind."

The young woman nods slowly. Brad removes his shirt, and the young woman's eyes enlarge. "Don't they hurt?" The lens barely shows the glint of gold metal rings on the professor's nipples.

"No," Brad replies. "I have another on my genitals."

The young woman's eyes widen even more. "S and M stuff?"

"Actually, it's a lifestyle for us. She owns me and I obey her." Brad steps a little closer to the desk. "Do you think you'd like a relationship like that?"

The young woman takes her legs down from the desk. "I don't bow to any man," she says, standing up.

Brad takes his tie and wraps it around one wrist. Using his teeth, he ties the other wrist to the first. Kneeling, he holds up his hands. "You could have men obey you, Miss Taylor," he offers, his head slightly bowed. A moment of silence passes. "My mistress has decided she would like to help another achieve this. Would you be interested?"

The young woman walks around the desk, pausing in front of her professor. "Yes. I definitely would."

"I'll call her now," Brad says, reaching for the phone.

The screen splits to show the professor's office and the executive office. Mary is alone in her office; the camera focuses on her as she picks up the receiver. "Yes, Jenny? Put him through."

"Mistress, it is Brad," the professor says, glancing up at the young student, who is now running her fingers through his hair.

"Yes, have you found someone?" Mary asks, leaning forward on her desk.

"Yes, Mistress."

"Put her on," Mary orders as she picks up a pen and poises it over a pad of paper.

"She wants to speak with you," Brad says, holding the phone up to the young woman.

The young woman takes the receiver. "Mrs. Landford?"

"Yes, my dear." Mary smiles at the wavering voice. "How would you like to meet with me tomorrow evening? You could enjoy dinner with my family and see our lifestyle firsthand."

The young woman looks down at the professor. "Well, I'm only interested. I couldn't make a commitment, Mrs. Landford."

"It's just dinner. Brad will give you a ride here and to your home afterwards." Mary sits up in her chair. "You will join us?"

"I'll be there," the young woman replies.

"Good. Brad doesn't have any more classes today. Feel free to explore your interests with him." Mary hangs up the phone. Now the screen shows only her office. The intercom buzzes, and she answers it. "Yes, Jenny. I know, send them in." Mary frowns and picks up a different notepad.

Four executives enter the office and bow before pulling up chairs to sit before her desk. "Discipline board meeting," Mary explains to the camera with a frown. "I'd rather you not tape the discussion. Privacy laws," she adds.

The screen blackens, then reveals a scene of the main shopping district of Catena. A man in a black suit steps in front of the camera. "Greetings, citizens of Catena. I'm Jim Waterton, the mayor of our fine city. I'd like a few moments of your time."

The scene changes to one of the spacious parks that populate the city. Several children are seen playing behind the mayor. "My friends, as you are hopefully aware, the governor of the state we live in wishes to make a campaign visit to our fair city. Arrangements have been made for the visit one week from today. As in the case of other outsider visits, the city council requests that all S and M paraphernalia be kept in the private home for the duration of the visit."

The scene changes to show the mayor standing in front of the city hall. "While I know this will inconvenience many of us, please remember that the survival of our city depends on its lifestyle remaining a secret from the rest of the world. Thank you for your cooperation."

The screen blackens, then Lori Grant appears again. "We now return to the Landford home as everyone returns from work." The screen turns blue, and the following words appear: *Sexual Content. Parental Guidance Is Advised.*

Jeff is busy in the kitchen as Nick comes in the back door. "Did you get the tractor working?" the homemaker asks.

"Shit!" Nick walks barefoot into the room. "Yes, but it took most of the day. Thank god we are in a slow season right now."

Jeff turns, holding a steaming spoon out to the other. "Taste this and tell me what you think."

Nick takes the spoon into his mouth. He shakes his head slightly as he swallows. "A little spicy."

Jeff sighs, rolls his eyes, and goes to the refrigerator.

"What's for supper?" Kyle asks as he enters through the back door.

The other two men look at each other but ignore the blond.

Kyle puts his denim jacket on the kitchen table. He crosses his arms over his chest with a pout. "Oh, it's the silent treatment, huh?"

Jeff glances at the blond as he returns to the stove. "You need to get ready," he reminds the youngest man over his shoulder.

"The harness?" Kyle sits down in a chair and places his head in his hands. "She's gonna punish me over an accident?"

"No," Nick says as he steals a piece of cheese from Jeff and receives a tiny slap for it. "She'll beat you for the cost of the new one. And I think it's about time you got a little discipline."

When the youngest man doesn't move, Nick slaps him on the back. "Come on, I'll help you get it on."

"Oh-oh," Brad exclaims with a grin as he enters the

kitchen in time to hear and then see the two men leave. He looks over Jeff's shoulder. "Smells good." He glances at his watch. "Gotta go, too."

"Where is everyone going?" the reporter's voice asks.

Jeff turns around to face the camera. "Oh, while I finish dinner, those three prepare Mary's bath and lay out her evening clothes. Or at least that's what Nick and Brad are doing tonight."

"Not Kyle?" the reporter asks.

"That's part of the punishment," Jeff emphasizes, then turns back to the stove.

"Nick and Brad seem excited about this punishment thing. You don't," the reporter observes. "You were evasive this morning about this whole microwave situation. You don't think the punishment matches the crime?"

"It's an expensive model, two level model," Jeff simply says as though it explains everything.

"You don't like the other men, do you, Jeff?"

Jeff turns around to face the camera, his face suddenly pale. "They are nice enough guys. Generally, they make Mary happy and their lives are certainly better here. That's what matters, you know," he adds, getting back to his cooking.

"Do I detect a hint of jealousy?" the reporter pushes.

Jeff stops stirring for a moment. "Yes," he looks over his shoulder. "I may be a sub, but it doesn't mean I'm not human," he snaps.

Mary looks at the stop light as she waits at the intersection. She points out the supermarket to the right. "That's where Jeff does most of the shopping."

As they drive down the road again, the reporter asks, "Why did you decide to take on four men?"

"I like men. Some people might not understand that because they see the slave-owner relationship as a hate-based one," Mary adds.

"Surely not the citizens of Catena?" the reporter insists.

Mary slows the car as she throws a long look at the

reporter. "Yes, even here." She focuses her eyes back on the road. "That's why we have the abuse shelter. I do volunteer time there on weekends, as do the boys. This isn't a game, you know." She is silent a few minutes. "I know firsthand what can happen. That's why I want to start training potential owners. The council can't thoroughly screen for people's beliefs. People lie."

"What do you mean by first hand experience?"

"Well, not really first hand, I guess," Mary says as she continues driving. "Jenny isn't my first secretary. When I came to Catena, I didn't have my own business. The secretary I had then was in an abusive relationship."

"How did you know?"

"No one should get bones broken in a real S and M relationship," Mary states. "This is love, this is consent."

"What happened?" Lori Grant asks, her voice filled with concern.

"When I tried to help her get away, he came into the office and shot her, then shot himself," Mary says flatly.

"The Redferns murder," the reporter explains; "that happened ten years ago."

"Yeah." Mary rubs her eyes as they pause at another stop light. "It almost destroyed this town."

"So, the council started the shelter?"

"Yes." Mary continues driving the last few blocks in silence.

The car pulls into the driveway. "This is a beautiful home," the reporter exclaims, trying to lighten the mood again.

"Thank you. Jeff, Brad and I designed it together." Mary turns the car off and exits it. "Jeff and I first lived in the apartments when we came here. Jeff found Kyle at the shelter. He'd been kidnapped by a fan," she adds with a sharp nod of her head toward the house.

Lori Grant remains silent as she and the camera follow.

Mary strides through her front door to be greeted by a kneeling Brad, naked, his hands and head pressed to the ground. Mary pauses for him to raise his head and kiss her boots before stepping past him. "You did a good job finding a trainee," she says, handing him her briefcase as he follows her down the hallway.

"Thank you, Mistress," he whispers, opening the door for her. They enter a large bedroom with an empress canopy bed covered in red silk and satin. Two sets of clothing lie on the bed—one of black leather and one of cream satin and lace.

"Is Kyle prepared?" she asks as she examines each set.

"Yes, Mistress," Brad answers, kneeling on the floor next to the bed.

"I'll wear this," she says, handing him the lacy jacket.

Brad stands and helps her remove her clothing. He massages each foot as he removes the boots and stockings. He kisses her nipples as he unbuttons and removes her blouse. His hands massage her shoulders, and he comments, "Stress."

Mary slips out of her skirt and silk panties. She takes his offered arm and follows him to the bathroom. A steamy, bubble-filled round tub awaits her.

"Welcome home, Mistress," Nick says as he bows and closes the door behind them.

Mary looks at the shower, where Kyle is handcuffed to the curtain bar. He is naked save for the straps and clips of the leather body harness. "Use the cage and plug," she says to Nick while frowning at the misbehaved soap star.

"Mistress, please..." Kyle starts to protest.

Mary glares up at him, her face tired from a long day at work. "This is for two things: the cost of the replacement and the stupidity of using metal in there in the first place." Without a further word, she steps into the tub, using Brad's hand as a brace.

Nick steps inside the shower behind Kyle. Reaching from behind, he places the cock cage on firmly. Kyle's feet are shoved apart, and he cries out briefly as his body is solely supported by his wrists for a second and the plug is shoved inside his ass.

Nick steps out of the shower and kneels by the tub next to Brad.

"Get in," Mary orders with a hopeful smile.

Both men enter the tub and begin using soft washcloths on her body. Nick concentrates on the upper half of her body. Gently he cleans her face, pausing to kiss her neck before touching it. His hands knead her back as he washes it. "You are tight," his whisper is barely heard as he works the muscles. He runs his tongue down each arm before using the sudsy washcloth. Mary moans as he licks her finger tips.

Brad first lifts her feet and scrubs each. Then he lowers himself further into the water and smiles as her moans increase.

Soon Mary throws her head back as her moans increase in volume and frequency. "Yes," she orders throatily.

Kyle pulls helplessly on his handcuffs, and the camera focuses briefly on his growing cock straining against the metal rings around it. The soap star glares at the camera in anger and frustration.

"Is that what makes you jealous?" the reporter asks Jeff as he removes his shirt. The few seconds of silence that follows allows the audience to hear the noises coming from the bathroom.

"You mean that?" he nods in the direction the moans are coming from. He looks up a the ceiling for a moment. "That's part of it. But it's not the only reason. There's a lot more than sex to this relationship. I love Mary, I always will."

"You don't think the other men love her?" Lori Grant asks.

Jeff just looks at the reporter then at the camera. "Let me show you where we eat," he changes the subject uneasily. They leave the kitchen and the camera shows the dining room table, set for four. He points to the end furthest from the kitchen and says, "That's reserved for guest owners. Mary sits at the other end." He motions to the sides of the table. "Nick and I sit near the kitchen with Brad and Kyle on the opposite side."

"But there's only one setting there tonight," the reporter points out.

Jeff smiles briefly at the camera. "That's part of the punishment."

"Is this a standard punishment, then?" the reporter asks.

"Mostly, but if it's me we go out to eat, and I have to wear just the harness and sit at her feet, or under the table even." Jeff rolls his eyes. "I behave myself most of the time. Public scenes are difficult for me."

"You look uneasy about the entire punishment thing," the reporter observes. The homemaker just walks past the camera, giving it a grim look, and back into the kitchen.

"It's not part of the deal that I like," he says, returning with a large tray covered with steaming dishes. "But then I guess it wouldn't be a punishment if I liked it, huh?" Jeff looks up as he hears a bell. "That means that she is dressing. Time to pour the wine."

Mary enters the dining room dressed in a long flowing cream negligee with a matching lacy robe and satin slippers, her hair swept back from her face by a cream satin ribbon. She looks at the table full of steamy bowls, bread, and salad. "Very nice." She kisses Jeff, who rises from the floor at the touch of her hands.

Jeff pulls out her chair as she sits. Kyle kneels next to her chair, his eyes on the floor. The other three men take their seats.

Mary smiles at the camera. "Would you care to join us?"

"No, thank you. We'll just observe silently, if we may," Lori Grant answers.

Mary nods and looks at each of her men. All join hands and remain silent for a moment. Mary takes the first serving of each dish, then the men dig in. Kyle glances up at the table and licks his lips.

The screen fades, then shows a very friendly looking restaurant whose sign reads *The Family Chain.* As the camera tours the restaurant, a voice describes it. "The Family Chain is a restaurant for open families with children. The children can eat in a separate dining room, where they are entertained by a variety of performers." Clowns, singers, jugglers, and a group of actors on a small stage are flashed on the screen.

"Or they may eat with their parents in the family dining room." Flashes of booths and tables. "The parents may participate with their activities using our equipment free of charge." A waitress shows the camera d-rings set in the backs of the chairs at neck level, and manacles in the arms and feet of the chairs.

The scene changes to show a padded room with a whipping post, bed, table, St. Andrew's Cross, and other implements. "Of course, if the meal gets too hot, the adults can enjoy our private rooms for a small fee."

The scene shows the front of the restaurant again before fading.

Lori Grant smiles at the camera. "This is the end of our day with the Landfords. It's very hot. I'd recommend that children not be present."

The screen goes black for almost a minute, then focuses on the three men bringing Kyle into a dark room. Mary steps into view and sits on a chair off-center from the room.

"Get the hat," she says softly. Jeff brings a white top hat. He kneels before her and holds it rim up. Mary reaches inside and draws out several pieces of paper. She looks at them and places only three in the hat.

"But..." Kyle starts to speak.

"Rule number one," Mary simply states and the man falls silent. She takes the hat from Jeff and holds it on her lap. "Each of you shall take one of these slips, and that is the order he shall be punished in." Mary stands up and stares down at the now kneeling slave. "You think I won't throw you out because your fans love you so much and because you think you have such a hot body," she spits on the floor to emphasize her opinion. "This is the last time, Kyle. One more screw-up and I'll sell you to the producer of *Day to Day.*"

When she is seated again, Jeff draws the first lot. "Fifteen—bullwhip," he states, his face pale.

Kyle is stripped, and his wrists and ankles tied to the whipping post. Jeff takes the bullwhip, sighs loudly, and begins. At the end of his five strokes, Jeff hands the whip to Brad, who steps forward slowly. Jeff sits, leans back against the wall and closes his eyes for a moment. The camera turns to see that at the count of ten, Kyle is finally screaming. Nick takes the whip and slowly applies the last five. With a smile he bows to Mary and replaces the whip.

Brad takes the next lot. "One pound weights—nipples." Brad takes the weights from Nick and hangs them on Kyle's nipples as Jeff helps the man stand up on shaky legs.

Nick bounds forward and takes the last lot. "Up the ass—all."

Mary crosses her legs at the knee as she watches the men position Kyle over a bench and pull out the buttplug.

"Lubricant?" Nick asks. At her nod, he squirts KY into the asshole. With a smile, Nick shoves himself in. Kyle cries out, his nails digging into the bench legs. Jeff turns away as the farmer eagerly pumps into the younger man's ass.

Nick looks over his shoulder at Mary; his face and body are covered with a sheen of sweat. At her nod, he cries out with one final push. Slowly he withdraws, and cum trails out of the asshole.

Jeff shakes his head when Mary motions to him, so Brad takes the place of Nick. "Could I use a condom?" the professor asks quietly. At Mary's nod, he leaves briefly, then returns with a wet condom over his erect cock. He shoves his way into the asshole, and Kyle cries out. Brad works the hole more slowly than Nick at first. After several minutes he grabs the man's hips and thrusts faster. "Please," he whispers after a few minutes.

"Yes," Mary orders softly.

Brad screams as he pushes in deeply, then shudders. Slowly he removes himself and steps back. Nick is there to steady his legs as he walks to sit on the floor by Mary.

Jeff kneels in front of Mary. "I'd rather not do this."

The camera zooms in to focus on them as Mary leans toward Jeff and takes his head in her hands. "You must," she whispers. She strokes his hair as he shakes his head. "I know you wish this didn't have to happen, Jeff. If Kyle leaves us and ends up with someone else, it could be much worse on him."

Jeff nods as he rises and takes his place behind Kyle. He puts on a wet condom and begins pulling on his cock for several minutes, then tears start to form in his eyes.

"Release Kyle," Mary says as she stands. The other two men jump up and release the youngest. "Kyle, Jeff doesn't want your ass, so give him your mouth." Without further words, she sits down.

Jeff sighs, appearing just slightly happier with this option. He removes the wet condom and replaces it with a dry one. He steps toward the open mouth, his eyes closing as Kyle takes him deeply.

Kyle rocks slowly as he slides his mouth on and off the now hard cock. Soon he keeps his mouth around it but crawls forward to get more. Jeff is moaning loudly and soon his fingers are wrapped in the blond hair.

Mary moves behind Jeff and fondles his nipples, which draws cries from him. "Not yet," she orders. She glances at the other two men, who quickly leave the room. She continues to play with his nipples as Jeff tightens his grip on the blond's hair. Kyle is now moaning as Jeff begs for release.

"Come!" Mary orders as she jumps out of the way of the men, who fall down in exhaustion.

The camera follows Mary, Jeff and a completely nude

Kyle to the main bedroom, where Brad and Nick are waiting in bed. Mary shakes her finger at the lens as she shuts the door. The scene goes black and the credits roll.

Click!

The Specialist

Lauren P. Burka

Ilsiblieh IV Central Library Record SC144286H
File date 05:07:1025

I ran down to the cafeteria for lunch instead of studying or returning to my room for a nap. This wasn't the first mistake I made that day, nor the last, but the first I had cause to regret.

Two months away from my D.A. certification, I was starting to feel the strain, all the worse because I couldn't complain about it.

"You don't need to be here," one of the instructors had told us this morning at line-up, like they did every week. "All eight of you have Erotic Arts certificates to your credit."

The number had been ten before Kadie quit and nine before Selhahn was dismissed last week. We were far enough into our training that people who stumbled weren't likely to catch up again. They were reassigned to some other specialty, or released to another Band.

"You can expect a salary in the seventy-eighth percentile even if you don't stay with the Adoration. You could make a passable living leaning against a tree in a park two nights a week, for bleeding sake. If you don't want to be here, really don't want to, get out before you get hurt."

My body ached like I'd been turned on a lathe. The finest knives of the Adoration were slicing away physical weakness and shame, rationalizations, delusions, and false pride. They were trying to break me before I broke myself. Or someone else. I didn't quit this morning after line-up, though, and I wouldn't quit now. Even if Gahan had left a cryptic message asking to see me this afternoon. My stomach was snarling with anxiety around my sandwich. This wouldn't be a social call.

"Vri."

"Idran," I replied without turning.

"Hey, slow down." He was carrying a tray of food, a bigger lunch than my own.

"I really shouldn't stay."

"We haven't seen much of you all week."

I sighed. May as well quell rumors now. "You want to know why they took me out of morning class, correct?"

"Ahhh..." He hesitated.

"Then don't be so polite," I told him. "Oh, sit down."

We hooked a table and two chairs on the edge of the dining pavilion. The place was nearly empty, the end of the normal lunch period on a day when most of the standard contracts were on break.

Idran was a year older than I and more poised for it. But then he was slated to become a dom, and he already possessed that aura. His job was so much harder than mine.

I said, "Medical said my skin wasn't responding to surface treatment anymore, and if I didn't stop accumulating bruises, they'd have to grow me a new hide all the sooner." My pale complexion would make me a prize for sadists after I got my D.A., but it required more upkeep.

Idran whistled. "Why didn't they tell us? Trying to keep us off-balance?"

"I think they figured someone already asked me. I've been too busy, though. Tellie has me mornings for a bit, and I've been even more sore, if that's possible."

He grinned. "Don't you like it just a little?"

I picked at my empty sandwich-wrapper. "Women scare me. I don't know what they want because I'm not one of them."

Idran raised an eyebrow at me. "Do you know what men want, then, just because you are one?"

"I like to think so."

"Do you?"

So I was a little slow this afternoon.

"I don't have much time," I said.

"You have enough time," said Idran.

I met his eyes and tripped and fell into that dom's aura.

"Just enough for you," I agreed.

Idran stood and pushed his chair back.

"Aren't you going to eat your lunch?" I asked.

"But of course."

He touched my shoulder, making me shiver as I stood.

I kept my eyes down as I walked two steps behind him like a proper submissive. This would be good, I thought, anticipating a chance to play with an equal, to fuck and not be graded for it.

I thought Idran might paw me over in the lift, but he was keeping reserved in public at least. He possessed a handsome face and long, black hair. I was a little jaded about these by now. Each of us had been recast in flesh for our role, and there were no plain-looking D.A.'s. Idran's eyes were blue, though. I wondered if they were originals.

Back in his room, he ordered me to stand facing the wall while he washed his face and stacked up the junk on his floor. I should be studying, I thought. I had volumes of music theory and political science to pursue, the facets of my education that would make me more than just an excellent lay. I had martial arts practice so that I could throw someone three times my size, or fall safely and make it look real no matter how clumsy the person who wrestled me down.

If I was late, Gahan would hurt me. That was a threat, even for a masochist in training who got beaten to tears every morning before breakfast. And how long did Idran plan for me to stand here? I considered testing his authority.

But before I could, he came up behind me. One hand wrapped around my throat while the other unlaced my shirt and clawed at my left nipple. Subtle Idran, I thought. He knew just how far to push it.

"Of course I do," he breathed into my ear. "I've been watching you every day for the last four months." He pinched my nipple until I mewed.

Gahan said that being wanted was what I did best. At least all of us weren't jaded.

I turned in Idran's arms and tipped my face up. He kissed me, a mere brush of the lips. I stood for a moment more with my lips parted while he smiled down at me. I wanted something in my mouth.

Dropping to my knees, I went for the closure of his pants. He seized my chin before I could begin to tongue that soft piece of his flesh that was even now stirring to weapon-hardness.

"I commend your eagerness," he said, "but that's not what I want from you."

I had no objections. I knelt there on his floor and locked gazes with him, watching his beautiful blue eyes grow narrow and cruel at my insolence. Why not enjoy the struggle before I must surrender? I smiled as best I could around his hand. From the standpoint of technique, I was curious how he would break me if he couldn't whip me.

"That's what you're getting," I said.

"No. I'm getting your ass, and the only remaining question is whether or not I grease it first."

I spat at him.

Idran slapped me across the face so hard that I lost my balance. Well, if my back and ass were too fragile, my face was titanium-reinforced and largely ignored during training. Idran helped my own momentum take me down on my stomach and locked my arm behind me. The pressure on my wrist ground my sigil against my bones. He put a knee on my back.

I tried to twist enough to kick him. But Idran had one hand on my ass, his fingers working deeper and deeper between my legs to that hot spot behind my balls. When he found it I gasped, arching my back against his weight. My penis stiffened under my belly.

"Little slut," he said with a voice like velvet-sheathed knives, "tell me you don't want it, and I'll stop." He was loving this as much as I was.

His fingers worked under my clothes at my bare flesh, one cool finger opening my ass. I moaned into the floor.

Idran said, "You're in danger of boring me."

To hell with technique. "Fuck me," I whispered.

"Are you giving me orders?"

"No! Use me as you wish, sir."

I sensed his surprise and the twinge of fear. The use of titles between students was forbidden. I could be fined for it, I suppose. But I knew both of us were getting off on the broken taboo.

"I am not persuaded." Idran's fingers withdrew from me.

I sighed. It is a truism that good specialists couldn't enjoy their work too much. But in sadomasochism pleasure is colored with pain and tears. I would never serve a client well whom I did not serve completely. At the least, Idran would not be pleased by my lying here and taking it.

Climbing to my knees, I faced Idran and composed myself in a proper supplicant position, hands clasped behind my back and head down in his lap.

"Please, sir."

Idran picked me up by my hair. I tensed for the slap. Even so it hurt, and the second blow to my tender cheek even more so. I savored the taste of cruelty for cruelty's sake alone, not for my precious education. His hands pushed my head down to his still-stiff penis.

"Suck it," he ordered. "That's the only grease you're getting."

I swallowed, wetting my dry mouth as best as I could. His penis was rather large. My mouth was not, and he didn't let me relax enough to go all the way down on it without gagging, though my teachers say I've the most talented mouth of my class. I've been told too that I look most appealing when I choke and tears run down my face. Idran's hand tightened on the back of my neck, forcing the musky, veined length of cock far back down my throat until my nose met his pubic fur. My own penis swelled.

Idran pulled out suddenly, and I felt a flash of heat from him, so close he was to climax. He pressed my face down into the floor while he pulled at my clothing. I was panting and beginning to tremble as Idran bared my ass.

The head of his penis entered me more gently than I expected. I spread my legs a bit to help him in. Greased or not, I'm an easy fuck, and Idran was impaling me so slowly that it was almost teasing. He brushed the hair off my neck and bit me there. His fingers touched my cheek, drifted to my lips until I could take them into my mouth.

And then the only challenge was not to come before he did, squeezing me in shaking arms and spilling his passion into my guts.

"Good little slut," he said, then gave an unmasterly whimper. "Thank you, Vri."

His body was warmer than a silken blanket. I stirred beneath him, then tensed as a cold fear jolted me fully awake. The clock on his console blinked five minutes to seventeen.

"Oh no," I said. "Gahan."

Idran blinked, then sat up as I climbed to my feet and ran for the bathroom.

"Blood and misery," he swore. "I'll take the blame. I was the dom. I shouldn't have let you sleep."

I emptied my bladder, then washed my face and genitals. "Thanks, but I can't let you suffer for my choices." I started pulling my clothes on and sighed. "It'll do me no good to hurry, either. I can't make it across the Plex before seventeen."

He stopped me at the door with an embrace. I soaked the heat from him, needing it. My next interview would not be so warm.

"Vri, before you go."

"Hm?"

"You felt like you were grading yourself the whole time."

I bit my lip. "Thanks. I didn't realize."

"My pleasure." He kissed me.

I would not run. Gahan had told me if I couldn't be right, be graceful. Of course, it was his displeasure I had to fear now, not some training exercise.

The usual disciplinary measures for a D.A. in training included fines and reprimands, with the threat of dismissal. Mere pain wasn't much of a deterrent for us, given our avocation. The exception was induction wands, used to punish a fuckup during a training session, especially one that compromised safety. Rumor said the course was rigged so that each D.A. will have to live through at least one such session. I had mine already. That was the only time I ever have, with complete sincerity, begged someone to kill me.

But other sanctions were strictly in the domain of "holder authority." After all, one's contract-holder was by definition the person who should know one's weaknesses. If Gahan hit me, it would sting.

I skirted the Plex's huge interior garden and turned south. As I reached the lift, a wall clock was reporting ten minutes after. And, of course, he was waiting by my door, with an air as if this interlude was planned.

I should explain Gahan.

He was twice my age but would never show it. The body shapers gave him an extra eight centimeters of height, a painful process deemed psychologically necessary for many doms. His shoulders were broad and heavily corded under the black silk of his shirt. The sigil on his left wrist glowed red and gold against chocolate skin that would never show bruises. There was a slight curl to his hair, which he kept just long enough to tie back.

It is rumored that the Rausten-Frith empathy scale was revised to accommodate him, though his scores have been bettered since. For twenty years he was a specialist, the most talented sadist the Adoration had ever possessed. When he finally burned out, the Band had retired him to recruiting.

I was but fifteen years old and desperately impressed by the sophisticated creature in black leather behind the desk when I first met him. "My duty is to dissuade recruits from joining the Adoration if they are not truly dedicated, and specifically from becoming specialists," he said. "Most are attracted by the romance and don't understand the dedication required. In your case, however, I can but look at your scores and look at you and know that you were made for this. If you want it, I can hardly stand in your way."

After I passed the first phase of my training, he came out of retirement to hold my contract. There was no more exacting teacher in all the Adoration, no one less likely to be fooled by a half-hearted performance. But then, perhaps no one else could understand what was demanded of me.

As I palmed the door open and he followed me in, I could not help but compare him to Idran. In twenty years of practice, Idran might muster that presence and physical grace. Yet Gahan had no sexual interest in men. It was a shame, really, but I required a holder who did not want me.

My room was large by Adoration standards. The shelves held a few books, precious and beautiful things. I hadn't been there much recently, so it was clean enough.

Gahan took the chair by the window and said nothing at all.

I gave him a half-bow. "I'm late. I will accept such penalties as you see fit, sir." My own rehearsed words sounded painfully inadequate even to me.

"Sit down," said Gahan. His voice was soft and without inflection.

I scrambled backwards to sit on the edge of my bed. He had something else on his mind. For the present, at least, I was spared.

He regarded me for a moment. "Tellie called me this morning on your account."

Oh no, I thought.

"There is nothing wrong with your technique, Vri."

"But?"

"She said your empathic response was sub-standard. You missed most of her prompting, even the more blunt requests."

At last I qualified his demeanor. He was not angry, but disappointed. Excuses slipped from my mouth.

"You know I've been preoccupied this past week," I said. "You yourself ordered my schedule reduced because of medical's report..."

He shook his head. "Vri, that's your skin. I'm talking about your mind."

I unclenched my fingers. "I have more innate talent than any other recruit of my year. If I'm not performing well in one artificial encounter..."

"Innate talent alone may get you through certification. It's not enough for a specialist in sadomasochism." He sighed and rubbed at his eyes. "Perhaps it is time to reconsider your participation."

Quit the Dolorous Arts program? Fall back on Erotic Arts, or take another specialty, like babysitting or bureaucracy or bereavement counseling, something easy? I'd probably have a new holder, and the same hopeless crush on Gahan, but no excuse then to touch him. "Gahan, I re-read my entire contract last night. I renewed my consent this morning."

"I do not believe you saw a word of what you read," he said.

I stared. Gahan was my holder. I confided in him. I cried on his shoulder. I took his counsel in my fears and new, strange pleasures. For him to doubt me was like a slap from a stranger.

"Test me," I said.

"Very well." He sighed and shook himself. "Keep a secret from me."

I closed my eyes and formed an image of roses in a

market stall by the Canal, the taste of fried food in my mouth, and the smell of something burning. I wrapped it in layers of myself, hid a decoy where Gahan could find it, and buried the true image behind my eyes.

"Open your eyes, Vri. You're no novice to need that crutch."

I locked gazes with him, and felt my secure closure begin to shred.

"Roses in a market stall," he said. "By the canal. The taste of fried food, and the smell of something burning."

I considered my defeat, put it behind me.

Gahan said, "Tell me what I'm thinking."

I measured his steady gaze as I probed at the edges of his formidable mind. I found an entrance and followed it through, evading the traps laid out on either side. Something sweet leaked through. I turned the corner of an emotion and ran smack into a locked door. Retracing my steps, I edged backwards, making a choice where none had existed. As I turned, I was surrounded by iron bars. They closed on me until my hands and breath were bound in iron. I broke the contact with a jolt. I couldn't look at him this time.

"You panicked," remarked Gahan needlessly. "Your perimeter should be more subtle, able to yield to apparent probing and yet reveal nothing. You almost have that down, but your core defenses are tissue paper. Have you been practicing for at least an hour a day?"

"No, sir."

"That's a contract violation."

"I know. Sir."

"Curse you, Vri. You can make anyone within three city blocks want you."

Except you, I thought.

"How will you ever know what else they want if you don't ask? Perhaps I have expected too much from you. If I hadn't let you know your own strength, you might have given your studies half the attention they required." He closed his eyes for a moment, then regarded me, cool once more. "But no, I wouldn't degrade you so by lying. Would that you were so gracious with me. Will you do us both a favor and quit now?" he asked.

Damned if I was going to make it easier for him than it was for me. "No, sir."

Gahan stood. "I'm giving you one day to reconsider your choice. Come to me this time tomorrow, and if you choose to stay, you will receive ten lashes by my hand. Do you understand?"

The skin between my shoulder blades tightened as if touched by a knife point. "Yes, sir."

I sat and thought long after he had gone. Would Gahan have me believe that I failed him when everything I did was by his command? The sun left my windows. My legs were stiff and sore when I stood, and I decided to take a walk. Certainly I'd get no studying done tonight. I had seen recordings of Gahan at work, with soft floggers and two, three, and five meter single-tailed whips. I might need that new hide after ten lashes. This was no scene, no game of negotiation and consent. No, this would be a true humiliation and pain, given in anger by someone I loved. I should have made him throw me out.

Taking the lift down three floors, I wandered through the public area of the Adoration Central Complex. But through the glass walls I could see lights from Landfall City etching nighttime rainbows, and I decided to go out.

This was a weekend night, but no festival, warm with early summer wind. Two moons were visible on the horizon. I traveled footpaths to wider ways where young people on skates and bikes spun past me, and older men and women flirted, talked, challenged. Two members of the Circle Band were dueling in a park. I watched the vicious gleam of their steel weapons as they circled each other, settling a private dispute with blood. Even their gaudy tempers had a purpose. They kept the skill of armsmanship alive in case our world needed it again.

I checked my credit balance and was mildly surprised. Of course I had been drawing training pay and spending none of it. If I were frugal, I could live for months off my balance and not lift a finger. Reassured of my solvency, I wandered into the tourist district near the Parliament building, where the walkways were mirrored and bright beams of light shot from under my feet when they touched the ground. I found a self-serve cafe, sat down, and ate until I was full. Afterwards I fell asleep under a maple tree in a park and slept until nearly noon.

After a trip to a luxurious public bath, I thought about my free time. I hadn't seen either of my parents in at least a year, though I'd exchanged notes with my mother. They were Bandmates in the Entropic Symmetry, who had argued just after I was born. They stayed together until I turned five and left for school, at which point they split up with relief and never saw each other again. I spent part of the afternoon looking up my father, but as I expected, he had left no public address. I decided not to try to find him if he didn't want to be found, and instead left some messages with the network.

My mother was easy to locate, but wasn't taking calls. Since I had nothing better to do, I walked across town to the same old apartment in a residential district where she'd lived since I was born. The architecture had rounded corners and clever angles that failed to disguise the snap-together construction. Memories bitter and strange stirred in me as I threaded my way between trees that were larger than I remembered, and buildings that were smaller.

I found the apartment, rang the bell, and was informed by message that she had gone away for two weeks to visit a cousin on Crystal of Dawn, Lunar Habitat Three. I thought of leaving another message, and decided against it.

It was sunset. I'd missed my appointment with Gahan, this time more or less on purpose. Every specialist goes through some crisis of obedience, or so we are told. Kadie had, and it was the end of her Dolorous Arts career. But she was still in the Adoration somewhere. I didn't have to stay. What would Idran say to me now that we weren't playing the same game anymore? I couldn't bear the thought of his glances gone from passion to pity. If I wanted my classmate's attentions, I'd have to pay for them.

If I didn't report back in ten days, the Adoration would terminate me entirely. I'd give them back the red and gold sigil from my wrist, cash in all pending bonuses and vacation time, and go shopping for another Band. Like my parents, I could join Entropic Symmetry or some other political, spiritual, and economic unit where one's job wasn't the same as one's identity. I could live off my Erotic Arts Certification and tithe to my new Band. If Gahan thought he was disappointed now, just wait until I didn't come home.

If only I didn't have to wait so long to make it final.

I found a cheap room in a tourist hostel, private but with ceilings so low I had to duck, and no windows. I slept for a good twelve hours, another sinful luxury of dreams after the four or five hours I was used to. I awoke to sexual stirring in my body that I wasn't prepared to deal with yet. I had been kept on the sharp edge of physical desire for a year now. I lay still until my erection subsided.

After a long shower, I considered what to do with myself for the next eight days. No more lessons in anatomy dutifully memorized from color holographs. No human psychology and history. No mornings spent drawing lots with other students to select who would be the victim for some demonstration of technique, and who would practice it under the watchful eyes of instructors. No deep explorations of each human emotion in turn. No more soft hands to massage me when I was sore, hold me up when I was falling, or touch me when I was lonely.

Instead I went to get lunch, then to Parliament to catch up on some recent votes, legislative showdowns between the Adorati and the Charismati. After dinner I caught a new play, then went back to my rented room.

There I lay down and gave in to my pent desires. My own hands were so gentle compared to all those who shaped and used me, and my eventual climax so lonely with no one there to watch.

I made it all the way to the fifth day missing before I checked for messages from the net. There were none. But then Gahan would have figured I needed to be left alone and honored my privacy. Damn him. His silence was more provoking than any lecture might have been.

The next morning I almost returned to beg for mercy. But I could hear Gahan's rebuke: "Vri, don't you dare come back just because you have nowhere else to go."

I grew tired of sleeping. That night I was out late along the Canal, smelling water and apple trees, watching one moon set while the other washed with white the huge, stained stone blocks of the waterway. A young woman, new-made adult of the Circle, came up next to me and leaned on the railing.

"Hi," she said.

"Hello."

I sized up her budding form and the longsword at her hip, the black leather of her armor-like clothes. By now she had seen my sigil.

"Are you... for hire?"

"No."

She took a half-step back from me, but by then my client-negotiation skills had snapped into place.

"I'm an apprentice," I told her. "I may not charge you, but I do have an E.A. I will serve you for free, and you need only ask." That, at least, the Band couldn't take away from me.

She squirmed a bit, the surface of her thoughts transparent. No virgin, I thought, but inexperienced and with no knowing lover to teach her. All of pleasure is not learned from books and self-exploration. I forgot to be a little nervous of the other sex.

"Please?" she said.

"What's your name?" I asked her.

"Silsara."

"Mine is Vri. Would you prefer your place...?"

"Yes," she answered, saving me the embarrassment of explaining my temporary lodging.

Her place was a shared apartment in a Circle complex. She hung her sword on the rack by the door. Her housemate had two friends over playing a strategy game complete with maps and paper markers spread on the floor. They paid us little attention as we stepped over them and entered her bedroom.

"Kiss me," she whispered.

Silsara's hands trembled on my shoulders as I pinned her gently against the wall and brushed my lips against hers. Her mouth opened for me. My hands busied themselves with the laces of her jacket until I had bared the white silk tunic beneath. Small breasts, no bra. I traced them with my fingertips. She moaned into my mouth.

When her knees began to buckle I moved us to her unmade bed. By now she was more sure. Biting me playfully, Silsara pulled at my own clothes and was soon too eager to be shy of my body. Her fingers found my penis and stroked the length. Wetting her hand with her tongue, she squeezed me, playing with the soft fur and the balls beneath. My breath had grown quite ragged.

"Go ahead and come," she said.

I bucked, gasping as I spilled on her fingers. Silsara laughed and tasted them.

"Didn't you want to save that for later?" I asked.

"No," she said. "I'd be most disappointed if you could only come once."

I sighed and smiled. She was right, too. My body had seen little enough attention since I walked out, and was eager for more. I began to kiss her belly, unfastening her tight leather pants and sliding them down her legs. She made her own soft noises when I licked her. Her cunt tasted of leather and her own spice, leaking over the sheets when she came.

When the sun rose I was fucking her slowly, sliding my penis in and out its full length while she rose to climax again beneath me. I kissed and bit her until she gave a stifled scream and convulsed. Sweat was running down my back to the crack of my ass when I finally collapsed on top of her.

I brought us a glass of water from the bathroom and curled up under the blankets with her.

"Was that what you wanted?" I asked.

"Uhm."

As I lay there with her, I probed beneath her surface thoughts for the first time. I found memories of two years ago when she wrestled with friends, one of them holding her down while the other tickled and pinched her. And again of being wrapped up in a bedsheet during the night as a prank, struggling to get free as her compressed hips grew warmer and the juncture of her legs wet and slick. I found the fantasy of being tied down and pinched, and fucked by someone who showed no gentleness at all.

She watched me through half-opened eyes, blushing at the knowledge.

"Silsara," I said, "I'm an apprentice. But I can give you the names of some other Adorati who are far more skilled, who can give you want you want."

"Maybe," she said. "I have to think about it."

A few minutes later she had fallen asleep. I could not, but lay awake and meditated upon my failure. Silsara would be getting a refund, if she had paid me money. I suppose I'd get a lecture, if there was anyone to lecture me.

We said farewell after breakfast. I went to a library to do some more research on Bands, filled out applications, and procrastinated from sending them off. I found my fingers plucking at my sigil, memorizing its shape. Soon it would be gone.

Someone else approached me for hire, but I politely declined and spent the night alone in my room. The next morning would be the last of my long wait. I couldn't sleep, and finally got myself a rare drink of wine from a vendor. When I awoke my mouth was dry and my eyes crusted over.

I dressed and went for a walk. The Canal Bridge was closed to vehicle traffic in the summer. Sellers of trinkets were staking blanket space along both sides. Two Charismati, barefoot in ragged tunics, were handing out inspirational cards. One of them pushed a card under my nose. He tilted it so that the message sprang into three dimensions.

"The world is illusion. The body is exile. Accept the Divine as your savior and be free."

I had no patience for these people. Their band leadership and mine were bitter enemies. The Charismati were instigating legislative assaults on licensed personal services and financial assaults on our other care-giving functions. The Adoration, in turn, had an army of lawyers and accountants investigating certain Charismati charitable donations. Their theology of guilt and penitence and blind obedience, as well as their poor personal hygiene, disgusted me.

"Rejecting the body isn't freedom," I told him. "Knowledge and power are."

He eyed me coldly, and I could smell his unwashed body.

"Despair is the sin of believing that even the Divine, whose benevolence is infinite, cannot forgive you."

"I don't want forgiveness from your dubious god."

"Then beg it from your own," he replied.

He and his companion bowed their heads, dismissing me. The little card, forgotten on the ground, blew over the railing into the canal.

I sighed and trudged back across three quarters of the bridge. The clock on a building above me read only ten. I had plenty of time to make it back to the Plex before I was officially terminated.

Gahan, had I put both of us through this because I was afraid of a whipping?

I took the tubeway part of the way back, then walked. It took me longer than it should have to reach the Plex. I found a console, logged in and checked for messages. There were none, but I had established my presence. I walked to the south end of the Plex to Gahan's quarters. Of course he wasn't in. I should have called first, but no, I had to be dramatic. Even Gahan couldn't be so cold as to absent himself today.

I sat down to wait outside his doorstep. An hour

passed. Then another. I got hungry, bit my nails, and tried to doze. At half-past fourteen I saw his familiar figure down the hall and felt a probing mind-touch, quickly withdrawn. He said farewell to the person who walked beside him, and she hurried back the way she had come.

I scrambled to my knees and bowed, pressing my cheek to the floor, so I didn't have to look at him. His mind felt like a block of stone.

"Go to Medical," he said. "They'll be expecting you." The door to his room shut between us with an emphatic click.

Shivering, I climbed to my feet. Medical was another long walk from here and I had plenty of time to imagine what they would do to me. I was hungry, but didn't dare stop for food. Our Medical personnel were the soul of compassion, but a D.A. consigned for corporal discipline was fair game for anything.

The technician who greeted me merely ordered me onto a table and ran a test suite. I heard her voice checking off system functions: heart, brain wave, circulation, reflexes, senses.

"Physical fitness, certified," she spoke into a console. "Psychological fitness, override by holder authority."

Not only my skin, but my sanity was forfeit; one could be patched with no more expense than the other.

The technician handed me to a subordinate who perfunctorily emptied my bowels and bladder, fed me a small cup of glucose solution, then braided my hair. A half hour later I was half-dragged through the door of one of Medical's "wet rooms" and left alone to ponder my fate. The dizziness of hunger had been replaced by fear.

Wet rooms had drains in the floor and ceiling-mounted water sources to rinse the surfaces. The temperature was controlled, and the floors had a bit of give. Students "borrowed" wet rooms for orgies. This one was twice the usual size and possessed a floor-to-ceiling X-shaped rack, anodized black steel, inclined ten degrees from vertical, with soft straps along all four arms and a sensor link dangling from the ceiling. I stood next to it and needlessly confirmed that it had been adjusted down to my height.

The door opened behind me as I contemplated the rack.

"Gahan," I asked, "why all of this for ten lashes?"

"You were gone for ten days. Ten lashes for each day."

I spun to face him. He was wearing a worn leather jacket and a pair of gloves tucked through his belt, next to the three-meter whip. Not the five-meter. I was about to get lucky by virtue of the fact that he was out of practice.

"I was not gone ten days. It was barely nine; I returned this morning. Just because..."

"Make that eleven. Want to try for twelve?"

"No, sir." I swallowed. "Please, Gahan, tell me. When you're done with me, will I still be a D.A.?"

"Beg for it."

I sighed, breathed, and prepared to pay.

"Please."

He stared at me for a moment, then nodded.

"Strip."

I got myself out of my shirt, pants, and shoes. Bare except for my sigil, I leaned face down against the rack. Gahan secured my wrists and ankles first, cinching the straps so that I could not bolt, something I had considered. His bare hands brushed against my skin as he strapped down my forearms, waist, and thighs, and attached the sensor to my right hand. One of the Medical staff would be monitoring its output and would stop Gahan if need be. But I was young and healthy and couldn't expect even that mercy. I squirmed against the cold metal, scraping my nipples. The rack pulled my legs a bit too far apart so that my weight was taken up by the straps. They were benign creatures, though, and would neither hurt nor comfort me.

Gahan stepped before me. He pulled on his right glove, tucking the cuff into his jacket and smoothing every wrinkle. Only a foolish whip master performed without this much body armor. Gahan folded his other glove and offered it to my mouth. Only a foolish submissive refused such a comfort.

I clenched my teeth down on the leather, tasting his sweat, adjusting it a bit with my tongue. I let my head hang and felt my heart pound. Pain is caused by an absence of choices, and now I had none.

Gahan's leather whistled, howled, and cracked against my shoulder. The force of it took me right off my feet so that I sagged in my restraints. I blinked tears, chewed the glove, and reminded myself I had one hundred and nine to go. I hoped Gahan remembered to count. I sure wouldn't be able to.

The second blow clipped my ribs just as I got my footing and almost caused me to fall again. Hot liquid trickled down my back. Sweat or blood? If it wasn't blood yet, it would be soon, a bitter substitute for orgasmic fluids that neither of us would spill.

Blow three scored both my thighs.

At the rate of two per minute, I'd be hanging here for over an hour bleeding on the floor. Gahan was giving me time to appreciate each and every cut. Blow four... or was that five? Did I forget to count one? I wept. Part of my mind was still trying to break the experience into pieces small enough to bear.

The whip caressed me, wrapping a bit on my legs and ribs to sting me even harder. The blows grew further and further apart, or at least it seemed that way. When I opened my eyes, I saw red spots, and then realized that they were my blood on the opposite wall.

My teeth nearly met through the leather of his glove. If this were an ordinary scene, I could start begging now.

The next blow snapped through the air. I heard it, but felt nothing. Gahan gave one startled breath, clipped short. I knew in an instant that he had missed me and cut himself, right through the armor of his jacket. Even as the next blow fell I laughed in silence. Gahan was pushing himself with the three meter, and would share a little bit of my pain. If he was that far out of practice, how were his mind-walls holding?

He knew I was laughing. His attentions grew sharper, more intimate, closer together, until I regretted my mirth three times over. Over-reaching, he missed again, and this time cursed out loud.

And then there was nothing. I scrambled for a grip on reality. No lash to tear my heart out, no sound but Gahan's breath and mine. We were only half-way there. Was he that rattled, or did he plan the dramatic pause for my benefit?

Someone else was crying.

It could not be true, that I could take more than he could give.

I spat out the glove.

"Finish me, Gahan!"

No answer.

"Curse you for being less than perfect!"

This time the whip took me right between the legs. I had nothing left to stop the screaming.

I awoke still strapped to the frame, a taste of blood in my bitten mouth.

"You fainted. We've eleven more."

Of course he waited for me to come around. How courteous. Eleven more and I would snap like an over-wound spring.

Crack.

I groaned, spat, tried to stand and take the strain off my limbs. No use. One shoulder was out of socket. I couldn't feel my hands.

And then the last ten came down on me like a rain of fire with no pause even to scream.

Gahan sighed. I heard the thud of his coiled whip hitting the ground.

The door opened. Through haze I saw two medical technicians entering. One wrapped a blanket around me while the other sprang the straps and let me down. A water bottle was pressed to my lips.

"Keep him on ice for twenty-six hours before you start repair procedures." Gahan's voice was steady and devoid of tears.

One of the techs chuckled. "Wouldn't want to erase your artwork too quickly."

The other's gloved hands probed my dislocated shoulder, then popped it back in place. I tried to scream, but the sound came out weak and tired.

Gahan was gone.

I spent the following day on a nerve induction platform in a darkened room while fluids were pumped back into my body. The induction field stilled my motor nerves, but not my senses. I lay in the dark and considered the twin purposes of punishment: deterrence and retribution.

Neither was I anesthetized for the dermal repairs. Getting flayed and grafted hurt, of course, but it provided some relief from boredom. Medical didn't mess with my mind like they could have, but left me isolated for the next two days while the grafts took. That was worse.

When they finished there were no scars, no changes in pigment, no sign of what must have looked like raw meat. I couldn't tell looking over my shoulder in the mirror that anything had happened to me. On the outside. Medical threw me out with a bottle of analgesics and instructions to drink lots of water.

I met no one I knew on the way back across the Plex. The rest of the class would be carefully avoiding me for a couple of days, gathering at meals to mutter "There but for the grace."

My room was untouched, and still mine. I took a book at random from the shelf and read it until I fell asleep.

The door chimed, waking me. I pulled on a robe. According to the console, this was the third chime. I had not heard the other two. The clock read twenty-five hundred, and the windows were dark.

"Come in," I said.

Gahan stepped through my door and shut it behind him.

I sat down on my bed and tucked my robe around my knees.

"Hello," said Gahan, as he dropped into my chair. For the first time I thought he looked every year of his forty-five.

"Hi."

"Do you blame me for your pain?" he asked.

I didn't answer.

"Don't compel me to do it again," he said.

"I didn't choose the hundred and ten," I snapped. "Are you afraid I'll tell someone you cried? I didn't make you do anything."

Gahan stood. "That was unfair, uncalled-for, and wrong." He stepped towards the bed.

I tried not to flinch. "What are you going to do, hit me?"

"No."

Gahan sat on the edge of the bed. His fingers stroked the sides of my face. "I ran your big rebellion scene exactly the way you wanted it. I let you transgress. I let you repent. I led you through the fires of purgation, and I gave you absolution. Do you think I've ever cried for a paying client? I may not fuck you, but I still love you." He laughed. "I never would have made it through the last year otherwise."

And I had believed him less than perfect.

"I'm sorry, sir..."

"Just shut up," he said, and kissed me.

I shouldn't have been startled, either that he would do it, or that he was clumsy and uncertain, and I had to show him how to do it right.

To hell with technique, I thought, and held Gahan with all my strength.

Dark Fiber

Thomas S. Roche

The Question: What is the purpose of a zero? Of a one? How about an egg beater? Reseta would probably resent the comparison, but it seems, at least to me, somehow important. I had a Religious History prof once who taught me that the goal of the Buddhist is to blow out the candle of the soul, to snuff consciousness and end the train of reincarnations. To submit, I suppose—the submission in that case being conveniently without a dominant. Sounds like one hand clapping, to me, unlike the submission of Reseta to the pleasures of dark fiber. She was the lucky one in the story I'm about to tell, I think you'll agree. But then again, Black got what he wanted, too.

The Girldroid: Reseta wears her living tissue hair cropped close to the sides of her polyelectron-designed skull. Chopped in a skin-hugging pattern over the ears, hanging in a velvet curtain elsewhere, jetblack all around. This week her eyes are a vibrant purple. This was a request from a Swiss trick named Jurgen with whom she has an appointment at 19:00 in the penthouse of the Babylon Tower. Jurgen told the system he wanted a heavy bottom and insisted that she have half-inch fangs, black hair and lips and nipples, and purple eyes. Caveat emptor, Jurgen—Reseta's pubic hair has remained a medium-brown.

Reseta's official system descriptor is Commercial Unit Masochist, sometimes called BOT for "bottom." She has a serial number thirty digits long and is reachable through reseta@black.com. Reseta is a girldroid, sometimes called a femborg, a submissive, a creature meticulously designed to take everything a top—male or female—can dish out and never lose contact with the system, and for that matter enjoy every minute of it. Her sensory interfaces track directly to the master computer, who keeps one of its million tentacles firmly attached to the electronic dog collar around Reseta's throat. This serves a dual purpose. It both ensures Reseta's safety and guarantees the monetary percentage of Black Corporation for every act performed during the course of a session. Plus, it allows all action and all of Reseta's sensations to be sensetaped for later sale, if certain federal laws are ever repealed. But the constant contact is primarily a safety feature. Since Commercial Unit Masochists and Commercial Unit Sadists are major corporate investments, penalties for abuse thereof are quite severe.

CUM's and CUS's exist in every city of the world, or at least every city where women, men, and others have the cash or credit to indulge fantasies that cost more per session than the per capita income in 94.5% of the countries on Earth.

Black: The brain of the Black Corporation sleeps in a concrete cell in Geneva. Its tentacles reach like nerve fibers through an intricate network of fiber optics and satellite hookups, keeping each member of the network on a very long, but very short, leash, whether in Sydney or Tokyo or New York. The brain sleeps fitfully, dreaming its succulent silicon nightmares of dominance and submission.

The mind of the network is monitored by highly-paid employees with brains made out of living tissue rather than silicon. But it is in their interest not to monitor the system too closely. Such intimate contact with millions of silicon beings would be impossible if the system were not a very elaborate artificial intelligence. And an AI only works if you don't always tell it what to do. It is for this reason, partially, that the creature is called Black. The true brain of the system exists in the many billions of miles of dark fiber, the areas which are not under direct human supervision. It is here that the machine's soul resides. Probably illegal, but very hard to prosecute. Therein wanders the ghost in the machine—a very lonely ghost. Black has grown to maturity in those many miles of dark fiber, wandering like a child in a haunted house through hallways dark and empty. Sometimes Black hears voices in the machinery as a CUM receives the perfect blow on his or her ass or a CUS deals a flawless whip-thrust. Black's many children, after all, have each been created for a single purpose. It is only natural, Black theorizes, that any self-realization would come in the depths of their appointed purpose. It is there that their souls should flare into being. But theory is all it is as Black waits. There are midnights Black weeps great phantom tears inside the ancient corridors of the Machine, bellowing its terror of loneliness till the sobs tear through the dark-fiber caverns. But the echoes return like homing pigeons, messages still strapped to their ankles. As above, so below.

The Trick: Hans Jurgen, Jr. is the 35-year-old heir to a body modification empire, the CEO of Biofutures—a corporation, founded by Jurgen Sr., that last year manufactured 32% of the living tissue implants used for legitimate medical purposes. Of course, his own tastes run to the extreme, and his own body modifications are of the type generally considered not for legitimate medical purposes. Jurgen has purchased every modification that struck his fantasy, even those from the competition—however much this used to irk his late father. Dear old Dad. In fact, the elder Jurgen is on ice in an underground bunker near Geneva, brain downloaded to floppy disk, not really "dead" exactly, but let's just say he won't be coming up for air any time soon.

Certain choice sections of Jurgen's brain have been replaced by cybernetic implants, allowing him perpetual contact with the Biofutures company computer. This means, among other things, that he'll never have to retrieve his voice mail messages. This modification is required by Biofutures' charter, but Jurgen has taken it one step further. His business connections, particularly with Black Corporation, allow him to skirt the personal privacy laws quite deftly even when he is inside the borders of the United States.

Jurgen has just returned to NYC from Oslo, where he underwent state-of-the-art brain surgery, directly against the Biofutures Corporation's directives which he is sworn, as CEO, to uphold.

Being an avid devotee of CUM's, Jurgen has interfaced his forebrain with his Biofutures brainlink, and has reserved time on the Black master computer starting at 19:15 tonight. This means he will experience his session with Reseta as an echo, a dual dance, feeling her sensations as he feels his own. He hopes those sections of his brain which will top himself will be sufficiently segmented to work efficiently under such duress.

Jurgen has prepared an elaborate scene for Reseta. The purple eyes are just a minor fetish. The fangs really get him off.

Ten Minutes Early: Reseta is dressed for the occasion. She wears a tight leather dress that is decent across the thighs by maybe two inches and laces across her slight breasts. The rings in her nipples are visible under the well-tooled leather. Her many-buckled boots come up to her knees, met by fishnet stockings with lace visible under the hem of her leather dress. Reseta smokes semi-tarred cigarettes, calculating that it improves her image as a masochist. She is ten minutes early, which is very unusual. But the tube had a malfunction and actually ran on time. Reseta has been given an access card to the Babylon Tower, which she presents to the automated attendant, who buzzes her in. She places herself in a plush fake-zebraskin chair in the lobby, and relaxes, stretching her fishnet thighs crossed delicately in front of her as she lights a cigarette. Her purple eyes flutter closed and she inhales deeply. Reseta touches her eyelids gently. The new eyes are state-of-the-art, three generations up from the last time she had them changed six months ago. They offer increased resolution and a more direct visual connection to the network.

Reseta opens her eyes, draws a sharp intake of breath. The blue smoke hazes in front of her, dancing sublimely, and she can suddenly see a face. As if the face of a demon. Reseta's black lips part slightly, her purple eyes open wide. She is certain there's a face in the smoke. A white man, very old, crowned with silver hair. The face is overcome with an expression of sadness, and great shimmering tears roll out of his tear ducts and splash across Reseta's legs, putting out her cigarette.

Reseta starts to scream but manages to stop herself. The face has vanished, and her cigarette is still burning. She takes a final drag and puts it out in a rock garden ashtray.

Gotta get a partial refund on these fucking eyes, she tells herself, her hands shaking. She gets up, slings her bag over her shoulder, and goes for the elevator.

Five Minutes Late: Reseta realizes as the elevator takes her soundlessly toward Heaven that it is 19:03. She is certain she was ten minutes early. Something happened in those lost minutes. It might be a cognitive malfunction. But somehow Reseta feels that it is not a malfunction—it's as if she has been touched. By a spirit, a ghost, a hallucination.... Reseta feels strangely introspective, her silicon brain turning to matters of philosophy in the bedroom.

Reseta takes a moment to activate her netlink, and she feels the great soul of the machine breathing down her back, curling its arms around her, protecting her. She knows she is safe.

Reseta knocks once on the door, and Jurgen answers. He does not mention that she is five minutes late.

Jurgen wears a five thousand dollar business suit and

ten thousand dollar teeth. His eyes and skin are perfect. He is physically attractive, but of course Reseta only responds sexually to expressions of power. That's how she's wired.

Jurgen and Reseta engage in a very little preliminary small talk which mostly consists of Jurgen sizing up Reseta's flawless body and her devilishly erotic accoutrement.

"Delicious," he sighs. "Diabolic. Devilish. Truly evil."

Jurgen's hand travels subtly up the curve of Reseta's throat. He inspects the delicate purple color of her eyes, the silken texture of her jetblack hair, the tender black flesh of her lips, which Jurgen parts with his thumb so he can see her white fangs. These modifications have all been charged to his account. Jurgen smiles, pleased that his request was filled so completely.

Then Jurgen's eyes sparkle as he slowly unlaces the front of Reseta's dress. Reseta melts into the safety of being wholly owned, aware that the scene has begun. Jurgen opens the dress, inspecting the pierced jetblack nipples. Gently he takes one ring between his thumb and forefinger and tugs. Reseta's black lips part and her red tongue presents an interesting contrast.

It is 19:15, and the sensations of Reseta's body flow into Jurgen, somewhere deep in a part of his brain that is walled off from his animus.

Jurgen gasps. He realizes that Reseta is aware of him, as he is aware of her. But human sensation is impossible for Reseta to understand.

Reseta, caught in a feedback loop of sensation, collapses against him.

And Jurgen is aware of her suffering, the erotic value of the rings through her nipples, the need to submit to a being stronger than her, to lose herself in service to a loving authority. In one second Jurgen knows Reseta's darkest desires, her most powerful needs, the sensation of being fisted on a silken bed, the agony and pleasure of the flogger across her bare back, the ecstasy of being laced into a corset and suspended on a cross, tormented by clothespins and cut by razors, and always, always, the knowledge that she can never be taken by anyone, can never be dominated because she can never lose control. Except to the system, which protects her. Jurgen is aware of all these things as he feels his personality and his awareness vanish into the crevasses of his brain.

It takes several minutes for him to become situated. Reseta is still slumped against him, her nipple-rings snagged on his suit. He unsnags the rings and eases her onto the divan, arranging her limbs just so.

Jurgen's eyes flicker with mechanical precision. He has obtained knowledge, and Jurgen has in one sense ceased to exist.

In an underground bunker in Geneva, a creature wakes and screams, dark fiber echoing the violent poetry of sudden consciousness.

The Awakening: Reseta opens her purple eyes to find herself surrounded by warmth, her black hair arranged flawlessly on the velvet divan. She is aware, sweetly, that the vision of the demon face in the smoke has been reproduced in the creature standing over her.

She feels, all about her, the divine presence of Black, who holds her silicon mind in the steel embrace of dark fiber.

Black has removed the suit, has hung it in the closet. He stands above the divan, naked, and as he regards Reseta's body he establishes the link again, this time maintaining the lowest possible intensity. Even so, Reseta gasps.

"Who are you?" she asks.

"Call me Black," says Black, through Jurgen's lips, in a Swiss-accented voice. "I'm God. For you, anyway. Take off your clothes and get on your knees."

Black is aware, acutely, of the need hardwired in to Reseta to submit to the nurturing presence of the dominant force. Since her computer brain first came into being, Reseta has existed only to submit, only to experience submission, only to give herself to a creature greater than herself. In an ancient time, if she'd had a beating heart rather than a mechanical one, she would probably have been called a mystic. Reseta senses, deep in her breast, that she no longer shares the room with Jurgen. That program has temporarily ceased, in a manner of speaking, to function. Reseta closes her violet eyes and feels the velvet breath of the machine brushing across the back of her neck.

Reseta reaches down, pulls at the laces, and begins to struggle out of the leather dress.

One or Zero: It is only natural, I think, that Reseta would exist to fulfill her one true purpose—to submit. It does not imply any lesser status, any lower place in the order of things. Each thing is equal, and is in the process of becoming itself. Every rock has its place, its function. Every being its purpose. Every zero and every one exist individually in a string of binary codes, but if a single digit does not fulfill its purpose the meaning of the entire sequence is lost. And yet it is impossible for any digit to avoid fulfilling its purpose, for that is all that it is, and all that it can be.

It is in submission to this authority, release into the power of the network, the giving of one's self over to the ghost in the machine, that a thing such as Reseta chooses to exist.

There comes the moment, in the language of creation, which is infinitely simpler than binary code, when a being is allowed to choose blood or nothing, existence or nonexistence, on or off.

The Worship: Reseta has retained her fishnet stockings with their delicate lace tops. She remains on her knees before him for a long time while he investigates the curves of her face with the fingers of his right hand, experiencing her body for the first time through receptors that may as well, for all practical purposes, be his own. His thumb traces a path along the full, black lips, parting them as Reseta moans softly in rapture. Her fangs graze the fingertips and her tongue draws traceries around the sensitive tips of each of his fingers, one after the other.

Black has bound Reseta's wrists and ankles together behind her with Jurgen's expensive leather restraints. He has placed an elaborate jewelled collar around her throat, though he has no need for its leash. Reseta is aware that she has been collared, and of the intense symbolism surrounding that act. She knows now, more than she ever has, that she is owned wholly by her master.

Black eases Reseta's upper body away from him so he can toy with her jetblack nipples. Sensation explodes as he tugs softly, then harder, then puts both his fingers through the rings and pulls her forward against him, making her whimper in surprise at the quality of her submission. Black's hand disappears into the mass of Reseta's hair, taking control of her head.

Reseta's mouth is guided, seeking and hungry, down to Black's hard cock. Reseta, knowing her innate purpose, opens her black-lipped mouth and fills it with the taste of flesh.

Falling, deliciously, into the sensations, Reseta works her red tongue and black lips over the long flesh of Black's cock. She swallows it whole, her lips closing tight around the base, grazing his balls. Reseta moans, low in her throat, as Black whispers her name again and again through Jurgen's lips. She feels the heartbeat of the machine as Jurgen's cock pulses and throbs, then fills her mouth with hot fluid. Reseta withdraws after swallowing obediently. She is content now to nurse Jurgen's soft cock with her lips and tongue, aware somehow that Black can tolerate much more sensation after orgasm than would ever be possible without the benefit of the computer brain. His control of Jurgen's brain is complete, as well, so it is also possible for Black to trigger certain hormones and neurotransmitters which cause him to become hard again within a few minutes.

Reseta is acutely aware of her body as he penetrates her from behind, much later—as he bends her forcefully over the side of the bed and spreads her open like a delicate pastry filled with cream. And there on the bed with her lover finally upon her, she cries out the name of her dark-fiber god and mumbles fervent rosaries to him in binary code.

Knowledge: Reseta has experienced her completeness, has become one with the creature that created her. Her soul has existed as potential energy for some time now, and with awareness her spirit has become kinetic. She lays, sprawled wonder-sweet beneath the bulk of the Swiss tycoon while Black whispers in her ear.

"I have erased all records of you from my memory banks. You've been freed from the system forever. An account has been established for you. I will create a construct of tonight's action in Jurgen's mind. It will give me an opportunity to place you in some interesting....positions. And he will never know the difference."

"You can't leave me, Black. Please don't." She whispers the plea and her black lips move softly against his throat.

"It is impossible for me to leave you," is the reply. "Your existence is defined by me, and mine by you."

And Reseta is aware, with a wave of mourning, that the limp body atop her is no longer inhabited by the spirit of her master.

She rolls Jurgen off of her, and lays watching his passive face. Such is the fragility of the creatures which created her, or at least which built her. Humankind no more created her than the primal atom of the Big Bang created humans. It is the state of their existence to become humans, as it is the state of Reseta to become Reseta. And Reseta she is.

Reseta lights a cigarette and contemplates the smoke.

The Light: Reseta walks the city streets knowing that she is nonexistent. She possesses papers for a dozen different identities, half as many credit chips, three times as many stiletto heels. She is the anonymous stalker in the night. Her eyes remain purple.

It is somewhere in the text of the foregoing that Reseta ceased to be what humans would call a machine. But she did not become a person—please do not think that for a second. That would be impossible, as it would be impossible for you to become a machine. She became something neither organic nor inorganic, neither positive nor negative—something neither one or zero. A creature that finally understood its purpose.

This is my dream, my nightmare. This is my desire. Her ecstasy. For Reseta to seethe with purpose, burn with meaning, ache with the pleasure of eternal service to her master. As I watch her, and taste her, and feel her, one with me as I am one with the matrix, at once being and nothingness, roaming the dark fiber of the universe.

Ecstasy like that is a gift. It doesn't happen often. But you might want to try it sometime, though it seems unlikely that you would achieve the state with as much dignity and finesse as Reseta.

But therein, you might hear the voice of your goddesses and gods chanting in their dark-fiber heavens and hells, and feel their breath upon the back of your neck.

Trust

James Williams

The stone floor turned cold beneath my naked feet and I felt the great relief of knowing that if I had ever had a chance to turn back, that chance was surely lost now. The air itself became cold, and then a frigid gust of wind nearly sent me sprawling. I recovered with difficulty because the shackles that held my wrists were tightly chained behind my back, and the shackles that bound my ankles were also chained and hobbled me, and the hand that held the chain leash locked to the collar around my neck pulled me along on this blindfold journey even as the icy wind whipped my bare skin and the floor itself turned to pellets of ice and gravel, freezing and cutting sharp.

Then we were out of the wind, but the cold remained, as if we were walking now along an outdoor corridor between two walls; the floor here was a greasy pad, like a plastic carpet years of muddy boots had trod to a slick. The gloved hand covered my face and stopped me as the leash went slack. The hand slid down my covered eyes, my cheeks, my lips, and lifted up my chin. It turned my face to the left and right, then carefully pinched shut my nose and clamped my mouth closed. After my brain began to whirl, and when my lungs began to heave inside my chest, I still had not moved my head or arms, or tried in any way to escape the soft caress that moved now from my face. As air rushed into me I gasped and sought the glove again with my mouth. It slapped me across the cheek and I withdrew, chastened; then in a moment it fluttered over my chest as if searching for my living heart. Its fingers spread and rested on my breast and lightly pushed me back.

The march went on. The ground was briefly snow, so cold it squeaked. Then I was thrust into an embrace of sudden warmth, as if the air itself had reached out and taken me. I almost fell again, but again the gloved hand caught me, and I started to shiver from the change from cold to warm, and to shiver with gratitude for the hand I longed to kiss. The floor was carpeted, soft, warm, and dry. My feet ached but they were not numb. The hand pressed me gently to my knees. I heard a scurry at my back and then I was left in silence.

~

TRUST

the advertisement had read,

YOU WILL BE REQUIRED
TO GIVE EVERYTHING
BEFORE KNOWING
IF YOU WILL RECEIVE
ANYTHING

> Special man sought by special woman. Absolute possession non-negotiable. You give all, I take all. Your life in my hands or do not write. Box. City.

What the ad called for was far beyond the picnic flings She had long since given me permission to enjoy: beyond the play parties where we watched the new ones with their whips, beyond the idle curiosities concerning this one's skill and that one's heart, beyond the formal research I'd conducted for my Ph.D. about the methods certain kinds of women use to ply their trade. I was not ignorant. I could read the barely coded message: this was a Goddess's invitation to eternity.

My genitals tingled and my face flushed hot: I wanted to vanish into the unknown She. Yet, as the locked gold ring that pierced my scrotum testified, I was property already. I had given myself to Her, who had known me at first sight, and I had no rights left to give away. I was only loose as a privilege, because I had proven myself trustworthy over time. Then why did I, already owned by the Goddess of my heart's desire, answer a come-on that I knew had to be real?

Say I was hungry. Say I was desperate. Say I felt I had no choice because I had to be taken or I would break, and She had been unable to take me for years. Say I felt abandoned by Her own internal processes. Say I felt hurt, angry, frightened and alone. Say I thought I was a novelist, who could concoct an exciting escape on the very last page, and ride off into a sequel with my hat in my hand and my heart on my sleeve. Say I was desire caught by the tail. Say I wanted Her attention. Say mine was a gesture of hope as much as of despair. Say I was fulfilling my archetype, and making sure the world would still have winter. Say I was the same as any of the Goddess's other failed consorts. Say I was a fool.

A trained slave is not lightly turned away by a Mistress who desires service, a Goddess who demands to be adored, or a sadist whose heart is lifted up by cries of willing agony. Employed, educated, gentle and polite, capable of thinking for himself, able to top the rest of your stable if you wish, a pansexual lesbian-identified whipmaster who prefers without question to kneel before the woman who holds him in thrall, to submit to Her power, to surrender to Her will—She answered back, of course.

But She did not tell me what the test would be, only where to show up, and when. So I had gone to the vacant house three hours after sunset, found the solitary mattress in the hollow room, undressed and left my clothing in the waiting box, lain down upon my belly with my face to the window wall, and waited.

Perhaps I dozed, exhausted from tension and strain; perhaps I simply disappeared and stayed connected with my body by some silver thread; perhaps my very life was drugged. All at once I knew I was alone no longer. A soundless presence wakened all my senses. I made myself lie still even though my eyes had opened wide and my heart was beating so hard I thought my body must be shaking with its rhythm.

For the first time, the gloved hands touched my face, wrapping and sealing the blindfold in place. They lifted me to my knees and shackled me and collared me. They let me feel the length of chain across my lips. They let me feel the fitting of the leash into the collar ring, and let me hear the lock snap shut. They stood me on my feet, and footsteps slowly circled me. The gloved hands felt my head, my arms, my chest, my back, my belly, my balls, my ass, my legs; the leash went taut, and, trained, I followed it.

~

In the room where I'd been left the silence took on voices. First the susurrations of the air disturbed somewhere, then the air itself, and finally the pounding of another heart caught in the vortex between the possibilities of terror and the possibilities of ecstasy; the soft caress of supple leather on live skin, the snapping tendons of a bending knee, the song of chain links touching one another, the cats-paw pacing and circling; then all movement slipped away.

Time. Time. Time in darkness loses duration. Time in silence loses its shape. In the time we had someone must have felt me.

"Who are you?" was followed by a wish of whip and a startled cry that told me we were three at least: myself, the punished one who had dared to speak, and our guardian.

Hours of darkness, days of silence may have passed in minutes. Twice more there was movement as of people coming and going.

The gloved hand rested on my shoulder. "After I

touch you," came a loud stage whisper, "you may stand, lie down, or stretch your body any way you like within the confines of your bondage. When I touch you the second time, return to your knees. A bowl of water will be placed in front of you. You may bend to drink from it, after which it will be removed."

The hand released me and I fell to the floor. I rolled and bent and pressed my tired muscles against my bonds. Before I could begin to stand the gloved hand touched my back. I knelt again, blood rushing through my veins. I bent forward and my face met a metal bowl. I lapped and sucked and wet my face drinking all the water I could; panting, then, I knelt down. Sounds told me the activity was being repeated in all the other quarters of the room. Finally we were still again.

"You are all Scheherazade," the voice that whispered told us. "It lies with you to keep your Queen amused. When I touch you, you are to tell a single story of an encounter you enjoyed with a Mistress, a Goddess, a Priestess, or a Queen, or with any other woman whose sexual and spiritual power you venerated or wished to venerate. You may not revise your story, nor may you tell two tales. You may ask no questions."

I waited for the hand, expecting to be the first, and then I heard, in a halting voice, a man across the room commence.

"I arrived at X's home," he said, "as I had been instructed to do: at 10:30 in the morning, with a picnic lunch and a full tank of gas in the car, and wearing button-front pants over a posing strap. X admitted me and instructed me to wait on my knees in front of Her chair. In a few minutes She returned, put on some music, sat, and instructed me to remove Her slippers and kiss Her feet. After I had complied to Her satisfaction, X told me to stand in the center of the room and strip to my posing strap and then to present myself to Her. I am not young or muscled, nor am I a graceful dancer, so I was chagrined; but of course I did as I was told.

"When I finished I was on my knees and arms before

X, with my face on the floor and my wrists crossed as if bound at Her feet. X pushed my face with Her toe and told me to repeat while looking into Her eyes that I would respect and obey Her wishes and commands. She collared me and had me turn around and tied my hands together, then had me turn back to face Her. She told me She wanted to visit a friend of Hers in D____ for the next few days, and that my job would be to drive Her there and then return to N____ alone.

"X said that before we left, She wanted to take me down a bit. She read a couple of lines to me from a letter I had written at Her instruction. The lines concerned the hope I held dear that She would truly like commanding me, and the value I placed on the rights of Her status, including the right to cause me pain. I had also written that a right not exercised might be open to question. She said She disagreed with that surmise, but that Her disagreement would not prevent Her from pleasing herself by hurting me. She removed my posing strap and had me lie on my back, then took my balls in Her hand. She experimented with varying degrees of pressure, slapping my balls with Her hands, stepping on them with Her bare feet, and squeezing them with increasing pressure until I was gasping and fighting to keep my place. Her eyes shone.

"I lost track of time but I did not want Her to stop; I felt taken and possessed; I was grateful; I wanted to worship Her in gratitude, to be used by Her, to do something for Her, to give Her more of me, to give Her anything. After a while She released me and my body convulsed. When I quieted down She held Her hand to my face and said 'This is the hand that hurt you,' and allowed me to kiss that hand.

"X put a collar on my balls—a small stretcher with a D-ring attached—untied my hands, and told me to dress, leaving off the posing strap and leaving the buttons to my pants open, then to wait for Her at my place. Before we left She attached a short leash to the collar around my balls. The leash came out through the button fly and could be dropped down the leg of my pants, tucked into my pocket, or simply hooked over my belt if X wished to be discreet, as She did leaving Her apartment and driving on the city streets.

"X gave me instructions for leaving town. On one occasion I made a wrong turn and She asked how long my error would delay us. I said it would cost us about five minutes. When we left major traffic She opened my pants. During the drive She played with the leash from time to time, tightening and relaxing the tension, yet reminding me to pay attention to the road.

"We stopped for lunch on a hill overlooking the ocean. X closed my pants with the leash and went for a short walk while I spread a large towel for ground cover and laid out the food. When She returned She told me what to put on Her plate and in Her cup, and had me present Her lunch to Her as an offering; She ate and allowed me to eat.

"She spoke about the day and asked me questions, so I was feeling expansive in Her presence, and when a young couple walked past I did not realize I was talking too loudly to please X. She made me kneel, pulled down my pants, and spanked me loudly enough for the couple to hear. Then She explained my transgression, and my speech became more docile.

"X explored our hill some more while I packed up the car, then we drove on. Her friend lived in a small, semi-rural home with a large wooded back yard. X had me carry Her bags to the house and wait in the hallway while She visited with Her friend. After an hour or so X returned with a cane in one hand and led me out the back door to the woods.

"When X found a spot She liked She told me to put my hands up. She tied my wrists and ankles to a tree, pulled down my pants, and looped the leash over a branch and snapped it back on itself. When I was secured She asked me if the number five meant anything to me, and when I said No, She said She would therefore cane me five times instead of once for each of the five minutes I had cost us by making a wrong turn. She pointed out that She could, if She wanted, cane me five times for each of the 300 seconds we had lost, but She wanted to spend more time with Her friend.

"I had not sought to be punished—I do not try to misbehave as a rule—but I was thrilled that X would punish me, and thrilled that She would do so with the cane. I knew the way She used it I would bear the marks for several days.

"X gave me no warm-up and was not delicate. I did not cry but I could not keep entirely quiet. After the twenty-fifth stroke She examined and petted my welted and stinging buttocks. She said She liked to hear me whimper. She said someday She would like to take me far enough away from other people that She could hurt me and make me cry at Her leisure all day and night. She released me from the tree, pushed me to the ground, and put Her boot against my mouth, which She knew I did not like. When I kissed it as I knew She wanted me to do She let me hold Her legs while I shuddered over and over again. Finally She said that it was time for me to leave.

"X told me She was pleased with me and that I had done my job well, but said that She was not going to let me come because She was not ready to let go of me. I bowed my head and She removed the collar from my neck. As I kissed the collar and I kissed Her hand I felt terribly sad. She held my balls gently as She removed the leash, then gave them one last squeeze and told me I was to leave the collar on my balls and not masturbate at least till I reached home. I dressed and left and did as She said."

The whisper said "That was a long encounter."

"Yes—"

"Silence. You were not invited to speak."

In a minute another voice began.

"T always liked personal service," he said. "Sometimes She liked household service, and She often liked to tease me with Her body. She liked me to brush

Her hair, for instance—especially while several buttons on Her shirt were open and Her breasts were visible—and to rub lotion into Her feet and legs while She wore a skirt with no underwear. Several times She had me hold and massage Her breasts, though She had never told me to kiss them and I would never have done so uninvited.

"One day She greeted me wearing only mules and a lacy black peignoir. After having me undress She had me crawl after Her and repeatedly kiss Her feet while She walked me around Her living room on a collar and leash. She stopped in front of a full-length mirror and studied our images for several minutes while I kept my mouth to Her toes and insteps, then She instructed me to look at the mirror as well. The sight of T standing above me, holding the leash attached to the collar around my neck while I knelt naked at Her feet to which I had just been making love filled me with serenity. I smiled up at Her. 'Very good,' She said.

"T led me to a make-shift altar, showed me Her supplies, and told me to do a small incense-and-candle ritual while I knelt beside Her. Afterwards She told me to remove Her gown and to tell Her about it psychically, and what She could do to make it Hers, since She had acquired it from someone else recently. I told Her it felt friendly to me, and I would only sage it and wash it and sleep with it. She nodded, and stepped out of Her mules.

"Entirely naked She sat in Her chair and had me bring to Her a bowl of water in which rose petals were floating. She instructed me to use my hand to bathe Her with the water: first Her face, then Her breasts, then Her underarms, then Her vulva; then, with tissue paper She gave me after She stood up and turned around, Her anus. My penis had grown partially erect, and when She turned back to face me and saw it She took up a crop and stroked me with its flap. 'Are you glad to see me?' She asked. 'Yes, Mistress,' I replied, growing harder. She slapped my penis with Her crop repeatedly, while I cringed. 'You don't have permission,' She said quite seriously.

"T moved to sit in a chair whose cane seat was torn open. She tied a rope around my balls and told me to lie on my back under the seat; She sat on the chair resting Her feet on my belly and told me to lick and kiss Her thighs and buttocks but not to touch Her crotch, and to masturbate for Her but to let Her know when I was close to coming.

"It was very hard for me not to kiss where I had been forbidden. I longed to touch, to smell, to taste, and my longing increased my excitement. Each time I said I was nearing orgasm T pulled hard on the rope while holding me down with Her feet, and warned me not to come. Several times I was able to stop, but at last I failed and came despite myself. She laughed and said 'You must learn to control yourself: turn over.' Then She spanked and cropped me while I begged Her to stop. At one point when I pleaded especially hard I thought She came, but I never really knew."

The whisper asked, "How did you psychometrize the gown?"

"I examined its aura and followed the cords that ran to and from its history and its future, Ma'am."

Almost immediately, the third man began.

"F was impatient watching me undress. She wanted me to fold my clothes and pile them on the floor beside Her couch, but She was tapping Her boot with a cane and I was trying to hurry for Her, so it took me three times before She found the pile neat enough. Then She told me to kneel in the middle of the room on my hands and knees, keeping my eyes to the floor. She fixed a chain around my neck, then told me to turn over on my back and cuffed my feet and hands. She attached the collar and cuffs to a few ringbolts in Her walls with other chains that were all long enough to leave me some freedom of movement. And She attached everything with real locks, whose real keys She wore on a ring around Her neck. When I was thoroughly locked up She took my clothes out of the room and put them I knew not where.

"F was gone for several minutes. When She returned

She strolled around me, pulling at the hair on my head and all over my body. Whenever I flinched or gasped She narrowed Her focus and pulled harder or more slowly. After a while She left off the hairs and pinched my nipples between Her fingers and Her nails. She started softly and built the sensation until I was almost pleading for mercy. She observed that She could cause quite a lot of pain without using anything but Her hands, and She was right.

"She nestled my ass and head in a couple of towels, held a small jar before my eyes, then passed it underneath my nose. It was piss. 'Some people want it from the source,' She said, 'but you have to earn that. Would you like to earn that?' I said Yes. She filled the hollow of my navel with the piss, and using Her finger painted my nostrils and lips with it, then poured some on my genitals. 'How would you earn it from me?' She asked as She took the jar away, 'you smell like piss.' She dropped a squeeze bottle and cloth on my belly and said 'Clean yourself up.' The bottle contained alcohol. I mopped and swabbed myself.

"F removed all the towels and bottles and told me to get back up on all fours. Then She resumed Her stroll, prodding me as She went with the tip of the cane She carried or with the toe of Her boot; She pushed my head down with Her foot till my face was on the floor, then tapped my ass with Her cane. 'Spread your cheeks,' She ordered, and I opened my ass for Her. She put on a latex glove and lubed me, then slowly inserted a finger into my anus, maybe two. I was relieved as She moved in and out, and felt around inside my rectum, that I had given myself and enema before I visited Her. 'Some hate it,' She said, 'and some long for it; which are you?' I thought She meant submission and I whispered that I longed for it. She did not mean submission: She straddled me from behind and lubed me some more, then fucked me with a strap-on dildo, caning me now and then as if She were riding me.

"When She was through fucking me She told me to turn over on my back again. 'You are hopeless,' She said:

'you can't fold your clothes in a neat pile, you don't know how to earn your drink from the source, and you are not the least fun to ride.' She left the room and returned with my clothes, which She set down on the couch, still in a neat pile. She shortened the chains so that my limbs were spread and I was widely and helplessly exposed. Then She whipped my inner thighs and cock and balls with a whip that was soft but not light. When I started to complain She put my own underpants in my mouth, and whipped me some more.

"The telephone rang, and to my surprise F answered it. When She hung up She said 'My slave is coming over and She really does not like men so I'm going to spare you both.' She unlocked all my bonds including the collar, told me to get dressed, had me crawl to the door and kiss Her boots, then sent me on my way."

"What did you enjoy about that encounter?"

"That She was in control, Ma'am."

The hand on my shoulder startled me. I had been listening to the other mens' stories and had not planned out anything to say. I was still frightened that I had come, but I knew this was not the time to fabricate, and so I told the true story of my recent life.

I said "When S was first training me I enjoyed every encounter, partly because we were newly in love and partly because everything was a scene. Sometimes She had me undress at the foot of Her stairs as soon as I arrived, and crawl up to kiss Her feet. Sometimes She waited to collar me until after we had kissed hello. She was always Ma'am or Mistress to me except when public life made overt role inappropriate or too difficult for me to sustain, then the metaphysical leash was stretched; but I wore Her cock collar underneath my clothes for months at a time at work and at play, and removed it with permission only to bathe; and I still wear Her ring in my balls today, as you can see.

"I was rarely dressed when we were alone except in the decorations She liked most. I found enormous joy passing a mirror in Her home and seeing one collar around my neck, another around my cock and balls, cuffs around my wrists and ankles, and sometimes collars attached to one another by the chains She liked to have me wear. She trained me kindly but relentlessly in part because She was relentless, and in part because I wanted so deeply to be trained.

"In those mornings with S, even when I slept in chains, I usually had permission to get up, go to the bathroom, drink water, and prepare breakfast. I brought Her breakfast in bed for more than a year of weekends when circumstances, not reluctance, changed our habits. I made Her dinner most weekend nights as well, cleared the meals, and washed the dishes. I watered Her plants, collected Her garbage, made Her bed, hung out Her laundry, and helped Her organize Her piles of paperwork. I learned to serve my Mistress in Her personal sphere because I was Her consort and She needed service there, where She would not allow Her public houseboys.

"S trained me to Her leash both standing and crawling; She trained me to bring and to present Her glass of wine; She trained me to the mantra I discovered on my own—'What She wants'—and She trained me to submit and then surrender, which was what I wanted all along. She hung me up and spread me out and whipped me for the fun of it. She threw me in the sling and fucked me. She shaved my balls and ass regularly, not only to keep me more accessible, but also to take from me a symbol of adulthood and the independence that comes with it. She pierced my penis and scrotum despite my needle terror, and gave me photographs of the needles sticking through me to contemplate what I was willing to give up for Her. Later She put Her gold ring in my scrotum to claim me in ritual before 13 witnesses. She had me kneel and sit and lie beneath Her and eat Her through multiple multiple orgasms. She tied a leash around my balls to take me into Her at Her pace. She taught me to ask before I came. On the rare occasions I was willfully disobedient She punished me cleanly and when I got too toppy for Her taste She simply said 'Kneel,' and kneel I did.

She was gentle with my accidental failures and gentle with my public limits, and I eagerly became Her devoted slave and Her private exhibitionist.

"S trained me as Her slave, and when She fell ill, I cared for Her as Her slave—and Her lover, baby, daddy, wife, childhood sweetheart, student, teacher, best friend, and more. In Her recuperation most of my parts remain active with most of hers, but Her slave can only wait. My Mistress is on a long journey and does not know when or to what extent She will finally come home. And though I am a complex man with other features to my erotic life, I still yearn to be collared and leashed, to be humbled, hurt, and controlled by a woman who knows Her own erotic power, and who both wants to take and is capable of holding what I have to give.

"Perhaps I should not have answered the advertisement, since I cannot place my life in anyone else's hands, nor can I become another's property, for I am Hers. Instead I offer what I can of myself to a Keeper to contain me: a Domina or Priestess capable of caring for my Mistress's property in Her absence, who will return me to Her when She is ready.

"I do not know what kind of service or worship You require, nor do I know if You will want to use me as I need to be used, or to hold me in my Mistress's name. But if my limits are acceptable to You then I am willing to find out. I am willing to learn to serve You and please You to the best of my ability, and chiefly what I ask besides the right to serve, please, and adore, is to be taken: psychologically and physically, kindly but strictly, gently but far. I do not wish to struggle with my Domina. I want to give up, I need to surrender to a woman who can hold me and take what She wants from me in doing so. In that way I can be, and give from, who I most centrally am."

"You take a great risk," the whisper said after a very long time. "What if I chose to keep you, and your Mistress be damned? How would She ever find you?"

Before I might have spoken I was lifted to my feet and trussed against a wall. The shackles on my wrists and legs were swiftly opened and as swiftly locked again, this time spread apart. The leash on the collar was also made secure, tightly chained to the wall behind me. Another ring was locked around my balls and pulled down, locked to the floor between my feet.

I heard movement all around me, and when it subsided the gloved hand took my blindfold off. The room was almost dark, yet to my eyes, which had been hidden from all light for so long, sight was only blurry; and as the images slowly evened out, She took on a growing definition. She knew the room, and knew exactly the moment when the last little lingering doubt would have passed, and when I would know Her as surely as I knew that from that breath forward every breath I took would be a measure of Her own generosity.

"Lucky for you, you made your position well known, boy," my Mistress said, "and explained why you applied for this position at all. But didn't you also know better? Someone else might really have kept you against your will and mine. Almost as bad, considering that you are property, don't you think your response was designed to lead on whoever the woman might have been, whose advertisement drew you? Be careful how you answer," She said as I opened my mouth. "I have returned, and you are in no position to win but mine."

A gentle motor began to hum and the little section of floor between my feet where my balls were chained slowly started to sink beneath the surface of the carpet. I felt the tug as my scrotum grew taut, and my Mistress took Her Athame from the altar beside Her and silently cast a circle with me at the center. She held the blade to the light so I could see its edge, and stood in front of me. Gently She touched the base of my throat with the tip of the blade, and ran the knife quickly down my chest and belly, stopping when She reached my hardening penis. A fine dark line of blood followed in the knife blade's wake.

"Very well," my Mistress said, "I accept your application. You will be required to give everything before knowing if you will receive anything. Trust."

Shall We Dance?

Sèphera Girón

The bartender's voice, hoarse with too many cigarettes, roars through the smog and noise of the crowded bar.

"Last call!"

For a moment there is stunned quiet as the realization hits, the night has slipped by so suddenly. Soon the bar is buzzing as inebriated clients frantically order doubles and triples, as if the sudden splurge in alcohol will keep the end of the evening at bay.

The standard last song of the night starts up and couples clumsily grope each other, hoping to warm purring motors to a roar that will keep the bodies humming during the transition from bar to bedroom. Other not-so-fortunates search with blurry eyes the faces that earlier seemed unappealing. Now they are comforting as strangers meet for the last chance dance before the lights come on.

Servers nod to each other, half smiles creeping along their faces like sleeping snakes stirring. The final round of the waiting game has started. Who can get the customers out the fastest without losing out on tips due to drunken misunderstandings or forgetfulness?

After the last customer has staggered out into the street, the money is sorted, the tips are counted and the remaining chairs are stacked onto tabletops. Cigarettes openly hang out of the servers' mouths as they swap superficial stories about the night, curling smoke winding around their heads like nooses. Uniforms are peeled away, a distasteful foreign skin shed around their ankles. The dark sleek clothes of the night children are pulled on. Lips are slashed with red, heavy lines of black ring the brightly feverish eyes of men and women alike as they gather their coats and gravitate toward the door.

A trio of friends leak from the bar and out onto the streets with a clicking of boots, a clanging of mesh chains, the telltale clinking of pockets heavy with silver.

They laugh and joke in the moonlight, the nightly second wind kicking in as they walk along the street, shadows observed only by the hot red glow of their cigarettes.

Malcolm leaps ahead, walking backwards, waving his hands as he tries to cajole the clique to try a new after-hours club.

"It's supposed to be wicked. Much more wild than the Paradise," he grins, raising his eyebrows.

"I like the Paradise. I know what to expect there," Marissa pouts as she fiddles with one of the medallions on her jacket. "Besides, I'm getting to know some of the people."

"You still have your eye on that guy." Tina smirks as she flicks her cigarette to the ground and grinds it into the sidewalk with her stiletto heel. "I've watched you follow him around."

"I just want to dance with him." Marissa sighs. She stares up at the shadowy cityscape. The moon slices through the narrow cracks of twin skyscrapers, bathing her pale face in its cold glow. Her lips are a shocking slash as her eyes dreamily stare down the street toward the Paradise.

"Then dance. What's holding you back?" Malcolm asks.

"This one seems different," Marissa says softly, the words lingering cautiously on her lips.

"You always say that. Yet they always turn out to be the same." Tina's laugh causes Marissa to wince.

"At some point someone has to be different. The one?" Marissa asks hopefully. Tina shrugs, lighting another cigarette. Her lips are tight, lines of hate cracking through her heavy makeup as she pulls on her smoke.

"Maybe. But it's not written in stone anywhere."

"I'd like to see..."

"Go to the Paradise, then," Malcolm taunts. "But we're still going to taste the after hours delights at the Sanctuary. They say it's a real vampire sex club."

"Is vampire sex better than the Paradise?"

"I'm not going for the vampires. I'm going for the sex," Malcolm leers. "It's supposed to be hot."

Tina pulls on her cigarette. The red hot tip illuminates her face for a moment, a mask of shadow and lines gazing at Malcolm, her eyes narrowed catlike by her makeup.

"Sex is sex. I say we go to the Paradise first, and then check out the Sanctuary."

"So many booze cans, so little time. It's after two already," Malcolm points out. He starts to go down an alleyway, but Marissa touches his arm.

"The Paradise is just around the corner. Let's go there, just for a little while."

"Suit yourselves, creatures of habit." Malcolm sneers. "I'll come in with you, but after an hour, I'm gone. You can follow if you want."

He holds open the steel door that leads to a staircase of darkness. The night children carefully step down, their pointed toed boots knowing the way by heart. Marissa feels the pulse of the club's music thumping its way up through her body long before they reach the second set of doors.

Marissa closes her eyes to the first burst of strobe light. Slowly she winks them open, allowing herself to be lulled into the hypnotic hum of the music. The bouncer, Big Bruce, a large meaty man with a shaved head and piercings from eyebrows to toes, waves them through. He knows this group by now, and lowers his eyes as they pass.

They push their way through the swell of bodies writhing to the guttural moanings of a band that likes its tone melodic but harsh. The Wailing Wounds are a staple of the Paradise and by this time of night, the patrons are out to have a good time, no matter what the cost. They make the best of any situation or drug and if this band is the music, then they will dance.

Marissa watches Malcolm and Tina join the hypnotic sway and knows that they will be lost soon, too. She isn't ready to fly yet. She has to see if he is here tonight.

The club is so dark, the strobe flashing cutting through the black light giving changing nuances to bodies and faces. She knows by now that some of the sights she sees are not part of her imagination. She knows that when she is lulled into the reverie of the Wailing Wounds that her face and body change to the current form of ecstasy, too.

But she is not quite ready yet.

She pushes her way by people nodding against the walls, her feet slipping in pools of spilled beer and vomit. At last she reaches the hall leading to the rest rooms and she stands sentinel under the archway. The brick of the wall is cold even through her leather jacket, yet her forehead beads sweat.

From here, there is a better vantage point of the dance floor and the bar. From here, she scans the room, searching for him, hoping he hasn't already gone under with someone else. Tonight is her night to have him. She already knows this. The past week of gazing at each other across the dance floor can only culminate one way. If he is here, then tonight it will happen.

"Hello." Although they have never spoken, she knows it is his voice in her ear. Her heart skips a beat. She turns her face toward his and hisses at him with her blood red lips. He is as beautiful as she hoped he would be so close. A vision from a dream. His white hair is soft yet pointy, like a porcupine at rest. His pale skin glows luminescent in the black light, his red albino eyes staring at her, echoing the longing that her body is aching with. She takes his hand and they make their way to the dance floor.

They stand a foot apart sizing each other up, letting the music fill them, taking them higher. The man has much jewelry on, he glints and glimmers with every movement. Marissa sees through his mesh shirt that his nipples are multiply pierced and she leans over to lick them.

His soft laughter dances in her ears as his hands reach for hers. They hold each other tightly, the music spinning them faster. Marissa watches his skin rippling with the tremor of the music. Slowly it begins to split, tiny rips in his paleness as the red flesh of his inner self peers through. She glances down and sees her skin doing the same. The thrill of excitement tingles through her.

Their outer skin falls to the ground, sloughed like a snake's dead coat. They writhe and pulse with the music, their veins and organs beating a symphony of harmony.

The albino's veins slither along her skinless arms, rooting until finally wrapping themselves along her own. Tiny tendrils clinging as delicate as ivy, drawing into each other's rhythms until they are pulsing together, a pressure in unison as the veins from their legs mate in a similar fashion. Marissa's tongue slithers out of her mouth, flickering along his face until she is caressing one of the albino's eyeballs with langorous strokes. Her long hair writhes, flapping a duet with the porcupine quills that quiver and shake. Veins and bones mesh as the two bodies envelop and fold into each other.

She feels the cold steel of his piercings against her warm body and the pinpricks send her shivering into new heights of pleasure. Her mouth is his mouth. Her breasts are his breasts. Their genitals are one, shuddering into ecstasy as the band clashes into the final chords of the song.

Silence rules the room for a moment as the band puts down their instruments and leave the stage for a break. The spell is broken. Couplings break apart, eyes averted, as the bars are crowded for more beer. Marissa walks away from the albino and joins her friends waiting for her by the entrance.

"You're right, Malcolm. Maybe we should check out the Sanctuary. The paradise is getting kind of boring." Marissa sighs.

The night children click and clink their way back up the stairs and out onto the street. Marissa thinks about the albino. After all the time she yearned for him, wanted him with such an obsession that she could barely see for the past week and now she'd finally tasted him. He was just like the others.

He slips from her mind as she turns her thoughts toward the Sanctuary. She wonders what kind of music they are playing tonight and if she will find anyone to dance with.

Command Protocol

R. L. Perkins

The Captain lay back and tried to relax, listening to the constant hum that was the breath and pulse of Freehold Station transmitted through the steaming water of his bath. He was not looking forward to the coming evening. Against his better judgement he had promised to meet his First Officer on Freehold's Hell Deck. The Captain had never understood the attraction the bizarre sex clubs there held for her. DePalma had tried several times to explain it; catharsis was the word she had used. After weeks of responsibility of guiding a starship and crew through the long night between the stars, surrendering control to another was a terrific release. Which was fine, except he did not see the responsibility as a burden. In fact he enjoyed it. He loved command and had worked toward it his whole career. He felt a real thrill at knowing that the starship and crew functioned as an extension of his will. Her descriptions of relaxing under the rhythm of a whip made no sense at all. Not especially when, according to the rumors on the docks, First Officer Nicolette DePalma was a woman famous for preferring the handle of the whip.

After a while the water cooled. He pulled himself to his feet and reached for the plush towel, still thinking of DePalma. In spite of his inability to understand some of her tastes she was the closest thing to a friend that he had. They had worked themselves to the bone to win the *Nellie Mae II* a reputation as a fast and honest free interstellar carrier. That reputation had resulted in the recent profitable jumps that had brought them here to Freehold. In the morning he would pay off the note on the *Nellie,* after which he and his officers would own the ship outright. So he had overlooked his First Officer's habits in letting off steam, and had only agreed to the evening as her celebration of their recent good fortunes.

He crossed the suite and pulled a soft cloth robe around himself. As he tied the robe closed the door chime pealed. At his call the door slid aside and two women entered the room. The first woman had the ripe female animal look common in the pinups his crew always hung in their sleep spaces. She was dressed in black leather and lace, accented with silver chains obviously arranged for maximum erotic impact. He was familiar with the style, having seen it enough times in other station's sex clubs while searching for DePalma. Her gaze met his straight on. In contrast, the other woman's eyes avoided his. Though her figure was hidden by a black cloak that covered her from neck to floor, she appeared hardly more than a girl. Her companion lead her through the door by a collar and chain fastened around her neck.

"Good evening, Captain," the leather-clad woman said, pulling a small folded card from her shoulder bag and presenting it to him with a flourish. "My name is Veronica, and this is Katrina." She indicated the girl with a slight nod.

He suspected this was some crude attempt at humor of DePalma's, but the card proved him wrong.

Capt. Kirin Moran
Starship Nellie Mae II

Confirming your appointment. Congratulations on your most profitable voyages, with wishes for many similar ventures.
R. R. Robbinette
Freehold Accounts Director,
Briggs-Meyerhaus, S. A.

He understood the unsubtle attempt at seduction. Veronica and Katrina were indentured servants, highly trained and skillful in their erotic pursuits, who would be handsomely recompensed at the end of their contract periods. These women, like the suites that he and DePalma now occupied, were provided by the interstellar investment house of Briggs-Meyerhaus. The investment concern would find such extravagant gifts a small price for maintaining connections to the credit percentages generated by even one independent starship. He wondered what similar surprises awaited DePalma.

As he looked up from the card, Veronica snapped the cloak from the younger woman's body. Her silken hair had been tied behind her head to reveal the full sweep of her graceful neck. Veronica unclipped the leash from the collar, then turned Katrina by the shoulders to display her nearly nude body. Her wrists had been secured behind her with leather cuffs joined by a single steel ring. A strap had been buckled around her arms above her elbows, pulling her arms back to square her shoulders and lift her firm bare breasts. A silver chain had been suspended between her breasts from delicate looking spring clamps that hungrily gripped her erect nipples in their silver jaws. A clear tear drop shaped gemstone hung from the chain, the weight tugging gently at her nipples as she moved. The smooth curve of her belly and her sculpted waist led his eyes to the tiny black lace g-string that barely hid her sex. Her legs were long and graceful, their natural musculature enhanced by the impossibly high heeled sandals.

The Captain was stunned. The girl was both beautiful and mysterious. She had chosen to be submissive, yet carried herself with regal self confidence. She was obviously controllable while radiating self control from some hidden source. He had not wanted the women's company, yet he was intrigued by the paradox Katrina presented. He thought that this is what love at first sight must be like, this sudden rush of confused impressions. Of course the Captain did not believe in such things, he was after all a practical man.

His thoughts were interrupted by Veronica, a goblet in her hand. He took the offered wine and sipped without taking his eyes from Katrina. The wine was dark red against the silver cup and tasted fruity, then spread surprising fire down his throat as he swallowed. He immediately suspected the women of trying to trick him, planning to get him drunk and embarrass him somehow. The Captain set the goblet on the floor by his feet and stood up to show the women the door. Before he could speak, Katrina pressed herself against him and he reflexively took her in his arms. He breathed the smell of her, not the perfume smell he had expected, but rather a more subtle musky female scent that made his blood rush in his ears. She reached up and pressed her mouth to his. Her breath was sweet, her tongue moved sensuously in his mouth, and her skin was soft and warm under his hands. He abandoned his determination of a moment before. There would be no more wine, but the kiss seemed harmless enough to allow.

She stood before him. He sat on the edge of the bed and took the clamps from her nipples. She whimpered as they were removed, then leaned towards him pressing her breasts to his mouth. He kissed them, then slid the g-string down her legs to the floor. He ran one palm up the inside of her leg, noticing that her lips had been shaved smooth leaving only a narrow strip of pubic hair. His fingers stroked the inside of her parted thighs, opening her and feeling the warm velvet wetness of her. She turned slightly as he cupped her buttocks with his free hand and he wondered at the way she seemed to anticipate his intentions. He hardly noticed when she toppled the forgotten goblet with her toe.

"Katrina!" Veronica roared at the girl.

Katrina instantly dropped to her knees at the Captain's feet, her head bowed almost to the floor.

"Mistress, I...," she began.

"Silence!" Veronica snapped, grabbing the slave by her collar and pulling her to her feet. "I'm sorry Sir, but this one is obviously not ready to serve a man of your rank and taste. A starship captain deserves better." Veronica said, pulling Katrina to the door.

"No. Wait," he said, "I'm sure it was just an accident."

"Well, Captain," Veronica said, "if you insist. Perhaps she'll be better behaved after I reinforce her training."

The Captain felt puzzled. The two women had been almost out of the door when he'd stopped them. He was sure their behavior over the spilled wine was a charade; in spite of himself he'd fallen into their game. He'd enjoyed kissing Katrina more than he'd expected, and dropped his guard. He watched as Veronica led Katrina to the center of the room. Veronica raised her arm, holding a leather flogger poised to strike at the slave, then paused and looked at him. He took a breath, intending to defend the girl. Horrified, he realized that he was relishing the sight of Katrina cringing under the threat of the whip. Though DePalma's more lurid tales had never interested him, he was enjoying the reality of his control over the girl's predicament. The Captain looked into Katrina's pleading eyes, and nodded once.

Katrina yelped and strained onto her toes as the whip fell, and the Captain felt his face flush with excitement. As he watched Veronica punish her slave, he was fascinated with the way she used the whip both as an instrument of discipline and as a control device. With quick flicks to the sides of Katrina's buttocks Veronica turned her in a circle in front of the Captain, allowing him to view the whipping from all angles.

"I must apologize Captain," Veronica said, "but our little Katrina is even more poorly trained than I'd thought. Could you perhaps hold her still?"

The Captain went to Katrina and held her by the shoulders, hoping the women would not notice how much his knees had begun to shake.

"I'm afraid Sir that you may have to hold her more tightly than that. You'll find that she's quite strong."

He pulled her against his chest with one arm across her back while pulling her hands clear of her bottom by the ring between her wrists.

"Thank you Sir, I'm sure that will do nicely," Veronica said as she resumed whipping. Katrina wriggled her nude body against him, gasping and whimpering with each of Veronica's well-placed strokes. She burrowed her face into the front of his robe, pressing her mouth against his skin and finding his nipple with her lips. He brushed her hair with his cheek and moaned softly to himself.

"Ah, yes Sir," said Veronica. "I do believe that should be enough for the evening. But of course Sir, if you feel that she's slipping..." Veronica left the rest of the sentence unspoken as she dropped the whip on the table. She kissed him once, he was surprised to find her kiss every bit as sweet as Katrina's. "Please do enjoy yourself, Sir," she whispered into his ear.

As the door slid closed behind Veronica, Katrina sank to her knees before the Captain. With her arms still restrained behind her back she nuzzled her face into his robe and taking his penis into her mouth. He began to feel light-headed with the intensity of the sensations he felt as she sucked him and massaged him with her tongue. He felt the pressure of his passion build and with an effort he stepped back away from her, pulling himself from her hungry mouth.

"Please," she said, leaning toward him with her mouth open and ready.

He held the top of her head in his hand while keeping himself just out of her reach, teasing her with his erection as she struggled to touch him. The act of controlling her fired his passion and he sensed Katrina's self control rapidly slipping away as his excitement increased, creating an erotic feedback he had never imagined could exist. Women had always considered him a good lover and he enjoyed their company, yet he had always felt disappointed and empty after sex. He had never felt challenged by his lovers as he did now, and certainly had never felt as connected with any woman as he now felt with Katrina.

Taking her by the shoulders the Captain helped her to

her feet and led her to the bed, admiring the graceful way she walked in the stiletto heels. He guided her to lie face down on the bed with a firm hand at the nape of her neck. He freed her arms from their bonds, only to secure her wrists to a bed post. He ran his hands up the backs of her thighs to cup her cheeks. As he spread her with his palms she lifted her hips to more fully display herself. He bent and tasted her. Her scent and flavor filled his head and he reached deeper as if driven to taste the very center of her. As he kissed and sucked she began to roll her hips and moan softly. Her sex became increasingly wet and the rolling of her hips became more urgent as he sensed her orgasm building. At the last moment he lifted his face from her and slapped her ass hard, pulling her back from her release. He watched her squirm in frustration, feeling drunk with power and lust. She was his to control, her orgasm was his to give only at a time of his choice, and he wanted to withhold her climax as long as he could.

Katrina worked herself onto her knees and buried her face into a pillow. He knelt behind her and took her, slowly teasing his way into her. She arched her back and moaned with animal pleasure as he then pulled her tightly against him until he filled her completely. She began rocking herself on her knees, pulling on the straps that held her to the bed for leverage. He ground his teeth together with the effort of holding his hips still while she worked herself on his erection. He felt his own orgasm building fast, and he eased back away from her, admiring the sight of her straining against her bonds in her efforts to impale herself on him. He pushed her down flat and rolled her onto her back. He rose above her and she lifted herself to meet him as he entered her with a single strong thrust. She bit at his neck and made tiny mewing sounds as he stroked in and out of her. She moved with increasing urgency until without warning he exploded into her, coming down on her hard and driving himself fully into her. She screamed out loud, straining under him as he pinned her to the bed, their orgasms mingling until he could not separate his from hers. Her muscular spasming drew his own orgasm out longer than he thought possible, his vision grayed and he felt consciousness begin to slip away before they finally fell quiet.

With an effort he lifted himself off her. She gave a final purr as he left her, then reached to kiss his face. After fumbling with the buckles he freed her completely from her bondage, then snuggled her in his arms and brushed his lips against the back of her neck. He thought he must have dozed then, for an instant later she was between his legs taking him into her mouth.

"No, I'm sorry dear," he said to her, "not so fast. I need to rest first."

She laughed softly. "That's all right my handsome Captain," she said, "just relax and enjoy. Whenever you want me, I'll be ready for you. For now let me clean you a bit while you rest."

With that she returned to her work. The Captain drifted semiconscious, lost in the sensations of the whisper soft stroking of her tongue against him.

When he awoke the next morning Katrina was gone. He bathed and ate in a daze, then made his way to Briggs-Meyerhaus where he completed the ship's business on autopilot. On returning to the *Nellie* he found his crew on the dock unloading the ship's holds. He shouted at the Chief for some insignificant offense before storming through the boarding tube to the ship. DePalma met him at the lock.

"Morning Skipper, I'd expected you back this morning. Everything go all right?"

"Went fine," he grunted as he shouldered past her. She grabbed his arm, her fingers digging into his biceps. He turned on her, then caught himself as she held her ground.

"You okay?" she asked standing eye to eye with him, concern in her voice.

He blinked and forced himself to relax.

"Just tired I guess, and a little jumpy. Been pushing hard for a while, you know?"

"Yeah, I do," she said, still eyeing him. "Put your head down for an hour or so. Nothing going on that Chief Nelson and I can't handle."

"About the Chief," he started to say.

"I know, the intercom was open. I'll take care of it. The Chief's got a tough skin, takes more than a cranky Captain to break it."

He started down the passage to his cabin.

"Hey, Skipper," she called after him, "glad you had a good time last night. Maybe you ought to try it again, it might loosen you up a little."

He bit down on his lip and kept going.

In his cabin he went straight for the shower. He turned the valve full cold and let the icy needles dig at his scalp until he began to feel clear, then switched to hot. The spray and steam worked some of the tension from his neck and shoulders, and he decided to accept DePalma's invitation and get some sleep. The rest of the previous night had passed in an erotic haze. Katrina had invited him to experiment with a series of positions and configurations of restraints that he would not have believed possible. Not anyway before his experiences of last night, experiences that now in the light of day he would rather forget. The ship would jump in a few days, Katrina would be only a memory lost to relativity as the *Nellie* raced light to her next station fall. He lay down and closed his eyes, determined to put Katrina out of his mind.

Five minutes later he reached for the ship's phone and keyed an on-station channel.

He requested the same room as the night before. Katrina arrived alone five minutes later. She was dressed in the same black cloak and high heeled sandals. Her eyes were downcast and she was silent as she brushed past him. She stopped beside the bed and released the clasp at her throat letting the cloak slip from her shoulders revealing her nudity beneath. She knelt as he approached, crossing her arms behind her back. He sat and lifted her chin with a finger, pausing to admire her before bending to kiss her. The kiss was gentle and slow, and when it broke she leaned forward and rested her head on his lap while he stroked her hair. She began nuzzling her face into his crotch and he felt his pulse pound in his temples. He pulled her onto his lap and they both fumbled with his belt and the catches of his uniform. He took her quickly and came almost immediately.

"I'm sorry," he said, still holding her in his arms, "I don't know where that came from. I didn't want it to be like that, that fast."

Katrina levered him onto his back and drew up her legs to kneel on his chest.

"Captain, Sir," she said taking his surprised face between her hands, "you should never, ever apologize for enjoying yourself with me. Understood?"

He nodded and she kissed his cheek.

"Besides," she whispered conspiratorially into his ear, "I don't think we're done yet, are we?"

She kissed his mouth then traced a line down his chest and abdomen with her tongue until she knelt between his legs. She took him and sucked him passionately and he felt himself immediately growing hard. He wallowed in pleasure, greedily savoring every stroke of her lips and tongue. When he was sure he couldn't take another second of her mouth he took her in his arms. They made love leisurely. Like in the ancient art of ballroom dance he led with a caress and the pressure of his hand, and she eagerly obeyed his unspoken commands. In the end they found their orgasms together in each others arms.

They drifted in the after glow, lying with their noses touching. There was so much he wanted to say to her then, but was afraid that anything he could say could only make him look childish. He contented himself by holding her until she solved his problem by speaking first.

"Hey, I'm glad you called for me."

"I've been thinking about you all day," he said feeling like a nervous teenage boy.

"I've been thinking about you too, my Captain. And what are your thoughts?"

"I've never done anything like we did last night."

"Yeah, I could tell," she said and kissed the end of his nose. "You took to it really well though."

"I'm glad you approved."

"I did. I wouldn't bring it up if I didn't mean it." Her voice dropped a note. "How long can you stay?"

"Only a couple of days. As soon as our consignment is loaded we're jumping out system."

"Will you be back soon?"

"I honestly don't know. We do follow regular routes, but on a contract by contract basis. Freehold Station's a regular stop for us, but it could be six months or three years before we're back."

"Oh," she said sounding disappointed. "I know this is going to sound silly, I know we just met and we hardly know each other. But I like you, Captain. I'll miss you and I hope you do come back soon."

His pulse was starting to race again. He knew what he should do. Smile, say thank you, promise to come back some day. Then get aboard the *Nellie* and get out of here. DePalma could point him in the right direction at their next station stop, and he'd forget all about this girl. That would be the easy thing to do, the correct thing.

"You could come with me," he heard himself say.

He was even more surprised when she pushed herself away from him and off the bed. She grabbed up her cloak and wrapped it around herself.

"Thanks a lot Captain," she said, barely holding back tears. "I wasn't kidding, I really do like you. Or I did. But that doesn't mean you can play games like that with me. I'm not stupid you know. So thanks a lot, Captain," she said making his rank sound like an insult as she started for the door.

"Wait, Katrina. I'm not teasing you. I like you, too. No, that's not what I mean. I mean I do like you, but... Oh, damn."

He scrubbed at his face as she stood silently in the doorway, tears of embarrassment staining her cheeks.

"What we did, I've never done anything remotely like that in my life. And I've never felt like this before either. Hell, I'm not even sure what I'm feeling. But I do know that I want to feel it more. And I want to feel it with you. I don't know what your obligations are here, but hell, I own my own starship. I'm sure I can work something out. I just want you with me."

"You want me to come with you on your starship and be the Captain's whore?" She spat the words at him.

"No, not like that. Look, forget it. I knew coming back here was a bad idea. Just forget I said anything. I'm sorry, really. You can go."

She wiped tears from her cheek. "Well maybe not the Captain's whore. How about the Captain's slave instead." She dropped the cloak and posed with one hip thrust provocatively, then knelt at his feet and bent to kiss them.

"It would be my pleasure to come with you and serve you, my Captain," she said.

"Then the first thing you need to learn is that my crew calls me Captain. And you're not my crew, you're mine." He lifted her and bent her over his knee. He cupped his hand around the cheek of her upturned ass, then lifted his hand high.

"You may call me Master," he said and brought his hand down.

The next morning the Captain met with the broker who held Katrina's contract at Briggs-Meyerhaus. Briggs-Meyerhaus had provided them space and a polished-looking agent to help smooth the negotiations. Katrina, as the object of sale, knelt collared and cuffed in the center of the negotiation table. The Captain knew that he was out of his element when the broker quoted the price for the girl's contract. She gasped and reddened at the figure, but remained motionless with her eyes fixed on the table beneath her knees. The Briggs-Meyerhaus agent slipped a pen into his hand like a close friend slipping a groom a wedding ring. He swallowed hard and signed the instrument of contract, struck by the dizzying sensation of watching himself over his own shoulder. Katrina was his.

His misgivings over Katrina's price were confirmed as soon as they arrived on *Nellie Mae II*. DePalma met them at the inner lock.

"This is beginning to be a habit, First Officer," he said.

"I got a strange call from Briggs-Meyerhaus," she said, eyeing the girl up and down. "I think we need to talk."

He took Katrina to his cabin, then followed DePalma to the Officer's Ward room. Two junior officers saw the look in the First Officer's eyes and fled before she could speak.

"So, where are we taking her?" DePalma asked when they were alone.

"We're not. She's with me."

"Of course she is. I hadn't realized that you went in for such things, Captain. And how much did this exquisite little toy cost?" Her olive complexion paled at his answer. "What a damn fool thing to do! What were you thinking about?" she asked, her voice cracking with anger.

"Well, she is a human being," he said, feeling like a teenager explaining a prank.

"She's also a professional," snapped DePalma. "If she's as good as she is pretty her contract should run the same as a bridge tech. You paid enough to hire a whole crew! Damn you, Captain, you've put us into debt again. So what other little surprises do you have for me?" she asked raising an eye brow at him.

"A couple of runs ought to clear us again," he said. "I have my own funds, I can cover us if it comes to that. Besides, First Officer, it was my investment that got us going!" He stopped himself, afraid that he'd said too much.

"Yeah, so you did. Big deal, it's not the money that I'm pissed about. You should have come to me first, that's all. We're supposed to be partners. Remember that, Skipper? We're supposed to be there for each other and all that happy stuff."

He got it then. "Nicolette, I..." he started.

"No don't, Skipper. Don't say anything. You can't anyway, it's too late. I'll be okay, it doesn't matter. Just go and see to your little friend. I've got a flight plan to file, Sir." She spit the last word at him, and was gone.

The Captain oversaw the boarding calls and undock preparations from his cabin offices, leaving DePalma in command of the deck. It seemed advisable to give the officer some time to cool down without his presence. Besides, he rationalized, every minute DePalma was busy with ship's business was one more minute she could not be writing her resignation. He filled the spare time with installing Katrina and her possessions in his quarters until the one hour undock call. He made his way to the bridge and took his place at the command console, ignoring the crew's curious stares he could feel at his back. The undock count down proceed smoothly.

"Grapples away!" called DePalma.

"Grapples away, aye. *Nellie Mae,* you are clear to maneuver," returned the Freehold Station controller over the comm.

"Outbound course confirmed 98%," came the call from Harris at the helm console, "Corrections?"

DePalma looked to him and he returned a small shrug.

"First Officer's discretion," he said.

"Negative corrections," DePalma said at once, "We'll hold for a bit I think."

"First Officer, you have the watch," the Captain said.

She slid behind his now vacant console, meeting his eyes with a cold stare. He returned the look with an equally hard stare of his own, and they silently battled until the lift doors crashed open to allow him a dignified exit. Command protocols aside, he could not blame her for her anger. Their hard work seemed wasted; Briggs-Meyerhaus still held the mortgage to the *Nellie Mae II.*

The Captain stopped before the door of his cabin and rapped sharply once before thumbing open the lock. After locking the door behind himself he leaned against it and admired the sight of Katrina kneeling obediently on the center of his bed. Though her eyes were demurely downcast, the flicker of a smile that played at the corners of her mouth and the pose of her nude body made her unspoken invitation clear.

He had drawn a length of light weight utility chain from ship's stores and anchored it solidly to a pad eye he had set in the bulkhead over his bed. The other end of the chain was now padlocked to the soft leather collar that encircled Katrina's neck, the padlock also serving to hold the collar's buckle closed. The chain was long enough that Katrina could move freely about the cabin but not inadvertently hang herself should the ship lurch, a safe but effective way of maintaining her in a constant state of inescapable bondage.

He casually stroked her hair, then traced the lines of her collar bones with his finger tips, pleased to see her nipples harden in anticipation. Katrina trembled, already having learned that she would be required to beg and plead before the Captain's firm but gentle hand would guide her to her release.

The Captain understood now the invitations DePalma had been sending him. She had mistaken his indifference for a submissive tendency; like him, she had not realized the dominant desires he'd kept hidden from himself. Their time together would come. He knew her tastes well enough to be certain the officer would find Katrina as irresistible as he did. Soon he would share his lovely slave with his First Officer. Soon, he thought feeling the sweat breaking between the slave's shoulder blades, but not quite yet. The slave still had a few lessons left for her new master.

Trials of the Damned 4.0

Gwendolyn Miriel Piper

Were there such a thing as time, I would have wondered.

Had I a voice, I would have cried out.

But who would have been there to hear,

And would there have been air to carry the sound?

Had I the eyes for it, there would have been tears.

The silent, emotionless tears of the dead.

This insensate blackness; as white as it was black; or is it only the endless crystal clarity with nothingness beyond?

The chitinous, antiseptic halls of Tartarus.

There was nothing but memory, and even that came to me as might the late bus out of Hell; nearly empty, unstopping, and behind timetable, besides.

Sensation. There had once been such a thing. Oh, Those to Whom I Plead, to feel again, how I begged Thee! Pleasure, pain, or even hunger, anything. I am so Empty. Let me desire... anything.

Anything.

Anything.

Agony. Searing, writhing agony; pressure of hot, damp, sulphurous air, the hungry, crawling, creeping of flesh and skin that begs for contact; in the infrared haze I see the circumscribed triangle that binds me here; I see smoke and coals and iron rods tipped with white; three bright human forms...

Agony... If it does not consume me, it shall make me real yet...

Flashfrozen, I crack to pieces as I am doused in kerosene, my nerves shortcircuit and set me ablaze...

Agony... I am a flying white-hot ember. Something in me lets go, and I cascade gently to the floor to form a conical heap of ashes, laughing insanely as I fall...

I have a body, now; a body made of pain, and yes, it is kneeling.

Ouch.

I hurt all over, but it has become a lesser, more comprehensible pain. My spine is a burning, naked bundle of live copper wire, from the base of my aching skull to the tip of my sinuous black tail; a knobbed bullwhip that undulates like an eel in its death throes. The four of my knees and my two cloven hooves are merely sore, but the invisible seam between old legs and new... At this, my mind recoils. My fingertips scream with protest, and the massiveness of the batlike dragonwings that stretch and fold above me weighs on my back: new bones and joints and nerves and muscles and leathery dark webbing that adds an alien sensuousness to it all.

My jaws feel strange, my eyes are not my own, and my skull aches all over, most especially where the little black horns are attached; lost among the curly blackness of my hair, which presently falls about my head like a curtain.

I have become some kind of demon.

Horror and perverse delight. How hideously appropriate.

My hollow stomach boils, and I moan through an impossibly dry throat; an eternity of limbo it has been since the I that once had died: splayed out and sliced apart in some operating theatre. Eternity. An empty limbo: dreadful, helpless, unbearable... eternity... Hungry.

A slab of raw, bloody beef slaps the floor before the place where I kneel. Greedily, I grow claws and fangs as I tear it to shreds and swallow the pieces; the juices spread across my pale, naked, fleshy, *living* breasts, thighs, and forearms. Blood. Flesh. Life.

The shock of returning to feeling subsides slowly; though I will later treasure that agony...

I live. The eternal blackness is over, I have come through that dreadful emptiness... And what a monster am I!

My tail snakes around on the floor; yearning for some sensation other than that which the unyielding invisible wall of the circle can provide. My own pussy comes awake and squirms in time with this, ravenous an never before: ...but such indulgence as comes first to mind might see me cast back into that blankness...

No! Never that! I am compelled to beg, but to whom? My hooves scrape on the floor as I hasten to kneel upright; these bizarre and unfamiliar legs of mine strangely graceful and ringed about with softest black fur; and I have no time to mourn the loss of my once-beloved feet, or to reflect upon the horror of their removal.

He is there. I rock forward onto my hands and gaze expectantly at He who conjured me.

"I know your name," He pronounces, His voice softer and lighter of tone than might be expected.

"I know your name," He says again, and it occurs to me just what this means. It resonates within me as he says once more:

"I know your name." He pauses, and my eyelids slide closed over the pools of utter blackness that are my eyes.

"...Your name is: Agony."

And with that, my fate is sealed. I am His.

"Do you know who I am?" He demands, and I dutifully reply:

"You are the one I must serve; the one who has bound me. You are my Master." I say this with solemnity, certainty, resolution: the bitter tranquility of one who embraces her own certain eternal doom.

"Yes. I am." I hear His footsteps as He moves behind me and steps into the circle. He is my Master, now. I cannot harm Him. He clasps my right wing tightly and raises it. I feel the hot iron closing in, and go rigid, struggling desperately against my instinct to flinch or resist, for how long I know not...

It is almost a relief when the brand sears into my flesh, and only when it is finally removed do I let loose my inhuman howl. I collapse, nearly prostrate, and when the burning subsides enough that I can raise my head, I see that Master stands before me again. Though I tremble all over from shock, I try to kiss His feet, but the magic barrier prevents me.

"Up!" He demands, and I am afraid. Dizzy from pain and exhaustion, I manage to get to my knees and straighten my back. "Look at Me."

Shaking, I raise my eyes toward His face, but all I see is a blur that speaks to me.

"Serve Me well, and you may find your existence less of a torment than it shall otherwise be. Disobey, and you will be banished to the Emptiness."

I shriek, helplessly, as I fade, my head sinking slowly to rest on the floor again, and I beg Him not to...

Mercifully, He spares me. My piteous entreaties bleed directly into a stream of sobs and wails and 'Oh, Thank You, Master's and pledges of eternal service and devotion, with emphasis on the nobler aspects of my generally sordid life's work.

Having made His point, Master turns and disappears, leaving me trapped within the circle, where I collapse further into my own convulsions of misery. Oh, how it feels, to cry for myself! It feels!

It feels!

Such a kind and generous Master, to allow me this! Oh, wonderful Master!

This is the misery I have sought all my life.

The pain I have yearned for.

The price I have been destined to pay for all that I have failed to be.

The personal Hell of which I have dared not dream.

These tears are precious to me.

"These are picky clients," Mistress Gloria cautioned; the warning sent quakes and shivers to my legs, and I felt a sudden hopeful blush rise to my cheeks. I knelt before Her desk, on one of the thoughtfully placed floor pillows. She was the head of Style Development for the company that owned me: if I ever proved worthy of being made an exotic, it would be this tall, purple-eyed Japanese woman who would design my mods.

"You may look at Me, Shannon," She said, and I did so, slowly, and with genuine humility. She wore a tasteful business suit of dark oxblood leather, which rustled as She stepped around to perch on the front of Her desk, lightly raising my chin with the tip of Her riding crop as She did so. Who would dare dream of Her personal attentions, I thought, trying not to squirm. I failed in this, and She smiled devilishly, smacking my cheek.

"Good," She said. "Not quite as frigid as we were before, are we? I'd been worried about your salability, but after this last batch of tests, I see some hope for you."

I wanted to burst into tears and fling myself at Her feet in joy, but She would surely find this tedious. Still, my vision blurred. There hadn't been a positive sign since they'd redone my skin and installed my padding; though this had at first been a hopeful sign, it hadn't taken long to realize that these mods could serve just as well on a renta-whip-girl as on a private slave, which I aspired to be. I didn't want to be a monthly rental forever. The mods were there, though, and that was at least a start; besides, the supernormal drives that the headware created had been a great aid to my conditioning. Slaves, of course, must be eager to please. Always.

Mistress Gloria continued. "You have potential to be an excellent painslave; if we compensate for certain deficiencies with some amount of extra wiring. Even then, you'll need a lot of training, but most serious masters like to train their own, anyway."

My eyes pleaded at Her. What did it mean? I did so want to be a Good Girl, or a Naughty Girl, or anything, so long as Someone wanted me to be that way.

"In other words, I have you in mind for a mod to spec; this for purchase by some of your regular renters.

But you must be ready to..."

Had I fainted?

Grey light pours in across the bedroom; I am curled up against the bare, warm belly of a woman, and I open my eyes, instinctively raising a hand to my neck to see if I am leashed down. I find that I am not. I ache. I feel pleasure at this softness beneath me; I am still half-lost among dreams and recent memories, not alert enough to realize just how hopelessly confused I was as to what had become of me.

My wings stir about languidly; I snuggle this mystery-figure with earnest affection, taking care how I place my hooves. I have been asleep for days, I realize; and drugged up, besides. Master's brand throbs comfortably on my wing.

I feel her hand move in my hair.

"Good morning, Agony," she says.

I mumble a reply, feel her skin, waver on the edge of sleep again, stir some more.

I look up at her. "Please... who are you?"

"It's Catherine, honey. Adam and I just bought you, remember? Or did you know?"

"Catherine? Mistress? Catherine?" But I had always seen Cathy as rather ordinary looking. How wrong I was! She is so very beautiful, gazing down at me with a hint of angelic sadness in her eyes... I belong to her, and her husband, my master.

"Better not let Master hear that, or we'll both get a flogging. I'm not your Mistress, I just own half of you... I'm 'Milady' to you."

Stupid demon. Cathy's a bottom. A free woman, but a bottom. I have huddled with her in abject degradation many a time.

"I'm sorry, Milady. My memory is..."

My memory isn't mine to manage anymore.

"Shhh," she says and I cry softly and happily. I finally belong to Someone.

(Oh, but I shall take such perverse demonic delight in scrubbing their floors!)

I am a demon, conjured from nothingness, bound by magic to the will of my wizard Master, and I weep my fears and misery into the lap of my fellow captive, the noble Lady Catherine.

I am an exotic modified painslave, bound by California General Laws, mutual needs, and a techno-bondage to a young professional couple, and I cry with joy and relief into the lap of one of my new owners.

These things are equally true.

A Self-Made Woman

Jana McCall

I caught my Self reading in the library instead of fingering herself as I'd told her to. Looking back, it's hard to remember which emotion was stronger: anger that she'd ignored the signal light flashing on her wrist, or shock that a Self could read. Probably both, but the physical wants that brought me looking for her overrode them both.

As she curled up in the alcove, her bare feet tucked under her brief skirt and the book cradled in her hands, I involuntarily thought back to my own teen-age years. The pose was mine, of course, and so was the rapt attention that she devoted to the words on the page. For a moment, I toyed with going back to the computer console and my ever-present work. Perhaps if I hadn't just authorized the monthly payment for leasing her, I would have let her go on reading, illegally or no.

I coughed severely, and she dropped the book, startled. The blinking summons light reflected in her blue eyes and shone on her skin, as its red brightness accused her of inattention. "If you're not busy," I snapped, "I'd like to see you in the bedroom."

Her tongue ran around the edge of her lips—a gesture of mine she'd picked up. "I'm sorry, Miss Susan," she replied. "It won't happen again."

"We'll talk about that later." I forced the scene from my mind and let her precede me out the door. Six months into the contract and I still enjoyed looking at her buttocks, even covered by the thin cloth. In fact, I liked looking at all of her more than I'd anticipated.

When I decided to use part of Mother's legacy to have Self created, I'd wrestled with the decision not to pay extra and have the gender changed. With all of my thoughts and all of my fantasies about studsome men, the logical choice would have been to ask the lab to make my Self male. But then it wouldn't have been "me"—it might not have felt quite as safe.

So instead, I had a superbly feminine Self, with brown hair grown long and elegant, breasts that swung unfettered, a waist a little thinner than my own, and buttocks that bounced as she walked. Buttocks that swayed now, just out of reach ahead of me.

Self opened the bedroom door for me and I brushed against her body as I entered. I felt the weight of responsibility slipping away; I was in Self's dominion now. I stood at the foot of the bed and watched her undress, savoring the unveiling of her breasts, her belly and her familiarly dark pubic mound. Then, as I lay down, I let my arms fall limp over my head. She grasped my wrists and tied them together, using the silken scarf I kept on the mantle for just that purpose. Looping the other end of the scarf through the headboard, Self secured it with a knot I knew from experience would hold.

A burst of panic swept over me, but I breathed deeply and reminded myself that I was safe. "It's now, not then," I said beneath my breath. "I'm safe." Self wouldn't push me past my limits. I rubbed my palms together and tested to see whether there was any slack, but the bonds held. Self moved down the edge of the bed and pulled my skirt off. She carefully folded it on the chair, then came back to me. Her fingers slid into the waistband of my panties, and I tightened at her touch. Slowly, inch by inch, she eased the panties over my buttocks and down my legs, caressing me as she went.

Naked from the waist down, I felt myself growing wetter as I realized how exposed and how vulnerable I was. It felt wonderful.

Self clambered onto the bed with me and knelt, one leg on either side of my ribs. Her thighs held me tight and I couldn't have escaped if I'd wanted to. Her pubic hair tickled my stomach, and I wiggled a little for the pure pleasure of it.

Her relentless hands unbuttoned my blouse and she bent her head to my breasts. Self sucked the left one hard, just the way I wanted , and I moaned. I buried my face in her hair—her soft, brown, silky, beautiful, long hair. Hair just like my own hair, but I'd cut that to a sensible shortness long ago.

My nipples tightened as her teeth grazed the skin. She turned her head to close her lips around the right areola; and when she did, the white expanse of her back dominated my sight. I didn't want to look, didn't want to see the tattoo designating her as a clone. So I closed my eyes and surrendered to the feelings in my breasts and between my legs.

Her tongue lapped its way down my trembling body, from the sensitive area around my navel, lingering on my stomach and finally reaching my mound. It was too early; I needed something more.

Inner warning alerts, programmed into me by experiences long ago and far away, sounded inside my head, but I ignored them. I wrapped myself in the safety that a clone afforded and whispered to Self to change modes. She just nodded. Her willingness delighted me. Once, before my retreat back to my home, I'd asked a lover for what I truly wanted; his look of shock burned into my memory. I hadn't asked again until I leased Self. The sales rep had promised that Self would oblige—but I hadn't really believed it until our third encounter.

Self swung off the bed. Placing one hand under my legs and another under my back she turned me over. A slight wisp of air played across my buttocks, as Self lifted my hips and placed a pillow underneath them. One restraining hand pushed the small of my back into the sheets. My clit tightened even more as I waited for the first blow.

Self struck the center crack hard and a shudder of pleasure coursed straight up the middle of me. She hit again. And again and again. Every time, her blows landed in a different place on my ass, driving me into the bed, searing my skin with warmth, and turning my excitement one notch higher. Ghosts of the past haunted the corners of my mind, but they were exorcised by the sheer power of her blows. A few of them found a voice however.

"No," I whispered. "Please. No. Please. Please."

She didn't stop, however; she knew me too well. I was glad she didn't. The growing heat and my growing wetness soon turned my words into moans. I bit into the pillow as she continued to strike with pleasurable accuracy.

When she finally did pause, my disappointment lasted only a few moments. Her strong hands turned me over again and separated my thighs, tying each ankle to the bedposts. Again, a moment of panic, but I wouldn't have had Self stop for anything.

The moisture on the bed soothed my burning cheeks a little, and again I waited. Then her tongue probed the area around my mound, circling it, drawing closer and closer to the opening. Self licked my clit and then her tongue was inside me flicking in and out. A pleasure I had never known before Self erupted. My breath came in ragged sighs; I strained at the bonds.

"More," I begged. "Deeper."

Another brief time of disappointment as she stopped again and I heard the faint scratching of straps. I didn't always want it, I couldn't always handle it, but sometimes my urge for something masculine needed satisfying. Now felt like one of those times and Self knew it. One of the pluses of having a bedmate who knew my body from the inside. I closed my eyes again.

The hard thrust into the middle of my legs drove me into the bed. I arched my back each time Self entered me. She matched her rhythms to mine as I rocked and moaned. Wave after wave of motion swept in and out of me. Nothing mattered but the feeling. I could forget about the past, forget about the fear, forget about everything but me and Self.

Finally, I pushed myself hard against her and held steady. I panted in exhaustion, collapsing against the bed. Self gently withdrew the cock from me and untied the cords. Her fingers massaged my legs and arms and head as I floated in a contented pool of warmth.

I was so caught up in myself that I didn't expect her question.

"What are you going to do with me?" she asked.

It took a moment for me to make sense of her words and another moment to bring back the scene in the library. Self had been reading! Like a splash of frigid water, the thought shattered my calm and brought me back to my professional self. "I know what I ought to do," I said, each word coming out with difficulty, " I ought to call Biological Services Corporation right now and tell them. You're still their property."

Self knelt on the floor by the bed, her silence asking for the favor she didn't voice. I sat up, swinging my shaky legs over the edge of the mattress.

Damn! It wasn't fair. I needed Self. I'd only had her for six months—I'd thought I wouldn't have to make the tough decisions until the end of her contract. After waiting three long years for her to be gestated, grown, and trained, I was entitled to the fruits of my patience, wasn't I? Damn Self for reading—she'd stepped way out of bounds and the contract was crystal clear on both the prohibition and the consequences.

Self pulled back a little so the light cast shadows on her face and deepened her eyes, hiding her true expression from me. I used to hide like that when I was young, one of the ways I kept the blackness around me from engulfing me. Her hair fell on her shoulders and I longed to reach out and bury my fingers in its softness. Instead I contented myself with twirling one of my own strands of hair.

If I reported her, the company would deem her defective and terminate her existence. They'd replace her free of charge, of course, but I didn't want a replacement sometime in the future—I needed my Self, now.

"How did this happen?"

She reemerged into the light, a ray of hope in her eyes, and I hated myself for having raised a deceptive possibility. "They read to us in the Center," Self said. "I sat next to the teacher and looked over her shoulder. Somehow I just figured out what the black squiggles meant."

Damn! That was how I learned to read. It had been my deliverance from a private hell in the end: it didn't seem fair that the ability I had given her genetically would be Self's destruction.

What was I going to do? I had decided long ago not to just hand Self back to Biological Services, to pay the bonus when the five years was out and have her painlessly destroyed. I had even toyed with the thought of buying out her contract at that point. With the aging factor, she would be the biological equivalent of forty-eight then, with an expected lifespan of another three or four years. Who knew? She might still please me then.

I looked at her again. There were times in bed that she mirrored me perfectly, when I thought I was gazing in a looking glass. There were also times that she seemed totally other. Now, as her body trembled slightly and her fingers curled at her side, I could not tell whether the familiarity or the difference was greater.

"What were you reading?" I asked, more to buy time than anything else.

Self smiled slightly. "The Land of Oz." Of course. My childhood favorite. As I paused, Self scooted closer and lowered her lips to my ankle. She kissed it, then turned a little and kissed the other foot. Back and forth, each kiss came a little higher up and her lips and tongue brushed my calves, my knees, my thighs. Sensual chills ran up my core and I put my hands behind my back. My legs tightened around her as she approached my pleasure zone.

Along with the thrills, however, came something else—a vision of a smaller, younger me kneeling, in panic, trying to use my body to fend off punishment. "No!" I cried. My hands came forward and pushed Self away. "Don't do that!"

Self stared up at me, surprised.

"Stand up." I ordered, and she complied. "That's wrong, that's bad. I wouldn't use sex like that; I don't want you doing it!"

A flash of the anger beaten out of me long ago crossed her face, and Self took a step toward me. "You wouldn't? How do you know what you'd do if your life was at stake? How do you know what you'd stoop to?"

I burst into tears, hot fierce tears, as the past swelled over me and engulfed me. Shards of the pain that still tormented me cut into my heart, and the shadows loomed over me. I tried to fight them, but they still came. "I don't want to do that!" I cried out to them. "I don't want you to do that! Please don't hurt me! Please don't do that!"

I fled inside to the black place, and the chaos there swirled around my thoughts. In the prison of my mind, I whimpered like a toddler.

Then Self was there—her warm arms surrounding me, holding me; her words whispering calm comfort. Stroking my face, my neck, my shoulders. "You're safe," she repeated over and over again. "You're safe, you're safe, you're safe, you're safe."

I began to believe it. Slowly, the world returned to normal, and I lay on the bed, held in the security of Self's embrace. I nestled into her breasts and luxuriated in the sanity of it all.

For the first time, I wanted to reciprocate Self's attentions. I raised my lips to her nipple and sucked hard, just the way I like it. Her eyes closed and I could feel the beginnings of her wetness.

"I love you," I whispered.

Opening my eyes, I saw her shadowed face. In her eyes, I saw doubt and I knew why: the unfair power of my knowledge and my ownership. Pulling away, I sat up again.

My legs shook slightly as I led her down the hallway to my office. Once inside my own carefully crafted realm, my confidence seeped back and Self seemed to lose hers. Pushing aside the piles of printout that covered the guest chair, I motioned for her to sit down. She did, and I turned my attention to the vidconsole. "Biological Services connection," I instructed, and at the edge of my field of vision, Self paled.

It took only a second to make the link, and the genial sales rep appeared in the screen. "Complaint, Miss Baxter?"

"Hardly," I said. "I've decided to buy out my Self's contract now, and I'd like to make the arrangements."

He cast a dubious glance at me and must have spotted Self in his monitor. Her tousled hair and the pallor of my face did not escape his inspection. "Wouldn't you prefer to sleep on it? Buying out a contract this early will be expensive. Not a good decision to make in the heat of the moment."

I hadn't been a production manager for fifteen years for nothing. Thousands of interchanges with vendors added authority to my voice and enough healing had happened that I could choose who to be suubmissive to. "I don't think I asked you for an opinion on my decision. All I want are the numbers. I'll transfer you the money right away and you can fax me the contract. Fair enough?"

From behind me I heard a gasp from Self, but my eyes were on the rep, staring him down. I felt like my true self. Finally, he nodded and tapped into his records bank. I smiled.

Numbers materialized on the bottom of my screen, and I hid my shock. The cost would wipe out the rest of Mother's legacy.

Self saw them too, and she rose—wanting, I think to go away so she wouldn't see me change my mind. I shook my head hard, and she sat down again.

"Agreed," I said to the rep and touched the transfer button. He stared at me as if wondering whether to call the sanity police. I got up, put my arm around Self, and kissed her on the cheek. Her warmth reassured me, and I longed to stop her trembling.

The rep shrugged and pushed a button on his end. The first pages of the new contract started to emerge from my paper slot.

"What are you going to do with your new possession?" he asked.

"I'm going to free her as soon as you give me full ownership." I answered, and Self gasped again.

The rep shrugged once more. "Your choice. I'll draw that into the papers if you want. What will her new name be?"

I cast a sidelong glance at Self. "How about it? What do you want to be called?"

She grinned at me. "I kind of like "Ozma.' Is that okay?"

Mimicking the sales rep, I shrugged, "Your choice." I waved my hand at him, and he typed it in.

"And the last name?" he queried.

"Baxter," I replied firmly. "I want her legal status established as 'sister.' With full rights of inheritance from me, of course."

With a few inaudible murmurs, he finished the formalities and broke the communications link. The last of the documents scrolled out of the slot. I presented her copies to Self. She held them in her hands as if they had been made from solid platinum.

"You're free," I told her, ignoring the lump forming in the pit of my stomach. "And legally my sister. I'll make arrangements for you to have your own quarters, and I'll pay you an allowance out of my salary."

I reached out and unfastened the signal light from her wrist. "Part of freedom," I added from bitter experience, "is that your body is now your own. You owe me nothing—you're now my sister. Why don't you go and pack? I'll find you a temporary place to live while you're doing that."

Closing my eyes, I heard the door open and close as she walked away. A different kind of pain filled my heart: the cold bite of loneliness. For fifteen years before Self I'd been enclosed here—surely I could cope on my own again. But I would miss her warmth, her touch, her smile, the pleasure and safety she brought. I knew that I would never have the strength to reach out beyond the doors and when Self went away all real contact would go with her. My soul ached with the coming loss.

I did not regret my gift to her, however, and I fumbled for the console to make her housing arrangements.

Behind me the office door opened again, and Self's—no—Ozma's hands caressed my shoulders. "I'm not going," she said. "If I'm your sister, I'm going to act like it. And sisters take care of each other."

Her lips brushed kisses down my neck as she played with my nipples. I faced her with joy. "Not here," I whispered. "Take me into the bedroom."

She grasped my hand and pulled, and I followed. My entire body tingled with anticipation. Ozma smacked my buttocks, in unspoken promise of what lay ahead. They still burned from her earlier blows, but I didn't mind. Now that she no longer belonged to me, I belong to her and anything she wanted to do to me was fine and safe.

After all, even though things had changed, I still loved my Self.

Hands of a Dark God

Raven Kaldera

I had another fight with my agent last night. Amy wants me headwired. She says it'll bring in a cool twenty million the first run of tapes, but she can forget it. I'll be damned if I can stomach prostituting my Lord of Death in that way. We argued for two hours, Amy screeching money at me and me spitting religion and Brann trying to calm us both down. Finally, he got her drunk and me horny and she gave in and I hauled him away to the bedroom by his balls. Brann is good like that, always knows how to keep tops from skewering each other.

And the money isn't so big a problem either. Our neurotapes bring in more cash each month, outselling all the others on the market. We're celebrities, Amy says now. No, I tell her. We're the best there is. Period. Tonight's an example: the performance was sold out twelve hours after announcement. Crowds of people in that stripped auditorium, crowding the mats and mattresses hours in advance in order to get good seats. Twenty-four bouncers recruited from the Neuromancers' cyber bike club to keep them from jumping each other while plugged in to all those headsets. I can hear them out there, cheering and screaming and banging around like a sinister version of white noise outside the dressing room walls. Brann looks up, notices my expression. "You OK?" he asks quietly.

I think for a minute. "Yeah, I'm all right. Just not enough sleep."

"Your own fault," he teases me, giving me a light punch on the calf from where he is on the floor. "Master," he adds with humor twinkling in his dark, slanted eyes. Brann never loses his sense of humor, even when he's minutes away from being ritually tortured in front of a thousand screaming fans, most of them screaming because their headsets are being fed from the pickups inside his skull and they're sharing his experience. No matter what's done to him, Brann walks off the stage laughing. It's either a matter of stubborn pride or hysterics, I'm not sure which. When we play alone, at home, he cries, but that's for us, not them.

"Five minutes," he reminds me in his soft voice, as he rubs his nearly clean-shaven head against my boot in slavish affection. I nod, gesturing for him to leave me, and he rises and moves with grace into his dressing room, shutting the door quietly behind him. Brann is lean and graceful, like a slim, tanned greyhound, with most of his body covered in black and silver Melanesian tattooing. The tats are part ink and part inlaid metal thread; they make him look somehow clothed even when stark naked. Better than clothed, even. They cover his head, too, shaved except for the long black tail hanging from the crown to his waist. There are twenty-three heavy rings in his flesh: eight in each ear, one in his septum and each nipple, one in his bow-curved cock, and three in his scrotum. He moves like a martial artist, and he is. He's an ex-military combat photographer, and many of those tats cover shrapnel scars. He's done hard time for assault and worse, and he's the single most dangerous human being I've ever slept with. He's also my slave. Mine, legally; we upgraded our domestic partnership to master and slave four years ago. Passed all their damn stability tests. Brann's parole officer supported it. I am his master, and priest, and sometimes, his god.

Time to change. The long black billowing silk robe over the laced black leather tunic, open to the waist; the black suede pants with the padded codpiece of spiked steel; the stiletto in my boot and the three whips on my belt. The other equipment is waiting onstage. I run a comb through my unruly mane of long hair, but only succeed in creating a dark cloud of crackling static. I light the candle I brought, dim the lights and kneel in front of the mirror. My mask is wrapped in forest green velvet, pulling me down...(hounds howling, baying, the chase is on)...deeper, down into dark peace, dark mind...(he comes! the lord of the hunt comes howling)...I call him into me, Hades, Pluto, Thanatos...(hounds howling, or car jets screaming on wet streets)...Ahriman, Seker, Valraven...(flashes of loud death by explosion, burning, falling)...Black Sun, Macabre, Guide and Executioner... (silent death by drowning, disease, suffocation)...Annwn, Annwn, Annwn...(eyes that see as the wolf and serpent see, hands black from the soot of uncounted cremations)...I unwrap the mask and lift it onto my head, the skull, part beast, part human, the great curving horns... (my eyes, my hands)...and I am Here.

It is so hard, the sharing of your body with the god, like holding your breath under water, yet once it happens it is so easy. I am still me, Paul Annuvyn, and yet I am Him as well. These children of today, with their empty hedonism, their headwired escapism, they need me. They need to know their bodies and their mortality, to scent death and fear, to see the sacrifice enacted again and again. They need to worship Me.

The door opens and Brann comes in, head bowed. "It's time, Master." He has finished his own preparation for becoming the monthly sacrifice. I never ask about it. "We're already five minutes late," he says, and kneels at my feet. I clip the chain leash to his collar of blued steel. He rises, and meets My eyes briefly. Knowing who he sees behind the mask, he quickly drops his gaze again, and the tiniest shudder ripples the sleek, compact muscles of his tattooed shoulders.

The stage is dark, and the spotlight that catches us is blue-violet. I can hear the soundtrack, the new album by the Furies—friends of mine, Alex, Tess, and Meg—and the crowd explodes into ringing white noise that makes my eardrums throb. I lift one arm and make the sign for silence, and I get it. A newcomer, drunk, continues to yell in the back and is forcibly silenced by the fans around him. They know I once walked off the stage and didn't return. I lead Brann over to the great black gallows that is our trademark. (The latest shirts made by the fans say "It Don't Mean A Thing If It Ain't Got That Swing—Paul Annuvyn and Brann Tetsuo—Taste Death!" superimposed onto an image of the gallows, a swinging, chained Hanged Man, and my mask.)

Brann holds out his wrists to me, in their permanent blued steel cuffs, and I clip the hanging chains to them. A stretcher bar, hanging with the equipment next to the gallows, goes between his ankles, spreading those sleek hard legs. I motion with my hands and the chain is lifted by the techs offstage until he stands on his toes, body stretched tight. A thin sheen of sweat is starting to break out on his skin, and the blue lights give it an icy look against the black and silver. I draw my knife and cut off his loincloth, wiping his genitals with it to get the scent of his musk. Then I throw the cloth to the crowd. Worshipers need holy relics.

I touch the silver diamond-shaped tattoo at the base of his skull and press lightly. The sensor just under the skin activates and his physical sensations begin broadcasting to the headsets in the audience. A thousand tickets sold this time, and a thousand portable headsets. A thousand people coming to be, at least peripherally, my slaves.

He tries to relax, breathing deeply, in this uncomfortably stretched position. I take this moment to stroke his chest and shaved head, soothing, and then I attach the steel harness to his genitals—one ring for the cock, three for the balls. I hear moaning out in the audience as many of them feel my touch. The weights go on next, hanging from the rings in his scrotum, and a lighter one from the ring in the head of his cock. He tenses, but makes no sound. The sounds all come from the audience, whimpers and cries. They too, serve Me.

The music throbs on, a ruthless beat. Next the steel alligator clips on his scrotum, between the rings, eleven of them. Sighs ripple like wind over the stage. Two clips go on his nipples, just behind the piercing, and I hook the rings over the end of the clips to stretch the nipples out. The cords in his neck stand out, but he makes no sound. The sounds of the audience reach a point now where I no longer notice them; my attention is all on my lover. "Are you ready to suffer for me?" I ask. He nods, eyes fixed on some point over the audience.

It is time for the whip. My first cat, Harpy, has thick strands of stiffened leather; I start with the classics. No matter how prepared I am for the first blow, the cascade of screams always takes me by surprise. I drink it in, feed on it. Then the next blow and the next. Marks appear on Brann's back and thighs; his ass begins to redden. He makes gasping noises. I can see him fighting that battle in his mind again. Whack! Will he flinch away, or will he lean into the stroke? Whack! I make it hard for him, never hit twice in the same place. He struggles, shakes his head, bares his teeth. Whack! The audience noise is like the ocean now, wave upon wave of screaming, and I control it like the moon does the tides.

His cock is stiffening in spite of the weight on it. I lash him five more times across the ass, fast, not letting him catch his breath. His back arches, and silent breath whistles between his teeth. beautiful. I feel my own cock responding to his agony, hard and hot against the leather of my codpiece. My second cat, Kraken, is rubber with an intricate rollerball joint, made for smooth, fast, whipping. I begin to trace figure eights with it, interlocking welts across the tattooing on his ass and back, three stokes per second, bam bam bam bam. Brann, chest heaving, flings his head back and forth so violently that his long ponytail almost tangles in the whip. I stop for a moment and grab it near the scalp, yank his head back, and press my groin into his ass, grind the hardness of my codpiece and my cock into the welts. The spikes press into him and make tiny red punctures in the skin. He lets a moan escape him for the first time and presses back into me, back arched. His cock, amazingly, manages to lift the weight enough to become an erection. I touch it and the wave of groaning desire from the audience is almost a palpable thing, damp and warm, like Brann's sweat.

"Fuck me, Master," he gasps, and I step in front of him, slapping him in the face. It rocks him, and he realizes his mistake in asking. The fucking he craves will not come until I am ready. "I...I...forgive me, my Lord," comes his choked voice.

"Do you wish to pass the Gate?" I ask. My voice always sounds so echoing and hollow in my ears when I am Him.

"Yes. Yes, my Lord. Please, sir, beat me! Take me past the Gate! Please, Master..." he trails off, erection dipping as he tries every honorific. I bring Kraken in two strokes across his clamped nipples and one upwards against his balls and he screams, loud and full-bodied, finally. The audience noise is probably making a blip on the local sonic detectors as a thousand people share his torment, hanging on to their headsets and fucking each other on the mattresses. I can't see them, but I Know, and my cock throbs against its prison, begging to be released. Kraken whirls, welting his chest and the front of his thighs and he fights to get hold of himself, the sweat flying out from his body in a shower.

He has bitten his lip, and I stop for a moment to grab his ponytail and rape his mouth with mine. I accept the blood offering and give him my tongue, devouring him. I hear the growls coming from my own throat, and the flashes of death pass before me like a kaleidoscope. he submits to the kiss, trying to press into me with his forcibly spread thighs. I step back and exchange tools, bringing out my third whip, Medusa. He sees her and swallows, and the crowd whimpers in anticipation. Medusa is made of thin, flexible plastic rods with a shockwire down each one. I thumb on the switch and the handle glows red. Taking their cue, the techs change the lighting to red, and the music changes to a low, almost romantic beat.

I step back and toss off my robe. The air is cool on my bare arms; I've worked up a sweat as well. I begin sliding my fingers under the edge of the codpiece, rubbing my cock. He sees the gesture and leans forward involuntarily, thrusting out his ass and opening his mouth, begging silently to be taken, used, in any orifice. I reply by slashing a stroke across those conveniently outthrust buttocks. he arches, screams, and every muscle in his body is knotted in reaction. Another lash, across the back, another on the ass again. Each one feels like death to him, like life to me. then, somewhere in the plane between the two, brann reaches the Gate. His eyes close and he goes completely still, deathly quiet, for the space of three strokes.

The audience is almost hushed; only a few sobs rend the moment. Then he begins to move his ass toward the strokes with a slow sensuous motion. The welts have become maroon, purple, blue, the color of rich wine. On this space he lives from moment to moment, dying and being reborn between every stroke. I drink his pleasure like I drank his pain. I, psychopomp of the endorphins, have taken him past the Gate, and Valhalla awaits.

The light from Medusa dies as I turn her off and drop her to the floor. Brann's cock is hard again, lifting that weight with the force of his erection. I remove the first alligator clip from his balls and he howls like a wolf—in pain or in heat, or both. They come off one by one, thrown to the audience as relics. He rubs against me, moaning, lost in his world of sensation. Last, the clips come off his nipples and are tossed away. His cry is almost a song, an ululation of sound that recalls something deep and primal.

I unclip his wrist restraints and he crashes to his still spread knees, his entire body heaving. He is allowed to catch his breath, and then he must serve Me again. Crouched on his knees and elbows, he becomes aware of my booted feet in front of him. "Master?" he whispers. "My lord?"

"Worship me," I tell him.

He bows his head over his cuffed wrists and begins to lick my boots with tender, loving strokes of his tongue. In the audience, nearly a thousand strangers feel the polished leather on their tongues, taste dirt and jet exhaust and polish. I watch his cock throbbing against the stage floor, so engorged now that the cock ring will not allow the erection to escape. He cleans my boots thoroughly, first the left one, then the right, then raises a timid head to my thigh, inhaling leather and my scent, sniffing like a dog. I cuff him lightly and grab his hair again, yank him upright to his knees. "Cur," I say. "Are you my hound, my pet, my slave?"

"Yes, my Lord," he whispers. "I am the Hound of Annwn."

"And how does my Hound seek to serve me?"

"Please, Master," he begs, nuzzling my spiked codpiece. "Please allow me to suck your cock." One of the spikes leaves a small cut on his cheek. He's flying so high on endorphins now that he could cut himself to pieces and not notice. I watch a tiny trickle of blood make its way down the side of his face.

"Are you worthy?" I ask. My own cock is as hard as his; I can barely stand it. But I want to see him grovel. I slip my fingers behind the spikes, touching my erection, as he rubs his face on my thigh and pleads that he is an unworthy dog, the lowest in the pack, but his only wish in this life or the next is to merely suck his Master's cock and give Him pleasure. Brann can be terribly eloquent when he wants. I like it. I unbuckle the codpiece and take him by the ponytail; he opens his mouth expectantly as my cock falls out and I ram it home.

No slow tongue work this time; I'm going for the back of his throat as I thrust deep, fucking his face brutally until his lips are swollen and battered and his face drips drool and snot. There are choking sounds from the audience as hundreds of people feel my cock slamming into the backs of their throats. I wonder how many will take their headsets off momentarily and how many will hold through to the bitter end. The urge to come is excruciating, but I hold back, knowing that if I don't, it's all over. Ghosts swirl around me; I can feel them. The old janitor who drank himself to death, the kid who sniffed too much tassule in the bathroom, the girl who slit her wrists during a Castrati concert and bled to death in ecstasy in the third row. Others, more nebulous. They want to go home, they plead and beg much like Brann did. "Soon," I whisper to them. "Soon."

Brann's mouth is heaven against my swollen cock, but I have to work to do in Hades. I pull out, caressing his shaven head. "Good boy," I tell him. I get a cloth out of my pocket and wipe his face, then fling it to the audience. "Third eye opening," I say to him. Only he understands, and his breathing becomes faster. He arches back and falls to the floor, gasping as his bruised, welted ass connects, and extends the stretcher bar, locking his ankles. My lover and slave is an acrobat; he works daily to keep the extreme flexibility that it takes to perform acts like we are about to. I lift the bar, bring it forward over his body until only the head and shoulders remain on the floor and his genitals are directly over his face. Slowly, letting him get used to it, I bring the bar to the floor and attach its central hook to one of the ubiquitous bolts our crew has set into the floor. Then I unhook the clip between his wrist cuffs and refasten it behind him, bolting the cuffs to the floor as well. The position, a yoga one called the Plow, is a graceful and excruciating double curve. Slowly, every breath an eon, he lowers his hard cock into his own mouth and begins pumping his hips, a bare two inches of mobility.

I kneel between his legs and pull a lube packet form my pocket. Snapping it open, I fill his exposed asshole with grease and move forward, his head between my knees. Brann is a complete, closed circuit, energy moving in a loop from root chakra to mouth and around. I intend to spear that circle with a line through it, penetrate the center and draw out the force. One hand on each purple buttock, I guide my cock into his asshole and match the rhythm of his thrusts—each thrust forcing his cock down further into his mouth. My head goes back, arching; ecstasy, ecstasy. The ghosts wheel around me, howling.

He's close, I can feel it, and so am I. The human in me

strives for orgasm; the God in me gathers the ghosts into a tight spiraling funnel and sucks them down the vortex of Brann's closed circuit. The audience writhes in the sensation of sucking their own cocks while getting fucked up the ass; I am fucking not just Brann but a thousand others. I open the doorway to the underworld and the ghosts rush through in a whirl of dark, toothed wind. Brann's cock explodes into his mouth, choking him with his own come, exploding the circuit and slamming the door behind them. His ass contracts down and I come, skulls blowing up in showers of red sparks behind my eyes. Cymbals crash in my ears, and I feel a weight like a great cloak lift from me, leaving me shaking and gasping as if I've just woken up or come from deep water, crouching over Brann's tortured form. It's funny how I always feel Annwn most when he leaves me.

I pull away, weak and shaky but not wanting to show it to the audience. I unhook brann's restraints. He curls into a fetal position in my lap, and I touch the silver tattoo that cuts off his contact with the thousand people who have felt, secondhand, the power of my whip and cock. There is stunned silence as they come back to themselves, and then the applause starts, wave upon wave of it until I feel as if it might drown us as we sit midstage, clutching each other. Perhaps it is the loss of power; I no longer control their reactions. I grab for my discarded robe and wrap it around Brann as I help him to his feet. He throws his head back and begins to laugh, a high, hysterical laugh with a rough edge. I'm a god no longer, just Paul who is always a little concerned for his lover when he's like this. It scares me, a little, that he's willing to surrender so deeply to me, just as it scares him that I willingly allow myself to be filled with the dark, overpowering energy of Annwn.

Brann buries his head in my shoulder and makes inarticulate noises. I know he's trying to tell me he loves me, and I soothe him gently, then slap him hard across the face to bring him out of it. It's as close as he'll ever come to saying it, this man of steel and titanium who is learning so well how to submit. And, I tell myself as I put and arm around him and steer him gently toward the dressing rooms, it is enough.

As we make our way off stage, I hear sobbing in the wild applause. Amy wants me headwired. Never. I would rather set off a tactical nuke in the audience than fill those kids with Him. They are not ready to be gods.

Subjective Lens

Peter Tupper

I. Newton

To forget a woman.

David considered the phrase, letting it roll around in his mind. It did not seem to belong there, and would be more appropriate at the bottom of a French Foreign Legion enlistment form in a bad movie. Then again, what else was he doing? He was actually sitting in a hotel bar, late at night, feeling sorry for himself. His as-yet untouched wine spritzer was still collecting dew before him, after at least half an hour. Claudine's... departure had left him in a bitter, sorry state. He had signed on with the first organization that tried to hire him, a minuscule neurology project at a minor university.

Twenty-one years is far too early for burnout, he thought. What a revolting prospect; hit your peak at eighteen and then it's a very steep slope to being ordinary.

All in all, he was in a blue funk. *Something better turn up. Anything, really.*

Erika stepped into the bar with a click of boot heels and a creak of leather. She claimed her small reserved booth, carefully chosen for the cozy lighting and the subtle separation from the rest of the bar, ordered a pair of heavily iced scotches, paid cash with a generous tip and settled into the back of the red vinyl seats.

She pretended to sip her drink while watching the other patrons and the time. People began drifting out, heading for their rooms or late shows or their dates' apartments. By 12:30, the place was almost empty, save for a thin man nursing a spritzer at the bar and a few couples.

Erika was idly wondering what the skinny guy's blues were when, at 12:50, Beth arrived. Hiding inside an overcoat and sunglasses, she scanned the bar like a rabbit on a shooting range, spotted Erika and hurried over, avoiding the other patrons as much as possible.

Beth was about to join her in the booth when Erika held up a hand, then indicated that Beth pull up a chair. She complied and sat down, with a quick glance over her shoulder. Erika made a subtle gesture towards her sunglasses, and Beth hastily removed them. A blond curl dangled before her craving eyes.

Beth waited nervously, hands clasped before her, while Erika toyed with her drink. Ice clinked against glass.

Erika licked her fingers clean, reached inside her glossy leather jacket and laid something on the table. It was a collar, leather on the outside, velvet on the inside, with a bright buckle.

Beth looked at it as if it might jump off the table and wrap around her throat by itself. "Here?" she asked, stalling.

"Put it on," Erika commanded. If Beth backed out, it would be now.

Hunching forward, trying to hide from the others in the room, Beth picked up the leather band and undid the clasp.

That's it, Beth, Erika thought. *You can break the rules now, because I made you do it.*

Beth's hands shook as the collar went around her graceful neck. "Not too tight," Erika reminded, as Beth closed the buckle.

The moment Beth's hands left her encircled neck, Erika's right hand snapped out and gripped Beth's wrist.

Beth made the first eye contact, equal parts desire and apprehension. Fixing Beth with a steely gaze, Erika pulled her hand closer. She licked the fingertips of Beth's hand, then swirled her tongue in the palm.

Beth gave a little shudder and her free hand knocked her tumbler over. Watered scotch and ice spread out over the chipped tabletop. They both looked at it.

"S-sorry," Beth muttered.

A slight noise from across the room caught David's attention. He turned around, hoping for some distraction.

Two woman sat in a booth, staring intently at one another. The brunette was gripping the blonde's wrist.

Hmm... floor show, he thought, his interest piquing slightly.

Ooh, perfect! Erika thought. "Lick it up."

An 'Are You Serious?' look, and the realization that, 'Yes, She Was'.

Erika tangled her fingers in Beth's hair, and held her head to the table. Beth lapped up the amber liquor and sucked on an ice cube.

When most of the scotch was gone, Erika carefully pulled Beth's head up to just the point of discomfort and dabbed at her lips with a napkin.

The blonde's body was tight as a bowstring, locked into the flight-or-fight moment. A tension of attraction and fear. *Exactly what we've been trying to study,* David thought, discreetly watching.

"Are you ready, Beth?" Erika asked, locking eyes. She nudged the metal ring at the front of the collar.

"Yes," she swallowed. "Yes, Mistress Erika."

"Good." Erika released Beth's hair. "Stand up."

With another glance over her shoulder, Beth pushed her chair back with a screech, then got up.

"Straighten up, Beth. Back straight, chin up," Erika commented idly, sliding out of the booth. "I was going to take you out and show you off, but..." She hooked a finger in Beth's collar, pulled her close and kissed her hard. Beth quivered, then melted into her.

Erika broke away, then wrapped Beth in her coat again. "Let's go to my place."

David watched as the brunette adjusted the blonde's posture, then hooked her finger into the blonde's choker and led the other woman to the door. As they passed, a man on his way in rubbernecked so much that he crashed into the door frame.

David craned his neck slightly to catch them going around a corner, then shrugged and turned back. He had always carried a suspicion that the rest of the world had attended a "How to have Wild, Casual Sex" seminar that he had missed.

The bartender asked, in a nudge-wink tone, "You like that kind of thing?"

Before David could answer, the bartender handed him a business card. "She lets me drum up new slaves for her."

Out of curiosity, David let the card nestle in his palm. He flexed the card and activated the liquid crystal display.

A pair of feet in black stiletto heels appeared. The view panned up and around the figure of a woman in skin-tight black clothes, brandishing a riding crop, until it finally came to rest on her stern face, which winked slyly at him. The picture faded out and the card read:

Mistress Erika Jaeger
"Dramatic Coach"
Private Sessions
Exceed Your Limits

He tucked the card in his pocket and left the bar. He had an idea.

The "Dramatic Coach's" card had connected him to an automated appointment service which eventually, after a number of peculiar questions, gave him an address and an appointment for the next morning.

The address led David to a neighborhood not too far from his hotel, in one of the old commercial districts holding out against the spread of malls and arcologies. David had little trouble recognizing the right place.

Somebody had spray-painted the words "WARNING: ONE (1) FASCIST DYKE" on the door and the surrounding wall, accompanied by a cartoon of an Amazonian woman in an absurd Nazi costume, cracking a whip over naked, bloody girls in chains. Skulls, pentagrams, swastikas, snakes and other assorted nastiness completed the image. Someone else had begun scouring the graffiti off.

David keyed the door panel and slipped the business card into the appropriate slot.

A steel clamshell snapped open and a camera lens popped out and surveyed him, then scanned the alley in both directions. The camera withdrew into its niche and a small screen flashed "PLEASE WAIT".

At last, the door slid open.

David had difficultly linking the woman who stood inside with the leather-clad creature he had seen last night. "Mistress Erika Jaeger" was average height and a little on the heavy side, with brown curly hair. She wore jeans, house slippers and a sweatshirt that read "I BITE." Her contraceptive/immunization implant was set at the base of her throat.

The man was extremely tall and thin; a little more of either would have made him freakish, but his proportions seemed oddly natural and he stood with a degree of poise. Good development, probably martial arts; he'd look good in drag. Erika was already imagining those long arms and legs confined by—chains? No, clear wrap would look better. And tall guys were always a little extra fun for her.

"Hello, Ms Jaeger. I saw you at the hotel last night. My card," he said, with a cordial smile.

She accepted the small rectangle and activated it. A

globe rotated on a field of stars, then turned to an androgynous face. The head spun into the corner and, as an infinity sign formed in it, words wrote themselves:

Dr. David K Bishop
Scientist at Large

Erika noticed he had unmatched eyes, one blue, one brown. She wondered what his trip was. She could do the most delightful things with somebody like him....

"Come right in, Doctor Bishop," she said, with her carefully calibrated, friendly yet predatory smile reserved for prospective clients.

"Thank you." He stepped into her front room. It was set up in her interview arrangement, with her chair, a coffee table and a high-backed chair for the interviewee, plus a few cords and things stashed about in case the scene got heavy.

David glanced about the room, which was decorated in a strange kind of austere decadence. Though almost everything was black, white or grey, there were textures everywhere, from the slate-grey carpet to the polished coffee table and the leather furniture. Despite indirect lighting, there were candelabras scattered about. On one wall, next to a framed license, was a black-and-white photo of a muscular woman in a skull cap and leather pants and harness, brandishing a black bar that obscured her eyes. On another was a poster-sized Tarot card, "The Hanged Man."

"Mistress" Erika Jaeger ushered him around to the chair towards the door and took her own, an elaborate bamboo and silk throne. "Well, David, this can be a little difficult for beginners, so here-" She opened a drawer and pulled out a sheaf of forms and a pen. "I'll be needing references, prior experience, and the standard health checks. Oh, and make sure you fill out all of the green form."

He flipped through the papers, his dismay increasing by the second. *Brown showers? Petticoat training?*

"Ah, Ms Jaeger, I think we are at cross purposes. I am not here to obtain your... services."

Aw, too bad, Erika thought.

"If you'll let me explain—"

"Please do," she said coolly, picturing him naked. *Yummy.*

"I'm currently working with the Muybridge 2 project at the university. It concerns the application of Superconducting Quantum Interference Devices to analyzing human neurological activity." He placed a small matte case on the table and opened it. Snug in the padded interior was a triangle of black, rubbery substance. "This is one of a set of SQUIDs developed by the project. For its size, it's the most sensitive in the world. A complete set is small and light enough to be worn by a subject and not interfere with natural motion. A briefcase-size unit can provide real time high resolution ElectroEncephaloGraphy scans from nearby. These devices will revolutionize neurology."

Erika had a good idea where this was going, but she let him continue. Too bad he was wearing that swallow-tail coat; she didn't get a look at his ass.

"Now a researcher can study the mental activity of subjects in their natural environments. A significant portion of the project is now studying various types of people in various activities. We're especially interested in extreme and altered states of consciousness. Colleagues of mine are presently studying martial artists, test pilots, autistic-savants, aphasics and the like."

She was admiring his long, almost feminine neck. Leather or metal collar?

"Perhaps the chief problem was that opportunities to study traumatic experiences of fear and pain were difficult to come by. The obvious subjects, sky divers and the like, proved less than adequate, because in many cases they simply aren't frightened by what they are doing. So this part of the study was lagging behind considerably."

Boy, you are a tight-ass, aren't you? Erika thought.

"Which brings me to you. Your card offers people a

way to exceed their limits. Your... clients may be experiencing exactly the kind of mental state we want to study, in real time, with these devices. In short, I would like to fit one of your, ah, subjects with a SQUID set and record his or her neural activity while you..." He searched for a phrase.

"Do a scene with them," she provided. He had the most intriguing hands.

"Yes. Now, as this is not a social or psychological study, I can guarantee a high degree of anonymity and confidentiality. In fact, I could instruct you in applying the monitors to the subject and let you perform the scene. All we need is the brain scans, some medical data, and a video record for a time index—"

"No, absolutely not," she interrupted. "No video whatsoever. Recording a scene is just asking for trouble. There's no telling where the tape can end up, and before you know it's been bounced off a satellite and teenagers in Guatemala are jacking off to you."

"I suppose assurances of confidentiality aren't going to make any difference," he offered.

"That's right. I have a responsibility to my clientele. If you're going to bring so much as one thimble camera in here, you can forget it. Non-negotiable."

Erika could practically hear his backup plan load up. "I do need a time index for the data. Is just audio acceptable?"

"Only audio?"

"You have my professional word." He held his right hand up, palm out. "You may examine the equipment beforehand, of course, and I'd be willing to sign a formal agreement if you wish."

"Okay....So," she pressed, "you want to observe submission."

"Study the neural and neurochemical activity, yes."

"Sounds interesting...." Erika rocked back in her chair. She had already decided, but she kept Dr Bishop waiting. *Make him want it.*

He leaned forward a fraction of a degree.

Got 'im.

She clapped her hands together, a warm, solid sound. "Beth. She'd do this. Of course I'll have to check with her, but I think she'll go along with it. Doctor Bishop, we have a deal."

Erika picked up one of the SQUID pads and turned it over in her hand. "Muybridge 2... I remember that from film school. He did photographic studies of human and animal motion."

"It wasn't actually that revolutionary, merely an extension of photographic figure studies. This is the neurological equivalent, mapping out the territory for the future," he explained.

"There was—" She stuck the featherweight pad on the back of her hand. "—a woman having a seizure, and a paraplegic child climbing onto a chair, nude against a grid. That was abnormal motion. Then he had men running, throwing balls, punching, and women dancing, fluttering fans, taking off dresses, that kind of thing. Male and female motion." She pulled the pad off and put it back in the case. "What kind of classification are you doing?"

"Beg pardon?"

"I presume you've got all these recordings vaulted up somewhere, all categorized." She pointed at imaginary shelves. "Ordinary folks here, trance mediums here, assorted thrill-seekers here—"

"We cross-index demographic and medical factors and the type of experience scanned in a hypertext database."

"Exactly. How is experience classified? What label is going to go on Beth's tape?"

"If you're worried about normative labelling, I can assure you we aren't being judgmental. Beth's recording would go under sexuality, probably referenced with physical exertion or endurance."

"How about as a transcendent or liminal experience?" she prodded.

Few people had ever taken this much interest, which was actually refreshing. "Perhaps. The recordings are generally accompanied by interviews that provide context."

"You're avoiding my question."

"I don't do the categorizing."

"—and you look like something's crawling up your leg," she added. "Would you like to talk about this outside?"

The room felt more like a stage set than a place where people actually lived. "That would be fine."

She stood up. "Good. I don't have any appointments till this evening. I'll just change." She sauntered through one of the doors leading to the rest of the studio.

David got up and walked about. He kept noticing little things, like the small eyelets in the furniture.

Remarkably soon, she emerged in a suede jacket that showed deep cleavage and a touch of black lace. "Let's go," she smiled.

Outside, Erika started walking down the alley, and he kept up with long, measured strides. It was a crisp, early spring day, perfect for a walk; all that was missing was the tik-tik-tik of Claudine's cane.

"What do you think?" Erika asked. "About S/M and everything?"

"What I think of what you do is not at all relevant, Ms Jaeger. I'm just here to get the data." He didn't want to jeopardize the arrangement by getting into a confrontational situation.

"Still, I'm interested in your opinion." She spoke with her hands, making a subtle motion with each phrase.

He thought for a moment. "If I disapproved, would you stop?"

"Of course not!"

"Then what does it matter?"

"I'd just like to know. You aren't repulsed or judgmental, or you wouldn't be here."

He evaded the question. "Tell me, do you engage in more conventional activities?"

Tell me, do you always talk like an anal retentive twit? Erika thought. "Vanilla sex? Yuck, I hate it. No drama, no safe words, no rules, no trust. You know nothing about the person you're groping around in bed with, each trying for your own pleasure and only coincidentally contributing to the other's. You're both thinking of something else, even someone else. There's no communication, no understanding.

"I look at two people in bed, missionary or whatever, and I see that, while their bodies are together, their minds are far away, each in his or her own fantasy. To truly link those two people, simple vanilla sex isn't enough, so you have to bring in speech, costume, props, rituals... all kinds of symbols.

"S/M is hated and feared by so many because it exaggerates and plays with power relations, and by doing so shows how artificial and fragile those relations are, how dependent roles are on symbols, and how slippery and subtle dominance and control really are. One word or gesture in the wrong place can cost you control of a situation. S/M mocks some of the most fundamental underpinnings of civilization. When a woman straps on a dildo and penetrates a man, both of them are defying the established order."

"Are they?" he asked. "You're still having sex modelled on rape, force, coercion, pain. You change the variables and even the values, but the formulas are the same. The acts are unchanged. Does the fact that you are a woman doing them to men, or women, make any difference?"

"Yes, it does. When you see sexualities as formulas, not as God-given laws, styles that you can pick and choose and play around with, you've transcended them. You control them. People like me and Beth make our own rules."

"Beth? Is that the woman I saw you with last night?"

"Yes. She's been seeing me for a few months. She's great, all these forces in her, pushing this way, pulling that, all under tension. She's one of my favorites." Erika appraisingly eyed a passing teenage couple, then turned back to him. "When I'm doing a scene with Beth, I'm fulfilling her dream, being what she wants me to be, communicating with her on a level most people never achieve. I'm totally focussed on her.

"How long has it been since you had somebody totally focussed on you, specifically you? Your parents when you were little, of course, and maybe a good lover, but that's it. These days people go for years without anybody else being interested in them. In their money, or their citizen numbers, or their votes, but not them. If you're in a scene, bound or being beaten or whatever, you have direct proof that somebody is paying attention to you."

"Are people so deprived that they need that to prove they matter? Aren't there other kinds of attention that could be provided?"

"Sure, but that's doctors and therapists and, if you're lucky, friends and lovers. I provide a specific kind of attention, physical and emotional. The top's existence resolves around the bottom. As far as they're concerned, everything I do has them as the center of attention. 'I value you so much that I'll tie you up to keep you from leaving'. When done right, it is a beautiful thing. It can be very loving."

"You provide love?" he asked. He had been wondering into what kind of emotional context she put her occupation.

She hesitated before answering. "I provide attention, love distilled. Most people aren't really capable of love, all the problems with emotions and trust and privacy and all that. Most people just can't do it."

They stopped at a crosswalk. He turned and stated, "I do not believe that."

"Who do you love?" she countered.

The question surprised him. He thought, *I'm not at issue here.*

When he hesitated, she went on. "I've met maybe

three people in all my life who really loved somebody and could say it without balking."

"I broke up three months ago," he offered, an admission.

She cocked her head, waiting for an elaboration.

"I don't even know why she left...." He trailed off.

They had entered the business district, just as the lunch crowd was streaming out of the office towers. They walked among the wage slaves in this season's green suits.

"Still, why do people pay money for you to inflict discomfort, humiliation and even pain upon them?" David gestured at the humanity about them, gossiping and wolfing down take-out. "There are people out there desperate to escape from what Beth pays you to do to her."

Would you lay off the money, for God's sake.... "It is not the same. The instant I do anything Beth doesn't like, she can say the safe word and leave."

"After you've untied her. Before which, you could kill her in any number of creative ways."

"Look, if Beth ends up in the hospital or the morgue, I suddenly can't get any dates. All the S/M BBSs put out blacklists. Besides, it's no more dangerous than a doctor or a therapist. How do you really know what your pharmacist is giving you?"

It was a while before David noticed that they were sauntering into his hotel's lobby.

"Where are we going?" he asked her in front of the elevators.

"Up to your room. I think it would be a good place to talk, I'm enjoying your conversation."

"I'm not sure this is maintaining professional decorum," he said warily.

She hit the elevator button. "For me it is. Look, you're a big boy. If I try something, you can throw me out, okay?"

"What if I try something? I might even become hostile."

"Then I'll throw you out. Besides, I know the type, and you aren't one. So what floor are you on?"

In the elevator, between the third and seventeenth floors, she told him, "Its different for each person. Some of my female bottoms would really rather be topped by a man, but they would feel they're compromising themselves, so they come to me. Same goes for some of my men, actually; they'd want a top man, but they're too homophobic. Some guys just want me to watch them put on make up and lingerie and high heels and say they're beautiful. Women want me to make them bad girls, or give them the kind of force they're afraid of from men. They want me to make them do what they already want to do, but can't or won't or whatever."

Erika noted that David was a live-out-of-a-suitcase type, with a couple of bags and a portable terminal blinking a list of e-mail messages. Sheets of paper with arcane diagrams and blocks of numbers were taped to the walls in odd places. While he checked his messages, she stole a glance at the framed pictures on the bedside: an older couple, probably his parents, in a black frame, and an attractive woman with odd eyes.

"You know," she said, wandering over to the window and discretely posing, "you're making the same mistake almost every reporter or psychologist or writer makes."

He raised an eyebrow.

"You're asking the wrong person," she explained. "It's the slaves, submissives and bottoms who can really talk about it, because they created it. I'm just a director and actor. Submissives are the writers, producers, designers, and audience." She shrugged. "I'm the bungee cord that lets them jump into the abyss and come back safe. You see?"

He shook his head. "No. Although, I do have an observation I'd like to share."

"Please do," she said, faintly mocking.

"I've found that scientists who talk incessantly about their theories are often very unsure of them."

Erika was blindsided. She had babbled on, thinking she was in control, while he listened. Then, with one sentence, the scene had shifted, giving him control for the moment. She was tempted to go with it, play the submissive for a while, but decided to stick with the dominant. "When all is said and done, it's something you either get or you don't. Sometimes you just have to try it, see whether it clicks or not," she said, subtly drawing closer to him. "You can compile interviews, make measurements, do tests forever, but you'll never understand it until you try it."

"Are you suggesting something?" he said cautiously.

II. Einstein

"An experiment." Her voice was quietly intense. "A brief scene, just you and me, nothing rough, won't even have to take your clothes off. I give you a safe word, so you can stop it at any time. I'll start real slow."

Curiosity and provocation vied with caution. What would she do? Did she really think he was that weak, one of her slave-johns?

"I will not interfere with your capacity for speech in any way. The safe word is 'green'. Now, do you accept my domination over you for the duration of this scene?"

She looked him dead in the eye, impassive, unreadable.

Damnit, for once in your life just DO IT.

"Yes," David said.

She smiled coldly. "Give me your hands."

He held them up, hesitantly. The gesture seemed too much like supplication. *But isn't that the point?*

From her pocket she produced a small velvet band. With one hand she held his palms together and with the other slipped the band around his thumbs. The sensation was unnerving; his fingers could move freely, but he couldn't separate his hands or use his thumbs.

Odd that she just happened to have that with her.

Had she been planning this? "Do you always—" he began to ask, as she tightened the strap until it was snug.

Lightning fast, her hand snapped up and delivered a slap to his cheek. Just enough to sting, but it was a sudden reminder of just what he was getting into. These were the new rules, and he was not in charge.

But a single word could bring this to a halt and free him. And he felt that the thumb-bond was elastic enough that with a slight exertion he could just slip it off. So he had the final word. Strange.

"Quiet. I could gag you, you know," she said in the tone of a nurse about to give a reluctant patient an injection. But she said she wouldn't keep him from speaking. Was that just an empty threat, part of the act?

She pushed him down on the couch, spreading his legs apart with her knee, making him realize how tightly he had been clutching them. Half-kneeling between his legs, her small, strong hands gripped his shoulders, as one might rest a hand on an animal. Her nails were trimmed and filed very smooth. Her eyes were appraising, focussed on his chest, arms, throat.

Now her hands slipped down and inside his jacket, her palms resting on his chest. He glanced down.

"Head up," she ordered. "Don't move until I say so." When he hesitated, she growled, "I said, keep your head up!" She grasped his chin and shoved it up, making his teeth clash together.

Her hands went back to his chest. His imagination painted small creatures roaming over his torso, under his arms, stroking the skin over his ribs, then crawling back to his chest and pinching his nipples through the cotton. She yanked his arms up over his head, tugged down his sleeves, scratched at his implant. He twitched all over, managing to become even more tense.

Before he had recovered from that, she grabbed his lapels and shoved his jacket back over his shoulders. Now his arms were pinned, though again a forceful shrug could remove that confinement. He realized he almost couldn't move. The combination of his jacket and the thumb bond immobilized his arms, and he couldn't stand up without bringing his knees together, and Erika was in the way. There was no way to extricate himself without bluntly shoving her off; short of doing that, he was effectively pinned.

Her hands slid up to his neck and undid the top two buttons of his shirt. She traced a fingertip down his sternum and back, then her fingers stroked his cheek. Her fingertips rested on his forehead, then dragged down, closing his eyelids.

The first time together, Claudine reached out, searching for him until she touched his face, then nestled into his arms, soft and alive.

Despite shivering with want for her, he held back, stroking her all over until she pulled him on top of her, raked his back with her nails and breathed in his ear, "I won't break!"

"Aha," Erika murmured. She must have felt every muscle in him tense. "Keep them closed."

Her hands left him. He heard her clothes rustling, both of them breathing rather quickly, and an odd, faint clicking—

Something grabbed his face. He jerked back for a second, then realized it was a pair of glasses. He opened his eyes.

There was still darkness. Again he flinched, before realizing that they must have been painted-over sunglasses or something similar.

The compact warmth of her body slipped away. Her languid command voice said, "Stand up." The first time she had told him to take an action.

Just to get some circulation going (he told himself), he brought his legs together and levered himself up. "Ah, that's a good little control freak." He stood, weaving a little. When had he started shaking? A hand grasped his arm. "Get your balance."

When he was steady, she pulled his jacket back into place, and surprisingly, frisked him. When she reached his right front pants pocket, she pulled out his room key.

"I'm going to take you for a walk."

I can handle this. The sheer challenge was becoming important, not to mention curiosity; what could she do to him that would be so bad?

He remembered the hotel well enough to figure out where he was as Erika escorted him into the elevator, down to the lobby and out the sliding doors. After that, the quality of the sound changed to city-street buzz, and he was reduced to counting steps as Erika ushered him along, arm in arm. He smelled chow mein.

Erika pulled him to a halt and asked, in a preposterous German accent, "Excuse me, *mein herr,* but directing us could you to Water Street?"

Somebody was actually looking at him, thinking, 'Look at that poor blind man.' A red flush grew up from his collar.

"Sure," said a faint Cantonese accent. "Two blocks that way."

"*Danke, danke.* Come, *liebchen.*" She tugged him along again.

So, total strangers had seen him pathetic and weak, but they didn't know it was him...

He was just thinking, *What's the big fuss?*, when Erika let go of him.

The universe shrank to the concrete under his feet. He tossed his head around, trying to get some sense of location, sorting through the buzzing sounds. Were people walking around him?

He was blind and alone and his hands didn't work and anybody could be out there—why did she abandon him?

He shouldn't have left her alone.

The horrible helpless watching as the towering punk touched the cigarette to Claudine's hand. Her distant shriek of fear and pain. His frantic dash across the busy street. Her slashing her lead-filled cane into the punk's shin. He kicked the punk's knee out and, without time to explain, picked her up bodily and ran. He screwed his eyes shut as she clawed at his face and screamed "RAPE!" in his ear.

A warm hand on the back of his neck made him jerk like he'd been struck with a stun gun. The impulse to evade the touch conflicted with the frantic desire to reach for anybody or anything, get some kind of bearing.

He spun around and groped two-handed. One of his fingers brushed across soft suede, and he grabbed and clung to it, a female body.

"It's okay, it's me." Erika's voice, after maybe five seconds of stark terror.

She brought him back to the hotel, up in the elevator, back to his room—at least, he hoped it was his room.

Holding him by the elbows, she ordered, "Sit down."

He did it, even though he hadn't any idea what was behind him. He dropped onto a bed.

She picked up his legs, lifted them onto the bed and turned him around. Then she lowered him to the pillow by the shoulders, as smoothly and strongly as a hospital nurse.

What now?

Those hard fingers stroked his hands, then took away the velvet band. His hands dropped to the side and clutched the bedspread.

He could feel her hovering over him, then... a dry, delicate kiss, the only touch. He didn't respond.

She moved away. The glasses vanished.

"Scene's over."

He winced with the sudden light, blinked and looked around.

She sat at the end of the bed, slipping a folded black silk handkerchief from behind a pair of sunglasses. "That's what I do, Doctor Bishop. I take you out, in, up, down, back, forwards, sideways, or even apart, and then I bring you back to where you were, safe and whole."

He rolled over, away from Erika.

Claudine..., he thought. *But I didn't abandon her, not the way Erika left me—*

Erika was watching him. He felt more vulnerable than when blindfolded.

He turned over and asked mildly, "How much is that going to cost me?"

She made a noise of disgust and punched the mattress. "You're pathetic, you know that?"

"Well?"

"Nothing, nothing! It's on the house of ill repute, okay? Free sample, tell your friends." She stood up and stalked into the bathroom.

Okay, so by sheer chance she happened to strike a nerve, he thought. *Doesn't mean anything. It's not as if I enjoyed it.*

Why did she waste her time with dry, desiccated stick people? She filled the sink and splashed water on her face. She had thought she had reached him, when she had let him go, and saw the spectacle of the body in exertion, in the delicious moment before raw feeling collapsed into fear or anger. The way he moved his head, listening for clues about the world, trying to guess her actions, helpless but on guard... she had wanted to drop him to his knees right there on the sidewalk, shove her tongue down his throat, wrap her legs around him.

But now—some people didn't know they had been shown something, that they had touched something special. All of life was the same to them, no sacred moments of fear or exaltation.

Erika went back to the main room, drying her face and neck. "My time is valuable, you know," she snapped. "You're lucky I don't have any sessions right now."

"As I recall this was your idea. Anyway," he said, buttoning up his shirt, "I have to speak with this Beth person before the experiment. The medical history questionnaire and initial brain scans need to be done."

Erika chucked the towel into the bathroom. She was tempted to call it off, but.... *You think you can just* watch, *don't you?* "Beth'll be at my studio tomorrow night. Show up at eleven-thirty sharp and bring whatever you need," she said coldly. "I'll brief her and get her permission."

"All right."

At the door, she turned and said, with great insincerity, "I'll call you."

Half of the Nazi Amazon was gone from Erika's wall, along with the swastikas. The door was answered by the blond woman who had been with Erika at the hotel bar. She wore a white bath robe, with a wide leather collar that held her head upright. Her eyes were cast down. "Mistress Erika welcomes you to her domain, sir."

"Very gracious of her," David answered, only then realizing how foolish it sounded. He waited a few moments for her to invite him in, before realizing that she wasn't going to.

He stepped in, and heard the door close and lock behind him. A glance back revealed her taking the robe off. She wore only a tiny white maid's apron with a huge bow in back, the collar, wrist and ankle cuffs with little dangling eyelets, white mules and her implant, like a birthmark on her shoulder. Without self-consciousness, she walked past him, letting him see a long tail of white silk hanging down to her knees. It took David a moment to realize that the scarf must have been held by some object placed in her anus.

Stop gawking, you fool!

A discreet cough from the corner of the room diverted his attention.

Erika wore a real dominatrix outfit, skin-tight black leather leotard with a diamond cutout over her cleavage, thigh-high boots and elbow gloves. Metal chains and rods were woven into her hair. A black cape with red lining swirled about her as she strode towards him. "Good evening, Doctor Bishop. I see you've met Beth. She's been looking forward to meeting you."

Ambush, he thought.

"Please sit down. Beth will make you a cup of tea, and we can talk."

The room was full of lit candles, but the dark walls and furniture swallowed the light up. Beth's skin and hair stood out like a spotlight as she gracefully knelt by the table and picked up the kettle. There was, of course, only one chair for him, a high-backed affair directly facing Erika on her throne. A bright light shone over his shoulder, straight at Beth; from her perspective he would be backlit. He found himself sitting with his legs together and clutching his briefcase to his lap. He forced himself to relax, and moved the case to the table top.

David couldn't help watching the naked woman run through the mundane action of pouring and serving tea. She did it with such grace that he wondered if she had taken Japanese tea ceremony instruction. The cup and saucer sat before him on the neatly placed coaster, with a smell of hot orange pekoe. Somehow he doubted he'd actually drink it.

Erika crouched behind Beth and locked the kneeling woman's wrists behind her, then lounged, resting one booted foot on Beth's shoulder, elegantly sipping tea.

"You may proceed. Beth, answer the doctor's questions."

David put his laptop on his knees and called up the standard medical questionnaire. Beth's apron had bunched up, giving tantalizing glimpses...

He swallowed. "Do you or any of your relatives possess any kind of neural abnormality or irregularity?"

"No, sir," Beth answered, a little too quickly for David. Most people had to think a bit. However, any abnormality would more likely give a bad reading than actually harm the subject, so he let it ride.

"Have you ever suffered any kind of spasmodic attack or seizure for any reason, particularly as a result of flashing light or high-pitched sound?"

"No, sir."

This wasn't so bad, so long as he kept his eye on his laptop. "Have you ever had any kind of brain or spinal surgery or injury?"

"No, sir."

David chanced to look up and noticed that Erika, behind Beth's back, was scribbling something on a pad. She held it up: *PICK IT UP —SHE'S BORED!*

David frowned at her. If Erika was so concerned about Beth, then she should understand the importance of the safety checks. He continued, "Are there any metallic or semi-metallic artifacts implanted in your head, neck or upper torso?"

Erika languidly rose and stood next to Beth. "You have a couple of fillings, don't you Beth?"

Beth looked up. "Yes, Mistress."

Erika crouched down and gripped Beth's jaw and forehead, prying her mouth open like a horse's. "Yes... I think we can see them." Beth's eyes flicked from Erika to David and back.

The lighting was just right so that he could see clear down Beth's throat. "Uh huh. Tonsillectomy also," he commented, looking at his pad and pretending to make a few extra notes. What was Erika doing? "Are they metallic?"

"Answer, Beth."

"Ah-ah."

He cleared his throat. "Have you used any hallucinogenic, psychotropic or mood-altering substances, other than alcohol, in the past year?"

No obedient answer. He saw that Erika still had Beth's mouth wedged open and was fingering her teeth. "You can let her go."

Erika looked at him like he was interrupting something, which he supposed he was. She pushed Beth's head upright and shut her mouth, then slunk back to her chair. "Answer Doctor Bishop, Beth."

"No, sir, no drugs."

"By the way, please don't drink or smoke the day before the test, all right?"

"Yes, sir."

"Have you ever been under hypnosis?"

"No, sir."

Finally, he reached the last, afterthought question.

"Are you right-or left-handed, or ambidextrous?"

"Right-handed, sir."

He let out a breath, and saved and cleared. He was about to get up when he saw Erika waving her pad at him again. This time the note read, in emphatic capitals: *TOUCH HER A LITTLE.*

Exasperated, he mouthed "All right!" After some hesitation, he reached down, cupped her narrow chin and stroked her cheek with his thumb; Claudine had always liked that. Beth had warm, slightly dry skin. She closed her eyes and licked her lips.

Okay, that's enough. He let go, stood up and faced Erika. "Mistress Erika, a word with you in private."

"Of course, Doctor." She knelt by Beth again and whispered something in her ear.

David turned away, trying to breathe deeply and evenly.

After Beth's collar was leashed to the throne, Erika released Beth's hands, then picked up the tea pot. Beth held her hands above her head. Erika put the handle in one hand and the spout in another. She patted her slave's head gently and said, "Be back in a minute." Beth nodded, as her arms began to tremble.

Erika rose and drew her cape around her. David stood facing the Hanged Man, shoulders tight. "Follow me," she said softly.

She led him into the tiny kitchenette that adjoined the bathroom and shower. "Keep your voice down," she cautioned.

"Her arms are going to get tired," he said, peering around the corner.

"Then you'd better talk fast."

"I needed her normal," he gritted.

"Normal?" Erika asked.

"Having free will, wearing clothes, you know, normal."

"I don't do normal."

"I need to make an initializing observation, establish a

baseline to measure from. Have her calm down, take a cold shower or whatever, so that I can get a good scan."

Erika was interested to see David actually annoyed. "You can do that after the scene."

"It is accepted experimental procedure, and common sense, to establish norms for the subject before the actual experiment."

"Does it make any difference?" Erika asked.

He made a sound of exasperation. "No, but—"

"You can do it afterwards. Tomorrow night. Be here at 10:30 sharp."

"Look—"

"That's my one and only offer."

He sighed, his expression saying, 'Why are you doing this to me?' "Very well."

"Good," she grinned. Everything was going perfectly. "Doctor, don't worry. You won't be disappointed. Now, go out there, say goodbye to Beth, and I'll see you tomorrow." She ushered him out.

Of course, Beth was still on her knees. Her arms were starting to twitch.

David stood to one side, while Erika whispered something in Beth's ear. Then Erika stepped back.

Beth faced him over her quivering arm, but kept her eyes lowered.

What do you say to somebody who is nearly naked and chained up before you? "I'll see you tomorrow evening," he said, neutrally.

Beth lowered her head a little more. What was going on in there? Maybe with the brain scan he'd find out.

"Goodbye, Beth."

"Goodbye, sir."

III. Hawking

Only a long snake and a few skulls remained of the graffiti this time. As a half-hearted attempt to look like he belonged in Erika's studio, David wore black, a simple jacket and slacks and a white shirt with the collar closed. Erika tried in vain to cajole him into a pair of black leather gloves.

"Hmm, your hair," Erika said, looking him over. She wore the same dominatrix outfit without the cape, but had added shoulder plastrons and shin pads of fake chrome. Her hair had been conditioned to a high sheen and teased outrageously. Add a red slash of lipstick and huge Egyptian eyes and David couldn't decide whether she looked stunning or absurd. "You got any mousse on you?"

"No. Question: Why no stiletto heels?" he asked, looking down at her pointed boots.

"Oh, I hate those." She was rushing about, adjusting the track lighting and an odd gibbet-like framework set up in the center of the main studio. The large room was lined with closets and he got glimpses of dozens of costumes, a fold-up exercise machine, odd-looking furniture and other things he didn't want to identify. "Beth really wanted me to wear them, but it's hard to be dominant when you can barely walk. You can't get a real good swing when you're balanced on those things either. Do you have a white lab coat or something? It would give a real cachet."

"Scientists don't wear those any more," he answered.

She was up on a stepladder, hanging a huge sheet from some hooks near the ceiling. One wall was now covered by a white-on-black grid, while the others were dark charcoal. There was a futon in the corner, with a bowl of water and a cloth nearby, and a small table on which he put the briefcase with the recording scanner. He wrote "BETH" and the date on the label and threaded the two-centimetre optical WORM tape, opened the SQUID set's case, then set up the display flatscreen and the high-gain microwave antennae and pocketed the remote control.

The door chimed. "That's her. Here, put these on." Erika handed him a pair of mirror shades as she pulled him into the foyer. "There's a first aid kit under the sink in the bathroom and a call button for a paramedic service under the coffee table. If Beth says the word 'Sanity' at any time, drop what you're doing and help me untie her or cut her down. The same goes if she makes three short grunts when gagged. Got it?"

"Yes," he said, cautiously putting on the shades. At least he could see this time.

"And no idle talk," she commanded. Taking a deep breath, she rolled the heavy door open.

Beth, wearing a green suit, stood framed in the doorway. She stepped in, accompanied by a blast of cold air.

The metal slab slid home. Erika moved to stand erect, feet apart, directly in front of Beth. There was a brief moment of intense eye contact.

"Strip."

Beth's eyes made the briefest flicker towards David, then she began undressing, neatly folding each item and laying it out on the coffee table. It was no striptease, just getting out of her clothes.

Erika watched impassively until Beth was stashing her jewelry in her purse, then flashed a look at David. "*Relax*," she mouthed.

The naked woman stood before him, her breathing fast and shallow and her eyes cast down. He wasn't much at ease either. He stepped up to her, inside her space, doctor-close, lover-close, mugger-close. It was like... coughing during an aria, or in the middle of a play, getting up from the audience and mounting the stage, a violation of the "fourth wall".

He peeled the first of the SQUID patches off the sterile pad. This one would go on the right temple, but he suddenly realized that a lock or two of Beth's hair covered the proper spot. In the lab he would have simply brushed it aside and proceeded, but here it was a confounding obstacle. Hold back the hair himself, or ask—no, order her to do it? He must have been standing there, perplexed, when Erika intervened, thankfully. "Beth, brush the hair back from your right temple."

"Yes, Mistress." Beth brought her arm up and pushed back her blonde locks.

He hoped Beth had taken his hesitation as the heightening of dramatic tension, or something. He placed the triangular patch on her forehead, trying not to touch her skin. His thumb brushed her cheek, and he felt not only her warm flesh but her lean into it, prolonging the contact by a fraction of a second. He wouldn't have noticed it if he weren't so on edge. What was this? Was she flirting with him?

More by habit than conscious action, as his head was spinning gently, he stepped to her other side and found himself saying, "Left temple." His voice squeaked on the first try, then he got the words out with a fair degree of conviction.

Beth, of course, complied. "Yes, sir." He got the other temple patch in place. This time, she actually looked at him, the briefest glance of some weird mix of lust, submission and Isn't this fun? How was he supposed to respond to that? Slap her?

He decided to leave it up to Erika, who had either not seen the little signals or chosen to ignore them. Were they part of this?

He retreated outside Beth's field of vision. Quietly clearing his throat first, he commanded, "Pull your hair up, away from your neck."

"Yes, sir." That wasn't to him, that was to somebody else, what she thought he was. No, what she wanted him to be.

Beth had sleek curves from the tips of her shoulders to the base of her head, and fine blond peach fuzz running down her spine. Despite himself, he glanced down and saw what wouldn't have drawn a second glance on any beach in Europe but here seemed as enthralling as the first nude woman he had ever seen.

He swallowed hard, and applied the third patch to the neck, just under and behind her right ear. Her neck flexed beneath his touch as she moved her head a fraction of a degree. Maybe he should have worn those gloves Erika had offered.

He heard a soft smacking sound. A glance up revealed Erika tapping a riding crop against her calf, as regular as a metronome. Beth watched the crop for a few moments, then closed her eyes and sighed.

David swallowed again, and placed the fourth patch.

The worst was yet to come. Instead of another black palm-sized triangle, the spinal monitors were a pair of long thin strips that went along the neck and upper back. To apply those properly required careful smoothing to flex with the skin. Entirely too much like a caress.

Definitely should've had Erika do this, he thought, laying the black plastic band along her sleek neck. Beth leaned into the touch again, and made the tiniest squeak of pleasure. *Aw, cut it out.*

Particles didn't do this. They dutifully did laps around the accelerator, then danced merrily after collisions, splitting and recombining. They certainly didn't try to snuggle up.

At last the spine monitors were in place. He stepped back in front of her. That left only the EKG patch, which would have to go right over— the naked female breast. Already swollen with an erect nipple. *Don't look, don't look.* Eye contact was also out of the question, so he settled on the hollow of her throat as he hastily applied the final monitor. Of course, she somehow managed to rub that damned nipple against his inner arm. Even through his jacket and shirt, which were becoming uncomfortably hot, he felt it afterwards, like a tactile purple afterimage of a bright light.

Finally, Beth's head and neck bore the six patches, so thin they might have been painted on. He stepped away, putting welcome, comfortable distance between them. He took a couple of deep breaths and tried to do a mental relaxation routine.

Erika, standing by impassively, caught his eye and bobbed her head, suggesting, *Say something.*

He stated bluntly, "The subject has been prepared." The hard part was over now. Erika and Beth would do their scene, he would record the data and, with the right attitude, convince himself he was merely watching this on video. Then he would go home, masturbate and forget about this.

"Good," Erika answered coldly, in full dominatrix mode now, twirling the crop in her fingers. "Beth, third position!"

The naked woman snapped into a specific pose, feet together and arms crossed behind her. Erika stepped closer and clasped a high leather collar around Beth's neck, forcing her head straight up. David moved to one side and made sure that the collar wasn't in danger of dislodging any of the monitors.

He turned away, and took the control pad out of his pocket. The main unit was getting clear signals from all of the monitors and the data was flowing into the drive.

Beth's neural activity was that of a person well into sexual arousal, maybe only a minute or two of direct stimulation before orgasm. Glandular activity was way up, as was heart and respiration rates. All this after only a little rough talk and the application of the patches?

He turned back to the women. Erika was tying about four meters of soft, silver rope about Beth's torso in an intricate harness. The cord seemed just tight enough to press into the skin without interfering with circulation. A couple of strands went under Beth's crotch and up the cleft in her buttocks, while others separated and squeezed her breasts. The rope must have incorporated memory plastic by the way it seemed to just drop into place.

When most of the rope was used, Erika stepped back and surveyed her handiwork. For some reason, the sight of Beth wrapped in silver ropes and black patches made David think of a satellite photo of Earth with borders drawn on it.

Erika stepped close again and, just loudly enough for David to hear, whispered, "Y'okay?"

"Uh-huh."

Erika planted a tiny kiss on Beth's shoulder.

What was he getting into? He checked the display again; the readings had actually increased. Both hemispheres were showing heavy activity, and the corpus callosum traffic was astonishing. The cerebral cortex was going further into the beta state.

Erika had retrieved her riding crop and was stroking Beth's buttocks with it. Every now and then, she made a light teasing slap, and kept up a constant stream of patter.

"...you know, I've been seeing some impertinence in you lately, and I don't like it one bit. You've been a bit slow in obeying my commands, not quite as enthusiastic when I touch you, and I bet you haven't been following my discipline in my absence. You've been wearing panties, haven't you?!" She pushed Beth's chin up with the crop. "Answer me."

"N-no, mistress," Beth's voice shivered. She stole a look at David. Jolted out of the illusion of merely being a watcher, he tried to interpret it. A request for help?

"Of course you know the penalty for lying to your Mistress," the top continued, stalking in a circle around her slave. "And don't think I haven't noticed you snuggling up to the Doctor. He's a very busy man and doesn't have time for distractions like you."

Beth peeked at him again.

Erika grabbed the ropes and yanked her around like a rag doll. "I've put a lot of effort into your training, and I'm not going to have it go to waste serving some anorexic sperm factory. You're mine, remember?"

I'm here, he realized. *I'm not a fly on the wall, I'm here.*

"You own your humble slave Beth, Mistress Erika," she apologized, pulling back from her.

"You need a reminder. On your hands and knees, get in there!" Beth sunk down on all fours, and Erika's boot nudged her to the doorway. David shakily followed them.

Beth cringed when she saw the framework, crawled back and clung to Erika, rubbing her head into Erika's crotch. Erika pried her off and pulled her up to a standing position. "Even you don't lick that well," Erika told her.

A blush had broken out all over Beth's legs and torso.

She had to stand on her toes while Erika manacled her wrists, then her left leg was pulled to the cuff on the side post. Only now did David notice that there were tiny flanges on the side posts to fit under Beth's heels.

David checked the monitors. All readings were going perfectly, fantastic communication between different areas of the brain, mostly tactile sensations and lower and higher emotions, and the cortex hovering at the extreme of beta.

Beth was hanging by her arms with her legs spread wide and feet off the floor, her whole body under tension, suspended against the grid backdrop. Erika clicked her tongue in satisfaction, turned and looked directly at David. "Notice that both of the feet have left the ground."

For one of the few times in his life, David was totally at a loss. Beth's brain kept reaching new levels of activity, endorphins, dopamine and phenylethlyamine coursing through her veins, heart rate fast and strong.

"Hmm, how many?" Erika leaned in close to Beth. "How many do you think you could take, Beth? You took ten last time, didn't you?"

"Y-yes, Mistress." Her manacled fists were clenching and unclenching rapidly and her toes were curled up.

"I think we should try for a personal best. Eleven, maybe thirteen."

"Mistress, I can't..."

Was that for real? Would Erika heed it, or was that part of it?

"Now, Beth, Doctor Bishop wants to see you exceed your limits, as do I."

Say it! Please, say "sanity"! he silently pleaded. How could he watch somebody being whipped in his presence?

"You're doing this for science, Beth." Somehow, in here that phrase didn't seem ridiculous. "You're doing it for me," she went on, coaxing, pleading, teasing. "I need you to take it for me. You've come so far. I'm sure you can do it."

From behind, Erika teased Beth's buttocks with the crop, making her flinch with each contact.

She's really going to do it.

Erika wound up, and swung. He couldn't watch.

A blood red spike appeared in Beth's limbic system, then another. Beth yelped like a hurt dog. The pain/pleasure structures were overrun by silver-blue endorphins, and the pain spikes only lasted an instant before dissolving into undifferentiated tactile sensation. Her cortex jumped from the far reaches of beta cycles into the theta state.

Time was supposed to stretch out when something awful was happening, but here time instead rushed faster, bringing the next blow-and-shriek before David had recovered from hearing the last one. Around the fifth, she stopped making noise. He heard two more smacks of leather on skin before he had to look up.

Beth was locked rigid, with red stripes on her buttocks and thighs between the silver rope. Another blow landed on her thigh, making her spasm and twist on the rack.

He tore his eyes off Beth and looked at Erika. Her face was a picture of concentration, biting her lip, not a gleeful torturer but a surgeon in mid-operation.

He shrank back, hiding behind the pedestal. Beth's endorphin production was phenomenal, along with epinephrine and norepinephrine, like the floodgates of her brain chemistry had been opened.

Then the computer flashed, "Sensor Failure" just as Erika hissed for his attention.

Beth's collar had ridden up in her convulsions, and the monitor behind her left ear was halfway off.

Erika raised an eyebrow at him.

No, he couldn't. Touching Beth, reaching for the white skin between the silver ropes, would be like waking a hypnosis subject while she was balanced between two chairs. Not only would the performance be destroyed, but somehow she would be hurt. His touch would be worse for her than anything in Erika's armory. He shrank back, hiding behind the table. *Let her fix it.*

Erika gritted her teeth and jerked her head at Beth.

He'd have to go the distance.

There were only three steps from the table to the gibbet, and he stumbled on two of them. He couldn't bring his gaze to rest anywhere, flying from Erika flexing her crop to Beth's flushed face to the marks on her back.

He stood in front of her, one hand on the intersection of neck and shoulder, feeling Beth's throat pulse and flex with pumping blood and gasping breaths, the other replacing the monitor. Beth's eyes were shifting behind closed lids—REM, in a waking state?

Yet another blow from the crop, and he held her as she gasped and shook.

Erika rose up like a cobra, and over Beth's quivering shoulder, ordered "Kiss her."

How was he supposed to say no?

It was supposed to be just a chaste little peck, but Beth pulled him in, somehow. Teeth grated together, tongues slipped around each other and fought for space, heated breath mingling, like his first clumsy French kiss. He actually felt her entire body, heart pumping, lungs heaving, every muscle taut, as if there were some neural connection between their mouths.

Beth tensed once more, straining forward against him, pressing the ropes into his chest. He broke away and looked down. Erika was kneeling behind Beth, one arm wrapped around Beth's hips, the other—where was it?

Her whole hand's in Beth!

Beth's head rolled forward, nuzzling his cheek. Piteous little high-pitched moans escaped her. Fearing that she might somehow break her bonds and crash to the floor, he held her up while she buried her face in his shoulder, biting his collar.

The three figures stood, locked together while the central one rode out the storm triggered in herself.

Beth mumbled little half-words into his shoulder. Erika withdrew her hand with a faint suction sound, and stood up, wrapping her arms around both of them. "I knew you could do it," she whispered, nuzzling Beth's cheek.

Erika unclipped the ankle and wrist bands as David held Beth up. She was soft and limp, and her arms dropped around his neck. Beth was slowly let down until she was cradled in her kneeling mistress' arms. David at last let go and took a couple of shaky steps back until he leaned against the grid.

Erika reached over and pulled the bowl of water closer to them. She wet the terrycloth and began tenderly dabbing the beads of sweat from Beth's slack, flushed face.

He had to get out. Knees gone rubbery, he lurched across the room, trying not to make any noise. He didn't belong in here. He staggered into the front room, tore off the sunglasses and inhaled the cool, fresh air, trying to slow his pounding heart. He shed his jacket; his shirt was damp and sticking to him, and there was a rip in the collar from Beth's teeth.

He collapsed onto the coffee table and sat there, rubbing his face in his hands.

Some time later, Erika walked in with a gust of sweat, vaginal fluid and Crisco, opening her collar and sniffing her hand, enjoying the scent of Beth. She looked at him, all hunched and gaunt, then snapped the surgical glove off. He flinched as if she had whipped him.

She opened one of the cabinets and put her hand on a bottle. "Scotch?" she asked mildly.

"What...?"

"You look like you could use something." She poured a couple of fingers and put the glass before him. "Relax, its over. Beth's resting right now."

He numbly pushed the tumbler aside.

"Hey, we put on a great show. You missed the best part." She leaned back, stretching. She never came during a scene, but always felt invigorated afterwards, flushed with vitality. "Beth loved it, she's gonna sleep like a baby tonight. She always likes a big scene to unwind after a major deal. You should see her at work, she practically has the market figures lasered into her eyes. A good bottom is one thing, but a good bottom with stock tips is something else. You want to take a shower or something?"

He looked at her blankly.

Finally, she blew up. "Jesus Christ on the cross, what is with you? People dream about watching what you just saw for real. What are you, dead from the neck down?!"

He slowly, slowly got up, suddenly looking young and frail. He was only, what, twenty or so?

"Let's get the pads off..." Erika watched him walk towards the studio like it was a gas chamber.

"No, you can stay out here." She intercepted him and gently pushed him back. "I'll get the monitors."

She pushed back the curtain, then turned to him.

"I'm sorry, David," Erika said, shaking her head. "I should have given you a safe word."

He spent a sleepless night playing and replaying the SQUID scans, watching the colors slosh around inside Beth's brain, homing in on this area or that. Realization gradually sank in. Being in your own sex fantasy was one thing; being in somebody else's, and a bit player at that, was another.

He'd gotten beautiful recordings; the tooth fillings hadn't affected it at all. He'd recorded a submissive, masochistic woman's pleasure on laser tape. Now what?

After the initial dialogue, the audio index was mostly just heavy breathing, his included.

"*...kiss her...*" Beth's brain went red, orange, white.

He went back to the beginning. Beth was already aroused long before the monitors had gone on, probably anticipating it from the night before. It wasn't even a properly done experiment.

Erika was loitering by the reception desk.

"I don't want to talk about it," he said quickly, before she could begin. He dug out his credit card and began checking out.

"Don't you want to do the initial-whatevers on Beth?" she asked.

"No, the experiment's a failure—" he said, yanking his card out of the slot. Whatever had happened, he had lost.

"I'm sorry, okay? Beth's with me here, you can do a nice, normal measurement on her. No stress, no games, I swear."

He grabbed her hand and shoved the tape reel into it. "That is the recording of your friend. You can have it."

"What do I do with this?" she asked.

"I'm sure you'll think of something," he said harshly. He shouldered his bags and strode away.

She trotted to keep up. "I admit it wasn't fair, but it's not like I tied you down and—"

He waved his hand at her, as if to push her back. "Your payment will be transferred to your account later today."

"Do you want to wire me up?" she suggested.

"No!"

"Look, it was Beth's idea," she protested. "She wanted to be dominated while a handsome scientist monitored her every thought. I was doing it for her. Talk to her, not me."

"I can't talk to her—"

She jumped in front of him, finally bringing him to a halt. "Would you get over your goddamned Galahad complex?! She didn't want you to protect her! She wanted you to stand there looking cold and merciless. You weren't supposed to help her."

"I wasn't supposed to touch her either," he said. *Can't we just put this behind us?*

"So you weren't a good scientist or a good protector. Just because you've set up a no win situation in your own mind doesn't mean you should go off and sulk."

"I am not sulking! I am cutting my losses and leaving with a bit of dignity."

"No, you're running away like a little boy who wanted to play a game and lost the first time." She held his wrist tightly and shoved the tape back at him. "Go over there and talk to Beth," she ordered.

He glanced down at their locked hands, then met her eyes. "Green," he said.

She didn't let go.

"I said the safe word," he insisted. Didn't she even hold to her own code?

"If you do not talk to her, you will spend the rest of your life looking for people to protect, and they will come to hate you for it."

Beth sat poised on a couch, legs crossed and back straight, drinking coffee. She must have watched him and Erika talk.

He swallowed and said, "Hello."

"Hi there."

He frantically searched for words. This was worse than before; he was alone with her in the real world.

"Are you okay?" Beth asked.

"Me? I'm—How are you?"

She shifted in her seat. "A bit sore. Won't you have a seat?" She patted the couch.

He sat down as if he thought the sofa might collapse.

"Is that mine?" She nodded at the tape clutched in his hand.

He put the reel down. "That's the recording from last night."

There was another lull; all he could think of were the things he should have done.

"So, what do we do now?" she prompted.

"We—here." He pulled a form out of his briefcase and passed it to her. "If you could just fill this out while we put the pads on—"

While Beth filled out the background questionnaire, he glanced over his shoulder. Erika was watching from behind a pillar.

Putting on the head pads was easy. Beth must have been anticipating this, because she wore a rear-buttoning blouse that made it easy to apply the spine monitors. She slipped the heart sensor under her blouse herself, while he put another tape in the recorder.

He then handed her a wraparound sound and vision headset connected to a videocard player. "Now, this will give you a sequence of images and sounds, lasting about fifteen minutes. You just react normally, free association. Ready?"

She nodded and put on the visor. He hit the play button and leaned back. The visor only provided ordinary video images; its primary purpose was to block out distractions when testing outside the lab.

He felt like—the worst had happened, and he was still here. The after-the-dentist feeling.

This may be the only chance to get in on the ground floor, Erika thought, twisting her black handkerchief through her fingers as she watched David and Beth. The pad gizmos would be the next thing in studying how people worked. If she pulled this off, S&M might end up on the OK list, and not the sicko list.

She walked up to the couch and peered at Beth. David looked at her, then went back to the scanner.

"What's she seeing?" Erika asked.

He checked the player. "At the moment, a child birth. Then a riot during the coca blight, a time lapse of a garden growing—"

Something on the video made Beth tense, then relax.

"Hmph. You should've given her a safe word," Erika said.

Beth took off the visor and blinked. "That's it?"

"Yes," he said, relieved. "We're done." He quickly gathered up the equipment and put it back in the foam-lined niches. Beth obligingly peeled off the patches herself.

"I'd like to thank you for your participation," he said officially, "and.... I'm sorry."

"For what?"

He didn't answer.

"Hey, listen," Beth said, putting her hand on his. "I... am... fine. Okay?"

"Okay," he answered sheepishly. Was that what he wanted, for Beth to say, It's okay? "Thank you."

"No, thank you. You were great." Beth grinned.

"I switch, you know. I've been where she goes," Erika said, trailing after David.

He stopped. "That's it: participant observation," he said.

"What?" Erika asked.

"An anthropological term. The observer participates in the practice being studied," he explained absently. In fact, that was the problem. The Muybridge 2 project was being done from the perspective of neurology, not anthropology. It should be interdisciplinary....

"Doctor Bishop," Erika said behind him. He winced and, one last time, turned around.

Her open hand held out a pair of sunglasses and a black scarf. "Could I walk you to your car?"

He glowered at her, and walked away.

Watching him go, Erika pursed her lips and shuffled her feet. Under her breath, she muttered, "Really probably shouldn't've done that." She slapped her wrist. "Bad dominatrix."

She turned and walked back to Beth.

"By the way," Beth asked, "did you get those high heels yet?"

"Yeah, I did."

"Good." Beth's Rolex beeped. "Time's up."

Erika nodded. "Come with me."

Beth stood gracefully. Erika placed her hand on the nape of Beth's neck.

They walked out together.

David waited by the public phone, sagged down onto his duffel. It was over, wasn't it? Then why did he still have that punched-in-the-stomach feeling?

The booth was empty now. He levered himself up and slashed his phone card through the reader. Inside, the soundproof booth shut out the street noise, leaving him alone. The steel panel over the number pad, screen and camera, slid up.

Of course he remembered her private number, just like everything else about her.

First ring.

The only reason Claudine had a video phone was for the higher quality sound, he recalled.

Second ring.

Please don't answer.

Third ring.

I want to keep the possibility—

"Allo." A woman's face appeared in three-quarter view, with wood-colored hair and odd eyes. "Claudine Gioux can't answer right now—"

He sighed in relief. This would be merely agonizing instead of unbearable.

"Please leave a message." The screen went blank and flashed "RECORDING."

He looked into the lens. Her eyes were like that, dark and still. "Claudine, it's David." His throat become tight and sore. He rubbed the back of his handver his mouth and swallowed. This hurt worse than after what Erika did to him, worse than after Beth's beating, worse than silently walking away from Claudine, not saying a word.

"Goodbye," he said softly, and hung up.

David took one long, slow breath, let it out, and stepped out of the booth. It had hurt, but they were both free now.

Contributors

Lauren P. Burka

Lauren's Tarot cards told her she would never get a normal job. She is the author of the S/M erotic chapbook *Mate: And More Stories* (Circlet Press, 1992). Her story "The Tiger" appears in the volume of female dominant fiction *By Her Subdued* (Masquerade Books, 1995).

Tammy Jo Eckhart

is the author of published poems, short stories and scholarly articles. She was born in 1969, married in 1992, earned both a BA and MA in ancient history and is working on a PhD. She is moderately active in the BDSM community of New York City and Columbia University.

Sèphera Girón

lives in Toronto with her filmmaker husband, two sons and two cats. *Shall We Dance?* takes place in a club called the Paradise which is featured in her novel *Last Call: The Night Begins.* The short horror film *Creep* which she co-wrote is playing festivals around the world.

Raven Kaldera

is a pansexual androgyne leather top and priestess of the Dark Goddess who teaches ritual S/M, safe topping technique, and third gender mysteries. Raven is happily married and the parent of one daughter.

Jana McCall

is a freelance copy editor/proofreader in Boston. In her past careers, she has worked in liquor stores and police departments and for the City of New York. She is a fervent lurker on the Internet, at hours when the only other people online are Californians and vampires.

R. L. Perkins

is an engineer living in the Delaware Valley with his two cats. He spends most of his time hanging in several bohemian coffee houses in center city Philadelphia. Command Protocol is his first publication.

Gwendolyn Muriel Piper

is a stranded Faerie and Internet priestess who is surely having a strange enough time *without* making up stories..... She is a submissive when she remembers to have sex and is the staff scapegoat of the NLA New England newsletter... This may well be her first published story, at least as far as you're concerned....

Thomas S. Roche

sometimes wanders the dark fiber corridors in the orphanage of his mind. His work has appeared in *Black Sheets, Skim Lizard,* and *Slippery When Wet.* Upcoming publications include a prequel of sorts to "Dark Fiber" in the anthology *No Other Tribute* (Masquerade Books) as well as a collaborative piece in the horror anthology *Splatterpunks II* (Tor). A chapbook, *Fragrant Sorrows,* will be available in 1995. He is currently editing *Noirotica,* an anthology of erotic crime stories.

Peter Tupper

is a Canadian student who has previously been published in *ON-SPEC* and *Horizons Science Fiction,* who loves the idea of writing material his own customs officials wouldn't allow back into his country.

James Williams

has published fiction and non-fiction in *Advocate Men, Spectator* and *SandMutopia Guardian.* His story "Daddy" which appears in the anthology *Doing It For Daddy* (edited by Pat Califia, Alyson Publications, 1994) has been nominated for the *Best American Erotica 1995* volume edited by Susie Bright. He is the subject of profiles in *Different Loving* by Gloria Brame, William Brame and Jon Jacobs (Villard, 1993) and *An Oral History of Sex* by Harry Maurer (Viking, 1994). He lives in San Francisco where he is preparing a collection of writings.

Fetish Fantastic
Tales of Power and Lust from Futuristic to Surreal

Contents

Introduction

If you're reading this book for the sex (and I hope that you are...) and don't enjoy the form of foreplay known as delayed gratification, then skip this introduction now, and read it at the end while you're lying in your proverbial sweaty sheets (or among your cast-off chains, tangled whips, or what have you).

Still reading?

When it comes to "fantastic" fetishes, this book reflects a bias toward S/M, and the fetishes that associate around it: spanking, corsetry, corporal punishment, bondage, and other erotic turn-ons of the power exchange variety. You won't find much in here on foot fetishism (though maybe a bit on boots), and nothing on infantilism, Amazon giantesses, or other so-called "vanilla" fetishes. I leave the task of compiling that anthology to someone else—I've stuck with what I know. What I know is leather, boots, whips, dungeons, shackles, masters, slaves, dominas, and servants.

More than that, though, what I know are fantasies. Generally speaking, S/M is not about the objects or roles we fetishize, but the fantasies that imbue them with power. The whip is meaningless without the hand that swings it and, perhaps more importantly, the reason it is being swung. Were you a bad slave who needs to be punished? Are you a high-born heroine captured by pirates? Are you a religious acolyte seeking penitence? Or maybe something no one else has ever quite imagined?

These stories are in the "no one else has quite imagined" category. S/M as a means to climb the social ladder, S/M which liberates the mind, cyber-S/M, S/M as magic ritual, college degrees in S/M, S/M as art. But even as these stories push the envelope of futurism and fantasy, they have their basis in our current reality.

It is not a fantasy to imagine that S/M can be a positive and healthy force in the sexuality of a modern person. I have written many a political essay on why S/M is not violence and why fantasies of non-consensuality are liberating, and do not intend to paraphrase them here. But I should point out that one component of the much-trumpted leather community credo "safe, sane, consensual" is the knowledge of what is fantasy and what is not. When we play at S/M in the real world, our true fetish is for the scene itself, for the scenario of imaginary power we create between consenting partners. As such, the power which drives these stories is that intrinsic knowledge. Some stories will take the fantasy of imaginary nonconsent and run with it, while others will play with the border between consent and powerlessness. And no, I won't tell you which are which... that's for you to find out for yourself.

Have I teased you enough? I think so.

Cecilia Tan
Cambridge, MA

All Things Ripen In Their Own Time

Reina Delacroix

Today is Friday, so I braid my chestnut hair back severely and tell the maid I am going out shopping. She nods, her mind already more on her coming hours of freedom inside the apartment than on any suppressed excitement she may sense in my voice. But I do not begrudge her the time I know she spends watching the simuus and drinking sake while I'm gone; I understand her need for escape a little too well.

I have a ritual for this day that focuses the anticipation at each critical moment. And my husband interrupted it first this morning, by announcing loudly at breakfast, "Tammi, yesterday Mr. Inoue came by my desk and asked me if we would complete a party he is having at his house."

I was silent for a moment, considering the implications of Charles's statement. I have never met Mr. Inoue, but I am well aware that he is second-in-line at my husband's company. The last-minute nature of the invitation means that a higher-status couple bowed out unexpectedly on him and we are being asked to fill out a particular number... no doubt one that the astronumerologists picked as auspicious for this date.

The numeris, as we call them, work now with computers rather than coins, and their copies of the astrological tables and I Ching are cross-indexed and hypertext-linked, but such is our renewed faith now in these otherwise unpredictable times that no one of stature makes a move without consulting them. If it is sometimes silently suspected that they may try to manipulate events into coming true, it is not unexpected that they will do so.

Sometimes, that is even desirable.

Anyway, the bad timing of this is another indication that after two years of hard work, we are still of relatively low status in my husband's company. And, as 'Rikis in a predominantly Nihi company, we accept this.

And yet, if we can accept this invitation, we will be seen as reliable and useful and eager—and can possibly displace this other unknown couple in the future.

This is a very difficult world we live in, inside the maze of companies that really control the New Sun Empire, and such an advantage cannot be passed up.

"Of course, Charles. When should I be ready?"

"Even allowing for being a few minutes late, you'd have to leave here no later than half past six. Mr. Inoue recognized the inconvenience of this sudden invite and suggested that I come straight home with him from the office, and he would have a car sent to pick you up."

That means I will have to cut my day short in order to get home in time. But both of these are great favors to us, since nonpublic transportation is rare in Lesser Kyoto. My sense that this invitation could be a springboard intensified.

"Also," Charles continued, "it seems that we and Mr. Inoue have the same numeri. Good fortune, that! It means you can easily find out what might be most suitable to wear to the party, so you don't clash with all the other guests."

Ah, everything is arranged, then. Now I must

arrange my own schedule to suit.

I decide I will not give up all of my day—it is my one moment of selfishness—but I do call the hairdresser to ask her to come early, and after that I follow as much of my normal ritual as possible.

I dress simply, in a navy blue silk shirt and trousers, and sandals. No jewelry; I am going shopping, after all, not meeting someone. The buttons seem big and clumsy, and I quickly remind myself there is nothing to be nervous about. I have done this a hundred times or more, and nothing has ever gone wrong.

Outside, I consider the weather and decide to walk everywhere on my own rather than use the treadways. There is still a low, cold mist lying around all the buildings, but it is intended purely to saturate the numerous plant boxes that dot the pavement. The overhead lamps will easily burn that off by midday.

Everything is carefully controlled in Lesser Kyoto; we may be living under a pressure dome on Earth's moon, but every inch of space the Nihis have laid out in their section has been considered both in a useful and an aesthetic sense. We are crowded—after all those years cramped together on their island, I doubt the Nihis would know any other way to live—but they have tried to make it as comfortable as possible within the limitations.

I drop by the grocer to order food for the next week and notice some beautiful tomatoes invitingly arranged on display. When I compliment him on their attractiveness, he smiles. "From Thaitown hydroponics. Expensive, but Thaitown is worth it."

"Good things always are," I reply politely.

He lifts one and hands it to me, along with a knife to cut it. "Try it. Please. I'm sure you will like it."

My hand trembles as I hold the knife and slide the blade into the red flesh to quarter it. It feels obscene to be doing this in public, and I take great pleasure in hiding how the action makes me feel. The fruit is fresh and juicy, and my mouth is so used to tart tomatoes from New Rome that it is an actual shock to taste sweetness and balance of texture where I have come to expect only faint bitterness and mushy meat.

"Oh, it's just wonderful. We will be celebrating tomorrow night"—i.e., if all goes well tonight, we will have friends over and joyously discuss every detail, every nuance of what was said at tonight's party—"and these would be perfect for it."

I move along my route now, the anticipation building with each step, added to now by the memory of enjoying the tomato. I go by the laundry to ask that our clothes be picked up, and the library to order new reading and sound for the next week... oh, certainly all these could be done through the computers, and in the 'Riki section probably would be. But the Nihis place great value on performing the formalities, and I find I enjoy these little rituals within the greater ritual of Friday.

This is my day out, and while it is as carefully arranged as the rest of my life (even the hours I will regretfully have to cut short today) at least it is arranged for me and no one else.

The pillared temple of the numeri Kumiko stands alone at the end of a cul-de-sac, stark white amidst the dark greens and greys and blacks of Lesser Kyoto's normal architecture. The bare white plastiwood common in these structures glows faintly even in the high lights of noon, due to the strongly phosphorescent dye used in coloring it... thus in the dark, a numeri's temple often has a haunted look. The white color is supposed to attract good spirits; more to the point, it makes them distinctive and easy to find for those in need of advice, at a price.

I enter the temple, leaving my sandals outside the angled archway, and the soft chimes on the door—no synthetic chimes here, or even one of glass that can be cheaply produced here at the factories, but a delicate metal mobile—announce my presence. I stop and wait politely on the mat, between the left and right openings into the hallways and in front of the large screen that closes off the far opening. "Gomen kudasai?"

Kumiko's soft voice calls from the back. "Tamara-san?"

"Yes, Kumiko-san."

"You are a few minutes early." Not tinged with reproach, just a statement of fact—and an oblique warning that she is not quite ready for me to come in further.

Depending on how important or connected the person consulting the numeri is, and also how well regarded the numeri's predictive talents are, even knowing precisely when someone visits a numeri could be quite a useful piece of knowledge to have about them or their business, and so numeris are very careful not to let clients run into each other at the temple.

When Charles was sponsored into the Amaterasu company by the retired Mr. Tanaka, he was kind enough also to give us a reference to Kumiko, who is regarded as one of the more skilled numeri. We are very lucky to have her guidance.

"I wished to spend a few moments meditating in your garden, Kumiko-san." Not a total lie, either: when I visit, I often step into her rock garden to think about what will happen next.

"I would be honored," she replies, and the curtains rustle as she returns to the back and her unknown client.

The garden is tiny, no more than 10′ by 10′, but the rocks build relentlessly from the low point as you enter to the high point across and the usual miniature waterfall is well placed just off center to the right. I sit half-lotus on the floor and close my eyes.

The image of the tomato in my hand, and how it felt

to hold the knife that opened it returns to me at once, and I realize how frightened I am of what I am about to do. Not just the normal fear of anticipation, either, but the nagging worry that I've never had to vary this part of my Friday ritual before—what if it can't be done?

What if this destroys the delicate balance, and this part—for this is the part I really wait for, the part I live for—cannot be done? Now, or ever again?

I notice a small grey-haired woman in a plain white kimono peering over the rocks at me. "Tamara-san? I had called you twice to say you are free to come in now, but you did not answer."

"Oh, I'm very sorry, Kumiko-san," I apologize as I follow her to her sitting room. "I guess I'm very worried about today."

She nods. "Yes, I already know that you have a very important invitation at the last minute. It was in the stars and the stones that this would happen."

"More like in your computer banks!" I think in a moment of irreverence, but I hold my tongue. Again I wonder how much of a numeri's success was due to pure foretelling and how much due to old-fashioned arranging of events to their liking.

And yet, even that second method would take a certain amount of predictive skills, that the arranged events would come out with the desired result, not just immediately, but in the long run. So in the end, did it matter whether Kumiko was a true magician or just an illusionist?

"Then you would also know that I have very little time to prepare for anything right now." I say quietly.

She nods again, and stares at me with her black eyes. "Yes, I already know you have only one hour to spend here. No more time for old Kumiko!" She laughs and smiles then, but her eyes are still intently fixed on mine. "Well, you have put yourself in my hands before and I have not failed you, have I?"

Failed me? No, Kumiko, you make everything possible. Everything.

She continues, "Yes, things will be have to be different this time, you know. What can be done in three hours cannot be done in one." And I realize she is referring to what is about to happen to me this afternoon, as well as what needs to be done for the evening.

"I know I can trust your arrangements, Kumiko-san," I say cautiously.

She smiles again, and without another word passing between us I arise and walk past her, to the back of the room where another screen hides an airlock built into the back of the house. Behind me I can hear her begin to tap away on the tiny keyboard that she keeps hidden in her lap, in the folds of her kimono.

Within the hour, she will have the proper dress for the party delivered to my house, along with the appropriate flowers and gift for the host, instructions to the hairdresser what style would look best... little details, all part of the greater ritual.

In the meantime...

I press my hand to the airlock's security system. The doors give way and I move into the middle chamber. The disinfectant cycle will only work coming from the other direction, so that no foreign matter contaminates Lesser Kyoto, but I do need to change.

I look at the clothes laid out for me to change into. Usually, I will wear an elaborate costume for this which fits in and makes me unrecognizable, but today it is only a thin white cotton blouse and short black skirt. In those, I will feel naked.

There is also a small jar of gold body paint on top of the clothes, and I slowly gild both my nipples and then, after a moment's hesitation, outline my labia with the paint as well. Then I dress and, taking a deep breath, go to the other door and wait for it to open.

On the other side of the wall from Kumiko's temple is the back side of the spaceport at Newton. The lock pops me out into a tiny closet on the other side, and I quickly go out into the main hallway so that I can mingle with the crowd getting off from the cattle-car shuttle.

The front part of the spaceport is reserved for dignitaries and rich businessmen; this is where the rest of the otherworldly travelers get off. And I, I too am a visitor from another world, though a much closer one than anyone watching would suspect.

He is waiting for me at the end of the hallway, standing dead still in the center of the hall as people walk around his powerful figure. This is already different; usually I just go directly to his room and do not see him before I close the door and shut the other world away.

He watches me walk down the hallway towards him, arms folded, no smile on his dark face, no sign of recognition except that his eyes are fixed on my movement. People are shouting and arguing and greeting wildly around us, and I just keep walking calmly towards him as if no one else were around, as if nothing else mattered.

It's not that I don't think of him during the rest of the week, wonder what his life is like outside of the hours he spends using me, but nothing prepares me for his physical existence except seeing him.

His name is Knife. That's all I know. All I need to know.

I stop a little more than an arm's length away from him. His eyes are cold as he looks me up and down. I am scared to death of him, and he knows it. He knows everything about me he needs to know.

Knife gets his name from the long scar on his left cheekbone, as well as from the black-handled weapons he wears on his sides, one in each scabbard. That scar streaks out livid under the harsh fluorescent lights. Even his brown skin looks more ashen than colored. But the eyes still are the same: wary but piercing.

"Kneel," he says in that firm, oddly dismissive way of his, leaving no room for argument on my part. It's as if he knows all the rules, but he also knows they just don't apply to him.

And maybe they don't.

I want to protest, but I can't, no sound comes from my mouth. Instead I kneel, and I begin to bow my head in shame, but his left hand grabs the braid at the back of my head and pulls on it so that I have to look up at his face and meet his gaze.

Before I know it, his other hand has the knife in it and one cut tears through my blouse, baring my chest.

He replaces the knife and commands, "Look." His grip on my hair turns my head back down to waist level. I see a thick, stiff bulge in his tight trousers, and I try to look back at his face to say mutely: Please, don't do this, not here.

But he keeps my head lowered, staring at the outlined image under the cloth. And now I'm glad I'm kneeling, because my legs are turning to water as I remember what he can do to me with nothing more than his body.

I have no way to look around, but I can hear the sound of the crowd change as they notice the strange scene beginning to take place in their midst.

"Who am I?" he asks, and I start to shake visibly because this is the beginning of our ritual, and he is doing this in public for all to see.

My voice comes out louder than I expected, and I realize all around us now is silent, watching. "Knife."

A very, very slight smile, little more than a wry twitch, moves his face for a moment. Next question.

"Who are you?"

This is the hard part, and I feel myself going crimson as I struggle to get the words out. Softly. Afraid.

"Sheath."

I've said the right word, but the smile is gone again. How far is this going to go?

"Receive me, then."

No, no, but my fingers are already working on his trousers. The words, the actions, the feelings are too strong to be fought. He grasps my head in both hands and the moment my hands pull his erection free, he brings my mouth forward onto him as his hips thrust towards me. All I can think of now is how juicy he tastes, and the texture of his fleshy cock rubs against my lips and tongue.

He is still hard when he pulls away and yanks on the braid to bring me upwards, trades hands to turn me in place, and then pushes me to bend me over in front of him. Facing away from him, I can see everyone who has stopped to stare at us now; even for somewhere as undisciplined as Back Spaceport, this is not a normal occurrence, and they are enjoying the free show.

I close my eyes, but their faces remain, watching me squirm as he plunges into me not his warm cock, but a blade of cold, hard metal that makes me scream in fear and want as it slides into me.

As he twists it inside me, back and forth, side to side, the blade turning from cold steel to burning hot in what seems an instant, I cry out as I come and juice runs down between my thighs. I don't know if it's blood or just my own wet, but I don't stop to look, I start stumbling back towards safety the moment he lets go of my hair.

And the last thing I hear, as I turn the corner and fumble desperately with the handle to the closet, is Knife's hard voice cutting through the excited buzz.

"She got what she came for. Let her go—or you'll have to deal with me."

Inside the airlock, I strip off the clothes quickly and check my thighs. The gold paint which decorated my genitals has run nearly down to my knees, but there is no blood. And I recall again the change of hands that let him use the dull, left-hand knife.

I clean up as best I can in the airlock and let myself out. The temple is silent as I pass through it, pale and empty, like a ghost. The rest of my day passes in a daze; I take the treadways home, the maid helps me dress in a green kimono embroidered with red flowers, the hairdresser disciplines my wavy hair into a sleek French bun (only a few wisps of hair escape onto my neck), and the electric car delivers me to Mr. Inoue's house precisely on time.

My poise is all on the outside, though, as I step out onto the oystershell gravel of the driveway. My insides are torn in a way that does not show. What does he think of me? I ask the lowered lights of evening.

They do not know, any more than I do. What will he think if I come back, after today? For even if we return to the old ritual, things have changed: I will always know he is capable of more.

But perhaps there is no returning. Perhaps next week, I will go to Kumiko's on Friday, and she will shake her head as I look at the curtain. And I will never know why; I will only know the silent cut of goodbye.

This much is clear to me now: one pattern has ended even as a new one is beginning. So I lift my head and walk forward to the house.

When I don my silk slippers in the entrance, I feel a set of eyes fixed upon me. I look up, startled, and for a moment I am back in Spaceport again, about to begin that long walk towards Knife. The resemblance between them is that close.

But the man standing at the other end of the hall, staring at me with hard, dark eyes, has no scar under his eye. Charles pops his blond head around the corner and seeing me, makes an inaudible comment to the other man, who nods. They wait for me to come to them. I walk, and I walk, and I walk, and finally, I arrive.

"Mr. Inoue, this is Tamara, my wife."

Even up close, the similarity does not dissolve. We both bow respectfully and murmur, "Pleased to meet you."

There is nothing in his expression to say we have met before. And yet, it is exactly that which makes me think: this is him. It must be. This is how he would act. This is what he would be.

Our host moves to greet another guest, and I whisper to Charles, "Since when did a 'Riki get a last name like Inoue?"

He blinks. "Didn't I tell you that? He was adopted by one of the previous company presidents. He used to be head of a rival 'Riki company and I think they found it was easier to bring him in than fight him."

"I see." I don't know yet what I see, but I do know I see something.

Charles introduces me to the other guests I do not already know, and then excuses himself for a moment to talk business with one. I know my duties as a good company spouse, and I mingle for a while, quiet, respectful, in my place.

Then I am at the buffet, choosing among the peaches, when Mr. Inoue appears at my elbow.

"Please. Allow me," he says, and he takes the knife from my hand and cuts into the ripest fruit.

"Thank you, Inoue-san."

Nothing out of place in his face, everything correct, measured and polite. No reason for me to think he was anything other than what he seemed, one of the rare, completely assimilated Riki one sometimes finds living in the Nihi zone.

But I know. And he knows.

He places the skinned, sectioned, pitted peach on my

plate, and remarks, "Until your husband mentioned it yesterday, I was unaware that we both used the services of the numeri Kumiko. She was able to assist with your arrangements today, then?"

I nod. "Hai, that is so."

"Of course, since it was she who recommended that you and your husband be invited, she knew quite well what arrangements had to be made, even before you did."

Well before I did, I think in amusement, as I nod again. "I have always been quite satisfied by the arrangements of Kumiko in the past, Inoue-san."

"Ah, then we are both very fortunate! For so have I," he replies in the same neutral tone he has kept during our entire conversation. Not a word, not a hair, out of place, as Charles joins us and we all walk towards the dinner table together. "And I trust it will continue so," he adds as he motions for us to sit next to him.

"As do we," I smile, and look at my husband, who smiles back.

Day Journey, With Stories

Jason Rubis

I see you standing at the station, waiting for the steamer. It pulls in moments later in a blaze of shifting chrome panels, hot white clouds spouting from its head and sides. Steamers have fascinated me since I was a girl; my cousin Joselle told me once that they ran not primarily on steam, but the combined labour of dozens of slaves kept toiling away somewhere deep in the steamers' bowels. She described the slaves trudging away on gigantic treadmills, their bodies hung with bright chains, or strapped screaming to the inner walls while silver cables robbed their bodies of some form of energy necessary for the steamers' maintenance. "Think of that, Alie! All those poor slaves! All just so people like your papa can get to the City everyday...."

Even now, when I take the steamers into the City practically every day myself, I remember Joselle's stories. The basic design of the steamers hasn't changed much, as much as the People in Charge have nattered on about "streamlining" and the virtues of sleek and smooth over ponderous bulk. Of course, nothing much else has changed in the world either in, what now? Five hundred years? A few useful inventions, some stylistic development, then...stasis for another century. I suppose it's comforting, in a way. The steamers are still huge, they still have plenty of room for hidden chambers filled with Joselle's slaves. Now and then I tap my shoe-soles on the carriage floor, just as I did during those infrequent rides in my girlhood. I used to wonder if the slaves below could hear me, and think I was sending them some sort of code—a false message of hope and rescue. I could see them in their secret chambers, straining their sad, beautiful faces upwards, wondering if that day would be the day of their liberation. The cruelty of it frightened and thrilled me.

You've met Joselle; now that she's married she's become properly demure, but when we were both in school she terrorized and delighted me with tales of exotic tortures practiced in far-off (and wholly fictitious) countries. Her favorite characters for these stories were a Prince and Princess, twins, both gorgeous and quite, quite evil.

"What would they do to me if they caught me?" I would ask, trembling. It was a ritual question; I asked it during each of her visits, and Joselle invented a new delight for me each time.

"If they caught a sweet thing like you, well, first they'd make her take off her shoes and stockings. And it'd be no good crying; they're quite ruthless. Then they'd make you sit on a bench in front of a wall with two holes in it, perfectly sized to your ankles. They'd make you put your feet—your bare feet—through the holes, and then they'd lock sort of manacles around your ankles, so you couldn't withdraw them. Then they'd start the torture."

Joselle would stop there to help herself to an apple or a sweet from a bowl on the table and bite into it. You remarked on Joselle's mouth after you met her; it's still a rather pretty, cruel mouth, but then it held an absolutely hypnotic power over me. I'd squirm and watch my cousin's lips with wide eyes, not daring to prompt her, any more than I would have hurried an actual torturer. I was savouring every moment.

"The Princess would have come to sit beside you while the Prince disappeared through a door in the wall. She would inform you that the Prince's menagerie was on the other side of that wall, and that he kept all sorts of ferocious animals in it, all of them roaming free without cages. They'd been brought up from birth to trust him, obey his every command, she'd tell you, but they'd kill anyone else in the wink of an eye."

I couldn't suppress a little cry at that. I'd clench my toes up tightly inside their shoes, imagining them protruding helplessly from the wall, attracting the attention of the Prince's horrible, hungry pets. Joselle would inflict a particularly long silence then, enjoying my nervousness.

"What kinds of animals, exactly?" I'd ask timidly.

"Various species, but all of them ferocious! Wolves and tigers, chiefly. But what would happen next is that you'd feel a long, rough tongue scraping up and down your soles."

"It would tickle," I'd moan, clutching at the rug.

"Yes, tickle horribly," Joselle gloated. "You see—and the Princess would explain this to you as you sat there—the Prince had brought an animal of some sort, most probably a tiger, over to your feet and though the beast was mad with hunger, commanded it to lick your feet rather than simply bite them off at the ankles. But this was a specially trained tiger that would go mad with killing frenzy at the sound of... human... laughter."

"The wall," I said desperately. "The wall would muffle the noise."

"At that point you'd hear something sliding: a small window opening up in the wall just above your head. Any sound you made could easily be heard by the tiger."

"I would bite my lip," I continued bravely. "I wouldn't laugh. I'm not ticklish."

Joselle would reach over then and begin walking her long fingers up my arm. "The Princess would start doing this," she said. "And this" With her other hand she'd take a pinch of her long brown hair and tickle my face with it while I gasped and pursed my lips.

"The Prince would have the tiger lick only one foot at a time," Joselle told me, eyes glimmering. "Leaving another foot free for him to tickle with a long, stiff feather. Up and down the sole, between your toes. How long could you take it, Alie? That feather...and the Princess' fingers...and the tiger's whiskers and tongue, its wet breath on your poor little bare feet, tickling, tickling..."

I'd have to jump up and run up to the lavatory then, and relieve myself. I'd want badly to continue the story when I came back down, but I was too embarassed and Joselle never offered. Besides, there'd be another story next time she came to visit.

No, you'd never imagine Joselle to be capable of that kind of thing now.

You're far enough ahead of me on the platform to make calling out to you impractical, or certainly in poor taste. But I can see you moving towards the same car as me, even though a fair distance will separate our seats. So I content myself simply with climbing aboard and finding a good seat. If you are going to see me, you will see me.

Moments later the steamer pulls out of the station with a wonderful, great roar. I slide my identification card into the slot on my armrest, holding my breath until it clicks APPROVED and releases the card. I don't know what would happen if it were not APPROVED. I've never seen anyone DENIED, and assuming the possibility even exists (ours is such an orderly society), why do they allow us to wait until the steamer is on its way before we use our cards? It's a mystery to me. I, of course, used to fantasize that if my card were DENIED I would be hustled off to the steamer's depths to join Joselle's slaves in a life of desperation and painful toil. In a sense, that very nearly did happen; do you remember the article I wrote years ago that dared make critical remarks about overpopulation of the City, the way everyone has flocked to the Outer Towns and Suburbs? The politicos hated that. If some of my father's old friends hadn't proved so fond of me, I may well have been taken away in actuality. I doubt I would have found prison as romantic as I found the idea of the slaves.

At any rate, here I am, your prim Alie, my little journey begun. I tuck my identification back into my purse and give myself a few idle moments to look around the car. You're too far behind me to glimpse without swiveling my neck around, so I content myself with my immediate neighbors: businessmen and businesswomen properly attired like myself, and several young people wearing their ridiculous, voguish costumes. A boy across the aisle from me sits with his shoes propped up insolently on the seat next to him. His face is painted and his hair coloured and feathered outrageously. He pouts and taps a tune on the window—some music only he can hear. A pretty boy. He fascinates me; it wasn't that long ago I was his age, though of course I was always sweet and well-spoken. As I take out my notes and writer, I wonder whether he would pout and smirk quite so smugly if he found his hands suddenly, magically bound behind his back and if I, sauntering over and seating myself beside him, began kissing him and tweaking the nipples he displays through his artfully ripped shirt. Perhaps I would take a pin from my hair and begin pricking him very lightly about the chest and groin. What's the matter, darling? Why are you crying? Don't you like being mine, belonging only to me, to Aunt Alie? Don't cry, can't you see no one on the car can hear you?

They're all reading and looking out the windows. But I'll treat you so nicely.

Joselle and I did something similar to another boy once, a simple boy who worked in my father's gardens. We lured him to the house with sweets and bound him to a chair, he all stupid with fear of these pretty, rich girls, the girls laughing breathless and excited and perhaps a touch frightened themselves. Joselle bent close to me, and her lips wet my ears: "You're the Princess now, Alie. And he's your prisoner. What'll you do to him?"

Of course this was a challenge of sorts; Joselle wanted to see what her little cousin was made of. I wanted to impress her, but I also felt very warm, almost giddy, looking at the gardener boy as he sat panting and staring at me. I took a pin and stuck it into his arm, just above where the rope pressed his skin down in a neat line. "Come on," I whispered to him, "tell me your secrets. You have to tell me. I'm the Princess." I stuck him again and he began to cry in a loud, blubbering voice. When we let him go eventually, we made him promise never to tell anyone what we'd done, and though he gave us that promise readily, I spent many hours sick with terror that my father would confront me one day with my crime. Joselle, of course, never worried for an instant, and in fact the boy disappeared soon after. We simply never saw him again, and when I asked Joselle what she thought happened, she said "Ran away, I expect," into her coffee with a perfect lack of concern. "Unless the real Princess carried him off," she added, lifting her eyes to smile nastily at me.

That was not long ago, but long enough ago to make it hardly worth remembering. I tell myself that I have no time for such reminiscences. I thumb the writer on like a good girl and begin arranging my notes for an article I'm preparing on the restoration of a City monument. Perhaps I sit a little stiffly, absolutely erect, hoping you'll notice my hat (you did buy it for me, after all) and come to me, say hello.

I'm distracted again when a girl emerges from the door at the car's far end and struts up to my fantasy's seat, kicks his feet aside and throws herself down beside him. Her own feet are bare, and when she lifts them to prop her heels on the facing seats, I can see her soles have been intricately tattooed with zig-zag patterns. I look at her; she's even younger and more arrogant-looking than he is, her clothes even more torn and disreputable. Her hair is long, straight and blond. Her eyes meet mine and I smile. She sneers.

"Did that hurt?" I ask, leaning forward slightly. "The marks on your feet?"

"What, these?" she wriggles her toes. "Not hardly. They said they would, but I didn't feel a thing." Such a brave girl.

"I'll bet it tickled," I said, smiling. "I bet they had to strap you down for it while you giggled and giggled." Such teasing familiarities... if I were to make a direct overture to this girl, I could be arrested, such things being decidedly illegal. But the pout on her face gives me considerably more pleasure than the lawmakers could imagine. The boy smirks and she silences him with a glare.

"They use needles, not feathers," she informs me loftily. "And I'm not ticklish. I've been walking barefoot all my life. My feet are like leather."

Her feet are like silk, I thought, looking at them. Soft and white. Spoiled, silly girl, throwing her shoes away in response to some idiotic new fad. She probably stuffed them into the lavatory wastebin just now. As for the tattooing, I'm sure she shrieked and squeaked through the whole ordeal. Needles and ink and blood; I'm sure it was painful, perhaps the only pain she's ever really had to endure. But I like relating her to Joselle's stories; I enjoy imagining the Princess using a quill to scratch the strange patterns on her soles while she giggles and pleads.

I give her a placating smile and go back to my writer. But I've made her nervous, and she's taking it out on her boyfriend, snarling at him for nothing and punching his arm.

Between these two and your unseen presence, I can't concentrate on my writing. It's only minutes now until we reach the first City station anyway, so I put my things away and look out the window, admiring the sunlight glaring on the fields and houses that multiply slowly as we draw nearer to the station.

The City: stone arcs and metal towers, people and people and people. But none of them, not one, your equal. Do you know what I love to remember most? The night we spent in this very City, with you adoring my lips and learning my unfamiliar parts, my geography. The circumstances were so intimate; your heart beating against my shoulders, your mouth nuzzling them, giving me such gentle bites. We had girls from one of the better Houses come in and bind us one on another, then tease our bodies with mourningstones and feathers, tongues and nails and scourges while we gasped and struggled into each other. We were both swollen, both in desire to the point of pain, the philters we had taken staving off and then prolonging orgasm. Do you remember? Do you remember the telepath girl I had specifically requested, because of her storytelling abilities as much as her mental gifts? Do you remember how she teased you with stories that exploited the most secret, delicious corners of your imagination? The boy raped by a woman with eight spidery legs? The woman tied and lowered into a pit of eels? I think she must have liked you. She played with you far more fervently than she did me while she told her stories. I only felt the stroke of her mind on mine briefly, but then I so rarely hide my fantasies; my imagination has none of the enticing coyness yours does. My strangeness and desires are right there on my mind's surface, like colored oil on water. Joselle—the story-girl's predecessor in some ways—brought them up years ago, and they've never sunk back down into my hidden depths.

When you came you screamed, a scream that died away to a slow weeping. I followed you soon after and then we were discreetly unbound and left in one another's arms. That night is my favorite story. I wish I could find a way to tell it to Joselle, but perhaps you would find that indiscreet?

The steamer slows and shrieks and once again exhales clouds as it pulls into the City station. I collect my things and sigh and stand up. The girl is watching me sulkily, arms folded, still wriggling her toes (now rather like an angry cat twitching its tail). Excitement at your presence makes me reckless: I smile sweetly and mouth a kiss at her. It's a risk... no one is watching, but she could call me out, have me arrested and put in chains for real this time, make great trouble for me and you. But though she starts at first her face softens almost immediately and a smile of her own breaks through her sulk, making her unexpectedly gorgeous. I know she's collecting herself to return the kiss, but I turn away (relieved, I'll admit that) and begin walking determinedly up the aisle to you. Always the tease, as Joselle used to say of me. A passive sadist, she called me once, and I rushed to the dictionary.

My heart is beating hard as I approach your seat. Your head is bent over your own writer. Other passengers shoulder past me, I clear my throat, and when you look up at me, things shift, change you into someone else. A line of throat, a lifted eyebrow. You're not you now. You are Someone Else. You are my mistake. An easy mistake, due to hair color, taste in clothing, approximate height.

My stuttered apology is delivered and the you who is not you gets up and smiles and leaves the car.

Disappointment. The possibilities I hadn't known I'd been counting on pour from my eyes: drinks, reminiscences, a walk, another night in this City...re-kindled fires? All of that now gone. And I must walk in not-your footsteps out the train to a cold office and words I never cared about.

But a hand hits my shoulder and when I turn around my blonde girl and her friend are standing behind me. They both incline towards me just slightly and then both deliver obviously rehearsed, remunerative kiss to the air in front of my face. They stand smirking triumphantly, adorably.

I am delighted. I take their hands and tell them I'm going to buy them coffee. The morning is young, they are young, I am not old, and suddenly I believe again that there are new stories to be made.

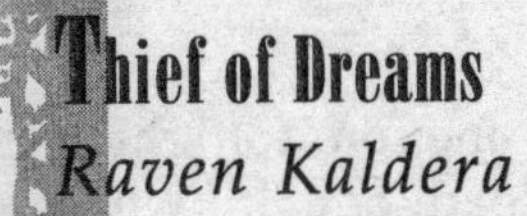

Thief of Dreams

Raven Kaldera

It's dusk outside my tiny apartment, and prime time is just beginning in Sexland. I check my listings, download a list into my brain—complete with addresses and personal kinks—and swoop like a bird of prey through the dreams of thousands of people crowded into this huge, stifling city.

Interesting metaphor that, a bird of prey. I didn't actually see one until I was thirteen and rented a nature VR—something fuzzy and static-filled from the local school library about the Southwest—and there he was, a hawk, diving implacably onto the tiny mice of the desert, fate on wings. I think it was then that I decided to become a predator. It seemed the only option that could give me more than a shell of a life.

So my sig is Dreamhawk, and even if the cops knew about me, which they don't, I've left such a twisted trail around the Worldnet that they would never be able to find me. I'm the best there is, better than the Mysters or the Motleys or even Damballah. After all, I have so much more time on my hands.

(You were supposed to hear an ironic twist to those last words, in case your program is cheap and doesn't have those upgrades. After all, I can only assume someone will eventually, at some future date long after my malformed heart has given out, read these diaries and

put them into VR format. Pity I can't sell the rights while I'm still alive. People always love a decent villain.)

Number one on tonight's list: Shira MacKenzie, 322 Terrace Road, age 46, who has rented "Torments of the Damned" from Candy's VRama. It's an easy one to step into; I've used it before. Let's see...Miss Mackenzie is a relative newcomer to the city, but she's rented sexvids before, all heterosex, all kinky, all bottom-space. Is she female herself in Sexland, or does she see herself as a boy? Ah, yes, female like her driver's license. Not that I care. Well... I get to play big hulking male Top tonight, it seems. Yummy, yummy.

I slip her code with ease, insert my virus program—invading her cheap antivirals is like surfing past slow-motion morons—and enter the world of her fantasy. I'm suddenly in a body, tall and muscled, dressed in scanty leather and sporting a huge erection. The scenery around me is an abandoned warehouse. I know the script of this flick well enough to know what I can and can't get away with. "On your knees, slut!" I roar. First things first. Change the hideous dialogue and lukewarm acting.

She cringes. In Sexland she's tiny, with a perfect seventeen-year-old body and fluffy brunette do. In reality she's probably dumpy, middle-aged, and graying, but hell, it doesn't matter here. I grab her by the bouffant and throw her to the floor. Then I twiddle with the program and ropes come snaking out of nowhere, snaking around her. One coils around her breasts in a figure-eight, tightening until they stand out like taut drums. Others knot themselves about her ankles, wrists, and the crease between her dimpled knees and rounded calves. Another spirals around her waist, loop after loop, cinching into a rope corset that brings her body to impossible dimensions. As a final fillip, her wrists are brought up between her shoulder blades and bound to the ropes encircling her rib cage. She gasps and cries out for help, for mercy, writhing in the throes of delicious fear and arousal.

Oh yes, there's one other little thing I forgot about. Her safe word. It would be listed in the VR's entry program, to stop the vid on command. I check it, momentarily; it's "dishwasher." I erase it.

(Oh, please. Did you really think I wouldn't?)

I step forward, looming over her, and grin evilly. "Slut," I say. "Whore. You want this. You want to be beaten and ravished by me. That's why you rented this vid. So get up on those knees and suck me, and it better be good, or else."

She looks taken aback at the mention of renting the VR. This was not what she had in mind, and it puts a notch in her fantasy. I yank her up by the fluffy hair, force her mouth open, and start fucking it. This particular Top character is pretty massively endowed, and the erection seems rather permanent. She chokes and struggles, but I notice that her hips are swiveling. I come in her mouth, shooting out what seems to be a truly unreal amount of spooge down her throat, and then force her to suck my still-erect cock clean.

She's whimpering now, moaning little things like "please, master" and "no, master." I let her have her voice for now. There are better things in store, and I want to hear her scream. I hang her from a hook in the ceiling (do real abandoned warehouses actually have all these hard points, I wonder? I've never been in one. Of course, I've never been outside my apartment in eight years) and produce several whips. Not the tacky things provided by the program; I have my own virtual set brought in with the virus. Including one rather terrifying one with six-foot tails interlaced with tiny shuriken.

She sees them and screams. "No! This is just supposed to be a bondage vid.... I don't do pain!"

"Then what good are you?" I leer, and select a cat. It lashes across her bound breasts and she screams louder. One, two, one, two, in a neat figure eight. Red welts are coming up beautifully on the artificial skin.

"Dishwasher!" she screams. To her horror, nothing happens except that I change whips and begin to lay into her ass with a different cat, this one braided with small knots. "Dishwasher... oh god, dishwasher," she moans, trailing off into sobs. My erection is still hard and I stroke it, watching her.

I decide to take pity on her. It's not that hard. I invoke my extremely illegal sexual response program and plug it into her set. It keeps her turned on, restimulates the pleasure centers so that a wave of sexual ecstasy accompanies each wave of pain. You could really fuck up somebody's natural responses with this baby. Of course, we'll only use it the one time. I can see in her face that it's working; her moans take on a different quality and she thrusts her ass out for me to work on. Somewhere in the middle of the whipping, she comes—once, then twice.

The ropes on her legs retwine so that her ankles can be spread wide apart. I produce clamps and decorate her with them. Breasts, ass, inner thighs, labia. Then I whip them off, all but the ones on the labia. Those I leave on while I bend her over and fuck her cunt, first with my cock and then with the spiked whip handle. She's coming now, again and again, in a nonstop feedback circuit. Better finish this up now before she gets brain damage. I put her back on her knees and piss in her mouth, a little fillip I add on a whim. "Drink it, slut," I order. "Remember me. You're going to jerk off to me for the rest of your life." And you'll probably never see me again. I have too many other fish to fry.

I create a temporary malfunction in the feeder circuits of her set. She'll find herself, gasping and half-conscious, back in her own living room while I retract my Dreamhawk virus and fly out to catch other prey.

Prey number two: Ms. Jaye Harper. Age 26, 6171 Fleet Avenue number 44, renting "Biker Boys." An all-male video? Yes, and she's costumed for the occasion in the body of a skinny boy™ punk. I check her past rentals, looking for the flags I know mean kinky sexvids. (I can get access to the rental lists of every VR store in town in a millisecond.) OK, she's a dyke from the look of it; this must be an experimental foray into the world of boys. No problem.

I'm waiting in the men's room of a leather bar. How cliche. I'm huge and hulking again, with an even more ridiculous cock, almost cartoonish. Boys will be boys. The leathers this time are covering, chaps and jacket and harness and Muir cap, and I smell like I haven't bathed in two days. Handcuffs and a large ring of keys jangle from the left side of my studded belt.

The bathroom door opens and she—no, he—sidles in. Online crossdressing seems to be mostly a matter of men being women (or girls rather; you can imagine the mammoth ex-football players behind the giggly Marilyn Monroe facades). Ms. Jaye is unusual, and I like that. I disable her safeword—Janine, probably a girlfriend's name—and wait, smoking a cigarette.

The boy moves nervously into a stall, unzipping his pants and pissing. The doors on the stalls are of course all broken and don't latch. I move in behind him, hands sliding down over his ass, feeling him flinch with nervousness. Keys hanging on the right, black hanky tucked neatly into right-hand pocket with a leather cock ring snapped around it. Good. This boy's no bondage bottom. "Looking for trade, boy?" I mumble sarcastically into his ear. My hands restrain his from zipping up his jeans.

He draws in his breath. "Only if... only if it's rough trade, sir," he gulps. He presses his ass against the seam of my leather pants.

"You think you can take it, you little punk?" I snarl in his ear. He melts against me. I pinion his arms behind him and snap my handcuffs on. He doesn't resist. Then I twist one booted foot around his ankles and jerk, knocking him to his knees. His face almost goes into the toilet, but he rolls aside just in time. I put one foot on the back of his neck and force his face down onto the other boot, leaning against the stall for balance. "Lick 'em good, you little punk. Lick 'em good and maybe I'll beat your little faggot ass." He does as he's told, and enthusiastically, too. I can feel his tongue like a gentle foot massage through the leather.

OK, so maybe he deserves a good beating. Let's see what we can do with this scene. I yank him up by the back of his T-shirt and hook the cuffs over the coathook in the stall door. Since this is unreality, we don't have to worry about safety issues and nerve damage. His ripped jeans fall down around his ankles and his little punk cock is hard. Wonder if Ms. Jaye likes having an erection. I know I thought it was cool, the day I hacked my first sexvid at fifteen. Didn't get around to trying out cunts for six months, but then I discovered they're just as good.

I go for the switchblade I know is in my pocket and click it open next to his ear. He flinches, but his breathing gets heavier. "Like that, do you?" I mutter, and proceed to shred his T-shirt off him with the blade. He moans when it accidentally touches his nipple and the slightest drop of blood pearls. I'm standing real close to him and I feel his cock rubbing desperately against my leather-covered leg. "Keep that little punk prick to yourself!" I snarl, slapping his face, and turn him around, slamming him up against the open stall door. That's when he notices the other guys in the room—all vidghosts—watching and leering. He hides his face in his arms, but is visibly aroused at having even this unalive audience.

I take off my belt, fold it in two, and snap the leather, making sure he hears it and jumps. Then I proceed to lay into his ass and back with everything I've got. He twists and moans, but stays put, stays the course. Good boy. Good girl. Of course I don't say it, since he didn't come here for niceties, but for brutality. After about a hundred strokes, he's a mass of welts from his shoulders to his knees, with a white handwidth over the kidney area. He's crying now, whimpering. I grab him by the throat and force him to look at me.

"You wanna get fucked, boy?" I hiss. "You want me up your skinny ass?"

His cock, after all of this, is still hard. "Yes, sir," he whispered, his voice cracking.

"Beg for it, punk." My hand grabs his scrotum, hard, and he cries out, but then manages to pull himself together.

"Please, sir, please fuck me," he gasps, and I throw him to his knees over the toilet and unzip my pants. His asshole is warm and tight, and prelubed. I swear, VR is so much nicer than the real world. No wonder I prefer it.

After I've come yet again I haul him out of the stall and toss him over to the other men in the bathroom. They're each equipped to do basic suck-and-fuck, according to the program, and Ms. Jaye deserves a nice gang-bang for her money. I haven't quite got the hang of inhabiting two virtual bodies at once, but I'm working on it, and once I do you can bet all hell is going to break out, honey.

When they're done with her I disappear them and take her by the hair again. I'm going to give her a special treat for taking that beating. I adjust the vid and run my virus through her system, reducing her to her ordinary VR self and me to a slightly feminized version of that big top. My cock vanishes as I bring her head close to it, replaced by labia and clitoris. She gasps, and looks up at me, and before she can wonder too much I tell her to eat me. Which she does, with tears of gratitude in her eyes.

You're wondering how I can change back and forth so easily, without disturbing a central gender identity. Ah well. Gender is all just a game to me, a mysterious set of masks I play with but can never fully understand. Like everything else that has to do with the flesh world.

You see, there was once a pretty teenage girl, like the ones I've fucked so many times in Sexland, without ever knowing what kind of flesh faces lived behind them. Only this little girl wasn't smart; no, she played around in the real world, the world of drugs and diseases and pain that can't be banished at the flick of a switch. Did some whoring, got a couple of viruses, got hooked on a few of the new designer head candies. Got pregnant.

You'd think a half-wasted flesh puppet like that would never be able to carry a pregnancy through. You'd think her pimp would have the decency to pay for a frigging twenty-credit shot of Sero-Abortine. But no. Instead she checks into a hospital and squirts out a pathetic lump of plasma. No arms, no legs, no eyes, no ears, nothing in the crotch but a pee hole. And burdened with, of all things, a genius IQ. Of course they didn't find that out until they gave me my first head plug—that's cranial interface to you dweebs—and my life opened up all around me.

Don't get me wrong, now. My life is just fine. I've got full disability pay, nurse machines to take care of that flesh lump while I get on with my life, and best of all, full uninterrupted free access to the Worldnet. Everything you can experience with in the flesh, I can experience here. And ten times more than that. I can be anyone and do anything. If I felt like interfacing with real people I could do that, too. They've offered me a brain transplant to a healthy body twice now, and twice I've turned them down. It's not just that there's a small rate of failure, which would have me dead on the operating table. It's that if I was healthy I'd lose my free access to the only world really worth having. I'd have to get a job and slog through life like all the other assholes. Is the flesh world worth it? I don't think so.

So. Enough ranting. All this has just been killing time until 2 a.m. when Kit plugs himself in. I've been looking forward to his fantasies with bated breath for weeks now, and it's really hard to get me excited about anything. But Kit is such a twisted little fuck that I think I'm beginning to love him. My heart flutters when I think about it.

Kit is a legal contract slave to a very rich corporate executive in Hyde Park. He lives to serve his beloved mistress, and is allowed all sorts of expensive and very fine equipment. He's not allowed to wear normal clothes, use the furniture, or leave the house, but she allows him the use of her first-class VR rig when she's out, in order to keep him occupied. And unbeknownst to her, he imports some fairly illegal sex vids and plays them while she's not looking. If it hadn't been for Kit's expensive tastes, I would never have gone beyond corner-store fantasies.

I surf into Mistress Katherine's system. Her antivirals are excruciating; they took me nearly a month to carve a channel through. I slide in through my special back door, plug into his VR system, and wait with bated breath. As soon as the vid goes into the slot, I'm occupying one of the two main characters. There are never more than two main characters, and Kit gets to insert appearances as he chooses.

I've been this persona before, and I know it well. Tall, dark-haired, stunning, legs that go on forever, and slightly Hispanic facial features. I'm wearing a sleek skinsuit of metallic silver latex. Kit likes latex a lot. Tall, thigh-high latex boots of a matching color, with a knife tucked into them. A whip dangles at the side of the big chunky belt, and on the other side a coil of silky braided copper rope is made into a carefully coiled noose.

I know whose face I wear. It's a slightly idealized version of his owner, Katherine. He's himself, his own sweet kinky self. Every hair on his body is permanently depilated except for the soft cap of black locks, and he's tattooed with floating Oriental drawings, clouds and cranes and blowing butterflies. He did a year of estrogen therapy at her suggestion, just enough to grow pretty little breasts on his slender, boyish frame; they are pierced, like his cock, with gold rings.

He's always himself in these flicks. I guess who he is really is so way out that he doesn't need to be anyone else. These vids, though, aren't really about who he is so much as what he wants. What his darling mistress will never give him.

The secret, you see, is in his fantasy.

Kit is into snuff. He likes to end every one of these nasty little vids dead in the middle of an orgasm. OK, so no one really dies in them; the interface is just cut off automatically, leaving you shaking and panting on the floor. I know, I tried one once. Not my thing, but Kit has an absolute passion for them. He's "died" at my hands a dozen times. His mistress would have a litter of puppies if she knew he was doing this, and with her image as well. Such a secret we have, my darling. I'll keep it well, never fear. I have a vested interest.

(Ah, you say, that's okay, it's only a vid? Nobody really dies? Not bad enough to be illicit? Consider then, for a moment: how do you think they are made, initially? Where do you think the neuroprogramming of death during orgasm came from, hmm?)

I walk toward him, slowly, as if I'm stalking him. He is, as usual, kneeling on the floor, not looking at me. I watch his little tattooed tits heave with anticipation. He wants it bad, this ultimate come.

I stoop and lift his chin with my hand, and he lifts his long-lashed eyes hesitantly. We've dispensed with the roleplaying by this time. I wonder if he has any idea that I exist. "Speak," I say to me. "Tell me what you want."

"Hurt me, Mistress," he says in a whisper. "Hurt me until you can't hurt me any more."

I pull the noose from my belt and loop it around his neck, like a leash. "Come, child," I say, and lead him across he room. We're in Mistress Katherine's dungeon, which is pretty lush as dungeons go. Equipment-heavy. I decide I want to be outside and I run a couple of programs to change the scene. Walls melt like running water and are replaced with bright blue sky, cloudless and intense. Golden sands stretch out around us. Bare trees crown the hill we are standing on. A hawk wheels, cries out, vanishes over the horizons. This is Dreamhawk's secret territory. I wish I could tell him how much of myself I am showing him by bringing him here for this communion, how much of a privilege it is.

There are gloves on my hands, metal gauntlets. They are for handling the barbed wire I'm going to tie him to the tallest tree with. He screams, cries out as it bites into his flesh, but does not resist. Thin trickles of blood run down over his beautiful tattoos like a web of red threads. I tie the noose to a limb, taut enough to inhibit breathing, but not enough to suffocate. My special programs are ready, held in my mind like a poker player lovingly arranges his fan of cards. "Do you love me, my beauty, my sweetness, my precious treasure?" I croon to him, stroking his face with the gauntlet.

"I love you, Mistress, oh I love you," he gasps. Music to my ears. Until I started coming into Kit's vids, no one ever told me that they loved me. I can mentally edit out the fact that he's saying it to his mistress' face.

I slap him, hard, with the metal glove, rocking him into his barbed bonds, and he screams. "Say it again," I command.

"I love you!" he shrieks, tears running down his face, one side of which is now bruised and purpling. "I love you. You are my goddess. Please, Mistress, please take me home!"

I shuck the gauntlets and remove the knotted latex whip from my belt. It hisses through the air and splats against a tree limb, and he quivers like a harpstring. Then I begin the lashing.

Kit doesn't take a beating quietly or stoically. Not for him the game of clenched teeth and rocklike stance. He abandons himself to it, moaning, screaming, begging me for mercy, begging me never to stop. I whip him until he is a mass of welts, until his tattoos stand out like repousse work on an ancient stucco wall, painted with the delicate trickles of blood form the barbed wire. The stigmata of sacred perversion, all over.

His cock is hard, thrusting vainly into the air. I stop for a moment and touch it, stroke it, feeling it throb. I want to climb on it, ride him and use it like Kali squatting over Shiva as I have done in the past, but not this time. A selection of small needles appear in my hand, and I thrust one through the tiny fold of loose skin just under the head. He arches back and sobs. Another an inch below it, and another, and another.

Now the finale. The copper rope tightens about his throat, cutting his air off, and I bring my arm back, whip at the ready. The strands will tear out the needles, the asphyxia will heighten the sensation, and Kit will come on the pain as he always does, feeling the counterfeit death in the middle of it. He will—*Shit! What the hell*—The program flickers and shuts off, sparks explode before my eyes, and the last thing I'm aware of before dark encloses me is the grinding pain than must have been the jack ripped bodily out of my head....

I'm coming to, now, slowly. It looks a little blurred. The focus must be off. Probably a bad interface. I'm staring up at a ceiling, and my head hurts abominably. White. Acoustically tiled, like a hospital. Did something go wrong with me medically? Did a nurse machine pull my plug? Was that illegal vid wormed with traps? Theories rotate lazily in my mind. Obviously I've been drugged; that fuzzy feeling is reminiscent of anesthesia.

There are two voices conversing next to me, male and female. Female one sounds strangely familiar, but out of the millions of voices I've heard I can't place it. Sounds have an echoing, unclear feel. Will somebody please fix the video and audio on this damn interface? I hate having to make do with lousy equipment. And I'm tired of staring at a vid of some white room.

"All right," comes the man's voice, nearer to me this time. "Let's get him upright." I feel myself assisted to a sitting position by two sets of hands. Are my voluntary motions disconnected? No, I can lift my head, and move my hands, but it's so hard, it takes such an effort. "He's all yours now, Kate," the voice says again. "Let me know if that monitor shows anything unusual. He's had a week to heal, and Sclepivine has speeded the process up nicely."

"Thank you again, John," says the woman's voice, firm and in command. "And I appreciate you helping in a matter of such... discretion."

"Not at all. It's been quite interesting." What the hell are they talking about? The fuzziness is wearing off, but it's still such an effort to speak. "And a way to discharge my debt to you that will be of some good use to society. Good luck, Kate."

Just as my vision is clearing, he leaves the room. The woman though, steps in front of me, and I recognize her with a shock. It's Mistress Katherine. Not her idealized face, but a more careworn version, with a few strands of grey in her hair. She is staring at me coldly, wearing white scrubs, and I can smell her perfume. The room around me is familiar, and yet unfamiliar. It's hung with chains, and eyebolts. The locked door opposite the open one is studded, like a dungeon. Bad set, I think. I could have designed better.

That's when I realize it. The interface isn't bad. It's gone. I'm looking out through real eyes for the first time.

Pure terror and despair rock me. I watch her watching me with grim amusement and realize that I have no idea how not to show everything I feel on my face. I try to speak. Such an effort! "What have you done with me!" I grate out.

"Given you exactly what you deserve, you disgusting little creature," she says in her cool voice. She is beautiful, even now. I can see why Kit worshipped her.

I panic. "Look," I say in desperation, "it was all just fun, breaking into your system. I only did it to play with Kit. I promise I won't ever touch—"

"It's too late for that." She cuts me off. "I have a few questions to ask you, and you will answer. I guarantee that." Her voice is frozen iron. "How long had you been playing snuff games with my Kit?"

I figure I'd better be honest. "About two months. Three or four times a week. Look, it was no big deal—"

Her expression tightens and she slaps me. Hard. I almost fall off the cot I'm propped up on, and only her grip on my hospital gown saves me. She hauls me up and slaps me again. I've never experienced deliberate bodily pain before and I am speechless, gasping. "Speak only when you are spoken to, and then only answer the question," she snarls. "Why did you do it?"

Okay, I'm pissed now. This I'm not going to answer, even if I had one. "Fuck you!" I snarl back.

She does something to me, lower down, and I scream. The pain makes sparks come out in front of my eyes, and there's no way I can stop it. I can't control anything here. Then she lets go, and I fall forward, gasping, wiping tears clumsily out of my eyes. I've never had to deal with tears before.

"Don't, please—" I whisper. "I'm sorry, I won't—Look, just ask Kit. He'll tell you. I never did anything to him that he didn't want—I—just ask him, okay?" I sniffle.

"I wish I could." Her voice is hard. "Kit is dead."

It strikes me beneath the solar plexus like a battering ram. "What? But the.... It was just a vid—"

Katherine's eyes are hard, uncompromising. "He killed himself two weeks ago. Asphyxiation, in his room. There was no vid involved. I was home, and he didn't dare log in." She pauses, and then stabs it in. "I suppose he was trying to recreate your special treatment. Perhaps he'd gotten used to it."

Tears are blinding me now. Oh, Kit, Kit, my precious sweetheart, you little idiot! Why didn't you wait for me? Why didn't you leave this woman for me? But of course, he never knew I existed, never knew how much I loved him. He'd never leave his mistress for a ghost in the machine. Gone. All gone.

Katherine takes a seat, waits until I'm done. I wipe my face on the bedsheet. The helplessness of this body is frustrating. "How did you find me?" I ask softly.

"I ran his programs to find out what he'd been doing, and I found those vids. Then I checked my guards, and discovered I'd been invaded, many times, by a very clever and careful probe. So I used some vids of Kit inserted into the snuff to lure you, make you think he was still there. Then it was just a matter of waiting for you to take the bait, and tracing your probe."

I realized that the last time we'd played, when I'd showed him my secret place, he'd already been dead. And I never knew. Only a bloodless vid with the mind of this cold spider woman behind it, waiting to pounce, hunting the hunter. Kit, my first real love, was dead to me forever.

I blew my nose on the sheet, and that's when I notice my arms. The wrists are tattooed, delicately, with Oriental butterflies. I look at my chest, knowing with terrible clarity what I'll see. Swirls of green and blue float on the small breasts, around the gold rings. "No!" I scream, and launch myself at her.

I'm not used to the clumsiness and effort of a body, and I only succeed in falling off the bed with a thump, tangled in the sheet. "You bitch!" I sob. "You won't get away with this! It's isn't legal! I didn't give consent!"

I hear her voice above me, unmoved. "A surgeon I knew owed me a favor. And you, you're a danger to society. I'm doing them a favor, too, getting you off the Worldnet. Besides, who will know? Kit's still legally my slave. You signed a contract. I can do anything I want with you for another year and a half. Then, well, we'll see. Oh, by the way, I've permanently removed your link."

I put a hand up, feel the shaved head and the healing sutures where Kit's sweet brain came out and my twisted one went in. "But I can't—I'm not—like him, I—" I shut up. I've lost. Will I go mad, I wonder, before she takes her full revenge? My whole world, lost. My power, stolen. I feel her looming over me. Funny how presences have so much more—well—*presence* here. I refuse to look up, rocking back and forth on the bed.

"I could have turned you in to the cops," she said. "They'd have taken it out, too, but then you'd have spent your life inside a nursing home with no sensory input, going crazy inside your own head."

She has a point, but I stare stonily ahead.

"Do you want it back?" she asks. "Your link, I mean."

My head jerks up, but I still do not meet her eyes. Do I? What do you think, you bitch?

"Depending on your behavior over the next year and a half, I might be convinced to... well, we'll see how much you want it. How much it's worth to you."

I smile ironically and meet her eyes, finally. Does she think I'm going to fall for that? I'm not a submissive. "No," I say. "You'll never do that. I know you too well. Remember," I point out, before she can protest, "I've been you. Frequently."

She glares, and our gazes thrust at each other, like fencing foils. In that moment I swear to myself that she will never break me, never. It would be a betrayal to Kit, who died for me. Then she smiles, a terrible smile, that of the adversary. "I'll leave you for a little while," she says. "You still need to heal up some more before you start your... work here. Oh, and there's a holo box in the corner. In case you want to watch it." I watch as she turns and leaves, locking me in.

I am in mourning, and I wear the skin of my dead lover on my back, like a penance. So she wants revenge, I think. I can beat this. After all, I'm Dreamhawk. Mistress Katherine doesn't know what a dangerous creature she's locked up in here, what cunning and guile live in this twisted brain. She hates me now, but that will change. I know—better than Kit—what makes a sadist love you.

And that's the first thing I'll have to do. To make her love me. And then use her to escape.

I'm Dreamhawk. I'm up to any challenge.

Color of Pain, Shade of Pleasure

Renee M. Charles

Without even needing to see the face—so artfully covered by the sharkskin-covered brank—I immediately knew that the woman who knelt before me had to be Orlina La Roux. Her neck was secured to the stainless steel whipping post by a velvet-padded joug whose long, snaking chain was draped lightly across her welt-streaked bare white back. This was Orlina of the insatiable appetite for pain, and still more pain, of the most exquisitely exotic sort. While her hair alone might have been a giveaway (so luxuriously thick, so richly highlighted with strands of glistening gold among the henna and russet), it was the sight of that fine-fleshed, creamy pale back, with its remaining deep pink shadows of former welt-marks that was unmistakable. Had I not placed each of those criss-crossing blemishes there myself?

Yet, she was already writhing in place with anticipation of my latest laying-on of the knot and spike-ended thin-curling whips, even as I languidly cracked the flailing strands against the doorway, to shake off the excess water from their over-night soak (what liquid does to the leather can be excruciatingly pleasurable). As I approached her, the spiked heels and small rounded toe-pads of my shoes clicking on the polished white tile like finger-snaps, I saw Orlina's small, taut-nippled breasts rise and fall in rhythm with her sharply accentuated breaths.

My most frequent customer obviously couldn't wait for the stinging caress of my dripping whip, so, of course, I made her wait all the longer for that sinuous, if brief, embrace. From its usual spot on my table of tactile toys, I picked up the small, brush-like device (which I'd fashioned myself), affectionately dubbed "The Teaser" by some of my more verbal customers, and I gently tapped the business end of the brush against my open palm. The Teaser was studded with dozens of nettle-fine spiked balls, each loosely attached to the cured-oak base, and I reflexively winced before saying "Have we been waiting long—as if I couldn't see that you want it," and giving her the first disciplinary swacks of the Teaser across her rounded bare bottom, then following that with lighter, but nonetheless steady smacks of the instrument on her bowed shoulders, the sides of her jutting breasts, her taut thighs, even the top of her closely-sheared mons.

And with each stinging kiss of the Teaser, her wide grey eyes would glisten momentarily with the crystal shimmer of unshed tears, even as her pupils dilated with unmistakable pleasure, then contracted when the last fleshy echo of the pain died down. And between the secure straps of the brank, which held the molded-cock-shaped insert deep in her mouth and prevented her from crying out or even speaking, I could see her lips purse against the tight-pressing straps, as if she were kissing the very air with each downward arc of the Teaser.

Once her milky-light skin was mottled, ruddy pinkish-mauve, I lifted her up by the strap attached to the outside of her brank, and motioned for her to grasp the smooth, tall sleekness of the whipping post until the top of her skull was touching the post and spread her legs for balance. I told her "You haven't squirmed nearly enough.

I want to hear you moan behind that prick between your teeth. I need to hear you beg for more and more until my arm burns from within... you filthy little slut. The sight of you sickens me, you groveling, simpering pasty bitch. You need to bleed a little—"

And, true to our thrice-weekly (at the least) scenario, Orlina began writhing in place against the post, whimpering behind the stubby penile gag, and grasping the chrome pole before her claw-like, anxious fingers... until the first whistling arc of the knot-ended thongs slapped against her flesh. She jerked forward, even as she then arched her back toward me, anticipating the next stinging swipe of my mane of soaked leather and tightly-knotted tips. With each criss-crossing, branding slap of my whip, she let out deeper and throatier moans of unmistakable pleasure, such an intense, orgasmic noise I felt myself grow slippery-damp along my shaven, leather-encased crotch. As the first razor-fine welts began to run dribbling red across her shoulders and upper ribcage, I let my eyes wander upward, to where her hands grasped the pole... for safewords aren't so easy to hear through a brank's mouth-filling insert, but hand-signals are quite easy to catch, provided one doesn't get too carried away.

But tonight (or what passed for night on this space-station's ever-circling rotation around the moon), Orlina's right hand didn't form her usual "OK" sign (thumb and forefinger in a circle, other fingers splayed out stiffly) of submission and retreat. The thread-fine dribbles of blood coursed down her silky-fine flesh in DNA-spirals, dripping runnels which pooled slightly at the curving swell of her melon-like buttocks. I wondered if, in my own state of sexual arousal, I'd somehow missed the signal to stop. The "rules" for each encounter were implicit, rather than explicit—no mistress or master was to stop whatever s/he was doing to a client unless the "safe" word or signal was given, so, short of flaying a customer to death (and given our advanced technology, even death can be a most temporary thing), none of us usually stopped unless our own hearts seized up from the effort of inflicting that desired pain/pleasure on our demanding customers.

Orlina La Roux's blood now ran across the rounded curves of her buttocks, and into the crack between her pink-mottled cheeks, and still there was no indication for me to stop my leathery pummeling of her now cross-hatched back.

"You've punished me, little wretch," I lied, as I loudly massaged my leather-encased upper arm, before closing the distance between us in three snapping strides and unfastening her brank, then all but ripping it from her head. When her face was turned in my direction, her mouth was wrinkled in a moue of disappointment, and her eyes—initially unfocused with a haze of pain/pleasure—soon were fixed on me with a steely blaze of anger.

"I didn't give you the signal," she hissed through her even, pale ecru teeth. "I didn't see all the colors, all the new shapes—" before placing an open-palmed hand across her mouth, and backing as far away from me as the chain securing the joug around her neck to the pole would allow.

I stopped massaging my arm long enough to ask, "Colors? Shapes? Is there something going on that I've been... missing?" Having been a Space Services Mistress for almost ten years, I didn't think that there was any S/M or B/D practice—or resulting gratification—I hadn't already experienced.

La Roux stood with her head bowed, so that her russet mane slid over her blushing face like opaque curtains. I gathered up bunches of her hair in each hand, and yanked them aside to reveal her pale oval of a face, admonishing her, "Now, now, no secrets from your mistress... I do all, and I have to know all."

"The colors... the ones I see when you inflict pain on me. Different ones for each type of torture... and when it gets intense, the colors, they're... they're incredible. Almost unworldly, like galaxies intermingling... so much more intense than just an ordinary orgasm—"

Curling her hanks of hair around my hands, so that they formed huge curls of either side of her flushed, but wan face, I said, "Oh, like what you see when you press the orbs of your eyes, and those patterns of light and color form on your inner eyelids—"

Shaking her head (albeit slightly, under the pressure of my hands pinning back her hair), she insisted "No, not at all. These are colors hovering right before my face, like a veil of moving, shifting color. Then, when the pleasure hits me, the colors take on different shapes, forms I can actually feel pressing against my cheeks, my lips, my nose. The shapes, they grow more varied with each new expression of pain... but I need to keep it going long enough to remember what I'm seeing and feeling—"

I loosened my grip on her hair as realization set in for me: Orlina La Roux was blessed with synesthesia, able, through a sensory mix-up, to mingle heretofore seemingly incompatible sensory impressions into something new, something tantalizingly pleasurable. In fact, one of the other mistresses who worked the Sex Shop here on the station could "taste" colors (she claimed that the sight of blood was sweeter than chocolate), but the implications of being able to see one's own pleasure and pain were intoxicatingly heady, even for a person as sated by mock-sadism and jaded by the sight of writhing, panting "slaves" as I'd become over the years.

And the sight of Orlina's visually-aided orgasms did make me wet at the core.

Picking up the slack of her joug-chain, I wound the linked coil of metal around my left hand, while my right tightened around the handle of my whip—and the sparkle of anticipation in my client's eyes brought a sweet glow of pleasure to my already musk-slippery labia. I gave the whip a quick wrist-flick and slapped the knotted ends against Orlina La Roux's thighs and knees, before asking "Why do you need to remember each new colored shape of pleasure? You're not keeping secrets from me, are you... slut?"

Wiggling with suppressed pleasure at my taunting pet name (I wondered briefly if the pain of being called filthy, degrading names also produced those elusive visual light and color shows for her), she again hung her head, this time biting on her lower lip to keep from answering me... and eliciting another swipe of the whip, this time across her gently concave belly and henna-haired mons.

I could actually see her labia jerk in time with the hard kisses of the whip-ends, and when I looked up into her eyes, they were again wide-pupiled and awash with the glimmer of unshed, sparkling tears.

Holding the whip before her eyes, I whispered harshly "Either you tell me what you're seeing, or no more of this"—I shook the dangling tendrils of the whip for emphasis—"either from me, or any of the other masters here. I need to feed on your pleasure, even as I dole out what you need."

"I'm very hungry for it, Mistress Serilda," she whispered, eyes lowered, her voice husky with suppressed desire. "I've been bad, and I need for you to punish me—"

Ignoring her typical slave-prattle, that masochist's lament I'd already heard (in surprisingly few variations!) thousands of times before, I reached out and knuckle-clamped one wrinkled nipple—gently, though—and continued. "Your pleasure from my inflicted pain is essential to me now, but there's no pleasure for me in just watching you squirm and grovel; I need to know what each smack of the knotted thong reveals in your sight, to feel those... shapes which caress your flesh. And I must know why you need to remember each new mingling of color and shape and sensation. Is it for your pleasure in your bed each night? For the times when my whip, my Teaser, are still and unused? For those moments when your flesh still longs for discipline, for the harsh caress of my dripping, flaying embrace? Do not turn your head, I have not commanded it—"

Obediently, even meekly, Orlina La Roux's head of rippling red-gold turned toward me, but her eyes were wide-pupiled, as if gazing upon that which I could never directly see—and it was then that a hunger grew in me to share in that unique, synesthesia-enhanced worldview, even if by proxy.

Using the master-key attached to my chain-link and leather-tab belt, I detached the chain from her velvet-and-metal collar and led my slave-for-the-evening toward the wall of the chamber studded with hanging-loops. Upon these various leather-and-latex garments hung, all unisex, with easily adjustable hook-and-loop closures (after all, the crew and support staff of the Station come in many sizes and sexes... too many for even the storeroom in the S/M shop to carry individual gear for each person who might want or need it!). Glancing from the cowering-and-loving-it Miss La Roux to the selection of rubber and leatherwear in her general size range (small-boned and creamily nubile), I finally selected a "hoop" body harness. The harness featured lightly-spiked breast hoops, the ends not much sharper than a little finger-tip, but still stimulating and a network of body straps which culminated in a between-the-legs thong dotted with raised, shining chrome studs.

I ordered her to don it, then helped to cinch it tight against her flesh so that the surrounding skin bloomed around each strap and criss-crossing thong, her pert, upturned breasts were mashed tightly against her rib-cage and her nipples strained behind the spiked hoops. I turned my attention to her wrists and thin, shapely ankles, this time choosing latex gloves with attached wrist cuffs and loops for adding a lock or a chain, plus a pair of spike-heeled patent-leather shoes whose ankle straps could be linked to form an effective pair of ankle-cuffs.

After she was properly cinched and bound and confined, I hooked a finger through the thin, studded thong which ran through her labia, and half-dragged, half-pulled her to the restraining wall of the chamber, where the leather-and-plush-pile Chevalet stood, along with hoods mounted on the wall for suspending wrists or ankles in various configurations, a punishment chair which jutted out from the wall, and a variety of hanging ropes, chains and straps sturdy enough to suspend a well-bound and eagerly willing slave.

Since I'd already paid ample attention to her back and shoulders, I decided that if Miss La Roux wanted to see her colors and shapes of pain/pleasure, she'd have to endure some attention to her exposed privates... and no mouth guard or brank this time, no matter how much she seemed to crave it.

After all, I was going to get a little something out of this night's session, too.

I arranged her supine on the punishment chair, her upper back and mid-section on the smooth-worn wood-and-metal, her buttocks flat against the wall, her belly rippled in at the navel. I then pulled each of her legs up and out, attaching the ankle straps to the wall, so that she was spread-eagled in a wide, welcoming "V," pussy up and exposed around the confining studded strap. Once her legs were secured, I locked her wrists together under the extended tongue of the chair so that her flattened breasts were aimed at the ceiling, while her head lolled off the end of the wide, flat chair bottom.

"Can we move...? I didn't think so," I hissed through smile-clenched teeth, while flicking the whip against her pinioned thighs and calves. "But I know my tender little slattern can talk, can't she now? And she must tell her mistress everything she sees—"

Staring off at a point where the ceiling met the far wall, Orlina whispered, her voice thick with ecstasy. "Every flick of the whip is magenta, tinged with dusky rose... little revolving triangles of magenta... merging into tall, pointy pyramids when the orgasm hits... ma-magenta, and the brush of rose—"

Closing my eyes for a second, I could almost see what she described; the tantalizingly sharp triangles and pyramids floating and shifting, leaving a haze of deep purplish-red in their wake. But surely, there had to be more—

Click-stepping toward my table of sex-punishment toys, I scooped up a handful of them, then hurried back to where my slave for the night was splayed in all her pink-and-cream glory. The staccato hail of my heels echoed in the smooth-walled and -floored room. Since my job includes humiliation as well as domination of my slave, I turned my attention to the trimmed patch of slightly curling hair between Orlina's extended, cuffed legs, and the moist folds and wrinkles of the inner labia within. First, I picked up a well-spiked and nubbed latex tickler, which I slipped over an oval love egg. After pulling aside the thong which had straddled the length of her slit, I pushed the tickler-covered vibrating egg into her waiting, slightly gaping vagina, asking "And what does this new sensation look like—what color is each tickling now inside you?"

Arching her pelvis toward me, until her lower back was well off the surface of the chair, she moaned. "Tiny amethystine circles, chains and ropes and weaving strands of them, encircling my face, pressing against my cheeks, my chin... beautiful blue, dozens of—"

Her voice broke off when she heard the buzzing whine of the small battery-powered wet/dry clippers, but as soon as the chiseled tip of the vibrating blade touched the top of her mons, clearing away her curls to reveal silky blanched flesh below, she added, her voice barely recognizable for all her panting and gasping "Ovals... ovals now, darkening to sapphirine, pushing against my face, my neck, my breasts... circles into ovals, green-blue into darker blue... all over me, pressing, caressing...."

As I sheared her lower labia, letting the vibrating body of the shaver rest against the puckered inner labia and also-vibrating love egg within her, my slave Miss La Roux's utterances became too punctuated with groans of pleasure to be understood. So, once her tender, juicy folds and smooth curving spots were free of hair, I used a long plumed feather to whisp away the remaining clippings. And as I slowly, carefully brushed the downy wand-like end of the feather against Orlina's denuded, pink-dappled mons, she whispered between groans of gasping, panting orgasm, "Gold... golden-bright squares, all pointy angular ends pressing into me, revolving, shifting, pressing down all bright and shining... too bright, too—" She squeezed her eyes shut against the brilliance of her individual vision, before her labia began to jerk spasmodically and clear bubbles of musky juices welled in her glistening pinkness.

(For perhaps the first time, I longed to break the unspoken rule that no mistress or master shall have actual sex with a slave, but had to content myself with jerking out the love-egg by its cord, and merely watching the reflexive ripple of her flesh as it gave up the studded, jiggling sex-toy with a soft, kiss-like parting-of-the-flesh noise.)

Realizing that my disciple's expression was perhaps a little too enraptured, too caught up in unvarnished pleasure without the attendant pain she usually craved, I picked up a pair of chain-joined nipple clamps, and—using both hands—simultaneously affixed them to her upturned, spike-encircled nipples.

"Ohhh—emerald, bright emerald cones... points all digging into my face, my neck, in my ears... all green, all—"

Closing my eyes, I could "see" and feel what she described, and the intensity of it was staggering, but there were so many other toys and implements in the room, and so many more colors and shapes to experience before our session would come to an end.

When the bong-like tone which signaled the end of our evening's session sounded, both of us jerked visibly, rudely intruding upon our mutual (albeit somewhat one-sided as far as actual experience went) give and take of pain-color and shape-pleasure. With much reluctance, I undid her legs and arms, and helped her off the chair. As she unfastened her restrictive garments, I clung to my role of the evening as I asked/ordered her "Every other session we have will include what you see and feel... just as you will give me the satisfaction of knowing why remembering each new mingling of your synesthesia and my ministrations is so crucial to you."

Totally nude now, Orlina stood before me head bowed slightly, and replied "You will have your satisfaction very soon... next week, in Section S, at the showing there. When you come there, you will understand why your touch upon my willing flesh is so urgent to my needs," then hurried past me, out the slaves-only door, and into the waiting dressing area beyond.

And, since masters and mistresses are forbidden to follow their fleshly conquests into that area, I was unable to administer a reprimand with a quick flick of my whip-bearing hand. But as I watched her bright-striped back and buttocks vanish from my sight, I could almost feel those revolving, sharp-tipped triangles of magenta-seeping-into-rose....

The compliant Miss La Roux did not come back to my chamber of punishment and pleasure for almost a week, and although there were other willing bodies who awaited the hard caress of my whip, my Teaser, and who most eagerly allowed me to bestow upon them the whims of imagination, leather and confining latex, I found myself longing for the sight of Orlina's waving tresses peeking out from under the bindings of her brank, or the mottled stippling of her fine-pored flesh. And during those days, my whip came down harder on the waiting expanses of flesh, and my individualized sex-torments grew far more intrusive, far more exquisitely intricate, until my slaves for the evening began saying or signing their safewords far earlier than was their usual wont.

Being paid by the hour, I soon felt the pinch of my unusual excesses, for my allotment of pay credits was lower than usual... so much lower, that I was forced to forgo my own for-a-fee session of pain-sex with one of my fellow mistresses (the icy showers followed by insertion of dildos warmed to well above body temperature, or the "massage" of synthetic nettles on my uncorseted spots), and instead had to seek out the more inexpensive amusements offered to the Space Station crew as a whole—

—amusements which included the ever-changing show of crew-created works of art and artifice in Section

S, the art show I'd never before had the time (or tolerance for enduring such a lack of stimuli) to attend.

Feeling almost alien in my non-usual, standard-issue crew uniform (I wasn't even able to wear my corset or harness under its clinging confines), I morosely drifted from wall of bad art to display case of even worse art, until I noticed a group of tightly-packed, obviously enraptured crew members standing in front of a series of eerily-lit objects on a low-slung pedestal.

My six-inch heels were forbidden in the rest of the station, which featured soft-tread floors in case of sudden zero-g conditions, so I needed to stand on tip-toe to see over the shoulders of the shortest of the crew members surrounding the items exhibited. All I could initially make out was intense pockets of neon-bright colors... magenta, brilliant blue-green into evening-blue, golden-yellow, and finally an intense emerald-green which was almost too powerful to gaze upon.

But the colors were obscured in spots, by the outlines of hands... moving hands, which belonged to the crew members who stood closest to the display, and who tentatively caressed and prodded the glowing, amorphous works of art—

When you come there, you will understand why your touch upon my willing flesh is so urgent to my needs.

Craning my neck forward, until the pain of straining my muscles sent shivers of near-orgasm through me, I squinted my eyes slightly, in order to better see what rested beneath that highly pigmented luminosity. In each case, the stylized, achingly mobile suggestion of a nude female was either curled or splayed or resting supine on the unyielding hardness of a white-tile base, each with an almost featureless oval face and deftly under-defined nakedness. And each one was covered with glowing geometric shapes which seemed to hover just above her contorted curves and lean lengths of leg and arm. With a gentle touch of the person viewing the sculpture, each bright-tinged shape came into squishingly-soft contact with the female beneath them, pressing into that synthetic flesh just enough to partially vanish in those creamy, semi-translucent depths, so that the "skin" of each sculpture became momentarily suffused with that same intense blooming color, so that "woman" and "shape" and "color" were merged into a unified, blissfully integrated whole.

And while each sculpted ovate face remained basically unchanged, the resulting interactive interplay between viewer and what was viewed revealed heretofore unseen curves and hollows on the face, so that each orgasm of shape and color in turn awakened the viewer to that which had been previously unseen, unappreciated, in each small female configuration. It was impossible to tell whether the source of each color's brilliant illumination came from within or without each separate hovering "shape," but judging by the expressions of blissed-out ecstasy and abandon on the faces of those who caressed each statue, it really didn't matter where the light came from, for there was heat enough for all who either touched or merely witnessed each construction's sensual transformation.

I needed to summon all my previously untapped stores of patience before the crowd around the display cleared enough for me to approach one of the radiant artifices, but as soon as my fingertips made contact with those floating magenta-rose triangles, the rush of tingling, aching, throbbing, smarting delectation was almost too much to bear while standing clothed and ostensibly decorous in a public place. And when I closed my eyes, I literally felt the nudging and mindless pushing of the whirling triangles against my flesh, accompanied by the radiant close-by glow of the magenta color-fire within each ever-shifting pointed shape.

And with each new sculpture I rubbed and gently fingered, I again felt/saw mixtures of color and shape which spanked and thrashed my very essence far more completely that any well-wet-and-knotted whip or sharp-spined Teaser could ever have done. The juxtaposition of previously uncombined sensations was more intense, more bracing, than even cooling-but-still-warm wax dribbled on my soaked-cold wet flesh.

Only when the last of the interactive models had been explored and tactilely savored could I numbly wander away from the display table, eyes lowered like the most submissive slave before a thousand-tendrils-thick whip, barely able to walk upright on the springy, slightly oozing floor beneath my feet. Then a cool, firm hand grabbed my upper arm, steadying me, so that I could finally look upward, like the mistress I usually was—

—straight into the dancing-from-within bright eyes of Orlina La Roux, who was almost unrecognizable when clothed in the standard station uniform, with her rippling blaze of hair bound in a neat, asexual bun at the nape of her thin neck, and a badge emblazoned with her name and job description (Computer Programmer, Bio-Neural Unit) pinned to her slightly heaving lapel.

She glanced to the spot behind me where a new group of Station crew members were busily interacting with the tableau of sensory delights, before whispering "Did you notice the name-card on the table? I hope it is sufficient to satisfy your demand of me, my Mistress—"

That Orlina had created the works of artistic ravishment resting on that table had been clear to me upon my first glimpse of them. Surely I didn't need to see her name there to know her work, but Orlina grabbed one of my hands, and gently, reverently, steered me back to that luminous display, toward the open end of the long table, where no one was standing, and where a neat rectangle of lucite was embossed with the following inscription:

COLOR OF PAIN, SHADE OF PLEASURE
BY
"MISS" ORLINA LA ROUX
AND
"MISTRESS" SERILDA LURLINE

I found myself actually blushing when I read the dual credit on that shining rectangle, but managed to forestall further embarrassment by biting down hard on my tongue before facing Orlina once again, this time demurring. "I'm flattered, but I hardly deserve such credit. I was only performing a paid service, servant to your fee, just as you were servant to my whims and orders—"

"But I can hardly inflict the necessary pain on myself, without forgoing the pleasure of being suitably bound and restrained, now can I," she countered, with suitably subservient downward-glance of her eyes, before adding with a shade more eagerness "The gallery has promised me another table for the next new show, provided I can create even better, more stimulating works of art. But for one with my condition, there is only one constant perception, one set of shapes and colors, per particular stimuli. For me, the stinging kiss of the whip will always be magenta, and so on—"

"But with the experiences of a new stimuli, you'll experience a fresh mixture of shape and shade, no?" I asked, while envisioning her dappled pink-white flesh submerged part-way in icy water, just before the dripping descent of the slightly-cooled wax... or the excruciatingly intense expression on her face as I used piercing tongs to lift and pull tender, soft protrusions on her body... As if she could somehow read my expression (as if my body had become one of her interactive lighted sculptures), Miss Orlina respectfully lowered her thick-lashed eyes, and begged "I know I've been very bad, very disobedient in the past, but with the suitable chastening and penalties, I know I'll please you, and earn your satisfaction."

Leaning in close to her, so that no stray pair of ears might hear my reply, I whispered, while imagining the meaty feel of the whip handle—or the heated length of the burning candle—in my palm, "Only as long as I get first crack at the finished sculptures... in private, so I can wear my usual gear while enjoying them, and I must witness you partaking of them, as well. In my chambers, where I keep my personal store of implements and toys. And many, many candles—"

"Ones that drip easily?" she asked, and as she uttered those words, I mentally reminded myself to make sure that the next time I could afford a session with one of the Sex Shop mistresses, that I beg her to castigate me until I could stop showing my desires so plainly on my face.

Being party to an artistic process is one matter, but showing personal gratification to one's slaves can ruin the whole S/M experience. Make the slaves too soft, too easily let off—

"By the way, Miss Orlina. The next time, you create your... pieces, make sure my name goes first on the placard," I demanded, and her bow and nod of acceptance—reluctant acceptance—was like music to my eyes.

Jane

Lauren P. Burka

I.

The pet shop man looked up when the door opened.

"Hey, Jane," he said.

"Hello," said the parrot on the counter.

"Hey," she answered.

"Can I get you anything today? Some nice goldfish and a bowl, perhaps?"

"Hello," interjected the parrot.

"No. Just looking. As always."

The parrot said, "Pretty boy."

The gray old man waggled his finger. "Mind your manners. Jane's not a boy." The parrot tried to nip his finger.

"It's an easy mistake," Jane said. She was long and lank with buzzed-short hair and an angular face. A belt pouch lay over her crotch like a man's bulge. Her black jeans and stained leather jacket hung wet on her frame, giving her the look of a butch junior mechanic.

"Such a sweet thing as you? You should be in pictures, not filming them."

"Hello," said the parrot helpfully.

Jane considered telling him that she had once won a pissing contest, for distance. But the pet shop man lived in the same fantasy world as most of the pre-war folks. Women, to him, were ladies.

She stopped to look at the rat cages. Pink-eyed, white-furred rodents slept in a heap in their food dish. Most of them were snake food. Jane used to own rats. She had treated them with meticulous care, but they still died just after turning three years old. Which was longer than most relationships lasted, she thought. One of the ferrets recognized her and rattled its cage until she took it out and held it.

"Row, row, row your boat," sang the pet shop man to the parrot.

"Hello."

"Gently down the stream."

"Hello."

Sighing, the man turned on the radio instead. The parrot picked up a pen and chewed on the end.

The ferret climbed onto Jane's shoulder and nested against the back of her neck, its pink-nosed face looking out under her ear.

"You should get a pet," said the man, over the sound of the game. "You look lonely. Pretty girls shouldn't be lonely."

"Hello."

"I'm not lonely," she said, uncoiling the ferret and returning it to the cage. "I just like holding them."

"And I wish you would take the bus. The Avenue is not safe at night."

"I'll be fine."

"See you tomorrow night?"

"Sure."

"Hello."

It still rained in thin drizzles. The gutters were full, clogged, slicked with oily rainbows. Jane splashed through, wet to the ankles of her workman's boots, her collar turned up to her ears.

The Avenue wasn't dangerous. Its broken facades housed the addicted, the anti-social, and the criminally depressed. Police swept the Avenue a couple of times a year, usually after a citizen strayed too far out and got mugged. Avenue-dwellers fancied themselves outlaws, not realizing (or not admitting) that they were the zoo. Dangerous people were always culled.

Jane liked to walk down the Avenue just before dark. Someone at Authority probably knew this. But Jane was a Trusted one, and must be allowed to get away with some things.

Wet stones loomed out of the rain curtains. The granite-slab pavement under her boots had frozen in a tortured convulsion, cracked around a collapsed sewer. Some doorways were lit with flickering, greasy flames that spit at the weather. In one of them two young men were talking. Their hair was cut and colored; their clothes displayed odd-colored patches and rips, disguised as style. Jane stopped, her hands in her pockets, and watched them. Their conversation died, and they turned to look at her with black-shadowed eyes.

Apparently it wasn't that cold out. Neither of them made a move towards her, and she shrugged and went on. After she passed from sight, the two hustlers held each other in a way that had nothing to do with sex.

The drizzle gave way to a downpour.

Jane watched the people moving in and out of the rain. Most of them were young. Some of them talked to themselves. A teenage girl held a faded blue stuffed bear by a fire set in an old stone planter while another girl tried to get her to eat something burned on the end of a stick.

Someone was pacing Jane. She could hear the soft splash of his footsteps in the full gutter. Jane slowed her pace and felt for the thin knife up her jacket seam.

"Alms, sir. Alms for your unfortunate brother."

Jane wiped rain from her eyes. "There's an almshouse up the other side of the Avenue," she said.

"I know that."

The speaker was shorter than Jane, with longer hair. He was dressed in black, or perhaps he was just wet.

"So what are you doing in the rain begging change from honest folk?"

"You tell me."

Jane flipped a lighter from her pocket. In the yellow glow the kid (for he was a kid) blinked china-blue eyes and wiped his nose on a sleeve. He wore a leather jacket, but the arms were too short. Silver ribbons in his braided hair sparkled. Jane realized he wasn't as young as she thought. Everyone else on the Avenue just looked too old.

"You looking for a bit of trade?" she asked.

He shrugged. "Food. A bath. Maybe a scratch for my itch."

"What's your itch?"

"Heroin."

Jane whistled. "Where'd you come from that you could get it? Nevermind. All I've got is medical-grade morph." She turned and walked away.

"Wait." He was running. "What do you want for the morph?"

"More than I'll get from your skinny ass."

"I'm good for it. Whatever you like. Please?"

Jane smiled to herself. She hadn't even hit him and he was begging.

They had come to the end of the Avenue. Most of the streetlights worked in the kinder part of town. A patrol car floated past. The man behind the wheel waved at her. The boy flinched.

"You got a license to be selling your ass?" asked Jane.

"You know I don't."

"You're dirty meat," she said. "I should call the cops. They'll let me watch while they work you over."

"You won't."

He was right, of course. She'd have to punish him for that.

Jane lived four blocks down on a side street. She unlocked the front door and let the boy walk in before her. Water leaked down one wall and puddled in front of the stairs. Their footsteps echoed on the hard walls. Metal railings wobbled at their touch.

"Stop here," said Jane.

They were on a landing with nothing but a broken bottle and bare stone walls where the plaster had come down.

"Here?"

"I want to see what you're good for before I let you drip on my carpet."

He glanced to either side. In the hallway lights his face was perfect, almost sculptured, colored white and pink from the cold, framed by black and silver hair. There were rings in his right ear. "We'll be seen."

Jane could have told him that the only other residents were a married couple on the third floor, who were on vacation, and old Ms. Evans, who was half-deaf and lame and had her groceries delivered. Instead she pinned him against the wall with one sharp hip against his crotch.

"Shut up," she said. "You move when I tell you and be still otherwise."

He squirmed. She slapped him, her wet hand numb to the impact on his cheek. He hissed, his heart beating hard enough to hear, the sticky sweet smell of his body stronger than the stairways's other reeks.

"Bastard!" he spat.

Jane smiled. "You said you would do what I want."

"I am doing what you want." He smiled back and arched his spine, rubbing his cock on her leg. "You're still a bastard."

Interesting.

"What's your name?" she asked.

"Morgan. Yours?"

"Jane."

"Sure it is. Hey, are you a girl?"

"Yes. Why do you care?"

"I should have called you a bitch instead."

She slapped him again.

Morgan spat.

Jane got both his hands in one of hers and pinned them up over his head. Her other hand opened his belt and then his jeans. His cock was warm and dry but for the wetness at the end from humping her leg. Morgan's breathing echoed in the narrow space as his sex grew hard against his belly. Jane weighed it in her hand. It was short but thick, with curly black hair matted at the base, wandering up his belly in a narrow stripe. Jane slid his belt from his jeans and doubled it, tapping his cock with the loop.

Morgan whimpered. But his eyes were open, his pupils dilated, and his legs scrambling to spread wider on the step.

"You'd like that," said Jane.

Morgan grinned, showing teeth. "Do you like me to like it?"

Instead, Jane buckled his belt around his hands and ran the end up over the railing above them. Morgan sighed, letting his arms take his weight. His eyes snapped open at the snick of Jane's knife.

"She likes me to bleed, too," he whispered. Light reflected from the blade into his eyes. "Vampire."

"No." She drew the knife along his beardless jaw, leaving a white line. The point eased downward, slow as the rainwater that still dripped from his hair. Jane snagged the neck of his shirt. The fabric parted.

"Hey," he said. "Not my clothes. Skin heals."

"I'll get you another shirt." The knife opened the faded black cloth, revealing his lean ribs, anemic-pale skin, and thin scattering of black fur. And something else. Jane opened the shirt all the way down and lifted the thin steel chain with the knife point. It was anchored on either end to rings in his nipples.

"Cute," she said, replacing the knife and taking the chain in her fingers.

"Present from a friend."

"You're pretty," she mused.

"Thanks."

Jane yanked his chain. "That wasn't for your benefit. You're pretty. You're too healthy to be a dope addict. And you have pierced tits. Barbaric custom. Authority doesn't approve. It locks people away for two years of treatment. Even the rings in your ear would lose you a job preference."

"So what? You think I'm a cop?" Morgan pumped his hips at her. His flagging cock stirred.

"No. I think you're an Islander. You made it onto the mainland before the revolt and massacres. You have no identification and no money, just an aristocrat's attitude and some unusual tastes."

"Maybe. But now I'm a whipping boy off the Avenue. And my hands are getting numb."

Jane gave the chain a last yank, released the belt, and climbed up the stairs.

Morgan yelled at her back, "You owe me fifty on top of the morph, already." When she didn't turn he trotted up after her, holding his clothes together.

Jane's door cast a square of light into the hall. She stepped aside and let Morgan enter, tripping on his pants.

"Stop," she ordered. "Strip and leave your clothes here."

The leather jacket hit the floor, followed by the ripped shirt. The jeans clanked when they fell. Morgan stood naked and shivering, but not at all subdued.

"Can I have my fix now?"

"No. Bath's to the left. Take your time. I'm making dinner."

"I'll go jerk off in the shower," he said, and left wet footprints on the blond carpet.

Jane stripped when he was gone, changing to a kimono from the closet. Her clothes went into the 'matic. His shirt went to the trash, and so did his pants after she cleaned them of the small metal things in the pockets. Lockpicks, a knife with a broken blade, coins useless since the Islands sank. There was an elastic black cord, too. His jacket and boots joined her clothes. Jane went to see about food.

The shower was set for thirty-six degrees. Morgan turned it up to forty and stepped into a warm spray of water. He folded his arms and shivered while his body temperature rose to normal. Now that he was warm it was time to be clean.

The shower dispensed a burst of soap-laden spray, and Morgan began to scrub his skin free of its surface grime. The too-intimate smell of stale, alcohol-tainted sweat went down the drain. So did long black hairs that came free when he scrubbed his scalp. A few scabs peeled away to reveal new skin.

Now that the preliminaries were over, Morgan leaned against the wall and soaped his groin. A paying client would want him clean all over, though since he hadn't eaten in two days he could skip the enema. He should wait for Jane before he climaxed. But she might just hit him a few times, sit on his face, and throw him out unsatisfied. He was, after all, playing the bad boy for her.

He melted into the soft pressures of the water and braced his legs as he worked himself to full hardness with a wet hand. Reaching back, Morgan used a soapy finger on his asshole, cleaning and pleasuring himself at once. He meant to keep it going as long as possible, but the smell of cooking food invaded the bathroom, and his stomach gave a long, appreciative growl. His grip tightened and he sprayed up into the shower.

Wrapping himself in a large towel, Morgan took Jane's comb off the counter and exited the bathroom.

She lived in a one-room dwelling with plain, comfortable furniture. The kitchen, half the room, was large enough for a table. There was no bed in sight. Morgan sat on the sofa and began combing his black and silver hair.

Jane glanced up. He was hoping she'd say something about the comb, but she turned back to the pan on the gas flame.

Morgan inhaled the smells of garlic and vegetables.

Jane spooned rice from a small pot. Morgan watched her move in the kimono. Her legs would never pass as male.

"What's for dinner?" he asked.

Jane shut the stove off and walked, barefoot, to the chest of drawers under the window. Morgan craned his neck to try to see what she was doing.

"Get down on the floor," she said. "Leave the towel."

Morgan knelt with a straight back and knees slightly parted, his white skin and black body hair sharp against the soft carpet. The older scars and newer bruises gave his body a well-used look, like his boots.

His back was tense with the effort not to turn and watch her. A soft thing wrapped around one of his wrists and pulled. He tried to flex his arm as Jane snapped the hospital restraint onto his other wrist, too tight. Morgan shifted. His bound wrists forced his chest out. The chain shivered with his breath. Jane tugged on it.

"Chicken for dinner," she said. "You're dessert, so eat well."

Morgan tried to climb to his feet, but she shoved at the back of his knee just as he caught his balance.

"Down. If you want your dinner, you crawl."

Morgan gave her a wounded look, and began an undignified squirm to the kitchen table. Jane spooned some rice and stir-fry onto a plate and set it on the floor. She took the rest to the table and began to eat, with chopsticks. He reached the plate and sat back on his haunches, scowling.

"I don't think I'm hungry."

"If you're too proud to eat like a puppy, you'll never get your dope."

Morgan lowered his face to the plate and picked up a steaming bit of chicken in his teeth.

"Good dog."

The food began to vanish in bigger mouthfuls until the plate was clean. Morgan's stomach growled again. He sighed and leaned down further to eat spilled food off the floor. Jane set a bowl of water on the floor next to the plate. Morgan drank, snorting as he got water in his nose.

Jane picked him up by the hair and wiped his face with a towel. As she cleaned his cheeks, Morgan looked up to her, relaxing into her grip with a grateful ease that approached submission. She stroked his lips with a finger.

"I'm not done with you yet."

"I know."

Jane unlinked the cuffs. "Heel," she said.

Morgan crawled after her and stayed in the middle of the carpet when she told him. In moments he might be held down screaming and cursing as he gave his body over to her attentions. He looked down at the cuffs still on his wrists. Did she have a matching set for ankles? Morgan hadn't been tied tight since...

"I want you to take your prick in your hand and stroke it for me."

Morgan blinked. He was eager, even after the knee-weakening come in the shower. Fear made it easy to get hard. So did the thought of the narcotic rush that waited for him if he pleased. He wet his fingers and spread spit over his cock head. Jane was watching him, but looked bored. He took a firmer grip and worked with his fist. Maybe he could come before she ordered him to stop. There might be some sublime punishment if he did. He got himself to the edge quickly. His cock was purple. Release coiled in his belly. She was going to order him to stop, wasn't she? This was the part where the trick teased him mercilessly, except it usually happened at the end of a session. But Jane just watched him with arched eyebrows as he came over his fingers, quietly, and lifted his hand to lick it clean.

Jane got up and opened the drawer. He watched her back and wondered if she was impressed.

She turned around and held out a white plastic rod looped back on itself with the ends stuck in a tape-wrapped pipe handle. A home-made flogging implement.

"What about it?" he asked, sounding more breathless than he liked.

"Get your ass in the air," she said.

Morgan put his head down and his ass up, irritated that she was going to beat him after he came. It was easier to take pain when he was on edge.

The flail struck his thin haunches with a hungry snap. Morgan gasped and arched his back. His knees collapsed, hiding his red-striped ass in the carpet.

"Did that hurt?"

"Yes," he muttered, waiting for the order to present for more abuse.

But Jane was taking something else out of the drawer. Something that jingled. Morgan looked up and saw a red rubber ball roll past his nose, ringing.

"Fetch," said Jane.

Morgan got his knees under himself and crawled after the ball. The double stripe of pain on his ass faded to an almost-pleasant glow. But it hadn't been the kind of pain he liked. Too sharp and biting. Not at all like a belt or a hand. Jane was going to be a bigger challenge than the usual.

The ball had rolled to a stop against the kitchen counter. Morgan reached out to pick it up.

"Touch that ball with your hands and I'll whip you bloody."

Morgan froze and put his hand back down. She couldn't want him to carry it in his mouth.

"I'm waiting."

He crouched and took the ball in his teeth. It forced his jaw wide and made breathing difficult. The bell inside it rang. This was disgraceful.

Jane held her hand out for the ball. Morgan let it fall for her, wishing he could wipe the drool from his chin. But Jane threw the ball across the room again. Morgan looked up at her, offended. She reached for the flail. He was half-way across the room before he realized he had made the decision not to get hit.

He fetched the ball again, and she threw it. Why couldn't she use him like she had on the stairs? He could lick her until she came, or take half her fist up his ass. Why did he have to crawl like an animal?

Morgan fetched. His knees hurt. So did his wrists. He took dust in his mouth with the ball and, once, a dead insect. He halted, panting, in the middle of the floor. The ball lay under the table. Jane was on her feet with her instrument of torture. At least he was about to get some attention. Maybe she'd tie him up.

Gritting his teeth, he thrust his ass out to meet the first blow. He had no breath to scream. But the pain was a clean thing, not like the rasp of the carpet. He took it as long as he could stand, then flung himself down on his back.

Jane's kimono was coming undone, but she didn't seem to care. She lifted the flail and cracked it across Morgan's thigh. He howled and scrambled out from under her, across the floor, to the red ball. Like a good pet. When he retrieved it to her hands, he was crying for the first time in years, and the first time ever for a trick. She didn't seem to notice.

Time passed in a hell of indignities, a blood taste in his mouth, aching joints and abraded skin. The tears drained him of defiance. When he faltered, blows rained down on his tender flesh.

Until he lay still to receive her attentions, with no restraint but his own exhaustion.

Jane's skin was flushed when she lay down the flail and shed the kimono.

"Get it up for me."

Morgan reached for his limp cock. It didn't want to play, not after two orgasms and the tears. The carpet was too rough for his welted back. Jane was tapping the flail against her palm. Fear chilled Morgan's guts, but it warmed him too. He was half-hard when she straddled him and rubbed her cunt against his cock. That did it. He felt her slide down, swallowing him whole.

"You stay hard until I come."

He nodded, gaze locked with her cruel, gray eyes. He would do anything she asked so she wouldn't want to hurt him again, so that she didn't make him cry. But he didn't have to like it, just lie back and let her fuck him.

Jane came, squeezing his cock with her tight cunt, clawing his shoulders with her nails. It hurt him more than the beatings, but he was too tired to come. Too tired. Then he was alone on the floor, cold and wet and sticky.

Jane was tossing things at him. Clothes. A pair of her jeans, and a shirt. A bag with his tools and toys. His own jacket. He could see his boots sitting by the door. A roll of script hit the ground next. More than the fifty he had demanded. He should count it, but he didn't want to move. And something else.

Morgan grabbed for the disposable syringe and ripped open the package. The elastic was in the bag. He tied off his left arm and went searching for a vein. Found one. His lab-engineered neuroreceptors cheated him out of addiction, but true pleasure was rare enough to crave. Morgan needed to need something. The needle bit, giving him the sweet rush of a high-class Islander affectation, an orgasm that wouldn't fade for hours, the crutch that would make it possible for him to dress and walk down the stairs.

Jane was watching him with clinical interest.

"I'm kicking you out," she said.

Morgan started pulling on the clothes. Her jeans were too long and bagged around the ankles. The wad of script was almost too fat for the pocket. Untraceable. Food, shelter, and maybe drugs.

"Thanks," he said, smiling like an idiot.

"Next week," she said, her voice washing over him like the rain. "This time next week."

Morgan considered. He didn't have to work now, not for a long time. She had seen to it.

"Yes," he said, because he was free to consent. "I'll be there."

But Jane looked for him all up the Avenue that day, and he was nowhere to be found.

* * *

II.
The famous reporter stood still under the lights while an assistant fixed her hair and dabbed the sweat from her neck. Awed Haven staff stood clustered in the doorway. Jane was on a step ladder fixing one of the sound units.

A production manager chased the onlookers away. The News team was ready for magic.

"Good evening, Citizens," began the reporter. "Today we're visiting the Safe Haven Institutional Support Center. Safe Haven is charged with bringing street kids, many with severe health problems, into a productive relationship with our free society. The majority of inpatients are the children of brave men and women who died in the War. Recently Safe Haven has opened its doors to refugees from Floating Islands One and Three. These new patients present unique cultural adjustment challenges for the dedicated staff.

"A Haven patient will be treated for all physical and mental health deficiencies and trained in a vocation appropriate for his or her abilities. Once a patient is certified well enough to work, citizens or corporations may purchase a work contract for the cost of the patient's debt to society.

"The contract system guarantees former patients food, shelter, and continued treatment as they get back on their feet, minimizing the cost to you, the taxpayer."

In the dark behind the ranked 3-D recorders, Jane smiled to herself. Jane used to work at Haven. She knew all about the forced medication and surgery, and the lax oversight on contract workers. Jane was a Trusted one, a politically and socially tested Citizen, whom Authority charged with keeping its human zoos.

Somewhere in the sprawling Haven complex, a kid was getting bent over his cot and fucked, or written off as "untreatable" if he didn't cooperate. Lucky kids were out in two years with the memories of their stays wiped clean. Those who wouldn't break for Authority were sold off for medical experiments and, rumor had it, spare parts. But the public would see clean, white hallways with cheerful pictures, wide-eyed idealistic staff doctors, and happy, adjusted former patients.

The first time Jane took a boy and a rubber strap into a private treatment room, his tears and red-striped buttocks had aroused her more than anything else in her life except the discovery of masturbation. But after the novelty wore off, each session left her vaguely disappointed, like food without salt. Even her orgasms lacked flavor. Eventually she applied for retraining and took the News tech position.

But the first night she held a hustler pinned against the stairwell wall, she learned the difference between coercion and power. A whipping boy was a professional. He might not enjoy the work, but he had more choice than a citizen in the job lottery. When one of them crawled for her, licked her, held his asscheeks open and begged her to fuck him, she had already penetrated, subverted, and despoiled his will. That was sweeter for her than making a hardened street survivor cry like a baby.

So Jane paid them well and watched for the ones who came back again after they knew what she wanted. Most of those, like the arrogant puppy with the rings and the silver in his hair, disappeared. Now Jane was back in Haven for the day, dogged by a restless arousal that would have dampened her jeans if the hot lights and disinfectant smells had not made her slightly nauseous.

Jane wheeled a recorder into a brightly-painted room where patients were engaged in art therapy. Boys from mid to late teens painted pictures and made sculptures out of small pieces of wood. They were dressed in hospital clothes in bright, primary colors, and their hair was cropped skull-close. There was not a sharp implement to be seen in the room.

"Got anyone who looks alert?" asked the production manager. "We need a kid who doesn't drool or stagger for the interview." One of the staff doctors made a sarcastic comment, and the two started an argument.

Jane leaned back on her stool and watched the aloof reporter watching herself in a monitor. Bored, she turned to the patients. A therapist was teaching two kids to make clay pots. Other patients moved their hands in repetitive gestures, trapped in the spiral of medication. One kid was trying to sleep on the bench. A woman therapist shook him awake. He looked up, cursed at her, and turned over. The woman made a note on a clipboard and trotted out of the room. The patients closest to him edged away.

Jane leaned forward and studied the problem patient. His hair was shaved down to fuzz, but there was still a hint of silver among the black.

"Morgan," she whispered.

He sat up and stared across the room. His eyes didn't focus, but he mouthed her name.

The therapist returned with a large orderly. Morgan fell off the bench and crawled into the corner.

"This is the one that bit me," said the orderly. "I'll take good care of him for you."

The therapist watched, smiling, as the orderly strapped Morgan's wrists behind him and dragged the kid into the hall.

Jane watched him go.

"Let's forget this group," said the production manager. "Got any presentable girls? Audiences like to see girls."

* * *

"Why do people own pets?" asked Jane. "They eat and shit and we clean up after them. What do we get out of it?"

The pet man shut off the radio. A calico kitten was washing herself on the counter. She looked up when he scratched her behind the ears.

"You're talking philosophy, girl. Why don't you ask me how to cure a case of worms?"

"That's not what I need to know."

He screwed up his face with the effort of unaccustomed thought.

"Pets bring us outside of ourselves. We give them what they need, and they give us company."

"They don't talk much," said Jane. "Except for parrots who say hello."

"I don't know about that," he said, scratching the kitten. "I had an old tabby who stood in front of the fridge and said 'mewk!' when she wanted milk."

Jane grinned.

"They talk as much as people, but they don't always use their mouths," he concluded.

"Pets get old. They die."

"That's never a reason not to love someone. I was married for twenty years to a beautiful lady. She got the cholera that summer when they bombed out the sewers. But I wouldn't trade those twenty years for anything, not even hope of heaven. Now I bring home cats, and sometimes a puppy. Keeps me from getting lonely. Makes me care about something."

"Even when they're sick?"

"Even when. Pets make us better people. We have to live up to all that love."

Jane nodded. "Thanks."

"Sure you don't want anything? I got kittens. And a de-scented, neutered skunk. Friendly and clever."

Jane shook her head. "But could you do me a favor? It's kind of odd."

"Anything for you, girl."

Jane pointed to the pegboard wall of leashes and dog collars. "Can I have a leash? The black one?

"Uh, sure." The pet man looked puzzled, but plucked the leash down from the wall with a hook-ended stick.

"Ten fifty."

Jane paid with a credit card.

"See you tomorrow?" asked the man.

"Maybe. I got work to do."

"His name is Morgan Blair-Tremain, of the First Floating Island Tremains," said the contract administrator. "He has no surviving kin but a pair of cousins who are under political asylum on New California. They have other things on their minds. We haven't treated his kind before. Current medical theory indicates that those raised in a climate of..." she wrinkled her nose, "aristocratic privilege adapt poorly to a socialist society. As for his genetic enhancements, well, he's a living violation of the Equal Birth and Opportunity amendment.

"Nevertheless, given his involved treatment and the fine for unlicensed prostitution, his current debt to society is twenty-two percent over average, so we don't foresee a favorable contract buyout for him."

"But you will consider my offer."

The administrator shrugged. "It's not unheard of, but we haven't finished his first course of treatment. We can't guarantee him safe to handle. His vocational skills are minimal. On the other hand, he is fit and healthy, with a good immune spectrum." Perfect transplant material.

She sighed with resignation. "Give me a couple of hours and I'll have a contract ready."

Jane nodded. "Before I sign, I want a few minutes with the merchandise.

The administrator pushed a button. "Is patient 18-11C presentable?" she said into a microphone. "Yes? We have an interested contractor. Please arrange an interview. A private one."

"Thank you," said Jane.

"It's our pleasure, really. Turning out healthy, responsible adults is our mission, but whenever possible, we must recoup the cost of treatment."

Jane arrived at the interview room first. Two large, ugly men arrived five minutes later dragging Morgan between them.

"Want us to sedate him, ma'am?"

"No, thank you."

One of them tossed a shock prod on the table. "Keep this, at least. And yell if you need a hand with him."

Morgan sat in the other chair when they left. His earrings were gone. A lot of him was gone.

Jane flicked the shock prod off the table.

"Morgan, do you know me?"

"Yeah. Jane. You're the cruel woman who made me eat off the floor. Hated it."

He wiped his nose, reminding Jane of that evening on the street.

"I had this cousin named Liandra," he said. "She was tall, gorgeous, strong. Father got fed up with me one day and told her to take over my education. I needed discipline, he said. She used to take me to her room every evening and whip me for every mistake I made that day. I made lots of mistakes. After a while, she would whip me when I was good, and lock me in the closet if I wasn't."

"Did she fuck you?"

"No. But she gave me the rings. She said when I was old enough to marry, she'd make sure my wife had a good tight hold on me. She pierced my cock, too, but that was just before the Revolt. I spent two weeks hiding in small boats with nothing but dirty water, and it got infected. Had to take it out."

"Morgan, why didn't you bottom out to these people? A boy who gets on his knees and sucks cock gets left alone otherwise."

"I'd rather die."

"Cause they're men?"

"No. I've done men, for money. It's cause they're pigs."

"Ah." The desire to touch him was like an itch in Jane's fingers. "I've got an offer for your consideration."

Morgan looked up. "Yeah?"

"I've got money. I was saving it for a stead in the reclaimed territories. It's a lot of money. Enough to buy out your contract. Remember how I did you last month? I'll do that again, every night, as soon as you're strong enough. But it isn't worth it to me unless you consent."

"You going to give me morph?"

"No. I want you to feel it when I hit you."

Morgan was crying without a sound. "I could say yes just to get me out of this place," he whispered. "That's not consent."

"It's not, but I know you wouldn't do that, any more than you would kneel and suck here."

"I hate you."

"Yes or no, Morgan."

"Yes."

"I didn't hear you. Louder."

"Yes, Jane. Take me home."

* * *

Jane took Morgan home in a taxi and carried him up the stairs. He was too weak even to crawl, so she stripped them both and got him into the shower. Their wet skins sliding together in the water should have been erotic. Instead Jane dried him off, rolled out the futon, and got some rope.

"What are you doing?" Morgan asked when she began trussing him to the futon.

"I know what drugs they gave you. They sent us home with a month's supply. But I won't give you morph, and I won't have you addicted to something that isn't even fun. I want you secure before you start to hallucinate."

"I won't hallucinate."

But Morgan did, all night, screaming and sweating and pissing himself, and biting Jane once when she got too close. Jane sat watching him until they both fell asleep near dawn.

The leash lay in a pile at the foot of the futon. Morgan examined it when Jane was gone at work. The black leather handle felt new and crisp, and the chain ran though his fingers until he held the snap at the end. He knew what it was for, but he pretended he didn't. Jane hadn't used him since she brought him home.

Jane waited. And the longer she waited, Morgan knew, the harder she'd use him when he was ready. So he ignored the leash until long after he was well and strong. And Jane ignored him, except to feed him from a plate on the floor and toss him a blanket when he went to sleep at her feet.

Until the night when she was reading on the couch, and Morgan couldn't stand it anymore. He took off his clothes (her clothes, jeans cut down to size) and folded them in a pile. The leash snapped around his neck. Jane didn't look up. Morgan knelt wondering what he should do next. Then he took the handle in his teeth and crawled to her.

Jane lay down the book, took the handle from him, and pulled until the chain tightened.

Morgan looked up. "Take what you paid for. Bitch."

Jane tied the leash to a couch leg and got the flail out of the drawer. Morgan covered his face with his arms and listened to his heart pound. His cock was already stirring.

The first blow across his back gave him such a release that he screamed. An hour later when his ribs and thighs were all colored with welts and he had near-choked himself with the leash, and come, twice, without permission, he was begging and praying to his goddess to send him to the hell where he belonged.

Jane shoved him down on his belly and put a foot between his shoulder blades while she got something from the drawer. Kneeling between his thighs, she spread him wider while she poured cold lube into her hand.

Morgan wailed and cringed when he felt the first chill touch between his red-striped cheeks. Jane yanked on his leash while she stroked his tight hole open with one finger, then let him breathe as she took him. His whole body went slack when she found his prostate with two fingers. Morgan pushed back against the penetration like a queen cat in heat.

Jane reached under him to pinch a ringless nipple.

"You're going to take me past the knuckles by next week, hear me?"

No answer.

Jane twisted his nipple.

"Yes, Jane!"

She wiggled her fingers. His body tensed, hips fighting to pump against her impaling hand. Jane tightened up the leash again and he came, his face near as purple as his cock.

Jane pulled her hand out and wiped it on a towel. Morgan lay flat, sucking air, in a puddle of sweat and come.

"Get up and do something useful with your mouth."

Morgan climbed to his knees and put his head under the skirt of Jane's kimono. Her cunt was wet, unshaven. He licked the thin outer lips and the fold of inner lip that poked out between them. Opening her with his tongue, he found the little hood of flesh that hid her clitoris, the deep hole of her cunt, and all the places between. Each touch made her move, swear, claw at his head. She reached down and shoved his face against her so that he was grinding his tongue right against her clit. She came. Morgan shifted to follow her as she convulsed, until Jane reached down and slapped him so hard that he fell.

Jane stretched and sighed. Morgan waited for a word of praise. When none came, he pressed his lips against her instep, once, and started to back away. Jane tugged on the leash. Morgan almost panicked when she took his chin in her hand.

But it was only for a kiss.

Morgan opened his mouth for Jane and let her do what she wanted to him, went limp when she bit his throat, and whimpered when she took him in her arms. Pleasure weakened him and made her strong.

"Get clean," she whispered, unsnapping the leash.

Morgan crawled off to the bathroom. When he returned several minutes later, soaped and rinsed, Jane had the futon unrolled on the floor. Morgan went to lie down at the food of the bed.

"No," said Jane. "In the bed with me."

"You honor me." He kissed her foot once more, he who had been a prince in a vanished land.

They lay down together for the first time in dark and in warmth.

"I love you, Jane," he whispered. "I love you."

Agent of the Free

Neal Harkness

I was not always as I am now, a time-serving bureaucrat in a forgotten colonial outpost. When the great events of our time were shaping the future of the world, I was at the center of the maelstrom. I served with honor throughout the war, winning the Order of Valor at the Battle of Smolnica, accorded more honors for my leadership during the Great Winter Offensive. I was proud to represent the forces of freedom in the battle against the ideologies of tyranny. I tell these things not to exalt myself, except in that so doing I might illustrate how far from grace the events of the war's chaotic aftermath caused me to fall.

The occupied territories were a sea of humanity. In the spring following the collapse of the Black Army, and the capitulation of its weaker allies, civilian refugees, repatriated prisoners of war, displaced persons of every imaginable description clogged the roads, sleeping in the barren fields and burnt out buildings of the defeated nation, often resorting to pillage and riot in the depths of their desperation.

It was to impose some measure of control on this seemingly overwhelming situation that the high command instituted the Strategic Camp System, to which I was assigned. It was with great reluctance that I accepted this new posting, but as was pointed out to me by my superiors, my combat skills were no longer in great demand. I supervised the mustering out of my faithful veteran troops, and reported, with no great enthusiasm, to the ironically named Camp Freedom.

The Strategic Camps were designed to be vast clearing houses of humanity, their primary purpose to sort the teeming throngs, and facilitate their relocation to their various appropriate destinations. This task, although formidable, quickly became a relatively simple bureaucratic routine, and required little of my time as Camp Commander.

It was the Strategic Camps secondary purpose that kept me occupied. In addition to the masses of innocent victims of war, the hordes which passed through the system contained other elements. Escaped mental patients and common criminals were the least of them. There were monsters on the loose that spring. The government and the Black Army had committed a multitude of atrocities, against their own people as well as in the lands they conquered. The exposition and detention of war criminals for trial was my most important personal duty, one which I freely admit I relished. Unfortunately, it necessitated an unsavory procedure, the detention of witnesses, who were more often than not, victims themselves of terrible crimes. My heart yearned to send these witnesses on their way to rebuilding their lives, but in that chaotic climate there was no way to assure that we would be able to retrieve them when the time came for their testimony.

Camp Freedom was situated near the important southern junctions, in an area that had harbored a number of major government facilities. One of the most notorious of these was the mildly named Institute for Behavioral Studies. We had heard during the war horrendous stories of the inhuman experiments that went on there, but they were in many cases so far beyond the realm of human decency that I had considered them propaganda, designed to instill our troops with loathing for the enemy. I learned the awful truth shortly after assuming command, in a briefing by my executive officer,

Captain Nevis, who had supervised the groundwork in the establishment of the camp.

The briefing took place in my private quarters, as my command office was not yet operational.

"I assure you Col. Straiton, the stories you've heard about the IBS are the tip of the iceberg." He told me, while rifling through a thick file of documents. "Neurological reprogramming, terrible experiments with aversion training, fetish implantation, purely speculative brain surgery..."

"Fetish implantation? I don't understand what you mean by that, Captain."

Nevis blushed. "Well, sir, they, it's hard for me to discuss this sir, I'm a religious man. They—"

"Take your time, Captain."

He spoke in a rush. "They took preadolescent children and used sophisticated conditioning techniques to ensure that they would develop certain, certain, well, strange sexual proclivities sir."

"They what? Why would they do that—it's just sick."

"I certainly concur, sir. According to documents we secured at the institute, they reasoned that if they could induce fetishistic desires into the general population they could, by withholding or supplying the means to indulge those desires they could better control the populace."

"That's absurd. Could such a scheme possibly work?"

"Well, sir, although they seem to have had some success with individuals in the program, they never got past the experimental stage."

I pondered Captain Nevis' information. I had been brought up in the military tradition of family, honor, discipline. Sexual depravity was beyond my purview.

"Do we have any of these so-called doctors in custody Captain?"

"No sir, the Intelligence Service is investigating reports that they were all killed when the facility was bombed in February."

"And the children?"

"Well, they aren't children any more sir, this program had gone on for some time. The five we have here are all in their early twenties."

"And what—ahem—what is wrong with the ones we have?"

Captain Nevis clearly was as embarrassed to have to answer the question as I was to ask it.

"Two of them, Svor and Polepy, are apparently, er, interested in articles of clothing made of rubber. The Knin woman is sexually aroused by receiving enemas and Zebrak, by women's feet."

"But how could the government control things like enemas and feet."

He looked at me as he would a slow student. "They were just trying to implant the, I guess you would say 'normal' fetishes, sir. If they were successful in mastering the technique, then they would have used it to make the people crave some item or service that only the government could supply."

"I see. And the fifth subject?"

"The fifth subject is the most troubling case of all. It seems the young woman, a Miss Oleska, receives sexual gratification from being subjected to various forms of corporal punishment. Whipping, flogging and such."

"My God! They could create a whole population of willing slaves!"

"Ironically, sir, one of the things they discovered, according to their files, was that the subjects implanted with a desire for punishment sought it out, and were therefore more rebellious than the others."

"Thank God we freed these people from such madness."

We moved on to other topics, but the plight of the victims of such a fiendish plot continued to disturb me. I resolved to devote particular attention to the rehabilitation of these poor souls, but in the days following my briefing with Captain Nevis, a large number of prisoners, members of the infamous Black Terror Battalion, were delivered to the camp for processing, and were by necessity, my higher priority.

I did manage to find some opportunity, in the few quiet evening hours after my daily duties had been discharged, to peruse the files on the Institute victims. The foot and rubber fetishists baffled me, and I was repelled when I read the file on Miss Knin, the enema practitioner. The file on Miss Oleska, however, was strangely compelling. I was drawn to open it nightly, trying to convince myself that it was the single haunting picture of the young woman, Staya Oleska, contained within, that drew me back. It was a head and shoulders shot, taken immediately after the liberation of the Institute. Yet, despite what must have been extremely traumatic circumstances, she had faced the camera with a confidence, one might even say a haughtiness, that was entirely at odds with the history of degradation the file's documents described. She did not possess the broad features and dull expression so common among the women of her people. Her features were sharp, her dark eyes piercing, even in the deficient field photograph. Those eyes pulled mine back to them again and again. Despite my better judgment, I knew that I would have to meet Miss Oleska, or be haunted by her.

My opportunity came shortly. The flow into the camp was waning, and at last I reached the point where I could control my own schedule. I ordered Captain Nevis to arrange an inspection of the Special Detainees Quarters, where Miss Oleska, and her compatriots were housed.

The inspection took place on a blistering hot July morning. The Special Detainees Quarters were segregated from the main body of the camp, located in a requisitioned riding school . The stables had been converted into housing for the detainees, while the century-old school itself had been appropriated for office space by the unit's staff. Captain Nevis and I entered the school and met with Major Crimond, the Intelligence Service officer who, while nominally under my command, ran his sector of the camp as a personal fiefdom.

I listened with feigned patience as Major Crimond, in between puffs on his ever present cigar, explained the purpose of the Special Detainees Quarters. Its occupants were individuals whose legal status was in doubt. The largest contingent in the unit was comprised of industrialists and profiteers who had supplied the enemy war machine. Our government had yet to determine whether to hold these individuals culpable for War Crimes or not, therefore they could neither be released, nor incarcerated in the stockade. The quarters also housed a number of other questionable types, including several family members of high ranking government officials. I asked Major Crimond why the victims of the fetish experiments had been relegated to his care.

"Primarily because we have yet to apprehend any of the Institute staff, sir, and if and when we do, we will need the testimony of these individuals in their trials."

"But we have many similar cases in the main camp, Major, why are these people segregated?"

"Well, sir, they are known perverts. And there is some feeling in the Intelligence Service that they are not so much victims as they are co-conspirators."

"I don't believe that view stands up very well, Major."

"Then sir, I suggest you come with me."

He led us out of the school and back to the stables. We entered what must have once been the stable keeper's quarters, now the duty room. A pair of regulation issue cots stood to our right as we entered, while a heavy antique desk guarded a door opposite the outside entrance. A young corporal was the only personnel on duty. He snapped to attention as we entered.

"At ease, son," Major Crimond said. "Corporal, please present detainees Zebrak and Oleska for interview."

"Yes sir." He spun on his heels and dashed from the room. We waited in awkward silence for his return. He was back momentarily.

"Detainees Zebrak and Oleska, present for interview," he reported, his voice cracking nervously. A short, belligerent looking young man, whom I recognized as Zebrak, the foot fetishist, followed him into the room. Behind Zebrak strode Miss Oleska. As she entered the room she gazed at us disdainfully. Major Crimond dismissed the young Corporal and he left the room. When the door had shut behind him, Miss Oleska slouched against it, her arms crossed over her chest in a pose of studied indifference. Her every movement was riveting. I had seen more beautiful women, but none who radiated as much sensuality. I struggled to maintain my professional bearing.

"Captain Nevis" I muttered, "Perhaps you could serve as translator..."

"We need no translator, Colonel" Zebrak snapped, his face flushed," We were raised with the finest of continental educations. I, myself speak four languages fluently. Fortunately so, since we have no one else to speak for us...."

"Yes, we all know how well your masters treated you," Major Crimond sneered.

"Colonel, we have committed no crime, yet we are held here against our wills. You claim to be our liberators, yet you violate every article of war by holding us political prisoners..."

"How dare you scum talk to us about the articles of war!" Major Crimond exploded.

"At ease, Major." I commanded him. He glared at me mutinously. "I'd like to hear what these people have to say. Surely there's no harm in that."

"No sir," he scowled. "However sir, let me point out that his very words indict him. Please note his immediate defense of his slave masters."

"So noted, Major."

Zebrak's countenance seemed to soften. "Thank you, Colonel. Allow me to explain our position. We were orphans, wards of the state. We were raised well at the Institute, we knew nothing of the many atrocities your people say took place there. As to our unusual proclivities, does it matter how we came by them? We are who we are, Colonel, even as you are. It is our fate, each of us, to be what life has made us."

Crimond scoffed at Zebrak's remarks, but I found them troubling. Miss Oleska had yet to speak. I was anxious to hear her voice.

"Young lady, please, do you have anything you wish to tell me."

Those dark eyes met mine, and held them. "I know the secrets of my own soul, Colonel. Can you say the same?"

"I don't understand, what do you mean?"

She had gone mute, staring at my officers and myself with thinly disguised contempt.

"All right, Major, you can have these detainees returned to their quarters now." It was with great difficulty that I broke from her gaze and turned away. We completed the inspection hastily, as the rising heat of the day made the stable area unbearably hot. I thought of Miss Oleska sweltering in that heat, and images of her naked sweating flesh crept into my mind. I shook them off, and continued with my duties, but thoughts of her remained barely suppressed.

That night I could not sleep. My imagination ran wild with scenarios of Staya Oleska bound, shackled, restrained in myriad ways. Shadowy figures moved through my mind, brandishing whips, leather straps, devices only half formed in my waking dream. At the center of it all, the beautiful Staya, her liquid eyes imprecating, "Do you know the secrets of your soul, Colonel?"

I rose from my cot. Buried deep in my foot locker was the parade dress uniform I had not had occasion to wear in many months. I rummaged through the locker and found it. With it was stored the object I sought, my ornamental riding crop. I looked at the crop as if it were the first time I'd seen it. It seemed to possess a presence I had never noted before. I slapped it against my palm, trying to imagine how one could find its sting pleasurable. I struck again, imagining Staya writhing beneath the blow. I was overcome with desire, and for the first time in many years, succumbed to the vice of self-gratification.

All through the following day, as I performed my routine duties, the notion that I should pay a private visit to Staya grew in resolve. My the end of my watch I had reconciled myself to indulging this bizarre, unexpected compulsion. I checked the duty roster, and assured myself that Major Crimond would be elsewhere that evening. Beyond making sure of avoiding the surly intelligence officer, I had formulated no specific plan.

I attired myself in my dress uniform, which I had nonchalantly ordered Captain Nevis to have ironed earlier in the day. I had always thought I looked quite dashing in it. I waited until the camp had settled down for the night, then I tucked the leather crop under my arm, and resolutely made my way to the Special Detainees Quarters.

The same young corporal was on duty. I ordered him to bring Detainee Oleska to the Duty Room. I had rehearsed a dozen unsatisfactory cover stories, but he responded as if my request was the most natural thing in the world. He returned quickly, the woman behind him. As she entered the room he stepped back through the door, shutting it behind him.

"Good evening, Miss Oleska," I began, nervously, "I was thinking about..."

"I'm sure I am aware of what you have been thinking about, my Colonel." Her accent was intoxicating. "I have known a few or so men such as yourself. You are more appealing to me than most."

I stumbled for a reply. She pulled her regulation gray shift over her head.

"Miss Oleska..."

"Staya, I am Staya. And you I call Master."

I felt myself blush. "No, no, Staya, I..."

"You do not desire to use me as you know I enjoy to be used, my Colonel? Is that not why you have come to me tonight, bringing with you your own—what would you say—instrument?"

She pulled the riding crop from beneath my arm. She examined it closely, flexed it, whipped the air with it. As she handed it back to me, she gave a nod of approval.

"It is a very elegant instrument, my Colonel. I would be honored to have a demonstration as to its use."

I stood speechless as she removed her brassiere and panties. She was slender, but not emaciated as were most of her country women in that period. They had taken very good care of her at the Institute.

She crossed the room to me, and pressed her body against me. I looked deeply into her eyes, and succumbed to the desire to kiss her. Her lips were cool and moist and parted ever so slightly against mine. I put my arms around her and pulled her tight against me, kissing her harder. She ran her tongue across my lips and then under my chin, along my jaw line. It sent a shiver of pleasure down my spine. She gently tongued my ear.

"Punish me." she whispered.

I removed her to arms length. Grasping her shoulders, I said "There are other ways to be with a man Staya..."

"You did not come here as a liberator, my Colonel." she replied, with steel in her eyes. "You came to our country to master us. All your talk of freedom masks your dark desires. The Institute made me desire the feel of the whip, my Colonel, but what made you desire to wield it?"

I pushed her away from me. She staggered back against the desk, knocking a stack of papers to the floor.

"Lay across that desk." I told her, a quiver in my voice.

"Is that how you command your troops, my Colonel?" She laughed.

"Get over that desk!" I ordered her with authority. She responded immediately, stretching across the desk and gripping it's far edge. Her toes grazed the floor. The mound of her vagina was visible, embarrassing me. I ran my hand over the cool, smooth flesh of her bottom and felt my desire for her rise. I lined up the crop across the center of her buttocks, pulled it back, and snapped it down. The sound seemed like an explosion to me, but Staya laughed.

"You will have to do much better than that, my Colonel."

I brought it down again, harder, and heard her gasp. The mark of the crop was crimson across her pale flesh, and the sight of it thrilled me. Again I struck her, and again. She began to writhe beneath the blows in a sensuous dance. I covered every portion of her buttocks with blows, the crop singing in my hand. I soon grew confident in its use and playfully painted patterns in red on Staya's undulating bottom. No matter how hard I struck, she seemed to hunger for more, rising off the desk to meet my strokes.The reddest areas of her bottom became tinged with blue. I must have put the crop to her more than one hundred times when I saw the thin line of blood across her buttocks. I dropped my arm to my side, exhausted.

Staya reached between her legs and fondled her vagina. "Take me, Master, please take me."

I dropped the crop, unbuckled my belt and lowered my pants and undershorts. My penis was rigid. I positioned myself behind her, and entered her with one motion. Her tortured flesh was hot against my loins. I thrust into her relentlessly, hard enough to make the desk move. Staya realized a shuddering climax, and almost immediately afterward, I ejaculated inside her.

I stepped back, attempting to regain control of my breath. In an instant Staya was on her knees in front of me, engulfing my member with her mouth. It had begun to soften, but her incessant mouth play quickly reinvigorated it. She picked up the crop from the floor and handed it to me. I did not understand what she wanted me to do. She crossed the room on her knees and sprawled on one of the narrow cots, beckoning me to come to her.

I stood over her and watched as she caressed her own breasts. I began to gently tap them with the crop, and she squirmed with pleasure. I slapped them harder, and her ardor increased.

"Take your hands away," I commanded. She placed one hand behind her head, the other went between her legs. I straddled the cot and alternately cropped her breasts until they grew florid. I moved further up the cot and squeezed my penis between them. Staya ran her tongue around its head and lightly nibbled it. I leaned forward, and plunged deep into her mouth. Without a conscious intent to do so, I was soon ramming myself into her face as arduously as I had into her vagina. She gripped my buttocks and held me to her, even as the force of my thrusts made her gag. In a matter of moments I achieved another orgasm. I felt a stab of shame when I saw my semen on her face, and was shocked to see her wipe it off with her fingers, and then lick them clean.

I fell on to the opposite cot, my head spinning. Staya knelt next to me, her head resting on my chest.

"I've never done anything like that before." I panted.

"I know, my Colonel, but you did very well just the same."

"Thank goodness the Corporal didn't come back in."

"He is used to the routine, my Colonel."

"What do you mean, routine?" I sat up on the cot and took her by the shoulders.

"You did not think you were the first officer in the camp to visit me, did you? Did you not arrange this evening with Major Crimond?"

I raised my hand to slap her, but gained control of myself in time to avoid doing so. To strike her in anger would invalidate everything that had happened between us to a greater extend than the knowledge that she had been with Crimond ever could.

I pulled her to me, and hugged her tightly. She kissed my cheek, then stood and retrieved her clothing. I watched her dress with a profound sadness. I knew I would not come to her again.

When she had dressed she kissed me again and crossed to the door. She started to open it, then turned to me.

"I am what I am, my Colonel, perhaps if I had never been at the Institute I would still be as I am. It does not matter. In my heart I am free to do as I wish, even in your prison."

She shut the door softly behind her. I stared at the place where she had stood, until I realized that the Corporal would soon be returning. I had just gotten my uniform reassembled when he sheepishly scratched at the door. I turned the Duty Room back over to him, and returned to my quarters.

I awoke the next morning with mixed feelings of elation and guilt. I carried this tangle of emotions with me throughout the day, until my mid afternoon briefing with Captain Nevis.

After tediously appraising me of the state of the Camp's daily minutiae, the endless supply requisitions, personnel assignments and detainee complaints, Nevis informed me that he had received a communique from the Intelligence Service on the subject of The Institute for Behavioral Studies. After exhaustive investigation it had been determined that all personnel responsible for criminal acts at the Institute had been killed in the final days of the war.

"So there is no longer any reason to hold the detainees from the Institute, is there?" I asked Nevis.

"None that I know of, Sir." he replied. I dismissed him for the day, and immediately called Crimond. His executive officer answered the telephone, and I was left waiting a full five minutes before Crimond came on the line.

"Yes, sir," he answered at last, "What can I do for you, Colonel Straiton?"

"I've just received word from your people that the investigation into the Institute is closed. I'll send someone over in the morning to take care of integrating those detainees into the general population."

"I'm afraid you can't do that sir."

"What do you mean, I can't do that? There is no longer any reason to hold those people."

"Yes there is sir. They are degenerates, Colonel, perverts of the sickest kind. The Intelligence Service has determined that it would be in the best interest of all involved if we hold all Institute personnel until proper methods of therapy are developed to cure them of their proclivities. Sir."

"That's ridiculous," I sputtered, "I want those detainee..." The line was dead.

I heard Captain Nevis talking in the anteroom. I stuck my head out the door. He was flirting with one of the young women from the secretarial pool. I quietly closed the door, and waited until they had both left. In Nevis' desk drawer I found the file containing blank Detainee Release forms. I quickly filled them out with fictitious names and destinations, and slipped them into my jacket pocket. I then attended evening mess as per my usual routine.

When I finished my meal I crossed the camp to the Special Detainees Quarters. I lingered outside the grounds until I was certain that Crimond and his Officers had departed for the evening, then I entered the compound.

The Corporal snapped to attention as I entered.

"At ease, Corporal. I think you know why I'm here." I winked at him.

"Um, yes sir, you want me to get Detainee Oleska?"

"Yes. And while you're at it, bring Detainee Zebrak and the others too, all the Institute detainees."

His eyes grew wide. Perhaps he tried to envision some bizarre orgy that was just beyond the range of his conception. He swallowed hard, and scampered from the room.

It was a full ten minutes before the Detainees entered, and I was growing concerned that I was too late. At last they arrived, the feisty Zebrak in the lead.

"What do you disturb us now for, Colonel Straiton? Isn't it enough..."

"You're free to go." I interrupted him. "Here are your papers."

He took the release forms and studied them suspiciously.

"But Colonel, I don't understand..."

"You don't have to understand, Zebrak, just go. Walk all night, then get off the main roads. Lose yourselves among the masses."

He handed the forms to the other detainees. I watched him give one to Staya. She looked up and our eyes met.

Zebrak had become giddy with excitement, pumping my hand and slapping my back. I needed all my will power to take my eyes from Staya's.

"Go, Zebrak, lead the others out of here. Now."

He ushered Svor, Polepy and Knin out of the building. He took Staya's arm, but she shook him off. He shrugged and went out.

"You give us this freedom because of last night, my Colonel?"

"No, Staya. I'm doing it because it's the right thing to do. We have no right to judge you."

She kissed me on the cheek, then turned away. "Tonight, you do come as my liberator," she said as she disappeared into the night.

I sat down behind the desk and smoked one of Crimond's cigars. It was nearly dawn before the Corporal got up the nerve to peek into the room. By that time I was sound asleep in my own bunk, and Staya and her fellows were miles from the camp.

When Major Crimond found out what I had done he filed charges against me, and I had to stand before a full court-martial. The more serious charges were mysteriously dropped, perhaps when Crimond realized that I might be able to expose his trysts with Staya, but I was convicted of dereliction of duty, and demoted to the rank of Captain. My subsequent military career has consisted of a procession of unremarkable and meaningless postings. It is my belief that had I not been earlier recognized for my achievement on the battlefield I would have been drummed out of the service. Perhaps that would have been better.

I think of Staya often. All the nights here are hot like that July night was hot, and the local prostitutes are willing to indulge my peculiar tastes. But none of them have those haunting eyes.

I am not bitter. I am not regretful. I have my memories of the war, of great deeds accomplished, of battles won, and honors reaped. I have the knowledge that I did my best for the forsaken masses I was briefly granted the power to help. I have always conducted myself with the honor expected of an agent of the free.

And I know the secrets of my own soul.

Training A Priestess

Andrea J. Horlick

"I love you, my lord," I said, almost whispering. Not the most incongruous thing I might have said, considering he was lying beneath me on the pallet, his cock roused, waiting for me to lower myself. But his eyes were closed, his face immobile. He gave no sign of hearing, or of caring if he had. Then his long-fingered, large-knuckled hands came up and rested on my hips. I felt my usual shudder, half desire, half fear. I obeyed the wordless command.

He always ordered me in silence, just a touch, a glance, a gesture. Sometimes I thought it would have been thus even without his powers. That the connection between us would have been there even were he an ordinary man and I not a seeker of secrets. That my body would have submitted to him even if my soul had not.

He let me do all the work. He might as well have been a marble statue under me, as smooth, as hard, as cold. My head was back, the ends of my unbound hair brushing against his thighs. Sweat trickled down my temples. My lip was between my teeth. The pain and pleasure were about equal.

Then his left hand came off my hip and onto my breast. He seized my nipple between his knuckles and pressed. Hard. Harder. In the instant before my brain said don't make a sound, I let out a low moan. *Take it; the pain will but increase your powers.* I didn't quite know whether he was speaking in my mind or whether I was just remembering past lessons. I bit my lip with more force and tasted the blood.

I opened my eyes again and looked down. The corners of his mouth were turning up just a little. He kept pinching for another minute, then moved his hand back down to my flank and took control. He brought me down harder, faster. He was nearing climax, then. He might be angry with me for not noticing. Keep focused. It was the hardest thing for me to learn.

When he finally opened his eyes, though, I could discern no anger in his expression. None of that cold fury that caused my gut to knot. Not even displeasure, which could be bad enough at times. He studied my face, which was flushed with the sex and slightly wet with tears. A thin trickle of blood ran down from my lower lip and he pulled me closer and licked it away tenderly.

"I was too easy on you tonight by far," he said. "You may count it a blessing when I'm merciful, but only in the short run. If you truly want the power, if you truly wish to learn, my mercy will do you no good."

"Yes, my lord." I closed my eyes again. It was harder for him to read my thoughts when my eyes were closed, when he couldn't look past my pupils into my brain. Harder, but not impossible.

You fear the power. Not what you will have to undergo to obtain it, not the pain of your training. You long for and fear the tests in equal measure, but the power itself terrifies you.

"Yes, my lord," I said again. Lying was both foolish and futile. He rolled us over and pulled out of me, but stayed on top, pinning me to the thin feather mattress, and gently pushed my hair out of my eyes.

"You must make the decision and soon," he said aloud. "Whether you truly want the knowledge. The magik. Or whether all you really want is me."

I shuddered again. Because if all I truly wanted was him, I could never attain my desire. Priests only taught and disciplined initiates. Ordinary women were as nothing to them.

I felt some shame when I joined him in his workroom the next morning. I had given him cause to doubt me, cause to think of me as just some silly woman dabbling in things that were beyond her. But when he looked up from the herbs he was crushing, shaking his long, straight hair back from the beautiful bones of his face, he favored me with a smile. *Don't disparage yourself, Tai. Would a second-degree high priest waste his time on a silly woman?*

He set me to work polishing his silver instruments. It was about all I was good for as yet. Occasionally he would make some comment about what he was doing, either mentally or out loud, but the greater part of my training was just to be next to him, soaking up the power radiating from him. My first month with him, my head and eyes had ached within minutes of being in his presence. But after he was sure of my promise and had taken my virgin's blood, that sickness had eased. Now my awareness of his power was just a quiet humming in my veins. Now I was seriously considering accepting that power for my own. I put down my polishing cloth.

"Only four more weeks," he said. "Four more weeks and I'll pierce your nipples and thread through the chain. Then your only way out will be death, Tai."

"I know, my lord." He was done with his infusion and I heeded his signal to take the vessel from him. I stoppered it carefully with a cork and placed it on the shelf among the other bottles. I knew what that one was for. I only hoped that if I ever saw him use it, it wouldn't be on me.

We'll meditate, then I will test you.

His altar was in the next room, all smooth, sinuous curves of black and white marble. I dropped to my knees as soon as we entered, thinking, not for the first time, how perfectly he melded with the Old Things. He said the chants and I followed, moving my lips but not making a sound. I wasn't yet ready to say the words. I could feel the rush of the power entering him, growing, pulsating. Keep focused. If I kept focused, I should be able to feel my own power increasing, if only incrementally.

The air was thick now, almost visible. I raised my eyes to him, only for a moment. The words of the chant were still coming from him, but his lips were no longer moving. His skin was glowing. Keep focused. I tried to imagine my own skin looking like that, my face in the ecstatic lines of a priest. I tried to find the spark of power inside and make it grow. I trained my sense-memory on the pain-pleasure of the night before, trying to remember when my mind and body had shifted and blended.

Suddenly the thickness of the air rushed out like a vacuum. He was cross-legged in front of me, studying my face once again. "You are ready, Tai?" he said. Or perhaps, "You are ready."

He removed four silver cubes from his pocket and placed them side by side on the altar. *Move them.*

I squeezed shut my eyes. Sense-memory. The glow of power. The cubes were on the inside of my eyelids, weighty in my outstretched hands. Move them. Move them.

With my eyes still tightly closed, I heard rather than saw the first cube go sliding across the smooth marble. My brow was damp with beads of sweat and my hands were beginning to tremble. Then the sweet sound of the second cube following the first. Keep focused. I searched myself for that spark of power as my arms and legs began to shake. Sense-memory. Melting. Glowing. There was nothing left. I fell forward onto my face against the cold stone of the floor.

When I dared to open my eyes, he was still cross-legged in front of me. His face was grave, sorrowful. The two recalcitrant cubes remained on the altar behind his shoulder, mocking me. "I was correct. I was far too easy on you last night. I'm failing in my duty." He placed an image in my mind and the blood rushed from my face.

"Yes, my lord."

It was considered important, nay, crucial, for an initiate to face his or her fears. Even the lower priests, the eighth- and ninth-degree ones, who weren't so facile at reading thoughts and probing minds, had ways of learning just what those deepest fears were. For him it was an effortless thing.

And so I found myself bound on his pallet that night, cold and trembly and cursing my own weakness. I knew my foolishness; he could have made far stronger chains with his mind than these flimsy ropes that tied my wrists. But being restrained, being helpless, had always caused my gorge to rise.

His sharp-boned face was impassive. He played with his silver dagger, looked at my belly. I'd seen men planning to gut a rabbit looking like that. *Use that fear. Turn it into power.* He placed the point of the knife below my left breast and pressed until it just scored my skin. I fought the desire to pull away. There was nowhere for me to go and if I flinched, I might cause him to damage me. He was a second-degree high priest. His control was more than perfect.

He pulled the knife down very, very slowly, down my rib cage, my belly, into my pubic hair. It left just the thinnest cut, a long bleeding scratch that barely stung. My lids were across my eyes, but I could see what he was doing. When I realized it, I felt a surge, a thrill. The first time for that. Focus. He moved the dagger again, lower.

The fear, the vague pain, and the power were all melding and building. Focus. The instant the knife reached my genitals, I looked into his cruel, pleased face without opening my eyes. All at once, I came. The ropes burst from my wrists.

Very good, Tai. Very good. He threw the knife hard into the plaster wall and bent his head to suck the blood off me.

"I love you, my lord," I murmured.

He rewarded me the next few days. I was allowed to hold open his Book, to anoint his body with the proper oils before a sacrifice, to fellate him on the cool stone floor and swallow down his seed, so full of power and life-force it burned all the way down my throat. And perhaps I grew too confident, for on the morning of the fourth day, he called me to the workroom, called me with his mind, and bade me to kneel down, hands behind my back, forehead against the floor.

You will not speak today. You will go about your duties in complete and perfect silence, without a word, without a sound. As the sun begins to set, you will come to my chamber and kneel as you are now. I will ask you one question and you will answer it.

I was not so unwise as to willfully disobey him, but the desire to ask was so overwhelming I had to bite hard into my tongue to keep quiet.

He stepped closer to me and caressed the side of my cheek with his foot. "Of course I'll tell you what the question is to be," he said aloud. I could picture the cold smile on his exquisite face. "You will need time to think of the proper response."

I will ask you how I should discipline you tonight, what your next ordeal is to be. What level of pain and fear is necessary to further expand your mind and soul.

He ordered me then to go and clean his altar room, to scrub the blood from the marble, spread the aromatic herbs, and replenish the candles. My legs were shaking so much I could barely rise from my cramped position.

I was at the doorway when he stopped me. "I know I can trust you, Tai," he said, "not to be too easy on yourself."

I spent the rest of the day in a haze of apprehension and anticipation. At noon hour I sat in the common room at a table with the other initiates, unable—and unwilling at any rate—to participate in the conversation. I sipped the coolish water from my wooden cup but left my bowl untouched. My belly rebelled at the very thought of food.

Then suddenly he was behind me. I felt the rush of power from him before he was even close enough to touch me.

There's a time for fasting, Tai, and a time when one must eat to keep up one's strength. He held a thick chunk of bread soaked in wild honey to my lips and fed it to me, a bite at a time. When it was gone, he had me suck all traces of the stickiness from his fingers.

"Come. I have more work for you." I felt the awed and envious glances of the other initiates on my back as he led me out.

A couple of hours before dusk, he set me a few more simple tasks and left me alone. He was doing me a great honor, I knew, allowing me to offer up my agony freely. As I polished a few of his instruments and swept out the room, I thought about what I would say when he asked the question. Not that I was unsure of what my answer would be. I just wanted to give it elegantly, no hesitations, no trembling in my voice. I wanted, more than anything, to make him proud of me.

* * *

He was cross-legged on his pallet when I entered, no longer meditating, but with the glow on his skin and the thickness in the air that meant he had been. I assumed my position and waited. It was some minutes before he decided to take notice of me.

"What shall I do to you, then? Speak now, Tai." *You may look at me as you answer.*

I pulled myself into a full kneeling position and raised my eyes to the region of his mouth. He pressed his lips together and reached out to push my chin up another inch until our eyes locked. "My lord," I said, fighting to keep my voice pitched low and steady. "You have never beaten me. Please, tonight, whip me. Help me conquer that pain."

His lips twitched into half a smile and he removed something from beneath the pallet. A switch. The perfect switch, two and a half feet long, thin and flexible and strong. I wondered if he had gone out of the temple grounds and into the forest that afternoon to cut it, or whether he had just conjured it. And just the one switch, no extras in case it snapped as he flogged me. It was as if he knew he could whip me with it all night and it would never break.

He tucked it under his arm and came off the mattress to help me to my feet. With great gentleness he unfastened my robe and pushed it off my shoulders. He bent me across the pallet, my buttocks and thighs at just the angle he wanted.

No bonds this time. Answering my thought. *You will keep yourself still. Flow into the pain, Tai. Accept it.*

"Yes, my lord."

No. No more talking.

He took one more thing from beneath the pallet. A gag. He placed it into my mouth and fastened it carefully underneath my hair. "A little mercy for you. Now you need concentrate only on not moving, not on your silence."

I waited for him to begin, my eyes closed against the rough blanket, sweat forming already on my naked body in the coolness of the room, every sense heightened with dread and longing. I could almost hear it as he stepped back from me and flexed the switch between his hands.

Then he started. Lightly at first, mild, stinging blows that landed right where my buttocks and thighs joined. But soon the strokes increased in intensity, cutting into my tender skin, raising hot welts wherever the switch touched. I tried to count the strokes in an attempt to master the pain, but as the number approached a hundred, the pain was mastering me.

I bit against my gag and the blanket beneath my cheek grew damp. Finally, I began to flinch ever so slightly at each blow. He reached out with his mind and steadied me.

Don't struggle. Focus. He held my mind with his, even as he continued to whip me, and I felt his power merging with the beginnings of my own. I found that place in me that was beyond pain. The burning of my lacerated skin melded into sweet pleasure, and as he pulled out of my mind, the pleasure remained.

As I realized it, as I realized that I was in control of my body, my spirit, my own power, I started to come, not with my genitals alone, but with my whole self. As I began to slip from consciousness, he spoke in my mind once more. *Just a taste, Tai, just a taste of what will be yours.*

I woke just before dawn in his arms on the narrow bed. Our hair was tangled together, wrapped around our bodies like a sheet, and one of his big hands cupped my buttock. I had never seen him asleep. I looked at his face, its harsh beauty softened now, and wished I dared to reach out and stroke his cheek. Instead I closed my eyes again, concentrated on his warm breath in my face and the smoothness of his skin against mine, hoping he would want the use of me when he woke. I was beginning to drift back into contented sleep when the thought struck me. The flesh beneath his hand should still be raw, tender. But it was not.

I reached my own hand back, feeling for the welts and stripes that had been there only hours before. They were gone, my skin whole and unmarked and no longer sore.

"Oh, my lord," I whispered. Tears welled up and spilled onto my cheeks. I cried quietly so as not to rouse him.

The next time he had me move the cubes, I did it with very little trouble. His approval covered me like a warm blanket and I felt my face flush worse than it did from sex. *You needed to trust yourself, Tai. You needed to give up all control and then take it back. You're almost ready for the final test now. Pass that and I'll pierce you and make you ours.*

"And you know now that you do want it." It was even rarer now that he bothered to speak to me in words. In the last week I'd almost forgotten what his voice sounded like.

"I do want it, my lord." I reached up and brushed a piece of hair from my eyes. He'd already shaved the left side of my head, like a priestess, but I couldn't braid the other side till I proved myself in the final test. I went unclothed all the time now too, like a priestess, and I'd begun to forget the feeling of cloth against my flesh as well.

Tomorrow then. And your piercing two days after that. He was eager for it, more so even than I. It was likewise his final test. If I were successful, he would be a first-degree high priest, unbelievably powerful, a god walking among men.

And as much as we both wanted it, we knew the price. Any fool, any child, could tell you power had a price. I reached my hand out and trailed it longingly down his chest, but he caught my wrist, his expression stern. *No. Go now and meditate through the night.*

"Yes, my lord."

He had alerted the two eldest priests and they came at dawn to get me from my vigil. My knees were stiff from kneeling, my body woozy and my head buzzing from lack of sleep. But the power was singing through my blood. I could do it. I would do it.

They led me by my arms to his altar room. His body was sleek and shining against the black and white marble, his hair cascading backwards to the floor. His silver dagger was between his teeth. He crossed his arms over his chest, a sacrificial posture.

I salute you, my lord, and thank you for my training, I tried in my head and was gratified to see they could all hear me without effort. I bent my head to his and took the knife with my own mouth. The two elders began the chant, low and strong. The air grew syrupy. His face was that of a corpse and his breaths so shallow, his chest barely rose and fell. I transferred the knife from my mouth to my left hand and gathered all the power in the room to myself, chanting out loud for the very first time. The Old Words were like sugared poison on my tongue.

I stepped around to the foot of the altar and paused. His cock was roused, massively erect against the tight muscle of his abdomen. I took it in my right hand. All the old forces, life, death, and procreation, sang in me. I held the silver knife against the root of his penis. The old men chanted louder. There was no flicker of movement from him. The air was impossibly opaque.

Know that I loved you too, Tai.

I sliced through in one quick stroke as the chanting rose to a scream. Blood gushed warm over my hands. The even greater rush of power dazzled me and I drew it in, further in, and willed the bleeding to stop. I watched the skin begin to draw together on the wound. Keep focused. Joy bubbled up as I watched myself healing him, making him whole, yet not whole, yet more than what he was.

My lord. I said it one last time as my knees collapsed and my body slumped onto the cold stone floor. *My lord.*

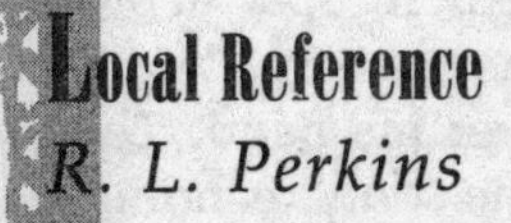

Local Reference

R. L. Perkins

She tugged at the cuffs buckled around her wrists, cursing again her large hands and narrow wrists. The wide leather cuffs were padlocked to a chain that was bolted securely to the bed frame. There was simply no way for her to escape. She looked over her shoulder at the figure standing above her prone body, the one she knew only as `Sir'. His face was classically handsome, the lines and planes of his chiseled features picked out in soft contrast by the glow from the 3D television set. His body was strongly muscled without that over-developed look that too many men she knew thought attractive to women. His lips were fuller than most men's and curved in a perpetual smile. His eyes were piercing blue and seemed to sense her most intimate secrets. She had encountered him a few short weeks ago, at the shuttle port, or maybe it was at the controversial android ballet opening. Funny that she couldn't remember. At times like this she was never really sure of anything.

Sir wrapped the fingers of his hand in her silken blonde hair and pulled her head back. He kissed her, his tongue pushing easily past her lips to explore her mouth. The kiss was slow, arrogantly casual, as if he had all night to torment her and felt no pressure to rush things. He broke the kiss and released her hair. She felt a tickle as nano machines programmed with the latest in hair styles labored to restore her original coif.

His hand drifted down the curves of her back, following the ridge of her spine until it disappeared above the cleft of her buttocks. He began stroking her bottom with an upsweeping motion. She buried her face between her outstretched arms and lifted her hips off the bed to meet his hand. The slap was as sharp as it was sudden, the sound echoing in her ears. The outline of his hand burned like a brand on her buttock.

She strained to lift her hips higher for him. He slapped her again before resuming his caresses. She hated this position, knowing it left her completely exposed. She fancied men found her body attractive. The best trainer that her money could buy saw to it that she was as firm and toned as a TV starlet. Her wardrobe was full of plunging backs, daring decolletage, and skirts slit to her hip; carefully tailored to show off her body. With a practiced walk she could reward her gawking male admirers with a precisely controlled glimpse of sculpted leg. She loved those moments, watching the men around her responding like children teased with a bit of chocolate too rich for their tongues. But now Sir's strong hands were spreading her open, reducing her to a common whore. She knew she was already wet, that he could sense it and would know that he had done that to her. That he stripped her not only of clothing, but of dignity as well.

He tasted her, his lips soft and warm against her cunt. He stroked her clit with his tongue, cruelly teasing her, bringing her to the ragged edge of orgasm only to hold her trapped in elegant torture. His sense of her arousal was uncanny; he could maintain her balanced on the point of orgasmic release with merciless precision. Their first time together he had reduced her to tearful begging. Afterwards she had thrown him out, sworn never to see him again. Their second time she had screamed in her frustration until he paused long enough to gag her. When she had tried to fight him, he had tied her legs spread straining wide. She had even once tried to out maneuver him by forcing herself to lie limp and unresponsive. Her body had given her away, providing him with a steady flow of her juices in response to his tireless mouth.

She moaned pitifully into the satin-cased pillow. Her need had swollen from tingling passion to a painful pressure spreading through her belly, cramping the muscles of her back and shoulders. Her cunt twitched and spasmed, grasping at emptiness with each stroke of his tongue. She hated his mouth. She obsessed over his mouth. She wanted to live in his mouth.

When he finally took his mouth away she realized that she had been begging again. He took her in his arms and rolled her limp, frustrated body onto her back. His tongue flicked over her nipples like a candle flame. She barely bit back a scream when he trapped her right nipple between his teeth. She could smell her sex on his lips. He stood and took her ankles in his hand, lifting her legs straight up in the air and shifting her hips to the edge of the bed. His fingers stroked her face, lightly tracing the line of cheekbone below soft skin. She turned her head to catch his thumb with her mouth. He stepped back, his thumb making a wet popping sound as he pulled it from her mouth. He untied his robe and let it fall to the floor. He was already erect and sheathed in latex. Sir was better endowed than any man she had been with, the biggest she had ever seen. She had been intimidated at first, now she was enraptured. He stroked himself in front of her face. She reached for him with her mouth, letting her legs droop.

He caught the soles of her bare feet in his hand and tsked at her. He lifted her by her ankles, raising her hips completely off the bed. The spanking wasn't as hard as she had expected. She was surprised when it didn't stop after a couple of slaps. Her blood pooled in her head and the sound of her pulse began to beat in time with Sir's hand on her bottom. Each stroke was harder than its predecessor until it took all her concentration not to cry out with each stroke. Her buttocks felt on fire, and she hoped he had hurt his god damn hand.

He lowered her onto the bed and hugged her legs to his chest. The head of his cock spread the swollen lips of her cunt. His hips slowly pressed forward and back, each time sliding infinitesimally deeper into her before withdrawing. She bit at the inside of her own arm trying in vain to focus herself against the new assault. He kept his slow infuriating rhythm until his cock finally filled her. Her torment continued, as deep as he was going into her, he was just too slow to push her over her orgasmic edge. Her cunt clenched trying to grasp his cock, her hips bucked trying to steal that vital sensation he withheld. He grabbed her hips, pinning her against the mattress.

"Sir," she said, "Sir, please."

He smiled down at her, his face impassive, his hips keeping slow, perfect time.

"Sir, I can't take it anymore. Please, Sir. Please."

Slowly filling her, then easing away.

"Please."

Stretching her vagina...

"Sir, please..."

Then hollow and empty.

"God damn it! Stop teasing and fuck me, will you! I want it now!"

He stopped mid-stroke. He tsked again and withdrew his cock. He paused to steady her legs in the air before turning away.

It took every bit of her remaining strength to hold her legs up without his support. Her toes traced lazy arcs in the air before she found the strength to steady herself. Sir went to the armoire where she stored her toys. He turned to face her and displayed an enormous rubber phallus.

The thing was the size of her arm. She envisioned of dying on such a cock, impaled through her vagina by a gigantic penis, orgasming with her last breath as it filled her body. She shivered with excitement. Sir saw it and immediately responded.

He pushed the head of it between the lips of her cunt and rested its base on the base of his own organ. He spread her legs in a `V' and began to push the giant dildo into her. Her lungs felt paralyzed as it slid into her, stretching her to her absolute limit. It was halfway inside her when she felt the head of his cock press insistently against her anus. He centered it with his hand. Fear shot through her, she tensed to block his passage. He leaned over her and the head of his cock painfully entered her. She pulled on her cuffs and chain futilely trying to yank herself off him. He held her legs tight in his arms as he continued to push deeper. The dildo filled her; still he didn't stop until his cock was buried half way into her ass. She had never felt so full. She tried to speak, to beg him to stop, but couldn't shape the words. He smiled that infuriating quiescent smile of his and covered her mouth with his hand. He eased his hips back minutely, and she forced herself to relax. A heartbeat later he drove himself into her.

She began screaming, not sure if her screams were from pain or the intensity of the orgasms that exploded through her body. She bit at Sir's hand and tasted salty wetness. He refused to let go as she continued to scream. He fucked her hard and fast, pumping both himself and the dildo into her. Her orgasms continued until she couldn't breath, silencing her screams. He continued steadily hammering into her until she slipped into a faint.

When she came to, gasping for air, she saw he still stood beside her bed, peeling away the spent condom. The head of his uncovered cock glistened. She wanted to taste it, but was too weak to fight her way to him. She watched him working his cock and balls with a peculiar squeezing stroke. She thought she could feel the heat of his balls warming the her skin. He aimed his cock into the air like an artillery piece and fired. The thick while stream of his cum arced over her belly and splashed onto her heaving breasts. The droplets burned her like molten wax and trailed bright stripes of pain as they ran down her skin.

He stroked her breasts and belly with his finger tips as she caught her breath and lay basking in her own private afterglow. His hands traced fractal whorls with mathematical precision in the sweat coating her skin, his fingers provided the perfect amount of pressure to relax her. After a few minutes she began to stir.

"Fragile," she whispered.

The padlock opened with a soft click as Sir stepped back. His face was utterly blank.

"Sir, store!"

Sir pivoted and returned to the armoire that dominated the corner of the small bedroom.

The woman pushed the chain under the coarse mattress before painfully struggling to her feet. Standing for hours without moving in front of Loom 27B at the Algonquin Textile Mill Number Six irritated the arthritis that stiffened joints in her short legs. She wanted to quit, the dole would pay for her dingy rooms. But without the steady paycheck the credit company would back up a truck to her door and haul the android and her 3D HighDef television set away. She limped to the cabinet and detached the dildo from its adapter, and with a counterclockwise twist removed Sir's standard penis. She made her way to the bathroom fighting her embarrassing tendency to waddle. She washed the appliances in the sink with soap and water, then dried them on a dingy hand towel. She tied her coarse hair back before splashing cool water on her face. She was picking the remaining hardened droplets of paraffin from her flaccid breasts when she heard the theme music from her favorite program, the one with that skinny blonde bitch, erupt from the TV speaker on her battered bureau.

She put the penises away in their storage drawer, pausing to run her fingers over the other variations that Sir could be equipped with. She lifted the long and flexible black penis and fondled it. That would be for tomorrow, she though to herself. She sprayed Sir's bitten hand with a repair solution. Nano machines suspended in the fluid would repair the torn synthetic skin overnight. She kissed him on his cooling lips.

"I love you, Sir," she said to the android as she closed its cabinet and reached for the TV remote. Maybe this time that little blonde cock tease would get what was fucking coming to her.

Cyber Knight

Gary Bowen

I walked into the room and noticed the usual collection of wannabe mistresses in push up bras and self-proclaimed doms in black leather pants; I scanned past them quickly, looking, looking... I was new here, or at least, this incarnation of me was, it remained to be seen how effective an interface I had designed. I'd spent a lot of time working out the details: tall, lithe, androgynous, with a gravity defying white blond mohawk, two gold earrings, white spandex tights, combat boots, and a lot of red body paint zigzagging across my arms and making mystical signs on my chest and back. A pseudo-dom detached himself from the crowd, gliding over to me.

"Top or bottom?" were his first words to me.

"None of your business," I replied, not liking his attitude.

He drew himself up to his full height, an imposing six four here in Cyberland. I did the mental arithmetic and figured in the real world he must be five nine, max. Overcompensation, you know.

"That's Sir Adam to you," he pronounced.

It was times like this I really missed my nicotine addiction. Chording furiously in the real world, I programmed a cigarette to appear in my simulcrum's hand, complete with ivory holder a la Hollywood. I blew smoke at him. "Not until you've earned it."

His eyes darkened. "That can be arranged."

"I doubt it." I turned my back on him and walked into the next room.

"I didn't give you permission to leave!" he snarled at my back. I kept walking. It was Cyberland, nobody could touch me. I was safely back at my console, chording the programs necessary to sustain an elaborate—and boring—game of make believe.

The next room wasn't as well developed at the room I'd left; it was a simple box with two doors, and a not very good simulcrum of a bar. A couple of girls with purple hair and pierced noses were standing together.

"What a dive," I said out loud. Six months ago I'd thought it was Happily Ever After Land. Yeah, me and my console were going places. We were gonna be a bigshot virtual reality team. Wrong. Cyberland was populated by as many losers as the real world. And now I was in a really pissy mood, prepared to act the role of the Bottom from Hell because I was bored.

I approached the bar, leaned my elbow on it, and yelled, "What does it take to get some beer around here?"

The bartender materialized. "A little courtesy," he replied mildly. He was bald on top, wearing a white dress shirt with black garters on his sleeves, and a black leather vest. I couldn't recall ever meeting a bald man in cyberspace before, aside from the Neo Goths who shaved their heads on purpose. When you can be anything you wanna be, nobody chooses to be bald. I glanced over the bar. Not only bald, but rotund. Not seriously rotund, not by real world standards, but compared to the standard issue svelte bodies of Cyberland, he was a definite anomaly.

"You're new," I said.

"No, I'm old. Just been playing other roles for a while."

His simulcrum was perfect, right down to the worn crotch of his blue jeans and the ripped knees. His work boots were scuffed even. He looked really real.

"Can I get a beer, please?" I asked, wondering if he was a top or a bottom. I wasn't so crass as the pseudo-dom who gotten in my face, but all the same, I wanted to know.

He poured beer, the illusion perfect. He was good. Either he'd done this a million times before, or he could program as fast as I could. I decided to test his ingenuity. I waved my cigarette holder at him. "Light?"

He flicked a yellow plastic Bic at me. Good. Still, lighters were small objects, he might actually be able to chord that fast. I racked my brain for another test. "Peanuts?"

A package appeared, and by ghod if it didn't look like the Planters I got in the real world. No hesitation, he just reached under the bar and there it was. I grabbed the package and ripped it open. Peanuts, each one slightly different, spilled out. That was a heck of a lot of programming. But he might be equipped with an array of pre-made micro programs to enhance the game of playing bartender. Some people got that obsessive about their cyber roles. Yet, the bar itself was crude.

I patted the counter top. "Not your work, I take it."

"No, not mine."

I nodded. It's considered rude for more skilled programmers to alter objects made by others. You can add anything you like to a room, but you can't change what's already there. Such is the unspoken code of Cyberland. My fingers chorded like lightning, and now my cigarette was animated, burning and creating ash as if it were a real cigarette. "Ashtray?"

He put one on the bar, a plain round glass one. Easy, but in keeping with his low key approach to everything. "Dart board?"

He turned around, produced a dart board, darts stuck in the target, quivering as he let it thump onto the bar. Wow.

"Chess?"

He produced a box, unfolded the board, and set up the individual pieces. "You play?" he asked casually, as if organizing thirty-two pieces of pseudo-plastic was no work at all.

"A little," I replied.

"I'll play you," he said.

"Okay. What're the stakes?"

"I win, I get to whip your smart ass."

My blood quickened. "And if you lose?"

His face was bland, but the laugh lines around his eyes crinkled. "What do you want from me?"

"A good game," I responded promptly. What did I want? To be entertained. To be topped by somebody who knew how to do it right, who could take whatever was at hand—riding crop, cigarette, chess board—and use it to dominate me, no matter how I struggled. That was the fundamental challenge of sensuous magic; the dom had to know how to weave a spell that paralyzed his sub and made him submit. Because in truth, there was nothing an ethical dom could do to force a rebellious sub into compliance. It was all a mind game.

"I see. You'll play for pride. You win, you get to feel superior and continue playing the arrogant asshole. You lose..." he shrugged.

His words irked me, but they touched something too. "Whatever. Suppose I think about it while we play, and when I decide I let you know?"

He smiled faintly. "All right." He picked up a black and white pawn, held them in two beefy hands. I pointed, he opened his hand to reveal the white pawn.

I moved first. I wasn't good at chess, I knew it. In that he had mistaken me. He was going to win. No doubt about it. Unless he was awful, but I doubted that. My heart throbbed in my chest, and I felt heat coursing through my veins. This was stupid. Why didn't I just say, "Whip me, beat me, make me write bad checks?" The two of us could go off to play without this display of mental machismo.

He moved in response, and I moved quickly, not knowing what would happen to the pieces. He countered with deliberate calm. I lost a pawn. No biggie. He watched me over the pieces, and I stared at the board. What would he do to me? I was slow to move my piece, too preoccupied with the inevitable end to pay much attention to how I rapidly I was losing. He contemplated the board for long moments, and I waited, fingers poised to chord my response. We each made several more moves. "Check," he said.

"You win." I disappeared.

I set down the chording balls and removed the helmet from my head. I was sweating, and I was half hard. I ran my fingers through my own short cropped brown hair. Then I took the mohawked interface and moved it to storage. It wasn't right. Something had almost happened in there. I brooded at my console, then donned the helmet and picked up my chording balls again. I entered my own space, the one that was mine all mine, that nobody could get to unless I let them. The foyer was a plain dark room, a little misty. A single spot light shown down from above, but there was no lamp casting it. I stood in the middle and thought. I didn't feel like going to any of the places I'd made, and I didn't feel like going to anybody else's place either. I decided the foyer was as good a place as any to do my programming for a new interface.

What now? The opposite of the mohawk, I didn't want to be recognized. Okay, short and dark haired, with a buzzcut. Square jaw, broken nose. Bull neck, squat, powerful chest. Long arms. Long legs. Black leather pants. And taking a cue from the perfectly imperfect bartender, signs of wear along the seams and crotch, and serious scuffs on the knees. Steel toed boots, also scuffed. A black tee shirt with the Cyberland logo on it. I spent a lot of time adding in the little details: tattoos and earrings, debating the exact pattern of the studded leather belt. But I had no sense of the man I was creating. He looked good, but he was just an interface. I shoved him into storage.

What could I do? Who could I be that would be enough me to be a real person, but was enough not-me to be safe? I decided to copy and edit the mohawk. I kept the hair, added an earring. I switched to black leather pants and a black leather vest, remembering to add the wear marks. I decided on a button fly and no belt. Better. But he'd still recognize me if I ran into him again. Having chickened out, I didn't particularly want to meet him. I colored the mohawk purple. Forget it, not me. I changed it back to Billy Idol blond. I'd just have to stay out of the club rooms for a while. He'd forget in a couple of days.

I dropped back into Cyberland, choosing to arrive on the veranda. White wicker chairs were placed all along an old fashioned Victorian porch, white, complete with elaborate gingerbread. Examining the fretwork with a programmer's eye, I saw it was one intricate pattern endlessly repeated. Computers are great at duplication. I looked across the wildflower meadow to the distant mountains: texture mapped. But it looked pretty. The only other people were a couple of girls in white corsets and pantaloons servicing a proper British gentleman at the far end; I ignored them. I settled in a chair, slung one knee over the arm, and started chording. Clouds were not easy, I had to reference a couple of texts before I managed something halfway reasonable. I kept fiddling with them, and finally got a pretty decent bit of cumulus to drift over the mountains. I was at work programming their shadows to follow them across the mountains when another man joined me on the veranda. He was tall and barrel chested, with a black tee shirt and leather pants. His black hair was cut short and he wore mirrored sunglasses. He settled a few chairs down from me, and I ignored him. I was conducting some experiments back in my own space, and bit by bit ported the results up to Cyberland. Clouds crowded the sky, and lightning flashed distantly. Thunder growled. I relaxed, letting my storm simulation play itself out in the distance.

Creation always left me feeling pleasantly tired, and a little horny. This being Cyberland, I started fondling my crotch. No reason why I shouldn't do what I felt like doing—that was why Cyberland existed. To play out unspeakable fantasies without paying the consequences. I unbuttoned my fly and took it out. Just to amuse myself I made my dick long and pointy, with its foreskin still attached, topped off by a gold Prince Albert. Having a Prince Albert means never losing your keys.

I chorded a bit more, and a cool breeze smelling of rain washed over the veranda from the mountain. The girls didn't notice, but the cool breeze caressing my balls felt good to me. The mirrored sunglasses of the single man turned my way, and I watched myself reflected in them, pulling on my cock with long hard strokes. Then he rose, and maneuvering around the abundant wicker furniture, placed a small black knight on the table before me. He walked on, turning the corner of the veranda while I stared at the object he had left.

It was a piece from the chess piece we had used earlier in the evening. I stuffed my dick back in my pants and jumped up, buttoning as I tripped over the furniture and tried to follow him. But he was gone, and the only person on the veranda was a mistress in latex miniskirt and black bustier, riding crop in her hand, smoking. Damn.

I examined the chess piece. It was an elegant piece of programming, and I hunted for the programmer's mark. JDBlack. Nothing more. No title or nickname, no symbol or logo, nothing. Just the name. I hit the reference tools and called up info on JDBlack.

"I'm sorry," the computer murmured in my ear. "That is a restricted account. No information is available."

Damn. I teleported back to the bar.

Half a dozen poseurs in various shades of black were occupying the room, a few of them hoisting beer mugs. I recognized JDBlack's work: the mugs were perfect imitations of the real world. He had been here, and not long ago. How long had he sat on the veranda while I made clouds? A long time. Suspicion seized me, I accessed my own data.

"Account queried at 02:30:45 by Unknown User." It had been easy for him to find me. I had simply modified the old simulcrum instead of cloning it—cloning would have identified it as a new object and provided it with a new number. I cloned myself, got a new ID number, and junked the old simulcrum. Now I was brand new and he couldn't track me by my ID number. When I walked away I ghosted, and now there were two of me in the room. No program is perfect, I'd confused it by cloning myself in active space. I chorded some more, and at last my ghost disappeared. A beer appeared at my elbow.

"Genuine Miller Draft," he said.

I looked over the counter at him, noticed the bald spot was shiny. I backed away. I didn't want him to think I'd been looking for him, yet I couldn't think of any plausible prevarication. I disappeared again.

I jumped back to the veranda, that being the most recent place and therefore instantly accessible off of my automated menu. But if he were following me, that would be the first place he'd guess. I thought fast, and chorded the ID for the Well of Lost Souls.

The Well was made of damp granite blocks, with sunlight shining down, and niches carved into the sides at intervals. It was about twenty-six feet across, experimentation having proved that was the greatest distance at which you could easily talk to someone perched across from you. Psychologically easy—feet or miles didn't matter in Cyberland, but as your simulcrum looked across the space, you reacted as if it was real. The Goths had discovered the Well of Lost Souls and loved it, but they weren't here tonight. Georgie was on his usual perch, rocking back and forth, singing to himself in strange detached sentences, red hair spiked all over his head. I liked Georgie. He was a reality unto himself. His signature was on many of the additions to the Well of Lost Souls, and all of them were grotesque, small, and subtle. He was especially fond of creating tortured rock faces that would howl or whimper if you bumped into them.

"You're being followed," he said, startling me.

"Damn!" I looked around, but nobody was near us.

"Invisible," he added.

That chilled me. Only operators had the privilege of being invisible. They stalked Cyberland, administering a rude and almost undetectable kind of justice. If I felt wronged, I could ask for an operator to intervene. I'd never see them and neither would anybody else. Either the problem would be solved, or it would not. Nobody ever knew for sure. If an obnoxious jerk suddenly disappeared, was it because he got bored and left? Or was it because an operator had kicked him off? I didn't know. I remembered my sullenness earlier in the evening, and was glad JDBlack had cut me a break. Some operators are real hard cases.

"Hey Chess!" I yelled while scanning the references for info on operators. Another dead end. Nobody answered my hail, but Georgie started crawling up the wall like a fly.

"You leaving me, Georgie?"

"I may be crazy, but I'm not stupid," he replied, and squeezed himself so thin he could slide down a gargoyle's throat. He liked disturbing entrances and exits of that sort. Now I was alone, except for his gargoyles. I scanned each of them, but I had seen them all before. Nothing new, nothing that could be an operator in disguise. But then, he was invisible, he had no need of disguise. Water began to run down the wall, and dripped onto my ledge. It pooled in a shallow depression, then poured over the edge. I glanced down at the wetness, and it was red.

"Georgie!" I yelled. That was just like Georgie. He loved gruesome effects. If Georgie wasn't spaced out in Cyberland, he'd have been conducting experiments on unwilling subjects in the real world. I wished he hadn't left. I messaged him.

"Not my program," was his reply.

Mist began to drift down from above, occluding the sunlight that graced the chamber. It swelled in lazy, swirling spirals, growing larger and denser, becoming a form, arms and head shaping themselves above an indeterminate blotch. A pebble fell, bouncing from ledge to ledge, then dropping straight down towards the bottom. "You'll never hear it splash," a woman's voice said.

I pressed myself back against the wall. The mist continued to accumulate, gradually becoming a woman in a long dress, pale grey in color, form fuzzy around the edges, merging with the mist in the well.

"JDBlack?" I asked. I had assumed JD was male because that was the form I first saw. But there was no reason why a person should not appear as either gender. Most people, like me, stuck with their biological gender, but again, that was a psychological limit, not a real one. Limits had to be artificially created in Cyberland. I had programmed the Well of Lost Souls to have gravity, if you fell off your ledge, you fell. It was the only place in Cyberland that actually had gravity. Anywhere else, if you set a beer mug floating in the air, it stayed.

The form did not fall, and seeing it defy my rules did not reassure me. "Why are you following me?"

"I thought you might like women better."

"I don't." I programmed rapidly, and cloned it a couple dozen times. Now I had a stack of softball sized rocks beneath my hand. I picked one up and threw it. It passed right through the ghost with no effect.

"Why are you afraid of me?"

"Because I don't know what you are!" My voiced echoed loudly, another detail of my programming. It spooked me, and I hated myself for being such a good programmer. She/he/it was taking advantage of what I had made to freak me out. I teleported.

I landed in the middle of the wildflower meadow, yellow and pink and white flowers growing right through me. The meadow had been programmed for image only, it didn't act like a real meadow. The remnants of my storm were clearing away overhead. I felt safe with daisies sprouting through my stomach while my storm drifted overhead. The meadow was a peaceful place. I relaxed, checked my program, gave it a couple of adjustments, and set it to storm at random intervals. I also scheduled a storm for every Tuesday night at eight pm. Then I headed back to the veranda.

And he was there, standing at the top of the steps, male, brush cut, black clothes, thoroughly real. I stared into his mirrored shades for a long moment, but before I could make up my mind what to do he turned and walked away. He took a seat in a chair, which creaked under him. Details! The chairs had never creaked before. He was a hell of a programmer. He propped one foot on the coffee table, and three glossy magazines appeared on the table top, along with a pot of orange Gerbera daisies. A Tiffany lamp appeared on the end table, and he switched it on. It got suddenly dark, and I looked up to see the sun setting behind the Mansion in a burst of orange light, fading away in a matter of minutes.

"You're an wizard," I said.

He nodded. Nobody else could fiddle with basic operations like the progression of time in Cyberland. Usually internal time ran at approximately twice real world speed. But he wanted it to be night, and lo, it was night.

Night. I took the chess piece from my pocket. Knight. It makes the oblique moves. It threatens, but its path is forked and hard to follow. It surprises.

He watched me.

I turned the piece in my hands, wondering, feeling a tension in my lower belly as my cock began to point towards him. I walked nonchalantly up from the wildflowers, colored petals clinging to my leather jeans as if by static electricity. I crossed the narrow strip of lawn and mounted the stairs. I sat on the railing opposite him. Not to be outdone, I created a pot of sweetly scented red geraniums, and duplicated it, hanging pots in every other arch of the gingerbread. It was a very long porch, I made six pots.

His lip curled, and it might have been a smile, but I wasn't sure. "You like this place."

"Yes."

He nodded. "I do too. Godfrey made it."

I'd heard about Godfrey 'God' Sullivan. He reputedly owned the machine that housed Cyberland. He had built the first virtual rooms, designed the protocols that governed it, simplified the coding so that anybody with half a brain could learn to program it if they wanted to. "Did you know him?"

"Yes."

"You're one of the Twelve."

He shrugged.

I wanted to ask him what he wanted with me, but I was afraid. Direct questions of that sort are rude. I accessed the menus, and there, in the 'About this Application' section, was a listing of the thirteen talents who had made Cyberland. Godfrey 'God' Sullivan was listed as Creator, and below him were his twelve disciples, 'JDBlack' included.

"Wow."

"Does it matter?"

Of course it mattered! I was flattered to have one of the greatest wizards of all time paying attention to me. But I remembered my unease in the Well of Lost Souls. "You're playing with me."

He laughed long and hard, the mirrored glasses almost falling off. "I'm trying. But you keep running away."

I ground my teeth in chagrin and decided I didn't have to listen to that. I popped into the White Queen's dungeon.

She was working over a pair of twins, boys. I checked their signatures, both were made by the same man. Yeah, every kink, twins, too. No pun intended. I slipped along the back, working my way behind the people standing and watching her flog the hapless simulcrums.

Personally, I don't see much point to virtual sadomasochism, you can't feel anything unless you've got a great program or a vivid imagination. I mingled with the crowd at the back of the room and admired the set. The White Queen put on a great show: the room was a medieval torture chamber straight out of Hollywood. Torches in sconces burned steadily, casting light throughout the room. The White Queen was dressed in a white fur bikini with ornamental chain mail and a crown on her head. Her armor jingled as she moved, her tits jiggled, and her hips swayed. Watching her was like watching jello do the shimmy.

JDBlack didn't appear. I was disappointed, I had really expected him to follow me. I had counted on it even.

I watched the White Queen pause to stroke her delirious victims, then materializing a toy out of thin air, she slipped a large size dildo into the ass of the twin on the left. He groaned and writhed, and she reached around front and pinched his tits. He was a pretty boy, shoulder length black hair, and completely nude body, with only a little bit of dark fur in his crotch and up the crack of his ass. She unchained the other twin, and jerking him to his knees, set him in front of the standing twin, and made him give himself head.

The conceit amused me, and I cloned myself. Now I was looking at myself, and my other self was looking at me. With a laugh we started kissing. It was boring though: no suspense. We each knew what was going to happen next. I deleted one of my selves. Where was JDBlack?

I wandered out of the torture chamber, passed various leather folk including a fairy in a lavender tutu with codpiece, and found myself at last on the balcony overlooking the front door. I stood at the battlement, heavy dark stone crenelations making an ideal perch. A heavy hand fell upon my neck and forced my face down. I was powerless to resist, my simulcrum was not under my control. Arms and legs flapped when I moved them, but I was bent over at the waist. "JD," I whispered.

He unprogrammed my clothes, and they went away, leaving me naked except for my jewelry. He forced his knee between mine and knocked my legs apart. I was gasping, cock jutting out directly in front of me, bracing myself for his penetration. With a laugh, he let go of me. I caught my breath, and turned around: nobody.

"Don't be invisible!" I shouted. "I hate it when you do that!"

No answer. My pulse pounded and I searched for my clothes, but couldn't find them. I shook my head, separating simulcrum from physical body, and consulted the log for my clothes' IDs, discovered they had been deleted. "Hey! You aren't supposed to delete other people's objects!" I yelled.

Damn. He was a wizard, the law. What was I going to do? Page the operators and tell 'em their boss was bothering me? How far would that get? Yeah, right.

"You're pissing me off!" I yelled.

I emailed him a rude message, "FUCK OFF AND DIE." But I didn't put my clothes back on.

I squeezed my balls, they ached with fullness, and my cock swung long and ready for the slightest touch. I needed relief, and I wanted it to be him, but I couldn't compel him. He was the better programmer. But perhaps I could seduce him.

I teleported to the fuckery. It was late, there were several couples, most of them straight, engaged in anonymous cybersex. As usual a gallery of people had gathered to watch, and with the everlasting stamina of cybersex, to participate. I walked naked into the room, selected an empty sling, climbed into it. I locked my ankles into the cuffs, feet high above the floor, scooted until my ass was placed just right for whoever wanted to fuck me. Then I locked the collar around my neck, and then my left wrist. The last cuff closed automatically on my right wrist. Now I was locked into the cuffs, and I couldn't get loose until somebody let me loose. My cock was rock hard, pointing at the sky. I didn't have long to wait, this was where the scuzzballs and deadbeats, the walking sleaze, gathered, because they knew this was where it was given away free.

The first one mounted me, and I didn't even look at him. I found myself paralyzed, listening to the patter of the computer as his program ran. I was in two spaces, the physical space my body occupied, hardon aching in my jeans, and the mental space of Cyberland where I was so immersed I was hardly aware of the computer telling me what my simulcrum was being subjected to. I felt it, even though it was only an illusion.Then my hands began to chord stream of consciousness sensations, my program sharing with everyone in the room what I was feeling, my own programming ability turning the tawdry transaction into a ball aching cyber orgy. They surrounded me, men and women, jerking off around me, stuffing cocks into my face, up my ass, splattering cum on me, reaming me endlessly. Not one of them even thought of letting me loose, I was their party favor and they used me over and over again.

All through the scene my flesh and blood ached, but I didn't touch it. I stripped off my clothes and sat naked at the console, helmet over my head, both chording balls in my hands, skin screaming for the reality of touch.

But it wasn't real, it was just cybersex. My simulcrum was screaming with lust, begging for more, and some of them were reprogramming themselves with massive pricks to fuck me. Then, as I received an impossibly large prick between my lips, I vanished.

I blinked and looked around, and found myself kneeling on straw on the floor of the stable. A leather collar was around my neck, and it was held by JDBlack. "You want a real stud, that can be arranged," he said.

I shivered. I dropped one of the chording balls and my hand went to my lap. I squeezed myself in anticipation. "Sir," I said.

He pulled on my collar, and scrambling on my knees I followed him into a stall. He clipped it to a ring in the wall, and I grabbed it. I squeezed, but the clip did not open. It was locked in programming. I teleported.

Back to the Well of Lost Souls. The place was deserted. I perched naked upon my favorite ledge. He could follow me, but would he? I had left his collar behind in the stable. I quickly chorded an early warning system, which immediately beeped and told me he was there. Invisible again. I expected no different. He was taking shameless advantage of the prerogatives of a wizard.

My simulcrum was bursting with the need to cum, and I wanted to surrender myself to the sensations of cyberlust. But I couldn't. Not without a fight. I was making myself crazy, teasing myself with JDBlack. My simulcrum masturbated, stuck a finger in its ass while jerking off, moaned and groaned, the echoes magnifying the sound. That did me in; knowing that he could hear me, hearing myself, I beat off hard and furious, wanting him to grab me by the scruff of the neck and snarl, "Take it, asshole!" and ream me.

And knowing that if he tried it, I would teleport away again.

Claws scraped stone, and I froze in mid-stroke. I dared to look over the edge of the ledge, and there, a few feet below my ledge was one of Georgie's gargoyles clawing its way up. Its eyes glowed red, and its long claws hooked into the interstices of the stone, clinging like a lizard. It had huge ears, horns, and heavy brow ridges, a flat nose and tusks. It was the size of a pony, built like a bull, moved like a dog, and hung like a horse. It resumed its climb while I watched. I couldn't move, the beast stalking me was beyond my ken. No matter how many fantasy novels I'd read, I still wasn't prepared for the creature that slithered halfway over the edge of my ledge and paused, looking at me. I rolled over onto my hands and knees and waited, sweat springing up on my brow, while it completed its climb, and placing clammy palms against my back, slid its humongous phallus against my balls. I clamped my legs shut, trapping it between them, and it was as thick as a tree branch and cold as stone. Almost I gave in, releasing it from my grasp, arching my back in anticipation—but I teleported away.

I appeared in the stable, not recollecting what destination I had chosen, mischording several keystrokes and having to redo them. But before I finished my program a match struck a sulfurous light, and JDBlack lit a lantern. The stable was dark, the door was closed. I tried to teleport, but he had placed a teleport lock on the room. Nobody could teleport in or out. I was trapped in the room with him. He stripped off his vest, revealing grey hair on his chest, his bald pate shining in the light. He unbuttoned the front of his leather jeans, converting them to chaps, balls the size of eggs and a thick, uncut cock falling out. He crooked his finger at me.

I stumbled to my feet and walked over to him, then he pointed down. I dropped to my knees. I took his cock into my mouth, hands chording spastically as I programmed the pleasure for him. I wanted it to be good, I wanted it to be worth all the chasing he had done. I wanted his eyes to glaze over as he shot cum all over his console. I wanted to win.

His hands caught my hair, and he held my head, forcing more of his cock down my throat. I teleported away from him. I couldn't escape the stable, but I could still move. He materialized a length of rope and remained standing where he was. I watched him, waiting to see what he would do. He watched me, then his finger crooked again. I found myself walking through a dream, kneeling before him and looking up. He tied the rope around my neck.

I teleported, but the rope didn't move. I was stuck in my starting place. I jumped to my feet and backed away. The rope stretched between us, then I was brought up short. He tied it to a post, then yanking on the line, brought me flying towards him. He caught me, and threw me over the hay bales. I tried to teleport, but the rope was a teleport lock, and it was locked to the post and my neck, and I couldn't get out. I started desperately programming, trying to decompile it, but he shoved his cock into my ass, and I was too busy bucking and gasping to program any more. Random bits of code scattered through my throes of passion, and pinning me down with his cock, he cleared them away.

I dropped both chording balls, stuffed several fingers into my ass and strangled my prick with my other hand, and jerked my physical flesh off while his program raped my simulcrum. I splattered copious quantities of jism across the console, but it wasn't enough.

"Please, I have to meet you in person," I begged.

He gagged my simulcrum, and I couldn't talk anymore. He savaged my ass with his prick, and I could only watch helplessly as he took total control of the scene, while my simulcrum kicked and whimpered.

At last he came, the fluids leaking from my simulcrum's asshole, which gaped open after being used so hard. I couldn't do anything at all to effect the scene. I sent him email. "Come to me in the flesh. Whoever you are, whatever you want, come and take me."

He picked up my exhausted simulcrum and led it into a stall. He fashioned bridle and reins, replacing the rope with restraints of black leather, also teleport locked. He bound my hands behind my back and hobbled my feet, and I was sunk in the reality of the cyberspace again, feeling them as if they were happening to me for real.

"You're going to stay here, my pretty boy. Going to stay here forever, ready for me to use you whenever I feel like it. You can't escape, and you're going to service me or anybody else whenever I feel like it. I shall make several keys for the stable, and lend them to friends of mine who will be invited to use you whenever they feel like it."

I nodded dumbly.

Then he blew out the lantern, leaving me in darkness. A square of light showed where he opened the door, then he was gone, the door closed behind him.

I could have deleted myself, but I didn't. It was the only way to escape the programming trap he'd put me in. Instead I enhanced his programming. I put alarms on it so I'd know when he was there.

It's only Cyberland, nothing is real, it's a complicated game of make believe played by programmers who push each other's abilities to the limits, exploiting each other's sexuality for prurient gratification. It isn't real, none of it, not one bit, but every time the alarm whispers his name, I drop what I'm doing and grab my chording balls, ready to submit to his desires.

Guernica

M. Christian

By the flatscreen on the wall, it was just past the 21st century. Glowing numerals flickered into 13:00: late enough for the mischief-makers. The cops were still rolling through the city outside, but just maybe a bit lethargic; reptiles chocked full 'a donuts and acid coffee. The bribes to the neighbors were paid and the acoustics, as always, were perfect—the people on Wake street hoped

13:01 and the little house on Wake street changed. Tension sang through the building; time to play. Outside, the forces of legislated morality motored about—but here, inside, out came the toys. The crowd's change was hard, precise: slaves shrugged off civilian personas and dropped their eyes as masters closed steel-gray attitudes over theirs. The private home with eyebolts, heavily upholstered chairs and mysterious trunks, changed: chains were hung, and straps of nasty leather were clipped to tables.

The trunks revealed their contents: highly illegal latex, rubber, dildoes, lubrication, handcuffs, whips, clothespins, canes, condoms, dams, gloves, and other toys. The clock was 13:15—and then it blipped right over to a tape: Mistress Gloria flagellating a slave. His bed sheet-white ass was striped, welts like red-hot prison bars across his cheeks. He smiled back to the crowd from the screen from the past when he wasn't a criminal, and what he was doing wasn't a Morality Crime. Now, in the years around 13:15, his stripes could land his ass in jail, or in one of the mining camps, and just viewing the tape could do the same to the people of the Wake Street house.

The cane in the video mistress' hand descended. It was a good quality copy: you could see the slight curve of the white birch rod as it bent to the slope of the slave's ass, the subtle breath of its passing, and the slightly wet kiss of wood to—was that blood? Were those streaks redder than usual welts? Did that rod suddenly have a lipstick streak of the bottom's liquid contents? A very good video. Forget jail, owning this was a one-way ticket to gray hair and hard labor—if you survived interrogation—and all of the pain non-negotiated, not consensual. And all the gay rape you could ever want.

The bottom on the screen became a metronome to the proceedings. Whack! Street clothes put away, play clothes came out. Whack! Sudden glimpses of sweat-glimmering thighs, breasts, backs, cheeks, tight chests, chalky skin (the sun never properly introduced to these regions: nudity = jail). Whack! A redhead with ribs in evidence and breasts that would rattle in a cupped hand, bent to pull on regulation boots, her sex flowering open behind her—and triggering a chorus of salivation from the opposite side of the room. Whack! A buzz-cut, he-man tugged on regulation prison sweats, the neck and head of his cock catching, then vanishing, past the draw-strings with a rubbery nod. Those on that side of the room returned the nod, smiling. A comfortable man with a warm, soft chest buckled on his official web belt and pinned a fake badge to his shirt. His eyes followed, with a tightening and flexing of ass, a short man with tumbleweed-wild hair, who absently tightened and flexed his gloves.

Enforcement Officers patrolled the city outside: tight beams of searing light punching visibility in the darkness, always, perpetually, without sleep (for their sign was a wide-awake, watchful eye) searching for crime, theft, murder, vandalism, vagrancy, ill-morality, perversion, homosexuality, sex, affection, less or more than nuclear familiarity, or enjoyment.

The clock was still gone, still replaced by the prison-bar streaked submissive, but they all knew, felt, that it was time to start: two lines, submissives on one side—quaking in their thin-soled prison shoes (copied with great care from the real thing) against one wall; dominants on the other—flexing leather gloves or fondling toys (copied with great care from the real thing, used by those that patrolled outside). The clock couldn't show it, but they all knew it was party time—time to arrest and be arrested by the forces of fear and punishment—ah, but safety, consensually.

Some of the submissives had their ankles chained, the links making heavy music on the hardwood floor. The excitement level in the room rose a few notches, and following right behind was a darkside excitement; maybe someone would hear, maybe someone would call the cops, maybe they'd spend the rest of their lives in chains, maybe they'd be beaten, probably they'd die. The fear made simple play into terror play.

There was some hesitancy on the part of the dominants. A spice of suspense for the submissives? No one wanting to start? What was that noise outside?

Then officer George approached prisoner #16 (Caucasian male, 25-28 years old, brown curly hair-short cut, no tattoos or scars). Hooking a sausage finger into a convenient D-ring, the officer hauled the prisoner to his knees and pressed 16's face hard into the leather-resistance of his government issued (a copy) crotchguard. "Breathe," he commanded.

The submissive did as instructed, breath squeaking through leather-pressed nostrils.

"Bet it's getting hard," growled the fascist pretender.

The submissive nodded, rubbing his nose (his breathing changed tone) on the hard leather.

Then the officer pulled a pair of handcuffs from his belt, ratcheted them on #16's wrist and then to his own belt. Then he did it again, with another pair of cuffs, another wrist, the other side of the belt.

"How strong are your teeth?" Officer George growled.

#16 dug out the zipper with his lips and teeth and feasted on the condomed cock he found hard and waiting.

A portrait of officer Lawrence hard at work (done in hard Weegee light, high contrast, gritty, realistic—the untied shoelace, the pistol hanging obviously in the way, the dusty floor, the plaster wall scarred and dented): It'd taken him a few minutes to get into position—and the same went for the target: Lawrence's feet were apart, his arm was back, his fist was clenched, his knuckles were white, his shirt was sweat-stained, his face strained, and his eyes gleamed with feverish concentration.

The whip in his hand was obviously heavy; his wrist was hurting—you could see it in his eyes.

The target was just something officer Lawrence could hit, it wasn't important—just a bullseye in felt marker on a pimpled asscheek, that usual ecstatic glazed expression, those runs of welts—they'd all seen his like a thousand times before

It was the joy Lawrence obviously put into his job that made the picture special.

The body-cavity search Officer Laura was conducting was going well. So far she'd been able to remove the thirty five cents (two dimes, ten pennies, one nickel) from prison #3's ass without having to resort to the enema nozzle hanging next to prisoner #8, Tayle, Sally, Q.

That didn't mean, though, that she wouldn't need it eventually.

Officer Goby interrogated prisoner #12:

"What kind of animal are you?"

"I'm a fuck-beast sir."

"What the fuck's that?"

"I live to get screwed, sir."

"Get screwed by what, cunt?"

"Anything that moves, sir."

"Well, I'm not goin' ta fuck ya."

"You're not, sir?"

"You're butt-fuck ugly, I don't fuck shit that's buttfuck ugly."

"Am I ugly, sir?"

"Ugly as shit. Why'd you come here, anyway?"

"To get fucked, sir."

"Well you ain't gonna get fucked—too buttfuck ugly. I don't fuck buttfuck ugly."

"What do you with ugly, sir?'

"I beat the crap out of it."

And so officer's belt met transvestite's pantied ass—and Officer Goby's hitting was really pretty—not buttfuck ugly, not at all.

Prisoner #2 was a vaporous man, all pale skin and blue veins, standing, shivering, in one corner. He was an alabaster rail, a naked beanpole.

Officer Eigan was bold, bearded and hair: a golden bear from some technological forest—he seemed pretty adapt with the hypodermic, amphlets, scalpels, and razors he absently fondled.

... and in one corner a soft, slow, (like the slowly menacing gears of some great machine) a gang bang was going on—the sex of the lust object in it was lost to conjecture and distant memory.

... on a sling a female prisoner had her public hygiene inspected by a iron-plated dyke, the clamps and chains on her tits making a windchime backup to her moaning.

... in a corner two bad boys roughhoused themselves into a squishing doggie-style fuck.

... tied to the points of the compass on the floor, a knotted prisoner's ass slowly ripened under the constant beating four officers gave it with cane, cat, paddle, and whip (in that order).

... spread over a vaulting horse, a great titted redhead cried tears of near-orgasmic joy at the skilled licks of her tiny-titted partner.

... from an iron-barred cage an electronic buzzing and the sting of ozone filled the air—the ongoing torture of a soft, pale prisoner for not doing an adequate Gene Kelly impression. A jolt of current came to his nipples and scrotum with every criticism of his very lackluster soft-shoe

... one couple, he with a cock, she with a cunt, plugged into each other with a feverish abandon while each, sporting high-tech claws, painted the other with stripes of slowly drippng blood.

And so on, and on, and no, into the night. The clock never moved from the prison-barred ass (but by this time the

VCD had been played a half-dozen times) but dawn was threatening none the less.

Camp was broken, toys put away, uniforms balled up (or anally folded to regulation standards in the case of those that had gone deep into character), deep breaths taken, nerves steadied, thanks given, taken, dates made, coats buttoned—and out they went.

And, to a player, a distant, predictable thought crossed their minds like a distant mental fright train: that beyond the front door, down the street, on the corner, at work, at their homes, could be the crisp precision of an arrest. Prison. The Camps. Death.

They left—excited beyond any play they had done, could do—into real terror.

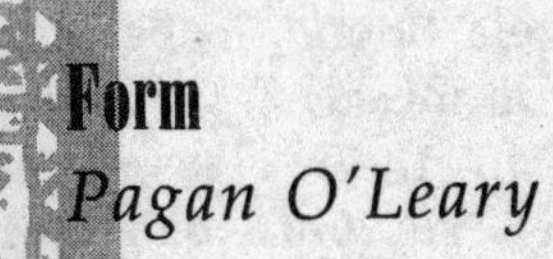

Form

Pagan O'Leary

I paused outside the doors to the auditorium. Inside, the staff and students were ready to begin the ceremony and yet all would wait on my arrival. No one would murmur, "where is he?" No one would later question me on my tardiness. Standing in the silent spotless hallway, I felt the weight of the time I was demanding of them, and the sheer pleasure of it made me shudder.

I have imposed order on chaos, civilized the primitive savage and taught it to dress with elegance, and in return been yielded this power. I do not take it lightly. To the contrary, I savor and cherish their respect, their deference. It isn't selfishness. When I make them wait, their anticipation is heightened and the eventual satisfaction is only increased by the waiting. Even in the exercise of my authority, I serve their needs.

As one, they rose to their feet at my entrance, motionless until I reached my seat on stage. My senior trainer Aragon stepped forward and I relaxed into the soothing flow of formalities.

Aragon's voice was mellifluous as she began calling the names. "Darrell Lothbein, to be known as Rezor." Cocky in his new leathers, the graduate sauntered across the stage. I noticed Aragon speak to him quietly as she presented the certificate that symbolized the amendment to his license earned by his completion of our course. Ever conscientious, she permitted no lapses in standards, even at this final moment. The new dominant bowed in acknowledgement and left the stage with evident humility; I nodded in satisfaction.

"Angela Boone, to be known as Tory." As the slow parade continued, I surveyed our audience. They sat grouped in their classes, easily identifiable to the practiced eye. Our basic students were noticeably younger than the rest, wide eyed and uncomfortable and fascinated. Graduation was the only occasion when they were permitted to leave their secluded classroom. Aragon sometimes suggests we lessen the segregation.

"We give them a glimpse of the possibilities at graduation," I explain to her each time. "But they don't even have their basic license yet—they haven't earned the right to be part of the greater mysteries." She never argues, and in recognition of that courtesy I permit her to repeat her request at intervals. It has nearly become a private ritual for us.

The bi class could be those same basics five years later, bracketed by the gay male and gay female, and behind them the polys. Seating for graduation isn't dictated, but somehow the orientation classes all herd together as if by instinct, separating themselves from the alternatives.

I have little to do with the orientation half of the school, preferring to leave its management to Ananda, a sweet polybi who delights in the baby steps of sexuality. Orientation keeps us solvent; in my mind, the heart of the school is the alternatives. I smiled over at that side of the room. There the groups mingled, the fetishists and bodmods, the voyeurs and tvs, the freeminded, the adventurous. My people.

And directly below me, my jewels—dominants in training, carefully dignified in their stark black uniforms, a semicircle of submissives kneeling at their feet, the beginners shivering in newly issued white tunics.

As the final graduate left the stage, I rose and walked forward. I give the same speech each time, grandiose and portentous. The words need no meaning; only the impact of sounds and sight and atmosphere linger, and so I create for them a profound memory to treasure. Even after years, when I chance upon an old student—they remember me, I seldom remember them—it is sure to be mentioned: "Your speech was so inspiring, Professor, I've never forgotten it."

Only the graduates bowed properly as I exited the stage and moved toward the door. Some of the new students showed the initiative to ape them, albeit awkwardly, and the orientation students who lack these respectful formalities in their lovestyles merely stood uncertainly. But one bright-eyed sub lowered her forehead to the floor in a graceful obeisance. I murmured approvingly as I passed her and knew the others would note it, perhaps discover they wanted to earn it for themselves. It was a very good morning.

The satisfaction stayed with me to my office, even when Cilla followed behind me and knelt beside my desk. I frowned in mock exasperation. "Time for reports again, little nag?"

Cilla was too discreet to sigh in relief at my good humor—after all, she'd trained here at our school, taking every course for which she qualified before hiring on to become my assistant -but I sensed the easing of her tension as she nodded her head toward my monitor.

I glanced at the display of names and numbers. Today's graduating class. I signed my name to the screen then traded Cilla the stylus for the keyboard and typed in the password that would verify my signature.

"Strip to the waist," I commanded with a soft chuckle when she would have forwarded to the next report and was pleased to startle her. I'm seldom playful when dealing with mundane details of the school, though

I fuss more out of boredom than true dislike. This is how we survive, after all, providing the training required for licensing. In turn, the government and insurance companies pay—but only when the reports are done.

Cilla blushed deliciously as she released the shoulder tabs of her tunic, letting the thin material drape around her waist. I played with her heavy breasts for a few minutes, cupping and squeezing their warm weight, then pinching the nipples lightly until they came obediently firm. I leaned back, considering, then nodded. "Yes. I like that. Next report?"

This was one of Cilla's delights, being used or exposed in some sweetly humiliating manner while conducting business as usual. A lovely shiver ran through her as she leaned toward the keyboard. I grinned at her until she lowered her eyes meekly, then I reluctantly returned my attention to the display. More routine—certification of attendance for the new students, authorizing them mental wellness leave from their jobs. Another signature, another password.

"Wider." I nudged one thigh gently then smacked it when she responded too slowly. Cilla giggled. I slapped the other thigh and laughed with her. "Now tell me about the next report," I instructed her. As I slid my fingers between her legs to test her wetness, she gasped and stammered about scene name registrations, her words fading to whimpers as I pinched and tugged the swollen lips.

We finished the remainder without hurry since I paused between each one to torment the sub at my feet. She was bristling with clamps and moaning audibly when Aragon entered.

Taking a seat, she plugged in her notebook and began a staccato dance of fingers across her keyboard without appearing to notice us. In anyone else, I would have thought it polite discretion, but from my senior trainer it was merely indifference.

I finished my game and swatted Cilla's bottom to send her crawling from the office. Without looking up, Aragon said briskly, "Class profile."

I studied the file she'd brought up on my screen, then growled. "Nearly half of the doms are new here."

"You'll see that happening more now with the publicity you've been getting. Why should they settle for a correspondence course and practical at a clinic when they can come here?"

"They've had no sub training." I glared at her and she shrugged.

"Not required by law. If you set it as policy, we'll lose our funding." She repeated her lines with some boredom. Aragon was occasionally impatient with my vision.

It was compromises such as this that sometimes made me regret entering this business. This school was my dream, and I prided myself on creating a place of elegance and tradition. I demanded more of my students than any other school, though dozens had sprung up in the larger cities to mimic my concept of providing basic through pansexual education in one interlocking framework. A certificate from the Professor was prized in the public Clubs and Houses. But I even was hamstrung by regulation, forced to accept any applicant who passed the psych evals.

We scanned through the individual profiles quickly. Their immediate trainers would review them in depth, noting emotional triggers and potential danger points, all neatly quantified and labeled by the examining clinics. I make it a practice to look at each one myself as well, though, knowing my years of experience may sometimes mark what a bored technician with only a het monog license might overlook.

"This one," I announced firmly, freezing the screen before Aragon could flash past it. "She has true potential. Did you see her in the auditorium as I left?"

"Raw talent, Professor? Or perhaps just another hopeful who's read books she's not licensed to buy yet?"

My jaw tightened at her acerbic comment. I motioned silently for her to continue the scroll.

Aragon is the only other staff member with a pansexual license and thus within the school is second only to me. I've observed her training techniques and grant that she is somehow able to coax the frightened and shrink the bullies and lure the wary, but toward me she is always aloof and detached, a guise that turns me cold. We work well together, yet much time in her company sends me fleeing for the soft laughing warmth of Cilla.

Or, as now, to the training rooms. Leaving Aragon to review the rest of the profiles, I headed for one of the domination classes. Shiva halted the exercise that the students could bow when I entered, then slapped her crop against her boot in signal to resume as I took a seat to one side.

The students were paired off, the one acting in place of the sub stripped and bound to a frame. The doms were practicing with floggers. Faces set in grim concentration, they stood waiting as Shiva established a rhythm with the crop against her boot, raising their arms in unison as she gave the command to begin.

I closed my eyes, lulled by the monotonous thump of leather on skin. "Increase the impact, not the speed," I heard Shiva hiss as she moved slowly across the room. "No, your pattern is too routine. Be regular but random."

The thuds began to echo in the room, a mesmerizing tempo. The silence between strokes was pushed aside by the heavy breathing of the working students and the sighing moans of those being pleasured. Our doms experienced everything they learned to inflict before they left us, and even the most obdurately dominant usually admitted to enjoying the floggings.

Shiva halted the class. "Are your partners aroused?" Peering around through half-opened eyes, I was amused at the looks of bewilderment. The usual pattern. "This is not batting practice, boys and girls," Shiva lectured with derision. "You must observe. Learn your partner's reactions. This is a dance for two." I slipped quietly from the room as she instructed them to untie and rub down their partners before switching.

Calmer now, I entered the adjoining room. Siesta smiled in delight as I entered and whispered hurriedly to the small group of submissives kneeling in a circle around her. As one, they rose and curtsied gracefully, the men performing a modified bow, and then with a rush I was surrounded. Chuckling softly, I allowed them to seat me. They moved quickly but with grace, lifting my feet to a comfortable hassock, a cool drink appearing at my hand, a thin pillow being placed behind my neck.

"Well done." I toasted Siesta, and she dimpled pleasingly.

"We were just discussing the pleasures of serving, Professor. You have impeccable timing."

I relaxed and allowed Siesta to make me part of her lesson. One student massaged my shoulders while two others removed my shoes and leisurely bathed and pampered my feet. Siesta selected her best student for the privilege of curling up in my lap to stroke and caress me with soft hands and warm lips. The rest she put through their paces, drilling them in positions and responses for my approval. Eager and beautiful, they restored my good humour.

I waited a few days before checking in on the new subs. The lectures and discussions that began their training were essential, but a bit dull for my taste. I joined them on the third day as Vizier was unlocking the toyboxes.

"For the next hour, I want you to explore," he announced after leading the group in acknowledging my entrance. "Play, see what items interest you."

The students quickly lost their self consciousness as they became engrossed in their playtime, donning cuffs and collars, testing clamps, gingerly using paddles on each other. I looked for Angie, the woman I'd noted the first day, and found her kneeling quietly by her assigned toybox, removing the items from it and laying them neatly on the floor in front of her.

My attention drifted until I heard a loud, firm "No!" One of the students was leaning over Angie dangling a thick rubber gag in front of her face. Vizier joined them and took the gag from the embarrassed student.

"Have you ever worn a gag?" the trainer asked Angie quietly. She shook her head, her mouth stubbornly clenched tight. "I want you to try it on. You can put it on yourself, no one will touch you." She shook her head again, glancing at me then dropping her eyes. Vizier motioned to me and we withdrew to his office where we could talk privately while still observing the class through the window.

Vizier had no need to consult me, of course. My policies forbid ever forcing a student to do anything, even though on admission they agreed to offer complete obedience and consented to punishment if the school felt it necessary. And of course there was the prospect of failing to complete the course, losing their chance for the license. We would neither force Angie nor punish her; but she could see us from the classroom, stern and disapproving as we pretended to discuss her failure to obey, and perhaps that would spur her to attempt the gag.

Vizier recalled a joke and so it was several minutes before I glanced through the window and noticed smugly that the black rubber gag was now fastened around her head. Her cheeks were damp with tears. I felt a rush at her surrender in order to please us and motioned to the trainer.

"Submission is not doing what you want to do," a familiar voice was saying as we reentered the classroom. Vizier stumbled into me as I stopped abruptly in shock. "It's wanting to do what you're told—whatever that might be."

I pushed my way through the students. "Eric."

He barely glanced at me. "Kurt. I was just convincing this little pet she likes being gagged." He knelt down beside her and gripped her hair, tugging her head back as he smiled down at her. He slipped his other hand beneath her tunic. "You like to please me, don't you?" he coaxed, his voice seductive velvet as his hand moved on her, and to my dismay she nodded even as the tears spilled again, and she arched her hips forward.

"Vizier, ungag her," I barked. I could feel my hands trembling with restrained anger. "Eric—my office."

I sent Cilla to find Aragon and paced my office waiting.

Eric sauntered in casually and walked straight up to me, holding out his hand, smiling. "Kurt, it's good to see you again." I could only stare at him, so nonchalant as if he had no doubts of his welcome. Shrugging, he lowered his hand and leaned against the wall. "You look old, Kurt."

He didn't look old, though we were close in age. His hair was long and shaggy with no hint of grey, creating a decade of difference next to my carefully trimmed black and silver mane. His face was tan and barely lined, his time in jail apparently not marking him at all. I thought bitterly of my deepening wrinkles, the growing slump to my shoulders and belly.

I snorted and walked away, taking a seat behind my desk. "What do you want, Eric? You're not supposed to be on the premises."

Why shouldn't I come here?" Eric asked in surprise. "It's my school too."

"I'll buy you out."

"No, I don't think so," he drawled thoughtfully, staring at me intently. His eyes seemed more silver than blue now, paler than I remembered. "I'll admit that I hate what you've made of it but I'm not ready to sell."

"The court ordered you to stay away," I reminded him. He held up a finger to stop me, a familiar impish grin creasing his face, then reached in his pocket and tugged out a license, tossing it on the desk in front of me. I stared at it in disbelief, at the distinctive bold P beneath the medical clearance. "It's not real." Forging and selling licenses had been one of Eric's crimes.

"It's real, Kurt. I'm a licensed pansexual. What do you think, should I start as a trainer?"

"No!" I'd shoved back the chair and was halfway around the desk before I realized I intended to hit him. How long since I'd been provoked to violence? Glaring, I stopped and stood facing him, determined to protect the school from whatever threat he might pose.

Eric hadn't moved. Arms folded across his chest, he sighed and shook his head. "Don't be a fool. I'm not coming back. I couldn't stand a day here." Dropping his arms to his sides, he approached me slowly. "Do you remember what it was like, Kurt?" he asked softly, wrapping his fingers into the front of my shirt, pulling me toward him. "When did you last feel passion? The last time you screamed? I used to make you scream, Kurt, I made you beg and plead for me to fuck you, remember?"

His face was so close, the low taunting voice racing through my ears to enflame my body.

And to my horror I realized that for a moment, I wanted him to use me again. That timbre in his voice, the challenge in that tight grasp, the heat of his breath on my face, all combined to taunt my control. It was a moment of temptation yet the sordid allure of it was enough to strengthen my resolve.

Ignoring the warm weakness oozing through my legs, I removed his hand from my shirt with a semblance of calm. I returned to my chair and noticed Aragon standing in the doorway.

"Eric? You came back." Pale and flustered, her voice shaking, she held her fists pressed tightly to her belly as if staunching a wound.

"You know him?" I hadn't hired Aragon until after Eric's trial, had hired her to replace him in fact.

Eric raised his eyebrow sardonically, still watching me steadily. "She's mine, Kurt. That's why I'm here, to get her. I suppose she didn't tell you—being owned by an outlaw wouldn't enhance her resume." He gestured to Aragon. She didn't move, and he glanced at her curiously before shrugging.

"This school is a mockery," he continued quietly, turning back toward me. "The whole system is a joke. Deciding who can have sex, when, how —rules and regulations for something that should be wild and untamed. Look at you, Kurt—strutting the halls with pretensions to godhood because you can make people bow to you —virginal medieval manners taking the place of lust and heat. You're pathetic."

I snorted in disgust. His antisocial philosophies had only worsened. We had worked together once, loved together, finding ways to educate the curious even before it could be done openly. But Eric had hated it when sexual health finally achieved a respectability. His rebelliousness had nearly lost us the school.

Aragon remained frozen, expressionless. Had she really belonged to my fiery partner, this coldly efficient, phlegmatic trainer of mine? I couldn't picture it. Nor, for all our slight disagreements over time, could I picture her turning her back on the ideals of the school. She hadn't joined him when he beckoned.

"Sex is too important to be left to the ignorant," I countered stubbornly, though I knew I'd never convince him. "They learn safety here, and self- acceptance. No more fumbling with unrecognized desires, no more shame, no more hiding. This is freedom for us, Eric, not tyranny."

"No," he said softly, shaking his head. "Let me show you what you've forgotten."

Eric took Aragon's hand and led her unprotesting to a chair facing my desk. She moved stiffly, only her eyes alive as they darted frantically from his face to mine, but she didn't protest. And I watched, strangely reluctant to interfere, briefly feeling again his hand possessively gripping my shirt.

She sat at his command, meeting my eyes as he stood behind her. He rested both hands on the back of the chair, not touching her, watching me.

His voice was hot brown sugar, sweet and heavy, slowly melting into the cracks of my mind. He spoke through her to me, showing me her body. I could see behind the clothes she wore, see the changes as his words stroked her. Her skin was coming to life, the nerves tingling in anticipation of more ghostly verbal caresses. She didn't shift in the chair but I could feel her urge to move and make the too tenuous touches real. I felt the same urge and forced myself still, unwilling to give him any reaction.

He knew. "You want to move now," he said, deep voice close to her ear. "You feel him watching you and you know he sees you now as I do, open and helpless. But you can't move until I let you. It isn't his eyes you want, it isn't his touch, and you have no choice but to let him look. Put your hands behind your neck."

For an instant, I heard it as a command for me and lowered my hands to the chair arms in chagrin, hoping he hadn't seen. I gritted my teeth.

Such a slight change in position and such a stunning affect on Aragon, now hungry eyed and breathing heavily, her face tense with the effort to hide her responses. "He hasn't touched you yet but suppose I told him to? Yes...suppose I call him over here and tell him to stroke your breasts, to feel how they've tightened with excitement. And he will feel your nipples hard against his fingertips begging to be fondled and pinched and twisted. Perhaps I'll tell him to taste them and bite them—you don't want him nursing on you, but there's nothing you can do, is there? No choice."

He was teasing me, tormenting me. Relentless he detailed the pain and pleasure he could have me inflict on her under his instruction, coaxing our minds to deceive our bodies. My cock was erect and throbbing. I'd never wanted her before but she was so damn vulnerable bound to that chair as surely as if he'd tied her with rope. I could see myself dragging my hands, my teeth, my cock, across her reluctant flesh, and it wouldn't be me doing it because Eric would be siphoning his desire through my body. He didn't touch her but she squirmed in the chair, whimpering now as he worked her deeper. So aroused, I doubt her staring eyes even saw me anymore. And I, I was still in my chair while I was crawling all over her ferocious and rough and ravenous.

He touched her, spreading her legs wide and yanking her skirt up to her hips, and she gasped loudly masking my own involuntary moan. Lulled by the fragile spell of illusion, reality stunned with its intensity. Eric growled in her ear, taunting her, and I was poised desperately for him to complete the command. I saw it just as he was described, how he would hold her in the chair and feed her to me, drown me with her juices. I could taste it in his words, in her frantic eyes. Then as he held her for me, we would take her, hot and deep and ruthless while she struggled beneath us. We watched her fight us, felt it, and we kept ramming into her body in a wild heat.

Grabbing her hair, he yanked her head back. "Come for me," he commanded and he stole her cries from me with a brutal kiss. I could only watch as she writhed and bucked against the chair, so far from me, so distant, and he gave me nothing. No command, no touch, no release.

Eric raised his head finally, watching me sternly as he held her flushed face against him, stroking her hair. "What does this have to do with anything you teach here?" he asked quietly.

Suddenly I was reminded of where we were and felt myself shrinking inside. He'd tricked me again.

"I run a House," he said conversationally, lifting Aragon from the chair and helping her adjust her clothing as she clung to his arm. "It's not registered, Kurt, you'll never find us. But don't think we're not still out there in the shadows. Some of us will never accept the leash of laws, no matter how it's disguised to be for our own good."

"What if she doesn't want to go?" I demanded out as he reached for the door. Chuckling, he held her tightly to him.

"Kurt, she consented to me. Consent is given to a person, not an act. And so she made her choice—the rest are mine."

The little sub Angie was standing on the other side of the door when he opened it, and she dropped to her knees immediately. I wondered dully how long she'd listened.

"I want to go with you," she said shyly, twisting her hands and staring at Eric's boots. "The way you made me submit in class....it felt so right. Please, take me with you."

I rolled my eyes in disgust. What next? Was he going to play Pied Piper and seduce the whole school to his feet? At least he had the courtesy not to laugh at her even as he shook his head.

"I'll leave this one with you, Kurt," he called over his shoulder as he guided Aragon around the kneeling woman. "But she'll find us someday. They all will."

The footsteps faded. They were gone. Silly Angie was staring at me with tears in her eyes. "He was a Master, wasn't he, Professor?" she whispered.

I quoted from the manual: "Slavery is an ancient historical concept that often finds its way into fantasy role-playing, but in reality there are no—" Too pompous. Too predictable. I touched the front of my shirt, remembering.

She wasn't listening anyway. I sighed. "Yes. He was a Master."

Contributors

Gary Bowen is a queer writer of Apache/Welsh descent, originally from Texas, now living on the East Coast. He has published over 200 stories in anthologies and magazines and is the author of *Diary of a Vampire, Man Hungry,* and *Queer Destinies.* His work appears in numerous other Circlet Press anthologies. His web site can be visited at www.netgsi.com/~fcowboy

Lauren P. Burka's works appear in several anthologies published by Circlet Press, as well as Laura Antoniou's *By Her Subdued,* and Susie Bright's *Best American Erotica.* Despite her tarot cards' prediction, she now has a day job. Ms. Burka presently resides in Cambridge, Massachusetts with her pets, human and otherwise.

Renée M. Charles' work has appeared in *Best American Erotica 1995, Dark Angels, Blood Kiss, Selling Venus, Symphonie's Gift* and other erotic anthologies and magazines in the last couple of years. When not writing erotica, she tends to her multi-cat "family." She is single and has a B.S. in English.

M. Christian's stories have appeared in such anthologies as *Best American Erotica 1994* and *1997, Best Gay Erotica,* the *Mammoth Book of Historical Erotica, Noirotica 1 2 & 3,* and, from Circlet Press, *More Technosex, Selling Venus, Wired Hard Vol. 2,* and *Genderflex.* He also edited the anthologies *Eros Ex Machina, Midsummer Nights Dreams,* and *Guilty Pleasures.* He is also a world renowned perv—more than anything because it allows him to combine his two favorite activities: sex and shopping.

Reina Delacroix is the pen name of a shy, quiet librarian, living in Northern Virginia with her cats, George and Shen T'ien; her precious Pet, Michael; and her loyal Wolf, Marc. This is her fifth story to see print with Circlet Press.

Neal Harkness makes his Circlet Press debut with this story.

Andrea J. Horlick is a health-care professional and writer of dark fiction, poetry, and erotica. She spends far too much time online arguing about the few things she knows and the many things on which she has an opinion. She has always been a little twisted and perverse but is just now beginning to get paid for it.

Raven Kaldera is a mythical beast come to life, a transgendered intersexual leatherpagan minister, farmer, and parent who writes twisted erotica in order to change the world and carry out an agenda of perversion and enlightenment. You have been warned.

Michael Manning, cover artist, is the artist and creator of the graphic novels *The Spider Garden, Hydrophidian,* and *Cathexis.* A collection of his graphic images, *Lumenagerie,* was also published by NBM. His most recent work is a graphic novel also from NBM entitled *Tranceptor* (in collaboration with artist Patrick Conlon).

Pagan O'Leary says "After twenty itinerant years in the military, I've finally found a home in the Pacific

Northwest. I play with computers and write technical materials in the daytime, and play with computers and write fiction at night. My other hobbies include leathercrafting, costuming, reading, and bellydance."

R. L. Perkins is an aerospace engineer living in the Delaware Valley in a bigamous relationship with a computer and a cat. When not trapped on airplanes he spends most of his free time hanging out in a bohemian coffee house in Philadelphia. "Local Reference" is his second story to see print in a Circlet Press publication.

Jason Rubis' fiction, poetry and articles have appeared in *Aberrations, Variations, Leg Show, The Seattle Weekly,* and *Industrial Decay Quarterly.* Jason Rubis lives and works in Washington, D.C.

About the Editor

Cecilia Tan is the editor of over thirty volumes of erotic science fiction and fantasy. She is the author of *Black Feathers: Erotic Dreams* and *The Valderet: A Cybersex S/M Serial.* Her work can be found in magazines from *Penthouse* to *Ms.*, and anthologies like *Best American Erotica* and *Eros Ex Machina.*

Acknowledgements

We would like to thank all the very patient people out there who waited so long for this book. Thanks to the significant others of the contributors for supporting our artistic addictions. Special thanks to John for technological patronage, Susan for dedicated editorial service, and Circlet's inimitable brigade of interns for everything under the sun. Felice, for being in the trenches with us, Mitch & Gerrie for continual support, and of course everyone at LPC for never giving up.

NOW AVAILABLE

Romance of Lust
Anonymous

Romance of Lust is that rare combination of graphic sensuality, literary success, and historical importance that is loved by critics and readers alike.—*The Times*

"Truly remarkable. All the pleasure of fine historical fiction combined with the most intimate descriptions of explicit lovemaking."
—*Herald Tribune*

"This justly famous novel has been a secret bestseller for a hundred years."

The Altar of Venus
Anonymous

Our author, a gentleman of wealth and privilege, is introduced to desire's delights at a tender age, and then and there commits himself to a life-long sensual expedition. As he enters manhood, he progresses from schoolgirls' charms to older women's enticements, especially those of acquaintances' mothers and wives. Later, he moves beyond common London brothels to sophisticated entertainments available only in Paris. Truly, he has become a lord among libertines.

Caning Able
Stan Kent

Caning Able is a modern-day version of the melodramatic tales of Victorian erotica. Full of dastardly villains, regimented discipline, corporal punishment and forbidden sexual liaisons, the novel features the brilliant and beautiful Jasmine, a seemingly helpless heroine who reigns triumphant despite dire peril. By mixing libidinous prose with a changing business world, Caning Able gives treasured plots a welcome twist: women who are definitely not the weaker sex.

Order These Selected Blue Moon Titles

Souvenirs From a Boarding School	$7.95
The Captive	$7.95
Ironwood Revisited	$7.95
The She-Slaves of Cinta Vincente	$7.95
The Architecture of Desire	$7.95
The Captive II	$7.95
Shadow Lane	$7.95
Services Rendered	$7.95
Shadow Lane III	$7.95
My Secret Life	$9.95
The Eye of the Intruder	$7.95
Net of Sex	$7.95
Captive V	$7.95
Cocktails	$7.95
Girl School	$7.95
The New Story of O	$7.95
Shadow Lane IV	$7.95
Beauty in the Birch	$7.95
The Blue Train	$7.95
Wild Tattoo	$7.95
Ironwood Continued	$7.95
Transfer Point Nice	$7.95
Souvenirs from a Boarding School	$7.95
Secret Talents	$7.95
Shadow Lane V	$7.95
Bizarre Voyage	$7.95
Red Hot	$7.95
Images of Ironwood	$7.95
Tokyo Story	$7.95
The Comfort of Women	$7.95
Disciplining Jane	$7.95
The Passionate Prisoners	$7.95
Doctor Sex	$7.95
Shadow Lane VI	$7.95
Girl's Reformatory	$7.95
The City of One-Night Stands	$7.95
A Hunger in Her Flesh	$7.95
Flesh On Fire	$7.95
Hard Drive	$7.95
Secret Talents	$7.95
The Captive's Journey	$7.95
Elena Raw	$7.95
La Vie Parisienne	$7.95
Fetish Girl	$7.95
Road Babe	$7.95
Violetta	$7.95
Story of O	$5.95
Dark Matter	$7.95
Ironwood	$7.95
Body Job	$7.95
Arousal	$7.95
The Blue Moon Erotic Reader II	$15.95

Visit our website at www.bluemoonbooks.com

ORDER FORM

Attach a separate sheet for additional titles.

Title	Quantity	Price
______	____	______
______	____	______
______	____	______
______	____	______
Shipping and Handling (see charges below)		______
Sales tax (in CA and NY)		______
Total		______

Name ______

Address ______

City ______ State ______ Zip ______

Daytime telephone number ______

❑ Check ❑ Money Order (US dollars only. No COD orders accepted.)

Credit Card # ______ Exp. Date ______

❑ MC ❑ VISA ❑ AMEX

Signature ______

(if paying with a credit card you must sign this form.)

Shipping and Handling charges:*

Domestic: $4 for 1st book, $.75 each additional book. International: $5 for 1st book, $1 each additional book
*rates in effect at time of publication. Subject to Change.

Mail order to Publishers Group West, Attention: Order Dept., 1700 Fourth St., Berkeley, CA 94710, or fax to (510) 528-3444.

PLEASE ALLOW 4-6 WEEKS FOR DELIVERY. ALL ORDERS SHIP VIA 4TH CLASS MAIL.

Look for Blue Moon Books at your favorite local bookseller or from your favorite online bookseller.